D1413094

1s.

GABORIAU'S
SENSATIONAL NOVELS

The Favourite Reading of Prince Bismarck.

INTRIGUES
OF A POISONER.

LONDON: VIZETELLY & CO.
42, Catherine Street, Strand.

Cover of an early English edition of
Les Amours d'une empoisonneuse, with a portrait of Gaboriau.

Emile <u>Gaboriau</u>

MONSIEUR LECOQ

Edited with an Introduction by
E. F. Bleiler

Dover Publications, Inc., New York

Published in Canada by General Publishing Company, Ltd., 30 Lesmill Road, Don Mills, Toronto,
Ontario.
Published in the United Kingdom by Constable
and Company, Ltd., 10 Orange Street, London WC 2.

This Dover edition, first published in 1975, is a
republication of the work originally published by
W. R. Caldwell & Co., New York, in 1908 as a two-
volume set. The first volume, *Monsieur Lecoq*, is
here reprinted complete; pages 618–639 of the
second volume, *The Honor of the Name*, are also
included in the present edition, where they are
renumbered 257–278. The illustrations facing pp. 6,
126, 136 and 218, by Bayard Jones, are taken from
the 1904 edition by Charles Scribner's Sons, New
York. The Introduction and Editorial Note (pp.
255–256) were prepared specially for this edition by
E. F. Bleiler.

International Standard Book Number: 0-486-22570-4
Library of Congress Catalog Card Number: 74-29016

Manufactured in the United States of America
Dover Publications, Inc.
180 Varick Street
New York, N.Y. 10014

INTRODUCTION
TO THE
DOVER EDITION

"Have you read Gaboriau's works?" I asked. "Does Lecoq come up to your idea of a detective?"

Sherlock Holmes sniffed sardonically. "Lecoq was a miserable bungler," he said in an angry voice; "he had only one thing to recommend him, and that was his energy. That book made me positively ill. The question was how to identify an unknown prisoner. I could have done it in twenty-four hours. Lecoq took six months or so. It might be made a text-book for detectives to teach them what to avoid." (*A Study in Scarlet*, by A. C. Doyle.)

T HIS was probably not Arthur Conan Doyle's own opinion of *Monsieur Lecoq*, but unfortunately it is the critical position that most of us who have read Doyle and not Gaboriau are likely to have accepted. Yet it is a very unjust judgment, since so much of Sherlock Holmes is based on this very Lecoq.

Monsieur Lecoq was the creation of Emile Gaboriau, who, with good reason, has been called the father of the modern detective novel.

Etienne Emile Gaboriau was born in 1832* in Saujon,

---

*Most standard reference works give other dates, but 1832 is correct.

France, a small town near the Atlantic, not too far from La Rochelle. His family were bourgeois, who had been lawyers, petty officials and physicians for many generations. A bright personable young man, Emile Gaboriau attended school at Saintes and Saumur, and then was placed by his parents with a notary to learn the profession. The life of a notary was not for him, however, and after about a year and a half of boredom, only partly relieved by devouring the Gothic and Romantic classics—Ann Radcliffe, Cooper, Dumas père and above all, Poe—he enlisted in the army. He was then twenty years old.

The duration of Gaboriau's service, which was in the cavalry, has never been settled, and precise dates are not known. It may have been two years, or three years, or even four. Nor is it known where he served his term. According to some nineteenth-century accounts he soldiered in North Africa; it is more likely, however, that he was stationed in the Pyrenees and never left France. In any case, he used material from his army days in an amusing short novel, *Le 13e Hussards* (*The Thirteenth Hussars*),* which describes the life of a recruit from fitting a uniform to doing K.P., to learning to ride, going AWOL, on up to discharge. Gaboriau is said to have risen to the rank of sergeant.

Around 1856 Gaboriau was in Paris, trying to make a living as a writer, although he is said to have accepted many strange commissions to keep alive. He managed a livery stable for a time, and he composed mottoes and ephemeral poetry to be printed on wrapping paper and shopping bags, and even on birthday cakes. All this alienated the sensibilities of his family, who were extremely rigid and proper.

By 1858 Gaboriau was reasonably established as a freelance writer and as an editor of minor periodical work. He sold a small but steady stream of articles, semifictional sketches and poetry. There was nothing in this early work to bring him credit or advancement, but it served to buy him time.

Gaboriau had his major stroke of good fortune around 1860, when he became acquainted and associated with Paul Féval, an extremely popular sensational novelist, successful dramatist, and publisher of periodicals. Féval employed Gaboriau as a secretary

---

*English titles following the French titles are those of the most important English editions. Additional titles are cited in the Bibliography.

and as editor for one of his newspapers, the weekly *Jean Diable*, which is not to be confused with Féval's novel of the same name.

It is often stated that Féval used to send Gaboriau to the police courts and to trials to gather material for sensational fiction, or that Gaboriau did ghost writing for Féval. There is no evidence for either claim, however, and both are rather unlikely. Féval's work is very different from Gaboriau's, and if Gaboriau did gather material from the courts, it certainly was not used in Féval's fiction.

During this period of literary apprenticeship Gaboriau composed a few books that are now forgotten, since they are obviously commercial journalism. *L'Ancien Figaro* (1861) was an anthology of periodical pieces collected by Gaboriau. It dealt with the Restauration, when the old nobility returned to France after the fall of Napoleon. *Les Cotillons célèbres* (1861) is a series of long, romanticized sketches of famous royal mistresses, while *Le 13e Hussards* (*The Thirteenth Hussars*) (1861) consists of amusing episodes in the life of a cavalry recruit. *Les Gens de Bureau* (*The Men of the Bureau*) (1862) is a weak, mildly ironic short novel about bureaucracy; its only present interest is that it illustrates Gaboriau's penchant for using the same names from novel to novel, even though the personalities are different. In this case the name is Caldas, later one of Lecoq's aliases.

Three more minor works followed. *Les Mariages d'aventure* (*Marriage at a Venture*) (1862) consists of two short novels that might be loosely described as comedy of manners, while *Ruses d'amour* (1862), which I have not seen, is said to be an anthology of various subterfuges and stratagems that have been used in pursuit of love. *Les Comédiennes adorées* (1863) contains short journalistic, biographical studies of famous actresses.

All through this period of ephemeral journalism, which also included much newspaper work, Gaboriau remained faithful to one personal interest: factual crime. In his youth he had read Poe's detective stories in a French translation, and had been sufficiently impressed to attempt a series of imitations, which are now lost juvenilia. He also collected volumes of celebrated French trials, and was aware of the memoirs of various famous detectives. He studied what literature was available on serious criminology, and may well have continued his legal studies into the area of criminal law. If, during this time, Gaboriau did frequent the police offices and law courts, it was unquestionably for himself, not for Paul Féval.

September 14, 1865 marked an important change in Gaboriau's life, for on this date began the serialization of Gaboriau's first major work, *L'Affaire Lerouge* (*The Widow Lerouge*), which has a very good claim to being the first modern detective novel. It was serialized in *Le Pays*, a struggling newspaper, where it attracted some critical attention, but it does not seem to have been remarkably popular. It was remembered, however, and when in 1866 another newspaper, *Le Soleil*, found its circulation sagging badly as a result of having serialized Victor Hugo's *Travailleurs de la Mer* (*Toilers of the Sea*), *L'Affaire Lerouge* was recommended as a palliative. Circulation soared, and Gaboriau suddenly found himself one of the most popular writers in France.

This success was not transitory, for when Gaboriau's second mystery novel, *Le Crime d'Orcival* (*The Mystery of Orcival*) appeared in serial form in 1866–7, it was printed simultaneously in two newspapers. The eventual result of this was a contract with *Le Petit Journal* for exclusive rights to future fiction, for 50,000 francs per year. In each instance serial publication was followed by book appearances, usually with Gaboriau's friend E. Dentu. In a relatively short time, what with periodical publications, book royalties, and reprints in provincial newspapers, Gaboriau became a wealthy man. This success did not disturb his habit of hard work, however, and he maintained the writing schedule of earlier years. His wife, about whom almost nothing is known, is said to have helped him.

For several years the stream of fiction continued. To cite book publication dates: *Le Dossier no. 113* (*File No. 113*), 1867; *Les Esclaves de Paris* (*Caught in the Net* and *The Champdoce Mystery*), 1868; *Monsieur Lecoq* (*Monsieur Lecoq* and *The Honor of the Name*), 1869; *La Vie infernale* (*The Count's Millions* and *The Vengeance of Baron Trigault*), 1870; *La Clique dorée* (*The Clique of Gold*), 1871; *La Degringolade* (*Catastrophe*), 1872; *La Corde au cou* (*Within an Inch of His Life*), 1873; and *L'Argent des autres* (*Other People's Money*), 1874.

As the reader will observe from the dates above, several of Gaboriau's works appeared around the time of the Franco-

Prussian War. What Gaboriau did during the war is not known, however, which would lead one to the conclusion that he did nothing important. A family tradition states that he was in Paris during the first part of the Commune, but that he managed to leave, hidden in a laundry wagon, before circumstances became too difficult. Comments in the later novels show that Gaboriau was rather strongly anti-Communard. It should be added, however, that Gaboriau was firmly opposed to Louis Napoleon's seizure of power and based much of his fiction on the theme of corruption in the Second Empire. In all probability Gaboriau was a moderate liberal.

Life seemed secure for Gaboriau in the middle of 1873. His work was going well. He had finished *L'Argent des autres* (*Other People's Money*), and he had two novels plotted out in detail. These were a new mystery novel involving a trial by jury, *Le Chef du Jury*—which seems to have been partly written—and a psychological novel, *Ninette Suzor*, which Gaboriau intended to be his first serious, non-sensational novel.

On September 28, 1873, however, Gaboriau died suddenly. The circumstances are not known, although he seems to have died of a heart attack, perhaps connected with a lung disorder he had suffered from while in the army. He was almost forty-one years old at his death, and his obituarists and funeral panegyrist, his old master Féval, found it a particularly sad circumstance that he died just as he reached writing maturity.

Gaboriau, in appearance, was tall and handsome, with a full, dark beard. An early British woodcut of him, if it is valid and not supposititious, indicates that his facial expression was not too dissimilar from that of the young Dickens. He is said to have been affable and generous, with a tendency toward extravagant dress, although this would have been nothing unusual in the Paris of his day. Mercurial in temperament, he sometimes spoke with the abruptness of the soldier, sometimes with the sensitivity of the artist. He delighted in spoofing strangers and his friends with fanciful arguments, often taking both sides in succession, like a better-natured Doctor Johnson.

One anecdote illustrates the mind that could create Lecoq and Tabaret:

One of his great amusements, Alfred d'Aunay records, was to study a passerby in the street and try to glean, by processes of reasoning and observation, his mode of life and social standing, and then to shadow his victim to see if his deductions were correct. ("Gaboriau: Father of the Detective Novel" by Valentine Williams, *National Review* [London], 1923.)

Like Sherlock Holmes?

I I

Did Gaboriau really invent the modern detective novel? The answer is a qualified "Yes," if each of the three words "modern," "detective" and "novel" is taken with precision. Generally speaking, in both English and French, there had been a considerable body of crime fiction before Gaboriau's day, and some of this contained the germs of later developments, including primitive detectives and detection. But most of this material, like Victor's *The Dead Letter*, could not be considered modern, being only curious ancestral effigies for future generations to look upon.

The elements that Gaboriau drew on for *L'Affaire Lerouge* —for Gaboriau did not create *ex nihilo* any more than does anyone else—may be listed in outline form:

(a) Edgar Allan Poe. Poe, in the early 1840's, had written pure detective stories that received international attention, and were translated into French by Baudelaire in the 1850's. As a young man Gaboriau read these stories with delight and enthusiasm. From Poe Gaboriau took the idea of the amateur consulting detective, the aspect of puzzling the reader, and above all, the ratiocinative method: that peculiar logical mechanism whereby the detective recreates a crime by means of minute observation and interpretation. It is difficult to define this process, but everyone who has read detective stories knows what it is.

(b) The French sensational literature of the day. Unfortunately, this remarkably broad jungle of minor works, filled with bloody and savage adventure, has never been explored, and is even less well-known than its British counterpart, the penny dreadful. Paul Féval, whom Gaboriau addressed as maître in his correspondence, wrote such novels which combined romance, manners, adventure, and crime elements. A curious example is Féval's *Jean Diable*, which appeared in book form in 1863, while Gaboriau was working for Féval. Among the characters of this long, complex novel is the detective Gregory Temple, superintendent of Scotland Yard, who is investigating the murder of a singer, in opposition to a master criminal, Jean Diable. Temple uses the ratiocinative method, and has even written a book about it. In brief summary this sounds like a detective novel earlier than Gaboriau's, but the detectional material is buried in a welter of romantic material, and the development is very, very thin. It has also been claimed that Gaboriau borrowed the name Lecoq from one of Féval's novels, but this is probably stretching too far.

Merging into and sometimes growing out of the sensational literature is (c) the higher literary tradition. Balzac stands at the top of a pyramid, beneath him standing Dumas père, Sue, Kock, on down to the nameless feuilletonists. Balzac used much crime material in his fiction, and several characters appear in his works who might be called proto-detectives. Vautrin, who appears in several stories, is based on the historical criminal and detective, François Eugène Vidocq, about whom more later. Gaboriau had obviously read *Une Ténébreuse Affaire* by Balzac, and it remained in his mind when he wrote the second part of *Monsieur Lecoq*.

(d) The French factual and pseudofactual crime memoirs and studies. These culminated in the memoirs (with embroiderings) of the ex-convict François Eugène Vidocq, a notorious criminal who eventually became the first head of the Sûreté. Vidocq's memoirs and the two novels that he had a hand in were extremely popular in France and the English-speaking countries, and set off a small chain of police stories. Canler, one of Vidocq's successors, also prepared memoirs which Gaboriau refers to.

In France such memoirs and studies of historical crimes have had a long and fairly honorable history, having been prepared on a higher level than the comparable English phenomenon, the *Newgate Calendar*. Many such collections of famous cases and the lives of malefactors have appeared in France, the best-known being those published under the name Pitaval, which has become almost a generic term. These French collections, it might be added, have been of some influence in the English development of the detective story, for individual pieces were often translated in early nineteenth-century periodicals. Wilkie Collins is known to have taken ideas used in *The Woman in White* from one of these French collections.

Like Poe, however, Gaboriau should not be seen as a collection of influences, but as a man who crystallized and solidified what may have been in the air around him. He unified a certain grouping of characteristics and created a form. Féval may have talked about ratiocinative deduction two or three years before Gaboriau, but he apparently did not care or was unable to develop the idea. Vidocq wandered about Paris in disguise, seeking criminals, and Balzac and Sue may have written long novels that combined comedy of manners with crime motives, but Gaboriau still has the distinction, in *L'Affaire Lerouge,* of having created the first modern novel that was clearly and unmistakably and consciously and primarily a detective story.

I I I

Monsieur Lecoq first appeared in *Le Petit Journal*, a Parisian daily newspaper, from May 25 through December 3, 1868. According to the data in Nancy E. L. Curry's excellent thesis, *The Life and Works of Emile Gaboriau* (1971), this newspaper version was slightly longer than the text we now have, Gaboriau revising it fairly extensively for book publication in 1869. It was extremely popular, and it went through several editions with great rapidity. It was also serialized in provincial newspapers throughout France.

The essence of the novel—the duel of intellect between the detective and the killer—is, of course, not new, for it had appeared in previous crime literature, from William Godwin's *Things as They Are (Caleb Williams)* (1794) on up through the *Jean Diable* that has already been mentioned. But Gaboriau added a new excitement to the theme.

The most important factor in *Monsieur Lecoq*, in the opinion of most critics, however, is the personality of Lecoq himself, here seen as a young man, just beginning to rise in the trade of which he is soon to be the great master. As Valentine Williams has nicely put it:

Here, through the jostling throng of desperately wicked dukes, incredibly noble maids, of *banquiers véreux*, Monsieur Lecoq, simple agent of the Sûreté, comes stepping, fresh as a bridegroom, *un beau gars, à l'oeil clair, à l'air résolu*, or as casual visitors saw him in his careful disguise, a sober personality of distinguished appearance, with his gold spectacles, his white tie, and his *mince redingote*. Against a canvas of tiresome puppets he stands out a living figure . . . He is as French as the crowing cock, which with its proud motto, *Semper vigilans*, he chose as his device. His limpid mind, his crystal-clear reasoning, his dazzling deductions, his fluttering *panache*, his ups and downs, his hopes and fears, all these are wholly French. ("Gaboriau: Father of The Detective Novel," *National Review*, London, 1923.)

All in all, Lecoq appears in five novels by Gaboriau, beginning with *L'Affaire Lerouge* (*The Widow Lerouge*) (1866), where he plays a very minor role. There he is a subordinate *agent*, jealous of his superior, Gévrol, and a follower of Père Tabaret. He appears only in the initial setting for the investigation, and is mentioned again later in passing. Did Gaboriau have an inkling, back in 1865-6, that Lecoq would swallow up the detective series? If he did, he made a bad gaffe, for in *L'Affaire Lerouge* Lecoq is not a bright young man of patrician origin, as in *Monsieur Lecoq*, but a reformed criminal who has joined the police force. This point is suggestive of Vidocq, as is the name Lecoq. But Gaboriau was often very careless about details, and he may well have forgotten the hasty image of Lecoq in *L'Affaire Lerouge*. In fact, in his next novel, *Le Crime d'Orcival* (*The Mystery of Orcival*), he made a similar error. He describes Gévrol as the favorite disciple of Tabaret, a description which could hardly have been farther from the mark in the other novels.

This *Crime d'Orcival*, which was serialized in 1866 and published in book form in 1867, marks Lecoq's second appearance, and it is the first novel to star Lecoq. Here Lecoq is an established detective who is summoned from Paris to solve what seems to be a double murder committed by a servant for purposes of robbery. Lecoq, using the same amazingly precise, imaginative deductions which the reader will see in *Monsieur*

Lecoq, soon uncovers a completely different solution, the background to which is shown in a long flashback. Some critics find *Le Crime d'Orcival* Gaboriau's best novel, but I find the characterizations inconsistent and insipid, the secondary novel somewhat unconvincing, and the general development a little hasty.

In his third appearance Lecoq dominates the famous *Dossier no. 113* (*File No. 113*) (1867). In this novel what seems to be a simple theft by a bank cashier of 350,000 francs is expanded to a cycle of crime and malfeasance, with conspiracy, swindling, illegitimacy and murder in the background. Lecoq, in disguise, intervenes to avert an act of injustice by the authorities, and further directs the activities of another detective. Lecoq is now the top man in criminal detection. The motivations for his actions in the case, however, are very curious to an Anglo-Saxon reader who is used to classical detective stories. Lecoq pursues his investigations not as a function of his official position in the Sûreté, not out of pity for an innocent man who is obviously being framed, not for the thrill of the chase as is often the motivation with British detectives and even with Père Tabaret, but for erotic reasons. Lecoq wishes to reestablish a liaison he had once enjoyed with a demimondaine who is now the suspect's mistress, and he wants to show the girl his infinite superiority over the cashier. By some standards this is not a particularly creditable motivation, but it is a very modern concept.

Lecoq's next appearance is in *Les Esclaves de Paris* (*Caught in the Net* and *The Champdoce Mystery*) (1868), where Lecoq enters toward the end of the novel to foil the machinations of Mascarot, a nicely imagined criminal mastermind. Mascarot (Mascarin in some American editions) has two other identities, and operates a servants' employment agency, which he uses to gather information for blackmail. Mascarot learns of an heir to millions who has been missing since childhood, and determines to establish his own candidate. Mascarot's dovetailed plans are sliding into place when Lecoq dramatically appears and destroys the conspiracy. This novel is followed by *Monsieur Lecoq* (1869), which is the last and best of the novels about Lecoq.

Besides Lecoq Gaboriau created three other detectives who are significant centers of attention. Of these the most important by far is the old amateur, Père Tabaret, sometimes called Tirauclair. Tabaret started to collect literature about crime, and ended by becoming a consulting detective who is invoked by the police or others when a case is perplexing. Lecoq recognizes him as master. Tabaret uses ratiocinative deduction, but presumably for reasons of age does not share Lecoq's penchant for disguises.

L'Affaire Lerouge (*The Widow Lerouge*), which marks Tabaret's first appearance, is concerned with a corpse found in a cottage. Tabaret, thanks to a suggestion from the proto-Lecoq who is present, is called into the case, and he immediately exercises his talents to reveal the "type" of the criminal. What then at first seems to be a chance occurrence brings Tabaret to the heart of the case, which is far more complex than it appeared at first. An ingenious resolution removes much of the taint of coincidence. This is the only novel starring Tabaret, although the reader will find him appearing briefly at the end of the first part of *Monsieur Lecoq*, where he sets Lecoq straight. His spirit, however, hovers over most of the other criminal novels of Gaboriau.

To remain with Gaboriau's detective fiction in the strict sense: Gaboriau's other major work is the nouvelle entitled "Le Petit Vieux des Batignoles" ("The Little Old Man of Batignoles") in the collection of the same name (1876). In this well-known story Mechinet, a member of the Sûreté, solves a murder very neatly, using clues in much the same manner as Sherlock Holmes did a little later. In the same collection also appears "Une Disparition" ("A Disappearance") in which Detective Rétiveau, also known as Magloire, discovers that a disappearance is really an insurance fraud.

Gaboriau considered all his later fiction as belonging to the same category, *le roman judiciaire*, which term he had arrived at in discussion with his publisher Dentu. This may be translated as judiciary novel, or perhaps legal novel. A modern purist, however, would prefer to separate the detective and mystery novels from those which only occasionally use the subject matter of crime. *Les Esclaves de Paris* (*Caught in the Net* and *The Champdoce Mystery*) (1868), despite the late appearance of Lecoq, is not really a detective story, but is a novel of society with crime elements. Similarly, *La Vie infernale* (*The Count's Millions* and *The Vengeance of Baron Tri-*

gault) (1870) buries a criminal conspiracy behind a complex, rolling surface of adulteries and deceptions.

La Clique dorée (*The Clique of Gold*) (1871) is also concerned with conspiracy. Here a quartet of criminals, led by a beautiful young woman, Sarah Brandon, preys on wealthy young men, first swindling them, then forcing them to suicide. Part of the plot is concerned with ensnaring a senile millionaire into marriage. *The Clique of Gold* was followed in 1872 by *La Dégringolade* (Catastrophe), which at first promises to be a detective novel, but soon wanes into a society novel. According to official report General Delorge fell in a duel, but his widow knows that he was assassinated during Louis Napoleon's seizure of power, and vows to obtain justice.

More concerned with detection in the stricter sense is *La Corde au cou* (*Within an Inch of His Life*) (1873), in which a young man, trapped partly by circumstantial evidence, partly by false witness, is prosecuted for arson and attempted murder. Proving his innocence is difficult, but toward the end of the book the defense hires a detective, a member of the Sûreté on leave. There are suggestions here of Sergeant Cuff of *The Moonstone*.

Gaboriau's last novel, *L'Argent des autres* (*Other People's Money*) (1874), concludes the major works published during Gaboriau's lifetime. After his death, however, several of his earlier works were printed in book form. These include the volume of shorter pieces, *Le Petit Vieux des Batignoles* (*The Little Old Man of Batignoles*) (1876); *Le Capitaine Coutanceau* (*Captain Contanceau*) (1878), a rather weak historical novel of the French Revolution; and *Les Amours d'une Empoisonneuse* (*The Marquise de Brinvilliers*) (1881), a historical fantasy in the manner of Dumas, loosely connected with the career of the celebrated poisoner. It is not known when these were written or if they were published previously in periodicals, but it is reasonable to assume that they date from before Gaboriau's days of success. It is possible that other material by Gaboriau still lies undiscovered in the ephemeral press of the 1860's.

I have discussed these novels separately, since this is the way that the American reader will encounter them. But Gaboriau in a vague sort of way seems to have thought of the later novels, from *L'Affaire Lerouge* on, as segments of a consistent universe, a small *comédie humaine*. As a result there is a certain carry-over of names and personalities from one novel to another. The reader often finds a familiar face among the newcomers. This situation, unfortunately, is complicated by the fact that Gaboriau was careless in his chronology and cross-references, and is inconsistent almost as often as consistent. A further complication is that Gaboriau simply liked certain names and used them over.

A common frame of mind, similarly, permeates all the novels of Gaboriau, both detective and social. The ultimate spring of all his major work is scandal of the sexual sort. Forbidden amours, illegitimacy, golddigging, adultery—all provide final motivation for action. This is in striking contrast to the British novels that are roughly contemporary. The collections of pseudo-factual "cases," like William Russell's, are usually founded on realistic economics or criminality. Wilkie Collins, in the two great novels, *The Woman in White* and *The Moonstone*, uses financial greed to motivate the stories. The ultimate in *The Woman in White* is Fosco's wish to obtain an inheritance, and the ultimate in *The Moonstone* is the monetary value of the gem. In Doyle's work, the ultimate is usually greed, with revenge a second consideration. For the other British Victorians —LeFanu, Miss Braddon, Mrs. Wood—the motivation is sometimes economic, sometimes the passion of anger, sometimes erotic, but never scandalous.

One could say simply and flippantly, that this simply means that Gaboriau was a Frenchman, and that his novels reflect the folkways of the time. But I do not know whether this is true. The psychologies of the characters—their violent passions and hatreds, their filial devotion, their raffishness, their strange innocences and pruderies—do they represent an aspect of life in the middle classes of Gaboriau's milieu, perhaps the ideals of his own pecksniffian family, or are they a literary convention, or perhaps both?

The motivations in Gaboriau are consistent and the personalities are consistent. A high problem of the generation before Gaboriau, one that entered very frequently in the fiction of the 1860's, was the haughty old revanchist nobility, returning in the post-Napoleonic restoration. There was the boom and bust of the Emperor Louis Napoleon; the extravagances of inverse machismo, when a chance act or word might ruin a girl's life, even though nothing significant had happened. Did this config- uration of folkways really dominate mid-Victorian bourgeois France? I do not know, any more than if British lords in the comparable English literature perpetually tried to swindle their relatives.

Let me cite an incident from the memoirs of Canler, one- time head of the Sûreté:

> At one period of my professional life I came to know a Monsieur V——, a wealthy clothier, retired from business, who lived many years since in the village of Plaisance, with his wife and two daughters, eighteen and twenty years old. The daughters were lovely and amiable girls, as modest as they were amiable, but their father cherished a fixed belief that a couple of rascals came regularly night and morning at the hour his daughters got up or went to bed, and hid them- selves behind the garden wall, where by means of a kind of mirror they brought with them, they made a practice of watching the young ladies at their toilets.
>
> "You can see," he said to me, "at a glance, how disastrous this circumstance must inevitably be to my poor girls. How can they ever hope to marry if it should be known that they are daily objects of inspection to a couple of low-minded scoundrels? Their characters are destroyed at once."

The point here is not the obvious fact that M. V—— was insane, and that the whole story was fantasy, but that it was socially recognized that the girls would be irreparably compro- mised simply by the glance of a stranger. Similar folkways abound in the works of Gaboriau.

IV

Gaboriau came close to being a best-selling author in France, and the great detective novels—*L'Affaire Lerouge, Le Crime d'Orcival*, and *Monsieur Lecoq*—went through many editions and remained in print for decades. Indeed, it is possible that certain of them have never gone out of print.

Paris, 30 juin 1869.

Mon cher Martin,

Je vous remercie, ou plutôt je ne sais comment vous remercier de votre bonne obligeance — les 200 francs que vous venez de m'envoyer me tirent du pied la plus mauvaise des épines. Ainsi que je vous le disais, j'aurai le plaisir de vous les rendre dans le courant de janvier.

Tout à vous
Em. Gaboriau

A. M. Paul Féval.

Letter from Gaboriau to Féval. "Paris, June 30, 1869. My dear Master, I thank you—rather, I don't know how to thank you—for your kind favor. The 200 francs you have just sent me remove a most painful thorn from my side. As I told you, I will have the pleasure of repaying the money some time in January. Yours, Em. Gaboriau."

Old Cap. Collier
LIBRARY.

No. 27.

MUNRO'S PUBLISHING HOUSE,
24 & 26 Vandewater Street, New York. – July 30, 1883.

5 Cents.

Old Cap. Collier Library is issued Semi-Monthly.—By Subscription $2.00 per Annum.
Entered according to Act of Congress, in the year 1883, by NORMAN L. MUNRO, in the office of the Librarian of Congress, at Washington, D. C.—[Entered at the Post Office, N. Y., as Second Class Matter.]

Old Tabaret, the Self-Made Detective:

OR,

"PIPING" THE LEROUGE CASE.

BY EMILE GABORIAU.

"HERE IS A SOILED TABLE NAPKIN," SAID THE GENDARME, "FILLED WITH PLATE, MONEY AND JEWELS."

Cover of an American dime-novel Gaboriau publication.

Old Cap. Collier
LIBRARY.

No. 37.

MUNRO'S PUBLISHING HOUSE,
24 & 26 VANDEWATER STREET, NEW YORK.—SEPTEMBER 14, 1883.

5 Cents.

OLD CAP. COLLIER LIBRARY IS ISSUED SEMI-MONTHLY.—BY SUBSCRIPTION $2.00 PER ANNUM.
Entered according to Act of Congress, in the year 1883, by NORMAN L. MUNRO, in the office of the Librarian of Congress, at
Washington, D. C.—[Entered at the Post Office, N. Y., as Second Class Matter.]

A GREAT ROBBERY;

OR,

"Piping" a Series of Bank Frauds.

BY EMILE GABORIAU.

MONSIEUR FAVORAL LIFTED HIMSELF UPON THE WIDOW-SILL WHILE MAXENCE HELD THE SHEETS.

Cover of an American dime-novel Gaboriau publication.

PRICE 10 CENTS.

Old Cap Collier
LIBRARY

Vol. 1. No. 52 Nov. 5, 1883. Subscription $10.

Entered at the post office, N. Y., as Second-Class Matter.

☞ Old Cap. Collier Library is issued Semi-Weekly.

LECOQ, THE DETECTIVE.

PART II.

By Emile Gaboriau.

Great
DETECTIVE
STORIES.

NEW YORK:
NORMAN L. MUNRO, PUBLISHER,
24 & 26 VANDEWATER ST.

Cover of an American dime-novel Gaboriau publication.

Gaboriau's friend and publisher, Dentu, apparently felt that
Gaboriau's work could be carried on by other hands, for in
1878 he published *La Vieillesse de Monsieur Lecoq* (*The Old
Age of Monsieur Lecoq*). This was written by Fortuné du
Boisgobey, a prolific hack who wrote many other mystery
novels, particularly *The Parisian Detective*, which was very
popular in the United States. In *La Vieillesse de Monsieur
Lecoq*, which was soon translated and published in America,
Lecoq, now an old man, has to save his son from execution as a
convicted murderer. All the evidence is against them. One of
the more amusing moments is when Lecoq, disguised as an
Indian rajah, interviews the true murderer, who in turn is disguised as a German genealogist. This novel is not to be taken
seriously, as Gaboriau's novels are, and apparently its sensation-
alism did not appeal to French readers, for there were no more
sequels.

For reasons now forgotten, Gaboriau's work was appreciated
in America before England. The first appearance of Gaboriau,
strangely enough, is in a disguise that Lecoq and Gaboriau
might have found amusing as well as annoying. This was *The
Steel Safe; or The Stains and Splendors of New York Life* by
Henry L. Williams, Jr. (1868), which was a barefaced plagi-
arism and adaptation of *File No. 113*. Williams follows Gaboriau almost sentence by sentence, scene by scene, but the whole
story is set in New York. Monsieur Lecoq has become Clayton
Newlife, and his disguised personality is Jehiel Sharpson of
Ohio. Lecoq lives on Prince Street.

Translations of Gaboriau's major works began to appear in
the 1870's in Boston, beginning with *The Widow Lerouge* in
1873. The dime-novel publisher George Munro, in his *Seaside
Library*, rapidly brought all the major and even many of the
minor novels into easily accessible form for the reader who had
five or ten cents. The first appearancee of *Monsieur Lecoq*, as
far as I have been able to trace, is in this dime-novel series, in
1879, a year before cloth editions appeared in America.

Before the appearance of Gaboriau's novels in America, the
American detective story had been on the trivial side numeri-
cally. There were prehistoric detective stories before 1840 by
Charles Brockden Brown and William Leggett; there was
Poe's crystallization of the form and invention of ratiocinative

deduction; but only a few minor successors to Poe. Then suddenly, shortly after the appearance of Gaboriau, the country was flooded with series after series of detective novels in dime-novel format. They were not modern detective stories, it is true; but they were novels that involved a crime, a detective (usually official), and some detection. I am inclined to think that this explosion of interest is the result of two foreign influences: to a lesser extent British detective casebooks (like "Waters"), as published by Dick and Fitzgerald, and to a larger extent, the long novels of Gaboriau.

In England Gaboriau's works began to appear in *Vizetelly's Sensational Novels* from 1883 on. Some of the translations may have been taken from American piracies; others may have been British in origin. This date 1883, it will be observed, is not far removed from 1887, the date of A. C. Doyle's *Study in Scarlet*. Doyle's diary notes reveal that he read certain of Gaboriau's novels, and in later years he recalled *The Widow Lerouge*, though somewhat dimly. Yet enough of the schema and details of Gaboriau's work remained in Doyle's mind that Doyle without Gaboriau would have been quite different. If Poe's Dupin was the father of Tabaret and Lecoq, Tabaret and Lecoq are the father and godfather of Sherlock Holmes. This is not to say, of course, that there were no other elements, or to deny Doyle's own ingenious contributions.

Let me quote a few Sherlockisms, which the reader can easily match in Doyle's stories:

He remained there for about half an hour, then came out running, then reentered and came out again; again reentered, and again reappeared, almost immediately. The judge could not help comparing him to a pointer on the scent, carrying his nose in the air, as if to discover some subtle odor left by the assassin. All the while he talked loudly and with much gesticulation, apostrophizing himself, scolding himself, uttering little cries of triumph or self-encouragement. (*The Widow Lerouge.*)

"The misfortune is that the art is lost, because fine crimes are rare. The race of strong criminals, fearless and ingenious, has given place to a mob of vulgar pickers and stealers, hardly worth hunting after—blunderers as well as cowards, who sign their names to their misdeeds, and even leave their cartes de visite. There is no merit in catching them." (*The Widow Lerouge.*)

Never was young libertine more irregular in his habits than this old man. He came or failed to come to his meals, ate it mattered not what nor at what hour. He went out at every hour of the day or night, often slept abroad, and even disappeared for entire weeks at a time. Then he received the strangest visitors—odd-looking men of suspicious aspect and fellows of ill-favored and sinister aspect. (*The Widow Lerouge.*)

Marguerite sprang to her feet at once agitated and alarmed. "How did you know this?" she exclaimed. M. Fortunat had left his armchair, and was now leaning against the mantel-shelf, in what he considered a most becoming and awe-inspiring attitude, with his thumb in the armhole of his waistcoat. "Ah! Nothing could be more simple," he answered in the same tone as a conjurer might assume to explain his feat. (*The Vengeance of Baron Trigault*)

These are all basic elements in the concept of Sherlock Holmes, although to my mind, Doyle developed them with greater clarity. There are many such small resemblances between the two sets of stories. If the modern reader has wondered at times why Doyle used the double-novel in *A Study in Scarlet, The Sign of Four* and *The Valley of Fear*—let him look to Gaboriau.

Gaboriau is obviously a historical link of the utmost importance. Is he more than this? Is he an author worth reading in his own right? My answer is a limited "Yes." While he has great weaknessess, he also has certain strengths that are almost unique.

Let us omit the question of Gaboriau's French style, which has been called alternately brilliant and whimsical, ironic and lyric. These qualities do not emerge in the translations, but the translations are admittedly bad. They are hastily, carelessly, insensitively prepared hackwork, which at times are neither French nor English.

Gaboriau is certainly one of the most accomplished plotters in the genre. He is capable of working out a complex group of life situations and interweaving them without boring the reader or confusing him.

Complex plots, of course, were a standby of Victorian popular literature, and in England G. W. M. Reynolds and Wilkie Collins specialized in comparable material. Yet it is safe to say that Gaboriau at his best excelled them both in ornateness. Such erector-set stories, however, may not be the highest achievement in literature (especially since the twentieth century is likely to seek other values), but they are still achievements that demand respect.

The detective novel is a notoriously difficult form to plot, since, to express it in the lowest terms, the author must devise something to fill in the space between the crime and the revealment or detection. It is greatly to Gaboriau's credit that in what is the first modern detective novel he solved the problem as well any one has done since. Where *The Widow Lerouge* has flaws, they are in other areas.

Gaboriau's second strength lies in his detailed factual backgrounds and in his criminological and legal accuracy. Strictly speaking, this is not purely a matter of literature, but the reader of one hundred years later can appreciate the care that went into the descriptions of judicial processes, quirks of law, detectional insights, and the whole philosophy of French criminal investigation. British jurists have been known to recommend Gaboriau's novels to juniors who wanted a rapid picture of French criminal procedure. Gaboriau's old chief, Féval, faked in such matters and relied on imagination to carry him through. Gaboriau was correct. If Gaboriau describes the powers of the examining magistrate, if he explains a point in the law of inheritance, if he describes a suicide by carbon monoxide from unventilated charcoal braziers, one can be sure that he has checked the point. For Gaboriau there are no giant sea anemones, no devil's foot. If a young man is sent to the war in French Indo-China, and a crime is committed there, as in *The Gilded Clique*, one can be sure that extradition and venue are correctly handled. All this mirrors a world strange to the American reader, a world where the prisoner is officially guilty unless he can prove his innocence, where police entrapment (as in the Epilogue to *Monsieur Lecoq*) is permissible.

Where does Gaboriau fail? His portrayal of people. His characters have been called cardboard, and the accusation is, for the most part, true. They do resemble the moving dummies in a shooting gallery. Yet this criticism is a little over-simple. While the various counts and barons, fake and real, that people the novels, the adulterous ladies and virtuous ingenues, the sincere young lovers with mistresses on the side—are statues or lay-figures that sustain a drapery of plot, Gaboriau did succeed in animating two major characters, Lecoq and Tabaret, the voices of realism, rather than of romance.

A little more consciousness of technique might have worked wonders for Gaboriau in this respect. When Gaboriau works through the mind of a single character, which he does to some extent with Lecoq and Tabaret, his skill at recognizing motivation and his ability to create small detail can work an animation. When Gaboriau, on the other hand, attempts to make his characters interact romantically, when he speaks remotely as a recording witness, he loses his honesty of emotion and de-sparks what might have been human. This is where melodrama comes in, and this is where disaster strikes.

Perhaps the safest judgment of Gaboriau as a whole is to call him an author with a fine lesser imagination and an excellent skill at research, hampered by a lack of large-scale insight. Too often he sets up trumpery effects that do not succeed, and too often he is false. This may seem to be a harsh judgment, but the reader can look at the works of Balzac to see what happens when a first-rate writer, even though he may lack smoothness, works on material somewhat similar to Gaboriau's.

Criticism should stay at criticism, and reading pleasure should remain reading pleasure. Despite a modern reader's occasional annoyance at Gaboriau's weaknesses, *Monsieur Lecoq, Part One,* is still very much worth reading; it is easily the most animated of Gaboriau's works. The ingenuity of the author's deductions; the piquant personality of the young man who is determined to make his way in his profession, despite obstacles of official stupidity and criminal cunning; the thrill of the psychological duel between the helpless prisoner in his cell and the imaginative detective—these are the factors that make *Monsieur Lecoq* a perennial classic. The detective has all the advantages except one: *Zugzwang*, but that tiny pressure is more powerful than all the powers of the prober.

The reader may not care who May really was; it makes no

difference in the long run—but it is a fascinating procedure to follow May and Lecoq and see how the role of May was sustained.

E. F. BLEILER

THE BOOK PUBLICATIONS AND TRANSLATIONS OF EMILE GABORIAU

1. *L'Ancien Figaro. Etudes satiriques, bigarrures, coups de lancette, nouvelles à la main, extraits du Figaro de la Restauration, avec une préface et un commentaire par Emile Gaboriau.* Paris. E. Dentu. 1861.

    An anthology of articles edited by Gaboriau. Not translated. Not seen.

2. *Les Cotillons célèbres.* Paris. E. Dentu. 1861. Two volumes.

    Journalistic lives of famous French mistresses and courtesans. Not translated.

3. *Le 13e Hussards, types, profils, esquisses et croquis militaires à pied et à cheval.* Paris. E. Dentu. 1861.

    Experiences of a recruit, followed by sketches of military life, types, and situations. English title: *The Thirteenth Hussars.* The second part has occasionally been published separately as *Military Sketches.*

4. *Les Gens de Bureau.* Paris. E. Dentu. 1862.

    Satire on bureaucracy. English title: *The Men of the Bureau.*

5. *Les Mariages d'aventure.* Paris. E. Dentu. 1862. Two volumes.

    Two short novels. The first, *M. J. D. de Saint-Roch, ambassadeur matrimonial,* is translated as (a) *A Chance Marriage* or (b) *Marriage at a Venture.* The second, *Promesses de mariage,* is translated as *Promise of Marriage.*

6. *Ruses d'amour.* Paris. E. Dentu. 1862.

An anthology of various stratagems used in love. Not translated. Not seen.

7. *Les Comédiennes adorées.* Paris. E. Dentu. 1863.

Journalistic lives of famous actresses. Not translated.

8. *L'Affaire Lerouge.* Paris. E. Dentu. 1866.

Detective novel. English titles: (a) *The Widow Lerouge.* (b) *Old Tabaret, the Self-made Detective; or, "Piping" the Lerouge Case.* (c) *The Lerouge Case.*

9. *Le Crime d'Orcival.* Paris. E. Dentu. 1867.

Detective novel. English titles: (a) *The Mystery of Orcival.* (b) *Crime at Orcival.*

10. *Le Dossier no. 113.* Paris. E. Dentu. 1867.

Detective novel. English titles: (a) *File No. 113.* (b) *Dossier No. 133.* (c) *The Blackmailers* (greatly abridged). See also 21 in Miscellaneous and Spurious Material, below.

11. *Les Esclaves de Paris.* Paris. E. Dentu. 1868. Two volumes.

Crime novel. The first part, *Le Chantage,* is translated as *The Slaves of Paris, Part One* or *Caught in the Net.* The second part, *Le Secret de Champdoce,* is translated as *The Slaves of Paris, Part Two* or *The Champdoce Mystery.*

12. *Monsieur Lecoq.* Paris. E. Dentu. 1869. Two volumes.

Detective novel. The first part, *L'Enquête,* is translated as (a) *Monsieur Lecoq* or (b) *Monsieur Lecoq, Part One* or (c) *The Detective's Dilemma* or (d) *Lecoq the Detective.* The second part, *L'Honneur du nom,* is translated as (a) *The Honor of the Name* or (b) *Monsieur Lecoq, Part Two* or (c) *The Detective's Triumph* or (d) *Lecoq the Detective, Part Two.* There have been two English translations of *Monsieur*

Lecoq. The first American translation was prepared by Mrs. Laura E. Kendall, and published in 1879. Other American publications are based on this translation, as reedited several times. The first British translation, that of Sir Gilbert Campbell, was published in 1888–9. The text used in this present volume is Mrs. Kendall's, as thoroughly revised and corrected for publication around 1908.

13. *La Vie infernale.* Paris. E. Dentu. 1870. Two volumes.

Comédie de moeurs, with crime elements. The first part, *Pascal et Marguerite,* is translated as (a) *The Count's Secret, Part One* or (b) *The Count's Millions.* The second part, *Lia d'Argeles,* is translated as (a) *The Count's Secret, Part Two* or (b) *The Vengeance of Baron Trigault.*

14. *La Clique dorée.* Paris. E. Dentu. 1871.

Crime novel. English titles (a) *The Clique of Gold* or (b) *The Gilded Clique.*

15. *La Dégringolade.* Paris. G. Paetz. 1872. 12 volumes.

Comédie de moeurs. English translations: (a) *Catastrophe* or (b) *The Downward Path.*

16. *La Corde au cou.* Paris. E. Dentu. 1873.

Crime and detection novel. English titles: (a) *Within an Inch of His Life* or (b) *In Deadly Peril* or (c) *In Peril of His Life.*

17. *L'Argent des autres.* Paris. E. Dentu. 1874.

Comédie de moeurs with crime elements. English titles: (a) *Other People's Money* or (b) *A Great Robbery; or "Piping" A Series of Bank Frauds.*

18. *Le Petit Vieux des Batignoles.* Paris. E. Dentu. 1876.

A collection. Title nouvelle and five short stories. "Bonheur passe richesse." "La Soutane de Nessus." "Une Disparition." "Maudite Maison." "Casta Vixit." English title: *The Little Old Man of Batignoles.*

19. Le Capitaine Coutanceau. Paris. E. Dentu. 1878.

Historical novel. English titles: (a) *Captain Coutanceau* or (b) *Captain Contanceau* [sic].

20. *Les Amours d'une empoisonneuse.* Paris. E. Dentu. 1881.

Historical novel. English titles: (a) *The Marquise de Brinvilliers* or (b) *Marie de Brinvilliers* or (c) *An Adventuress of France* or (d) *Intrigues of a Poisoner.*

MISCELLANEOUS AND SPURIOUS MATERIAL

21. *The Steel Safe; or, The Stains and Splendors of New York Life* by Henry L. Williams, Jr. New York. DeWitt. 1868.

A plagiaristic adaptation, with a New York setting, of *Le Dossier no. 113.* This translation was abridged to a short story, reset in Paris with the original names, and issued in Great Britain as *Warrant 113* (London. Crown Publishing Co. Ltd. 1884).

22. *La Vieillesse de Monsieur Lecoq* by Fortuné du Boisgobey. Paris. E. Dentu. 1878.

Pastiche, published under du Boisgobey's name. English translation, published under several imprints, *The Old Age of Monsieur Lecoq* by Fortuné du Boisgobey.

According to bibliographic records this book has also been published under Gaboriau's name in the United States. The following titles are recorded: (a) *The Old Age of Monsieur Lecoq* by Emile Gaboriau or (b) *The Last Adventures of Lecoq the Detective* by Emile Gaboriau. It is possible that (c) *Perils of Lecoq the Detective* by Emile Gaboriau is the same work. These three editions have not been seen.

23. *Famous French Criminals* by Emile Gaboriau. New York. Frank Tousey, Brookside Library. 1883. A collection of factual French crimes, probably of British origin. Spurious.

24. *File No. 114 or Young Earnest.* Chicago, Laird & Lee. 1887. This is said to be a "sequel" to *File No. 113.* It is not clear whether it is a separate spurious work, or a

retitling of a second portion of *File No. 113*, a situation that frequently occurred in dime-novel publishing. It is known from bibliographic records, but has not been seen.

25. *File No. 115* by Harry Harper. New York. Ogilvie. 1886. Presumably connected with the Gaboriau novel. Not seen.

BIBLIOGRAPHY

The French have neglected the study of Gaboriau greatly, and the only documents worth examining are two English papers.

"Gaboriau: Father of the Detective Novel" by Valentine Williams. In *National Review*. London. December 1923. This gathers together most of the early biographical material and offers critical comments.

The Life and Works of Emile Gaboriau by Nancy E. L. Curry. Unpublished doctoral thesis, University of Kentucky, 1971. Mrs. Curry has studied the periodical publications of Gaboriau and sums up French research since Valentine Williams wrote his essay.

MONSIEUR LECOQ

MONSIEUR LECOQ

AT about elèven o'clock in the evening of the 20th of February, 186--, which chanced to be Shrove Sunday, a
party of detectives left the police station near the old
Barriere d'Italie to the direct south of Paris. Their mission
was to explore the district extending on the one hand between
the highroad to Fontainebleau and the Seine, and on the other
between the outer boulevards and the fortifications.

This quarter of the city had at that time anything but an enviable reputation. To venture there at night was considered
so dangerous that the soldiers from the outlying forts who
came in to Paris with permission to go to the theatre, were
ordered to halt at the barriere, and not to pass through the
perilous district excepting in parties of three or four.

After midnight, these gloomy, narrow streets became the
haunt of numerous homeless vagabonds, and escaped criminals
and malefactors, moreover, made the quarter their rendezvous.
If the day had been a lucky one, they made merry over their
spoils, and when sleep overtook them, hid in doorways or
among the rubbish in deserted houses. Every effort had been
made to dislodge these dangerous guests, but the most energetic measures had failed to prove successful. Watched,
hunted, and in imminent danger of arrest though they were,
they always returned with idiotic obstinacy, obeying, as one
might suppose, some mysterious law of attraction. Hence, the
district was for the police an immense trap, constantly baited,
and to which the game came of their own accord to be caught.

The result of a tour of inspection of this locality was so
certain, that the officer in charge of the police post called to
the squad as they departed: "I will prepare lodgings for our
guests. Good luck to you and much pleasure!"

This last wish was pure irony, for the weather was the most
disagreeable that could be imagined. A very heavy snow storm
had prevailed for several days. It was now beginning to thaw,

and on all the frequented thoroughfares the slush was ankle-deep. It was still cold, however; a damp chill filled the air, and penetrated to the very marrow of one's bones. Besides, there was a dense fog, so dense that one could not see one's hands before one's face.

"What a beastly job!" growled one of the agents.

"Yes," replied the inspector who commanded the squad; "if you had an income of thirty thousand francs, I don't suppose you'd be here." The laugh that greeted this common-place joke was not so much flattery as homage to a recognized and established superiority.

The inspector was, in fact, one of the most esteemed members of the force, a man who had proved his worth. His powers of penetration were not, perhaps, very great; but he thoroughly understood his profession, its resources, its labyrinths, and its artifices. Long practise had given him imperturbable coolness, a great confidence in himself, and a sort of coarse diplomacy that supplied the place of shrewdness. To his failings and his virtues he added incontestable courage, and he would lay his hand upon the collar of the most dangerous criminal as tranquilly as a devotee dips his fingers in a basin of holy water.

He was a man about forty-six years of age, strongly built, with rugged features, a heavy mustache, and rather small, gray eyes, hidden by bushy eyebrows. His name was Gevrol, but he was universally known as "the General." This sobriquet was pleasing to his vanity, which was not slight, as his subordinates well knew; and, doubtless, he felt that he ought to receive from them the same consideration as was due to a person of that exalted rank.

"If you begin to complain already," he added, gruffly, what will you do by and by?"

In fact, it was too soon to complain. The little party were then passing along the Rue de Choisy. The people on the footways were orderly; and the lights of the wine-shops illuminated the street. All these places were open. There is no fog or thaw that is potent enough to dismay lovers of pleasure. And a boisterous crowd of maskers filled each tavern, and public ballroom. Through the open windows came alternately the sounds of loud voices and bursts of noisy music. Occasionally, a drunken man staggered along the pavement, or a masked figure crept by in the shadow cast by the houses.

Before certain establishments Gevrol commanded a halt. He gave a peculiar whistle, and almost immediately a man came out. This was another member of the force. His report was listened to, and then the squad passed on.

"To the left, boys!" ordered Gevrol; "we will take the Rue d'Ivry, and then cut through the shortest way to the Rue de Chevaleret."

From this point the expedition became really disagreeable. The way led through an unfinished, unnamed street, full of puddles and deep holes, and obstructed with all sorts of rubbish. There were no longer any lights or crowded wine-shops. No footsteps, no voices were heard; solitude, gloom, and an almost perfect silence prevailed; and one might have supposed one-self a hundred leagues from Paris, had it not been for the deep and continuous murmur that always arises from a large city, resembling the hollow roar of a torrent in some cavern depth.

All the men had turned up their trousers and were advancing slowly, picking their way as carefully as an Indian when he is stealing upon his prey. They had just passed the Rue du Chateau-des-Rentiers when suddenly a wild shriek rent the air. At this place, and at this hour, such a cry was so frightfully significant, that all the men paused as if by common impulse.

"Did you hear that, General?" asked one of the detectives, in a low voice.

"Yes, there is murder going on not far from here—but where? Silence! let us listen."

They all stood motionless, holding their breath, and anxiously listening. Soon a second cry, or rather a wild howl, resounded.

"Ah!" exclaimed the inspector, "it is at the Poivriere."

This peculiar appellation "Poivriere" or "pepper-box" was derived from the term "peppered" which in French slang is applied to a man who has left his good sense at the bottom of his glass. Hence, also, the sobriquet of "pepper thieves" given to the rascals whose specialty it is to plunder helpless, inoffensive drunkards.

"What!" added Gevrol to his companions, "don't you know Mother Chupin's drinking-shop there on the right. Run."

And, setting the example, he dashed off in the direction indicated. His men followed, and in less than a minute they reached a hovel of sinister aspect, standing alone, in a tract of waste ground. It was indeed from this den that the cries had proceeded. They were now repeated, and were immediately followed by two pistol shots. The house was hermetically closed, but through the cracks in the window-shutters, gleamed a reddish light like that of a fire. One of the police agents darted to one of these windows, and raising himself up by clinging to the shutters with his hands, endeavored to peer through the cracks, and to see what was passing within.

Gevrol himself ran to the door. "Open!" he commanded, striking it heavily. No response came. But they could hear plainly enough the sound of a terrible struggle—of fierce imprecations, hollow groans, and occasionally the sobs of a woman.

"Horrible!" cried the police agent, who was peering through the shutters; "it is horrible!"

This exclamation decided Gevrol. "Open, in the name of the law!" he cried a third time.

And no one responding, with a blow of the shoulder that was as violent as a blow from a battering-ram, he dashed open the door. Then the horror-stricken accent of the man who had been peering through the shutters was explained. The room presented such a spectacle that all the agents, and even Gevrol himself, remained for a moment rooted to the threshold, shuddering with unspeakable horror.

Everything denoted that the house had been the scene of a terrible struggle, of one of those savage conflicts which only too often stain the barriere drinking dens with blood. The lights had been extinguished at the beginning of the strife, but a blazing fire of pine logs illuminated even the furthest corners of the room. Tables, glasses, decanters, household utensils, and stools had been overturned, thrown in every direction, trodden upon, shivered into fragments. Near the fireplace two men lay stretched upon the floor. They were lying motionless upon their backs, with their arms crossed. A third was extended in the middle of the room. A woman crouched upon the lower steps of a staircase leading to the floor above. She had thrown her apron over her head, and was uttering inarticulate moans. Finally, facing the police, and with his back turned to an open door leading into an adjoining room, stood a young man, in front of whom a heavy oaken table formed, as it were, a rampart.

He was of medium stature, and wore a full beard. His clothes, not unlike those of a railway porter, were torn to fragments, and soiled with dust and wine and blood. This certainly

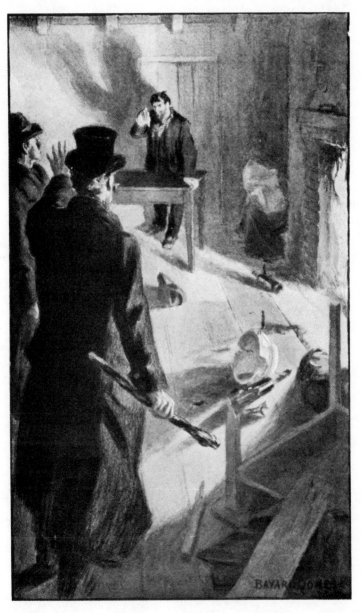

Facing the police . . . stood a young man.

was the murderer. The expression on his face was terrible. A mad fury blazed in his eyes, and a convulsive sneer distorted his features. On his neck and cheek were two wounds which bled profusely. In his right hand, covered with a handkerchief, he held a pistol, which he aimed at the intruders.

"Surrender!" cried Gevrol.

The man's lips moved, but in spite of a visible effort he could not articulate a syllable.

"Don't do any mischief," continued the inspector, "we are in force, you can not escape; so lay down your arms."

"I am innocent," exclaimed the man, in a hoarse, strained voice.

"Naturally, but we do not see it."

"I have been attacked; ask that old woman. I defended myself; I have killed—I had a right to do so; it was in self-defense!"

The gesture with which he enforced these words was so menacing that one of the agents drew Gevrol violently aside, saying, as he did so; "Take care, General, take care! The revolver has five barrels, and we have heard but two shots."

But the inspector was inaccessible to fear; he freed himself from the grasp of his subordinate and again stepped forward, speaking in a still calmer tone. "No foolishness, my lad; if your case is a good one, which is possible, after all, don't spoil it."

A frightful indecision betrayed itself on the young man's features. He held Gevrol's life at the end of his finger, was he about to press the trigger? No, he suddenly threw his weapon to the floor, exclaiming: "Come and take me!" And turning as he spoke he darted into the adjoining room, hoping doubtless to escape by some means of egress which he knew of.

Gevrol had expected this movement. He sprang after him with outstretched arms, but the table retarded his pursuit. "Ah!" he exclaimed, "the wretch escapes us!"

But the fate of the fugitive was already decided. While Gevrol parleyed, one of the agents—he who had peered through the shutters—had gone to the rear of the house and effected an entrance through the back door. As the murderer darted out, this man sprang upon him, seized him, and with surprising strength and agility dragged him back. The murderer tried to resist; but in vain. He had lost his strength: he tottered and fell upon the table that had momentarily protected him, murmuring loud enough for every one to hear: "Lost! It is the Prussians who are coming!"

This simple and decisive maneuvre on the part of the subordinate had won the victory, and at first it greatly delighted the inspector. "Good, my boy," said he, "very good! Ah! you have a talent for your business, and you will do well if ever an opportunity—"

But he checked himself; all his followers so evidently shared his enthusiasm that a feeling of jealousy overcame him. He felt his prestige diminishing, and hastened to add: "The idea had occurred to me; but I could not give the order without warning the scoundrel himself."

This remark was superfluous. All the police agents had now gathered around the murderer. They began by binding his feet and hands, and then fastened him securely to a chair. He offered no resistance. His wild excitement had given place to that gloomy prostration that follows all unnatural efforts, either of mind or body. Evidently he had abandoned himself to his fate.

When Gevrol saw that the men had finished their task, he called on them to attend to the other inmates of the den, and in addition ordered the lamps to be lit for the fire was going out. The inspector began his examination with the two men lying near the fireplace. He laid his hand on their hearts, but no pulsations were to be detected. He then held the face of his watch close to their lips, but the glass remained quite clear. "Useless," he murmured, after several trials, "useless; they are dead! They will never see morning again. Leave them in the same position until the arrival of the public prosecutor, and let us look at the other one."

The third man still breathed. He was a young fellow, wearing the uniform of a common soldier of the line. He was unarmed, and his large bluish gray cloak was partly open, revealing his bare chest. The agents lifted him very carefully— for he groaned piteously at the slightest movement—and placed him in an upright position, with his back leaning against the wall. He soon opened his eyes, and in a faint voice asked for something to drink. They brought him a glass of water, which he drank with evident satisfaction. He then drew a long breath, and seemed to regain some little strength.

"Where are you wounded?" asked Gevrol.

"In the head, there," he responded, trying to raise one of his arms. "Oh! how I suffer."

The police agent, who had cut off the murderer's retreat now approached, and with a dexterity that an old surgeon might have envied, made an examination of the gaping wound which the young man had received in the back of the neck. "It is nothing," declared the police agent, but as he spoke there was no mistaking the movement of his lower lip. It was evident that he considered the wound very dangerous, probably mortal.

"It will be nothing," affirmed Gevrol in his turn; "wounds in the head, when they do not kill at once, are cured in a month."

The wounded man smiled sadly. "I have received my death blow," he murmured.

"Nonsense!"

"Oh! it is useless to say anything; I feel it, but I do not complain. I have only received my just deserts."

All the police agents turned toward the murderer on hearing these words, presuming that he would take advantage of this opportunity to repeat his protestations of innocence. But their expectations were disappointed; he did not speak, although he must certainly have heard the words.

"It was that brigand, Lacheneur, who enticed me here," continued the wounded man, in a voice that was growing fainter.

"Lacheneur?"

"Yes, Jean Lacheneur, a former actor, who knew me when I was rich—for I had a fortune, but I spent it all; I wished to amuse myself. He, knowing I was without a single sou in the world, came and promised me money enough to begin life over again. Fool that I was to believe him, for he brought me to die here like a dog! Oh! I will have my revenge on him!" At this thought the wounded man clenched his hands threateningly. "I will have my revenge," he resumed. "I know much more than he believes. I will reveal everything."

But he had presumed too much upon his strength. Anger had given him a moment's energy, but at the cost of his life which was ebbing away. When he again tried to speak, he could not. Twice did he open his lips, but only a choking cry of impotent rage escaped them. This was his last manifestation of intelligence. A bloody foam gathered upon his lips, his eyes rolled back in their sockets, his body stiffened, and he fell face downward in a terrible convulsion.

"It is over," murmured Gevrol.

"Not yet," replied the young police agent, who had shown himself so proficient; "but he can not live more than two minutes. Poor devil! he will say nothing."

The inspector of police had risen from the floor as if he had just witnessed the commonest incident in the world, and was carefully dusting the knees of his trousers. "Oh, well," he responded, "we shall know all we need to know. This fellow is a soldier, and the number of his regiment will be given on the buttons of his cloak."

A slight smile curved the lips of the subordinate. "I think you are mistaken, General," said he.

"How—"

"Yes, I understand. Seeing him attired in a military coat, you supposed—But no; this poor wretch was no soldier. Do you wish for an immediate proof? Is his hair the regulation cut? Where did you ever see soldiers with their hair falling over their shoulders?"

This objection silenced the General for a moment; but he replied bruskly: "Do you think that I keep my eyes in my pocket? What you have remarked did not escape my notice; only I said to myself, here is a young man who has profited by leave of absence to visit the wig maker."

"At least—"

But Gevrol would permit no more interruptions. "Enough talk," he declared. "We will now hear what has happened. Mother Chupin, the old hussy, is not dead!"

As he spoke, he advanced toward the old woman, who was still crouching upon the stairs. She had not moved nor ventured so much as a look since the entrance of the police, but her moans had not been discontinued. With a sudden movement, Gevrol tore off the apron which she had thrown over her head, and there she stood, such as years, vice, poverty, and drink had made her; wrinkled, shriveled, toothless, and haggard, her skin as yellow and as dry as parchment and drawn tightly over her bones.

"Come, stand up!" ordered the inspector. "Your lamentations don't affect me. You ought to be sent to prison for putting such vile drugs into your liquors thus breeding madness in the brains of your customers."

The old woman's little red eyes traveled slowly round the room, and then in tearful tones she exclaimed: "What a misfortune! what will become of me? Everything is broken—I am ruined !" She only seemed impressed by the loss of her table utensils.

"Now tell us how this trouble began," said Gevrol.

"Alas! I know nothing about it. I was upstairs mending my son's clothes, when I heard a dispute."

"And after that?"

"Of course I came down, and I saw those three men that are lying there picking a quarrel with the young man you have arrested; the poor innocent! For he is innocent, as truly as I am an honest woman. If my son Polyte had been here he would have separated them; but I, a poor widow, what could I do! I cried 'Police!' with all my might."

After giving this testimony she resumed her seat, thinking she had said enough. But Gevrol rudely ordered her to stand up again. "Oh! we have not done," said he. "I wish for other particulars."

"What particulars, dear Monsieur Gevrol, since I saw nothing?"

Anger crimsoned the inspector's ears. "What would you say, old woman, if I arrested you?"

"It would be a great piece of injustice."

"Nevertheless, it is what will happen if you persist in remaining silent. I have an idea that a fortnight in Saint Lazare would untie your tongue."

These words produced the effect of an electric shock on the Widow Chupin. She suddenly ceased her hypocritical lamentations, rose, placed her hands defiantly on her hips, and poured forth a torrent of invective upon Gevrol and his agents, accusing them of persecuting her family ever since they had previously arrested her son, a good-for-nothing fellow. Finally, she swore that she was not afraid of prison, and would be only too glad to end her days in jail beyond the reach of want.

At first the General tried to impose silence upon the terrible termagant: but he soon discovered that he was powerless; besides, all his subordinates were laughing. Accordingly he turned his back upon her, and, advancing toward the murderer, he said: "You, at least, will not refuse an explanation."

The man hesitated for a moment. "I have already said all that I have to say," he replied, at last. "I have told you that I am innocent; and this woman and a man on the point of death who was struck down by my hand, have both confirmed my declaration. What more do you desire? When the judge questions me, I will, perhaps, reply; until then do not expect another word from me."

It was easy to see that the fellow's resolution was irrevocable; and that he was not to be daunted by any inspector of police. Criminals frequently preserve an absolute silence, from the very moment they are captured. These men are experienced and shrewd, and lawyers and judges pass many sleepless nights on their account. They have learned that a system of defense can not be improvised at once; that it is, on the contrary, a work of patience and meditation; and knowing what a terrible effect an apparently insignificant response drawn from them at the moment of detection may produce on a court of justice, they remain obstinately silent. So as to see whether the present culprit was an old hand or not, Gevrol was about to insist on a full explanation when some one announced that the soldier had just breathed his last.

"As that is so, my boys," the inspector remarked, "two of you will remain here, and I will leave with the others. I shall go and arouse the commissary of police, and inform him of the affair; he will take the matter in hand: and we can then do whatever he commands. My responsibility will be over, in any case. So untie our prisoner's legs and bind Mother Chupin's hands, and we will drop them both at the station-house as we pass."

The men hastened to obey, with the exception of the youngest among them, the same who had won the General's passing praise. He approached his chief, and motioning that he desired to speak with him, drew him outside the door. When they were a few steps from the house, Gevrol asked him what he wanted.

"I wish to know, General, what you think of this affair."

"I think, my boy, that four scoundrels encountered each other in this vile den. They began to quarrel; and from words they came to blows. One of them had a revolver, and he killed the others. It is as clear as daylight. According to his antecedents, and according to the antecedents of the victims, the assassin will be judged. Perhaps society owes him some thanks."

"And you think that any investigation—any further search is unnecessary."

"Entirely unnecessary."

The younger man appeared to deliberate for a moment. "It seems to me, General," he at length replied, "that this affair is not perfectly clear. Have you noticed the murderer, remarked his demeanor, and observed his look? Have you been surprised as I have been—?"

"By what?"

"Ah; well! it seems to me—I may, of course, be mistaken— but I fancy that appearances are deceitful, and-- Yes, I suspect something."

"Bah!—explain yourself, please."

"How can you explain the dog's faculty of scent?"

Gevrol shrugged his shoulders. "In short, he replied, "you scent a melodrama here—a rendezvous of gentlemen in disguise, here at the Poivriere, at Mother Chupin's house. Well, hunt after the mystery, my boy; search all you like, you have my permission."

"What! you will allow me?"

"I not only allow you, I order you to do it. You are going to remain here with any one of your comrades you may select. And if you find anything that I have not seen, I will allow you to buy me a pair of spectacles."

II

THE young police agent to whom Gevrol abandoned what he thought an unnecessary investigation was a débutant in his profession. His name was Lecoq. He was some twenty-five or twenty-six years of age, almost beardless, very pale, with red lips, and an abundance of wavy black hair. He was rather short but well proportioned; and each of his movements betrayed unusual energy. There was nothing remarkable about his appearance, if we except his eyes, which sparkled brilliantly or grew extremely dull, according to his mood; and his nose, the large full nostrils of which had a surprising mobility.

The son of a respectable, well-to-do Norman family, Lecoq had received a good and solid education. He was prosecuting his law studies in Paris, when in the same week, blow following blow, he learned that his father had died, financially ruined, and that his mother had survived him only a few hours. He was left alone in the world, destitute of resources, obliged to earn his living. But how? He had an opportunity of learning his true value, and found that it amounted to nothing; for the university, on bestowing its diploma of bachelor, does not give an annuity with it. Hence of what use is a college education to a poor orphan boy? He envied the lot of those who, with a trade at the ends of their fingers, could boldly enter the office of any manufacturer, and say: "I would like to work." Such men were working and eating. Lecoq sought bread by all the methods employed by people who are in reduced circumstances! Fruitless labor! There are a hundred thousand people in Paris who have seen better days. No matter! He gave proofs of undaunted energy. He gave lessons, and copied documents for a lawyer. He made his appearance in a new character almost every day, and left no means untried to earn an honest livelihood. At last he obtained employment from a well-known astronomer, the Baron Moser, and spent his days in solving bewildering and intricate problems, at the rate of a hundred francs a month.

But a season of discouragement came. After five years of constant toil, he found himself at the same point from which he had started. He was nearly crazed with rage and disappointment when he recapitulated his blighted hopes, his fruitless efforts, and the insults he had endured. The past had been sad, the present was intolerable, the future threatened to be terrible. Condemned to constant privations, he tried to escape from the horrors of his real life by taking refuge in dreams.

Alone in his garret, after a day of unremitting toil, assailed by the thousand longings of youth, Lecoq endeavored to devise some means of suddenly making himself rich. All reasonable methods being beyond his reach, it was not long before he was engaged in devising the worst expedients. In short, this naturally moral and honest young man spent much of his time in perpetrating—in fancy—the most abominable crimes. Sometimes he himself was frightened by the work of his imagination: for an hour of recklessness might suffice to make him pass from the idea to the fact, from theory to practise. This is the case with all monomaniacs; an hour comes in which the strange conceptions that have filled their brains can be no longer held in check.

One day he could not refrain from exposing to his patron a little plan he had conceived, which would enable him to obtain five or six hundred francs from London. Two letters and a telegram were all that was necessary, and the game was won. It was impossible to fail, and there was no danger of arousing suspicion.

The astronomer, amazed at the simplicity of the plan, could but admire it. On reflection, however, he concluded that it would not be prudent for him to retain so ingenious a secretary in his service. This was why, on the following day, he gave him a month's pay in advance, and dismissed him, saying: "When one has your disposition, and is poor, one may either become a famous thief or a great detective. Choose."

Lecoq retired in confusion; but the astronomer's words bore fruit in his mind. "Why should I not follow good advice?" he asked himself. Police service did not inspire him with repugnance—far from it. He had often admired that mysterious power whose hand is everywhere, and which, although unseen and unheard, still manages to hear and see everything. He was delighted with the prospect of being the instrument of such a power. He considered that the profession of detective would enable him to employ the talents with which he had been endowed in a useful and honorable fashion; besides opening out a life of thrilling adventure with fame as its goal.

In short, this profession had a wonderful charm for him. So much so, that on the following week, thanks to a letter from Baron Moser, he was admitted into the service. A cruel disenchantment awaited him. He had seen the results, but not the means. His surprise was like that of a simple-minded frequenter of the theatre, when he is admitted for the first time behind the scenes, and is able to pry into the decorations and tinsel that are so dazzling at a distance.

However, the opportunity for which he had so ardently longed, for which he had been waiting during many weary months, had come, he thought, at last, as he reached the Poivriere with Gevrol and the other police agents. While he was clinging to the window shutters he saw by the light of his ambition a pathway to success. It was at first only a presentiment, but it soon became a supposition, and then a conviction based upon actual facts, which had escaped his companions, but which he had observed and carefully noted. He recognized that fortune had, at last, turned in his favor when he saw Gevrol neglect all but the merest formalities of examination, and when he heard him declare peremptorily that this triple murder was merely the result of one of those ferocious quarrels so frequent among vagrants in the outskirts of the city.

"Ah, well!" he thought; "have it your own way—trust in appearances, since you will see nothing beneath them! But I will prove to you that my youthful theory is better than all your experience."

The inspector's carelessness gave Lecoq a perfect right to secretly seek information on his own account; but by warning his superior officers before attempting anything on his own responsibility, he would protect himself against any accusation of ambition or of unduly taking advantage of his comrade. Such charges might prove most dangerous for his future prospects in a profession where so much rivalry is seen, and where wounded vanity has so many opportunities to avenge itself by resorting to all sorts of petty treason. Accordingly, he spoke to his superior officer—saying just enough to be able to remark, in case of success: "Ah! I warned you!"—just enough so as *not* to dispel any of Gevrol's doubts.

The permission which Lecoq obtained to remain in charge of the bodies was his first triumph of the best possible augury; but he knew how to dissimulate, and it was in a tone of the utmost indifference that he requested one of his comrades to remain with him. Then, while the others were making ready to depart, he seated himself upon the corner of the table, apparently oblivious of all that was passing around. He did not dare to lift his head, for fear of betraying his joy, so much did he fear that his companions might read his hopes and plans in the expression of his face.

Inwardly he was wild with impatience. Though the murderer submitted with good grace to the precautions that were taken to prevent his escape, it required some time to bind the hands of the Widow Chupin, who fought and howled as if they were burning her alive. "They will never go!" Lecoq murmured to himself.

They did so at last, however. Gevrol gave the order to start, and left the house, addressing a laughing good-by to his subordinate. The latter made no reply. He followed his comrades as far as the threshold to make sure that they were really going, for he trembled at the thought that Gevrol might reflect, change his mind, and return to solve the mystery, as was his right.

His anxiety was needless, however. The squad gradually faded away in the distance, and the cries of Widow Chupin died away in the stillness of the night. It was only then that Lecoq reentered the room. He could no longer conceal his delight; his eyes sparkled as might those of a conqueror taking possession of some vast empire: he stamped his foot upon the floor and exclaimed with exultation: "Now the mystery belongs to us two alone!"

Authorized by Gevrol to choose one of his comrades to remain with him at the Poivriere, Lecoq had requested the least intelligent of the party to keep him company. He was not influenced by a fear of being obliged to share the fruits of success with his companion, but by the necessity of having an assistant from whom he could, in case of need, exact implicit obedience.

The comrade Lecoq selected was a man of about fifty, who, after a term of cavalry service, had become an agent of the prefecture. In the humble office that he occupied he had seen prefect succeed prefect, and might probably have filled an entire prison with the culprits he had arrested with his own hands. Experience had not, however, made him any the shrewder or any the more zealous. Still he had this merit, when he received an order he executed it with military exactitude, so far as he understood it. Of course if he had failed to understand it, so much the worse. It might, indeed, be said of him, that he discharged his duties like a blind man, like an old horse trained for a riding school.

When he had a moment's leisure, and a little money in his pocket, he invariably got drunk. Indeed, he spent his life between two fits of intoxication, without ever rising above a condition of semi-lucidity. His comrades had known, but had forgotten, his name, and his partiality for a certain beverage had accordingly induced them to call him "Father Absinthe."

With his limited powers of observation, he naturally did not observe the tone of triumph in his young companion's voice. "Upon my word," he remarked, when they were alone, "your idea of keeping me here was a good one, and I thank you for it. While the others spend the night paddling about in the slush, I shall get a good sleep."

Here he stood, in a room that was splashed with blood, that was shuddering, so to speak, with crime, and yet face to face with the still warm bodies of three murdered men he could talk of sleep!

But, after all, what did it matter to him? He had seen so many similar scenes in his time. And does not habit infallibly lead to professional indifference, making the soldier cool and composed in the midst of conflict, and rendering the surgeon impassible when the patient shrieks and writhes beneath his operating knife.

"I have been upstairs, looking about," pursued Father Absinthe; "I saw a bed up there, and we can mount guard here, by turns."

With an imperious gesture, Lecoq interrupted him. "You must give up that idea, Father Absinthe," he said, "we are not here to sleep, but to collect information—to make the most careful researches, and to note all the probabilities. In a few hours the commissary of police, the legal physician, and the public prosecutor will be here. I wish to have a report ready for them."

This proposition seemed anything but pleasing to the old police agent. "Eh! what is the use of that?" he exclaimed. "I know the General. When he goes in search of the commissary, as he has gone this evening, there is nothing more to be done. Do you think you can see anything that he didn't see?"

"I think that Gevrol, like every one else, is liable to be mistaken. I think that he believes too implicitly in what seems to him evidence. I could swear that this affair is not what it seems to be; and I am sure that if we like we can discover the mystery which is concealed beneath present appearances."

Although Lecoq's vehemence was intense, he did not succeed in making any impression upon his companion, who with a yawn that threatened to dislocate his jaws replied: "Perhaps you are right; but I am going to bed. This need not prevent you from searching around, however; and if you find anything you can wake me."

Lecoq made no sign of impatience: nor in reality was he impatient. These words afforded him the opportunity for which he was longing. "You will give me a moment first," he remarked. "In five minutes, by your watch, I promise to let you put your finger on the mystery that I suspect here."

"Well, go on for five minutes."

"After that you shall be free, Father Absinthe. Only it is clear that if I unravel the mystery alone, I alone ought to pocket the reward that a solution will certainly bring."

At the word "reward" the old police agent pricked up his ears. He was dazzled by the vision of an infinite number of bottles of the greenish liquor whose name he bore. "Convince me, then," said he, taking a seat upon a stool, which he had lifted from the floor.

Lecoq remained standing in front of him. "To begin with," he remarked, "whom do you suppose the person we have just arrested to be?"

"A porter, probably, or a vagabond."

"That is to say, a man belonging to the lowest class of society: consequently, a fellow without education."

"Certainly."

Lecoq spoke with his eyes fixed upon those of his companion. He distrusted his own powers, as is usual with persons of real merit, but he felt that if he could succeed in making his convictions penetrate his comrade's obtuse mind, their exactitude would be virtually proved.

"And now," he continued, "what would you say if I showed you that this young man had received an excellent, even refined, education?"

"I should reply that it was very extraordinary. I should reply that—but what a fool I am! You have not proved it to me yet."

"But I can do so very easily. Do you remember the words that he uttered as he fell?"

"Yes, I remember them perfectly. He said: 'It is the Prussians who are coming.'"

"What do you suppose he meant by that?"

"What a question! I should suppose that he did not like the Prussians, and that he supposed he was offering us a terrible insult."

Lecoq was waiting anxiously for this response. "Ah, well; Father Absinthe," he said gravely, "you are wrong, quite wrong. And that this man has an education superior to his apparent position is proved by the fact that you did not understand his meaning, nor his intention. It was this single phrase that enlightened me."

Father Absinthe's physiognomy expressed the strange and comical perplexity of a man who is so thoroughly mystified that he knows not whether to laugh, or to be angry. After reflecting a little, he decided to adopt the latter course. "You are rather too young to impose upon an old fellow like me," he remarked. "I don't like boasters—"

"One moment!" interrupted Lecoq; "allow me to explain. You have certainly heard of a terrible battle which resulted in one of the greatest defeats that ever happened to France—the battle of Waterloo?"

"I don't see the connection—"

"Answer, if you please."

"Yes—then! I have heard of it!"

"Very well; you must know then that for some time victory seemed likely to rest with the banners of France. The English began to fall back, and the emperor already exclaimed: "We have them!" when suddenly on the right, a little in the rear, a large body of troops was seen advancing. It was the Prussian army. The battle of Waterloo was lost."

In all his life, worthy Father Absinthe had never made such a strenuous effort to understand anything. In this case his perseverance was not wholly useless, for, springing from his stool, and probably in much the same tone that Archimedes cried *"Eureka!"* he exclaimed, "I understand. The man's words were only an allusion."

"It is as you have said," remarked Lecoq, approvingly. "But I had not finished. If the emperor was thrown into consternation by the appearance of the Prussians, it was because he was momentarily expecting the arrival of one of his own generals from the same direction—Grouchy—with thirty-five thousand men. So if this man's allusion was exact and complete, he was not expecting an enemy, but a friend. Now draw your own conclusions."

Father Absinthe was amazed but convinced: and his eyes, heavy with sleep a few moments before, now opened to their widest extent. "Good heavens!" he murmured, "if you put it in that way! But I forget; you must have seen something as you were looking through the shutters."

The young man shook his head. "Upon my honor," he declared, "I saw nothing save the struggle between the murderer and the poor devil dressed as a soldier. It was that sentence alone that aroused my attention."

"Wonderful! prodigious!" exclaimed the astonished old man.

"I will add that reflection has confirmed my suspicions. I ask myself why this man, instead of flying at once, should have waited and remained there, at that door, to parley with us."

With a bound, Father Absinthe sprang again to his feet. "Why?" he interrupted; "because he had accomplices, and he wished to give them time to escape. Ah! I understand it all now."

A triumphant smile parted Lecoq's lips. "That is what I said to myself," he replied, "and now it is easy to verify my suspicions. There is snow outside, isn't there?"

It was not necessary to say any more. The elder officer seized the light, and followed by his companion, he hastened to the back door of the house, which opened into a small garden. In this sheltered enclosure the snow had not melted, and upon its white surface the dark stains of numerous footprints presented themselves. Without hesitation, Lecoq threw himself upon his knees in the snow; he rose again almost immediately. "These indentations were not made by the men's feet," said he. "There have been women here."

III

OBSTINATE men of Father Absinthe's stamp, who are at first always inclined to differ from other people's opinions, are the very individuals who end in madly adopting them. When an idea has at last penetrated their empty brains, they twist and turn it, dwell upon it, and develop it until it exceeds the the bounds of reason.

Hence, the police veteran was now much more strongly convinced than his companion that the usually clever Gevrol had been mistaken, and accordingly he laughed the inspector to scorn. On hearing Lecoq affirm that women had taken part in the horrible scene at the Poivriere, his joy was extreme— "A fine affair!" he exclaimed; "an excellent case!" And suddenly recollecting a maxim that has been handed down from the time of Cicero, he added in sententious tones: "Who holds the woman holds the cause!"

Lecoq did not deign to reply. He was standing upon the threshold, leaning against the framework of the door, his hand pressed to his forehead, as motionless as a statue. The discovery he had just made, and which so delighted Father Absinthe, filled him with consternation. It was the death of his hopes, the annihilation of the ingenious structure which his imagination had built upon the foundation of a single sentence.

There was no longer any mystery—, so celebrity was not to be gained by a brilliant stroke!

For the presence of two women in this vile den explained everything in the most natural and commonplace fashion.　Their presence explained the quarrel, the testimony of Widow Chupin, the dying declaration of the pretended soldier.　The behavior of the murderer was also explained.　He had remained to cover the retreat of the two women; he had sacrificed himself in order to save them, an act of gallantry so common in the French character, that any scoundrel of the barrieres might have performed it.

Still, the strange allusion to the battle of Waterloo remained unexplained.　But what did that prove now?　Nothing, simply nothing.　However, who could say how low an unworthy passion might cause a man even of birth and breeding to descend?　And the carnival afforded an opportunity for the parties to disguise themselves.

But while Lecoq was turning and twisting all these probabilities in his mind, Father Absinthe became impatient.　"Are we going to remain here until doomsday?" he asked.　"Are we to pause just at the moment when our search has been productive of such brilliant results?"

"Brilliant results!"　These words stung the young man as deeply as the keenest irony could have done.　"Leave me alone," he replied gruffly; "and, above all, don't walk about the garden, as by doing so, you'll damage any footprints."

His companion swore a little; but soon became silent in his turn.　He was constrained to submit to the irresistible ascendency of superior will and intelligence.

Lecoq was engaged in following out his course of reasoning. "The murderer, leaving the ball at the Rainbow, a dancing-house not far from here, near the fortifications, came to this wine-shop, accompanied by two women.　He found three men drinking here, who either began teasing him, or who displayed too much gallantry toward his companions.　He became angry. The others threatened him; he was one against three; he was armed; he became wild with rage, and fired—"

He checked himself, and an instant after added, aloud: "But was it the murderer who brought these women here?　If he is tried, this will be the important point.　It is necessary to obtain information regarding it."

He immediately went back into the house, closely followed

by his colleague, and began an examination of the footprints round about the door that Gevrol had forced open. Labor lost. There was but little snow on the ground near the entrance of the hovel, and so many persons had passed in and out that Lecoq could discover nothing. What a disappointment after his patient hopes! Lecoq could have cried with rage. He saw the opportunity for which he had sighed so long indefinitely postponed. He fancied he could hear Gevrol's coarse sarcasms. "Enough of this," he murmured, under his breath. "The General was right, and I am a fool!"

He was so positively convinced that one could do no more than discover the circumstances of some commonplace, vulgar broil, that he began to wonder if it would not be wise to renounce his search and take a nap, while awaiting the coming of the commissary of police.

But Father Absinthe was no longer of this opinion. This worthy man, who was far from suspecting the nature of his companion's reflections could not explain his inaction. "Come! my boy," said he, "have you lost your wits? This is losing time, it seems to me. The authorities will arrive in a few hours, and what report shall we be able to give them! As for me, if you desire to go to sleep, I shall pursue the investigation alone."

Disappointed as he was, the young police officer could not repress a smile. He recognized his own exhortation of a few moments before. It was the old man who had suddenly become intrepid. "To work, then!" he sighed, like a man who, while foreseeing defeat, wishes, at least, to have no cause for self-reproach.

He found it, however, extremely difficult to follow the footprints in the open air by the uncertain light of a candle, which was extinguished by the least breath of wind. "I wonder if there is a lantern in the house," he said. "If we could only lay our hands upon one!"

They searched everywhere, and, at last, upstairs in the Widow Chupin's own room, they found a well-trimmed lantern, so small and compact that it certainly had never been intended for honest purposes.

"A regular burglar's implement," said Father Absinthe, with a coarse laugh.

The implement was useful in any case; as both men agreed when they returned to the garden and recommenced their investigations systematically. They advanced very slowly and with extreme caution. The old man carefully held the lantern in the best position, while Lecoq, on his knees, studied each footprint with the attention of a chiromancer professing to read the future in the hand of a rich client. This new examination assured Lecoq that he had been correct in his first supposition. It was plain that two women had left the Poivriere by the back door. They had started off running, as was proved by the length of the steps and the shape of the footprints.

The difference in the tracks left by the two fugitives was so remarkable that it did not escape Father Absinthe's eyes. "Sapristi!" he muttered; "one of these jades can boast of having a pretty foot at the end of her leg!"

He was right. One of the tracks betrayed a small, coquettish, slender foot, clad in an elegant high-heeled boot with a narrow sole and an arched instep. The other denoted a broad, short foot growing wider toward the end. It had evidently been incased in a strong, low shoe.

This was indeed a clue. Lecoq's hopes at once revived; so eagerly does a man welcome any supposition that is in accordance with his desires. Trembling with anxiety, he went to examine some other footprints a short distance from these; and an excited exclamation at once escaped his lips.

"What is it?" eagerly inquired the other agent: "what do you see?"

"Come and look for yourself, see there!" cried Lecoq.

The old man bent down, and his surprise was so great that he almost dropped the lantern. "Oh!" said he in a stifled voice, "a man's footprint!"

"Exactly. And this fellow wore the finest of boots. See that imprint, how clear, how neat it is!"

Worthy Father Absinthe was scratching his ear furiously, his usual method of quickening his rather slow wits. "But it seems to me," he ventured to say at last, "that this individual was not coming *from* this ill-fated hovel."

"Of course not; the direction of the foot tells you that. No, he was not going away, he was coming here. But he did not pass beyond the spot where we are now standing. He was standing on tiptoe with outstretched neck and listening ears, when, on reaching this spot, he heard some noise, fear seized him, and he fled."

"Or rather, the women were going out as he was coming, and—"

"No, the women were outside the garden when he entered it."

This assertion seemed far too audacious to suit Lecoq's companion, who remarked: "One can not be sure of that."

"I am sure of it, however; and can prove it conclusively. If you doubt it, it is because your eyes are growing old. Bring your lantern a little nearer—yes, here it is—our man placed his large foot upon one of the marks made by the woman with the small foot and almost effaced it." This unexceptionable piece of circumstantial evidence stupefied the old police agent.

"Now," continued Lecoq, "could this man have been the accomplice whom the murderer was expecting? Might it not have been some strolling vagrant whose attention was attracted by the two pistol shots? This is what we must ascertain. And we will ascertain it. Come!"

A wooden fence of lattice-work, rather more than three feet high, was all that separated the Widow Chupin's garden from the waste land surrounding it. When Lecoq made the circuit of the house to cut off the murderer's escape he had encountered this obstacle, and, fearing lest he should arrive too late, he had leaped the fence to the great detriment of his pantaloons, without even asking himself if there was a gate or not. There was one, however—a light gate of lattice-work similar to the fence, turning upon iron hinges, and closed by a wooden button. Now it was straight toward this gate that these footprints in the snow led the two police agents. Some new thought must have struck the younger man, for he suddenly paused. "Ah!" he murmured, "these two women did not come to the Poivriere this evening for the first time."

"Why do you think that, my boy?" inquired Father Absinthe.

"I could almost swear it. How, unless they were in the habit of coming to this den, could they have been aware of the existence of this gate? Could they have discovered it on such a dark, foggy night? No; for I, who can, without boasting, say that I have good eyes—I did not see it."

"Ah! yes, that is true!"

"These two women, however, came here without hesitating, in a straight line; and note that to do this, it was necessary for them to cross the garden diagonally."

The veteran would have given something if he could have found some objection to offer; but unfortunately he could find none. "Upon my word!" he exclaimed, "yours is a droll way of proceeding. You are only a conscript; I am a veteran in the service, and have assisted in more affairs of this sort than you are years old, but never have I seen—"

"Nonsense!" interrupted Lecoq, "you will see much more. For example, I can prove to you that although the women knew the exact position of the gate, the man knew it only by hearsay."

"The proof!"

"The fact is easily demonstrated. Study the man's foot-prints, and you, who are very sharp, will see at once that he deviated greatly from the straight course. He was in such doubt that he was obliged to search for the gate with his hand stretched out before him—and his fingers have left their imprint on the thin covering of snow that lies upon the upper railing of the fence."

The old man would have been glad to verify this statement for himself, as he said, but Lecoq was in a hurry. "Let us go on, let us go on!" said he. "You can verify my assertions some other time."

They left the garden and followed the footprints which led them toward the outer boulevards, inclining somewhat in the direction of the Rue de Patay. There was now no longer any need of close attention. No one save the fugitives had crossed this lonely waste since the last fall of snow. A child could have followed the track, so clear and distinct it was. Four series of footprints, very unlike in character, formed the track; two of these had evidently been left by the women; the other two, one going and one returning, had been made by the man. On several occasions the latter had placed his foot exactly on the footprints left by the two women, half effacing them, thus dispelling all doubt as to the precise moment of his approach.

About a hundred yards from the Poivriere, Lecoq suddenly seized his colleague's arm. "Halt!" he exclaimed, "we have reached a good place; I can see unmistakable proofs."

The spot, all unenclosed as it was, was evidently utilized by some builder for the storage of various kinds of lumber. The ground was strewn with large blocks of granite, some chiseled, some in the rough, with numerous long planks and logs of wood in their midst. In front of one of these logs, the surface of which had been evidently wiped, all the various foot-prints came together, mingling confusedly.

"Here," declared the young detective, "our fugitives met the man and took counsel with him. One of the women, the one with the little feet, sat down upon this log."

"We ought to make quite sure of that," said Father Absinthe, in an oracular tone.

But his companion cut short his desire for verification. "You, my old friend," said he, "are going to do me the kindness to keep perfectly still: pass me the lantern and do not move."

Lecoq's modest tone had suddenly become so imperious that his colleague dared offer no resistance. Like a soldier at the command to halt, he remained erect, motionless, and mute, following his colleague's movements with an inquisitive, wondering eye.

Quick in his motions, and understanding how to maneuvre the lantern in accordance with his wishes, the young police agent explored the surroundings in a very short space of time. A bloodhound in pursuit of his prey would have been less alert, less discerning, less agile. He came and went, now turning, now pausing, now retreating, now hurrying on again without any apparent reason; he scrutinized, he questioned every surrounding object: the ground, the logs of wood, the blocks of stone, in a word, nothing escaped his glance. For a moment he would remain standing, then fall upon his knees, and at times lie flat upon his stomach with his face so near the ground that his breath must have melted the snow. He had drawn a tape-line from his pocket, and using it with a carpenter's dexterity, he measured, measured, and measured.

And all his movements were accompanied with the wild gestures of a madman, interspersed with oaths or short laughs, with exclamations of disappointment or delight. After a quarter of an hour of this strange exercise, he turned to Father Absinthe, placed the lantern on a stone, wiped his hands with his pocket-handkerchief, and said: "Now I know everything!"

"Well, that is saying a great deal!"

"When I say everything, I mean all that is connected with the episode of the drama which ended in that bloody bout in the hovel. This expanse of earth covered with snow is a white page upon which the people we are in search of have written, not only their movements, their goings, and comings, but also their secret thoughts, their alternate hopes and anxieties. What do these footprints say to you, Papa Absinthe? To me they are alive like the persons who made them; they breathe, speak, accuse!"

The old agent was saying to himself: "Certainly, this fellow is intelligent, undeniably shrewd; but he is very disagreeable."

"These are the facts as I have read them," pursued Lecoq. "When the murderer repaired to the Poivriere with the two women, his companion—I should say his accomplice—came here to wait. He was a tall man of middle age; he wore a soft hat and a shaggy brown overcoat; he was, moreover, probably married, or had been so, as he had a wedding-ring on the little finger of his right hand—"

His companion's despairing gestures obliged the speaker to pause. This description of a person whose existence had but just now been demonstrated, these precise details given in a tone of absolute certainty, completely upset all Father Absinthe's ideas, increasing his perplexity beyond all bounds.

"This is not right," he growled, "this is not kind. You are poking fun at me. I take the thing seriously; I listen to you, I obey you in everything, and then you mock me in this way. We find a clue, and instead of following it up, you stop to relate all these absurd stories."

"No," replied his companion, "I am not jesting, and I have told you nothing of which I am not absolutely sure, nothing that is not strictly and indisputably true."

"And you would have me believe—"

"Fear nothing, papa; I would not have you do violence to your convictions. When I have told you my reasons, and my means of information, you will laugh at the simplicity of the theory that seems so incomprehensible to you now."

"Go on, then," said the good man, in a tone of resignation.

"We had decided," rejoined Lecoq, "that the accomplice mounted guard here. The time seemed long, and, growing impatient, he paced to and fro—the length of this log of wood—occasionally pausing to listen. Hearing nothing, he stamped his foot, doubtless exclaiming: 'What the deuce has happened to him down there! He had made about thirty turns (I have counted them), when a sound broke the stillness—the two women were coming."

On hearing Lecoq's recital, all the conflicting sentiments that are awakened in a child's mind by a fairy tale—doubt, faith, anxiety, and hope—filled Father Absinthe's heart. What should he believe? what should he refuse to believe? He did not know. How was he to separate the true from the false among all these equally surprising assertions? On the other hand, the gravity of his companion, which certainly was not feigned, dismissed all idea of pleasantry.

Finally, curiosity began to torture him. "We had reached the point where the women made their appearance," said he.

"Yes, indeed," responded Lecoq, "but here all certainty ceases; no more proofs, only suppositions. Still, I have every reason to believe that our fugitives left the drinking den before the beginning of the fight, before the cries that attracted our attention. Who were they? I can only conjecture. I suspect, however, that they were not equals in rank. I am inclined to think that one was the mistress, the other her servant."

"That is proved," ventured the old man, "by the great difference in their feet and in their shoes."

This shrewd observation elicited a smile from Lecoq. "That difference," he replied, seriously, "is something, of course; but it was not that which decided me in my opinion. If greater or less perfection of the extremities regulated social distinctions, many mistresses would be servants. What struck me was this: When the two women rushed wildly from Mother Chupin's house, the woman with the small feet sprang across the garden with one bound, she darted on some distance in advance of the other. The terror of the situation, the vileness of the den, the horror of the scandal, the thought of safety, inspired her with marvelous energy. But her strength, as often happens with delicate and nervous women, lasted only a few seconds. She was not half-way from the Poivriere when her speed relaxed, her limbs trembled. Ten steps farther on she tottered and almost fell. Some steps farther, and she became so exhausted that she let go her hold upon her skirts; they trailed upon the snow, tracing a faint circle there. Then the woman with the broad feet came to aid her. She seized her companion round the waist; she dragged her along; their footprints here are mingled confusedly; then, seeing that her friend was about to fall, she caught her up in her strong arms and carried her— for you will see that the footprints made by the woman with the small feet suddenly cease at this point."

Was Lecoq merely amusing himself by inventing this story? Was this scene anything but a work of imagination? Was the accent of deep and sincere conviction which he imparted to his words only feigned?

Father Absinthe was still in doubt, but he thought of a way in which he might satisfy his uncertainty. He caught up the lantern and hurried off to examine these footprints which he had not known how to read, which had been speechless to him, but which yielded their secret to another. He was obliged to agree with his companion. All that Lecoq had described was written there; he saw the confused footprints, the circle made by the sweeping skirts, the cessation of the tiny imprints.

On his return, his countenance betrayed a respectful and astonished admiration, and it was with a shade of embarrassment that he said: "You can scarcely blame an old man for being a little like St. Thomas. 'I have touched it with my fingers,' and now I am content to follow you."

The young police agent could not, indeed, blame his colleague for his incredulity. Resuming his recital, he continued: "Then the accomplice, who had heard the fugitives coming, ran to meet them, and he aided the woman with large feet in carrying her companion. The latter must have been really ill, for the accomplice took off his hat and used it in brushing the snow off this log. Then, thinking the surface was not yet *dry* enough, he wiped it with the skirt of his overcoat. Were these civilities pure gallantry, or the usual attentions of an inferior? I have asked myself that question. This much, however, is certain, while the woman with the small feet was recovering her strength, half reclining upon this board, the other took the accomplice a little on one side, five or six steps away to the left, just beside that enormous block of granite. There she talked with him, and, as he listened, the man leaned upon the snow-covered stone. His hand left a very distinct imprint there. Then, as the conversation continued, he rested his elbow upon the snowy surface."

Like all men of limited intelligence, Father Absinthe had suddenly passed from unreasoning distrust to unquestioning confidence. Henceforth, he could believe anything for the very same reason that had, at first, made him believe nothing. Having no idea of the bounds of human reasoning and penetration, he saw no limits to the conjectural genius of his companion. With perfect faith, therefore, he inquired: "And what was the accomplice saying to the woman with the broad shoes?"

Lecoq smiled at this simplicity, but the other did not see him do so. "It is rather difficult for me to answer that question," replied the young detective, "I think, however, that the woman was explaining to the man the immensity and imminence of the danger that threatened his companion, and that they were trying to devise some means to rescue him from it. Perhaps she brought him orders given by the murderer. It is certain that she ended by beseeching the accomplice to run to the Poivriere and see what was passing there. And he did so, for his tracks start from this block of granite."

"And only to think," exclaimed Father Absinthe, "that we were in the hovel at that very moment. A word from Gevrol, and we might have had handcuffs on the whole gang! How unfortunate!"

Lecoq was not sufficiently disinterested to share his companion's regret. On the contrary, he was very thankful for Gevrol's blunder. Had it not been for that, how would he ever have found an opportunity of investigating an affair that grew more and more mysterious as his search proceeded, but which he hoped to fathom finally.

"To conclude," he resumed, "the accomplice soon returned, he had witnessed the scene, and was evidently afraid. He feared that the thought of exploring the premises might enter the minds of the police. It was to the lady with small feet that he addressed himself. He explained the necessity of flight, and told her that even a moment's delay might be fatal. At his words, she summoned all her energy; she rose and hastened away, clinging to the arm of her companion. Did the man indicate the route they were to take, or did they know it themselves? This much is certain, he accompanied them some distance, in order to watch over them. But besides protecting these women, he had a still more sacred duty to perform—that of succoring his accomplice, if possible. He retraced his steps, passed by here once more, and the last footprint that I can discover leads in the direction of the Rue du Chateau des Rentiers. He wished to know what would become of the murderer, and went to place himself where he might see him pass by with his captors."

Like a dilettante who can scarcely restrain his applause until the close of the *aria* that delights him, Father Absinthe had been unable during the recital to entirely suppress his admiration. But it was not until Lecoq ceased speaking that he gave full vent to his enthusiasm: "Here *is* a detective if you like!" he exclaimed. "And they pretend that Gevrol is   shrewd! What has he ever done to compare with this? Ah! shall I

tell you what I think? Why, in comparison with you, the General is a more John the Baptist."

Certainly the flattery was gross, but it was impossible to
doubt its sincerity. This was the first time that the balmy
dew of praise had fallen upon Lecoq's vanity, and it greatly
delighted him, although he modestly replied: "Nonsense, you
are too kind, papa. After all, what have I done that is so very
clever? I told you that the man was of middle age. It was
not difficult to see that after one had examined his heavy, drag-
ging step. I told you that he was tall—an easy matter. When
I saw that he had been leaning upon that block of granite there
to the left, I measured the block in question. It is almost five
feet five inches in height, consequently a man who could rest
his elbow upon it must be at least six feet high. The mark of
his hand proves that I am not mistaken. On seeing that he
had brushed away the snow which covered the plank, I asked
myself what he had used; I thought that it might be his cap,
and the mark left by the peak proves that I was right. Finally,
if I have discovered the color and the material of his overcoat,
it is only because when he wiped the wet board, some splinters
of the wood tore off a few tiny flakes of brown wool, which I
have found, and which will figure in the trial. But what does
this amount to, after all? Nothing. We have only discovered
the first clues of the affair. Still, we are on the right scent
—so, forward then!"

The old officer was electrified, and, like an echo, he repeated:
"Forward!"

IV

THAT night the vagabonds, who had taken refuge in the
neighborhood of the Poivriere, had a very bad time of it;
for while those who managed to sleep were disturbed by frightful dreams of a police raid, those who remained awake witnessed
some strange incidents, well calculated to fill their minds with
terror. On hearing the shots fired inside Mother Chupin's
drinking den, most of the vagrants concluded that there had

been a collision between the police and some of their comrades, and they immediately began prowling about, eagerly listening and watching, and ready to take flight at the least sign of danger. At first they could discover no particular reasons for alarm. But later on, at about two o'clock in the morning, just as they were beginning to feel secure again, the fog lifted a little, and they witnessed a phenomenon well calculated to arouse anxiety.

Upon the unoccupied tract of land, which the people of the neighborhood called the "plain," a small but very bright light was seen describing the most capricious evolutions. It moved here and there without any apparent aim, tracing the most inexplicable zigzags, sometimes sinking to the earth, sometimes rising to a height of four or five feet, at others remaining quite motionless, and the next second flying off like a ball. In spite of the place and the season of the year, the less ignorant among vagabonds believed the light to be some *ignis fatuus,* one of those luminous meteors that raise from the marshes and float about in the atmosphere at the bidding of the wind. In point of fact, however, this *ignis fatuus* was the lantern by the light of which the two police agents were pursuing their investigations.

After thus suddenly revealing his capacity to his first disciple, Lecoq found himself involved in a cruel perplexity. He had not the boldness and promptness of decision which is the gift of a prosperous past, and was hesitating between two courses, both equally reasonable, and both offering strong probabilities of success. He stood between two paths, that made by the two women on the one side, and that made by the accomplice on the other. Which should he take? For he could not hope to follow both. Seated upon the log where the women had rested a few moments before, with his hand pressed upon his forehead, he reflected and weighed the chances.

"If I follow the man I shall learn nothing that I do not know already. He has gone to hover round the party; he has followed them at a distance, he has seen them lock up his accomplice, and he is undoubtedly prowling round about the station house. If I hurried in pursuit, could I hope to overtake and capture him? No; too long a time has elapsed."

Father Absinthe listened to this monologue with intense curiosity, as anxious as an unsophisticated person who, having questioned a clairvoyant in regard to some lost articles, is waiting the oracle's response.

"To follow the women," continued the young man, "to what would that lead? Perhaps to an important discovery, perhaps to nothing."

However, he preferred the unknown, which, with all its chances of failure, had chances of success as well. He rose, his course was decided.

"Father Absinthe," said he, "we are going to follow the footprints of these two women, and wherever they lead us we will go."

Inspired with equal ardor they began their walk. At the end of the path upon which they had entered they fancied they observed, as in some magic glass, the one the fruits, the other the glory of success. They hurried forward. At first it was only play to follow the distinct footprints that led toward the Seine. But it was not long before they were obliged to proceed more slowly.

On leaving the waste ground they arrived at the outer limits of civilization, so to speak; and strange footprints mingled constantly with the footprints of the fugitives, at times even effacing them. In many spots, either on account of exposure or the nature of the soil, the thaw had completed its work, and there were large patches of ground entirely free from snow. In such cases they lost the trail, and it required all Lecoq's sagacity and all his companion's good-will to find it again.

On such occasions Father Absinthe planted his cane in the earth, near the last footprint that had been discovered, and Lecoq and himself hunted all over the ground around this point, much after the fashion of a couple of bloodhounds thrown off the scent. Then it was that the lantern moved about so strangely. More than a dozen times, in spite of all their efforts, they would have lost the clue entirely had it not been for the elegant shoes worn by the lady with the little feet. These had such small and extremely high heels that the impression they left could not be mistaken. They sank down three or four inches in the snow, or the mud, and their tell-tale impress remained as clear and distinct as that of a seal.

Thanks to these heels, the pursuers were able to discover that the two fugitives had not gone up the Rue de Patay, as might have been supposed. Probably they had considered this street too frequented, and too well lighted. They had only crossed it, just below the Rue de la Croix-Rouge, and had profited by an empty space between two houses to regain the open ground.

"Certainly these women were well acquainted with the locality," murmured Lecoq.

Indeed, the topography of the district evidently had no secrets for them, for, on quitting the Rue de Patay, they had immediately turned to the right, so as to avoid several large excavations, from which a quantity of brick clay had been dug.

But at last the trail was recovered, and the detectives followed it as far as the Rue du Chevaleret. Here the footprints abruptly ceased. Lecoq discovered eight or ten footmarks left by the woman who wore the broad shoes, but that was all. Hereabout, moreover, the condition of the ground was not calculated to facilitate an exploration of this nature. There had been a great deal of passing to and fro in the Rue du Chevaleret, and not merely was there scarcely any snow left on the footpaths, but the middle of the street was transformed into a river of slush.

"Did these people recollect at last that the snow might betray them? Did they take the middle of the road?" grumbled the young police agent.

Certainly they could not have crossed to a vacant space as they had done just before, for on the other side of the street extended a long factory wall.

"Ah!" sighed Father Absinthe, "we have our labor for our pains."

But Lecoq possessed a temperament that refused to acknowledge defeat. Animated by the cold anger of a man who sees the object which he was about to seize disappear from before his eyes, he recommenced his search, and was well repaid for his efforts.

"I understand!" he cried suddenly, "I comprehend—I see!"

Father Absinthe drew near. *He* did not see nor divine anything! but he no longer doubted his companion's powers.

"Look there," said Lecoq; "what are those marks?"

"Marks left by the wheels of some carriage that plainly turned here."

"Very well, papa, these tracks explain everything. When they reached this spot, our fugitives saw the light of an approaching cab, which was returning from the centre of Paris. It was empty, and proved their salvation. They waited, and when it came nearer they hailed the driver. No doubt they promised him a handsome fare; this is indeed evident, since he consented to go back again. He turned round here; they got into the vehicle, and that is why the footprints go no further."

This explanation did not please Lecoq's companion. "Have we made any great progress now that we know that?" he asked.

Lecoq could not restrain an impulse to shrug his shoulders. "Did you expect that the tracks made by the fugitives would lead us through Paris and up to their very doors?" he asked.

"No; but—"

"Then what would you ask more? Do you think that I shall not know how to find this driver to-morrow? He was returning with his empty vehicle, his day's work was ended; hence, his stable is in the neighborhood. Do you suppose that he will have forgotten that he took up two persons in the Rue du Chevaleret? He will tell us where he drove them; but that will not do us any good, for, of course, they will not have given him their real address. But at all events he can probably give us a description of them, tell us how they were dressed, describe their appearance, their manner, and their age. And with that, and what we already know—"

An eloquent gesture expressed the remainder of his thought, then he added: "We must now go back to the Poivriere, and go quickly. And you, my friend, may now extinguish your lantern."

While doing his best to keep pace with his companion, who was in such haste to get back to the Poivriere that he almost ran, Father Absinthe's thoughts were as busy as his legs, and an entirely new train of ideas was awakened in his mind.

During the twenty-five years that he had been connected with the police force, the good man—to use his own expression —had seen many of his colleagues walk over him and win, after only a few months' work, a promotion that his long years of service had not gained for him. In these cases he had not failed to accuse his superiors of injustice, and his fortunate rivals of gross flattery. In his opinion, seniority was the only claim to advancement—the only, the best, the most respectable claim; and he was wont to sum up all his opinions, all his grief and bitterness of mind in one phrase: "It is infamous to pass over an old member of the service."

To-night, however, Father Absinthe discovered that there is something else in the world besides seniority, and sufficient reasons for what he had formerly regarded as favoritism. He secretly confessed that this newcomer whom he had treated so carelessly had just followed up a clue as he, veteran though he was, would never have succeeded in doing.

But communing with himself was not this good man's forte; he soon grew weary of reflection; and on reaching a place where they were obliged to proceed more slowly on account of the badness of the road, he deemed it a favorable opportunity to resume the conversation. "You are silent, comrade," he ventured to remark, "and one might swear that you were not exactly pleased."

This surprising result of the old man's reflections would have amazed Lecoq, if his mind had not been a hundred leagues away. "No, I am not pleased," he responded.

"And why, pray? Only ten minutes ago you were as gay as a lark."

"Then I did not see the misfortune that threatens us."

"A misfortune!"

"A very great misfortune. Do you not perceive that the weather has undesirably changed. It is evident that the wind is now coming from the south. The fog has disappeared, but the sky is cloudy and threatening. It will rain in less than an hour."

"A few drops are falling now; I just felt one."

These words produced on Lecoq much the same effect as a whip-up on a spirited horse. He sprang forward, and, adopting a still more hurried pace, exclaimed: "Let us make haste! let us make haste!"

The old police agent followed him as in duty bound; but his mind was, if possible, still more troubled by the replies of his young companion. A great misfortune! The wind from the south! Rain! He did not, he could not see the connection.

Greatly puzzled, and not a little anxious, Father Absinthe asked for an explanation, although he had but little more breath than was absolutely necessary to enable him to continue the forced march he was making. "Upon my word," said he, "I have racked my brains—"

His companion took pity on his anxiety. "What!" he exclaimed, as he still hastened forward, "you do not understand that our investigation, my success, and your reward, are dependent upon those black clouds which the wind is driving toward us!"

"Oh!"

"Twenty minutes of merely gentle rain, and our time and labor will be lost. If it rains, the snow will melt, and then farewell to our proofs. Let us get on—let us get on more quickly! You know very well that in such cases words don't suffice. If we declare to the public prosecutor that we have seen these footprints, he will ask, where? And what can we say? If we swear by all the gods that we have seen the footprints of a man and of two women, the investigating magistrate will say, 'Let me see them.' And who will feel sheepish then? Father Absinthe and Lecoq. Besides, Gevrol would not fail to declare that we were saying what was not true, in order to enhance our own value, and humiliate him."

"What an idea!"

"Faster, papa, faster; you will have all day to-morrow to be indignant. Perhaps it will not rain. In that case, these perfect, clear, and easily recognizable footprints will prove the culprits' ruin. How can we preserve them? By what process could we solidify them? I would deluge them with my blood if that could only cause them to congeal."

Father Absinthe was just then thinking that his share of the labor had hitherto been the least important; for he had merely held the lantern. But here was a chance for him to acquire a real and substantial right to the prospective reward. "I know a method," said he, "by which one could preserve these marks in the snow."

At these words the younger man stopped short. "You know —you?" he interrupted.

"Yes, I know," replied the old detective, with the evident satisfaction of a man who has gained his revenge. "They invented a way at the time of that affair at the Maison Blanche, last December."

"I recollect."

"Ah! well, on the snow in the courtyard there was a footprint that attracted a detective's attention. He said that the whole evidence depended on that mark alone, that it was worth more than ten years' hard work in following up the case. Naturally, he desired to preserve it. They sent for a great chemist—"

"Go on, go on."

"I have never seen the method put into prastise, but an expert told me all about it, and showed me the mold they obtained. He explained it to me precisely, on account of my profession."

Lecoq was trembling with impatience. "And how did they obtain the mold?" he asked abruptly.

"Wait: I was just going to explain. They take some of the best gelatine, and allow it to soak in cold water. When it becomes thoroughly softened, they heat it until it forms a liquid, of moderate consistency. Then when it is just cool enough, they pour a nice little covering of it upon the footprint.

Lecoq felt the irritation that is natural to a person who has just heard a bad joke, or who has lost his time in listening to a fool.

"Enough!" he interrupted, angrily. "That method can be found in all the manuals. It is excellent, no doubt, but how can it serve us? Have you any gelatine about you?"

"No."

"Nor have I. You might as well have counseled me to pour melted lead upon the footprints to fix them."

They continued their way, and five minutes later, without having exchanged another word, they reentered the Widow Chupin's hovel. The first impulse of the older man would have been to rest to breathe, but Lecoq did not give him time to do so.

"Make haste: get me a dish—a plate—anything!" cried the young detective, "and bring me some water; gather together all the boards and old boxes you can find lying about."

While his companion was obeying him, Lecoq armed himself with a fragment of one of the broken bottles, and began scraping away furiously at the plastered wall that separated the two rooms.

His mind disconcerted at first by the imminence of this unexpected catastrophe, a fall of rain, had now regained its equilibrium. He had reflected, he had thought of a way by which failure might possibly be averted—and he hoped for ultimate success. When he had accumulated some seven or eight handfuls of fine plaster dust, he mixed one-half with a little water so as to form a thin paste, leaving the rest untouched on the side of the plate.

"Now, papa," said he, "come and hold the light for me."

When in the garden, the young man sought for the deepest and most distinct of the footprints, knelt beside it, and began his experiment, trembling with anxiety. He first sprinkled upon the impression a fine coating of dry plaster, and then upon this coating, with infinite care, he poured his liquid solution drop by drop.

What luck! the experiment was successful! The plaster united in a homogeneous mass, forming a perfect model of the impression. Thus, after an hour's labor, Lecoq possessed half a dozen of these casts, which might, perhaps, be a little wanting in clearness of outline, but which were quite perfect enough to be used as evidence.

The young detective's alarm had been well founded, for it was already beginning to rain. Still, he had plenty of time to cover a number of the footprints with the boxes and pieces of board which Father Absinthe had collected, thus placing them, as it were, beyond the reach of a thaw. Now he could breathe. The authorities might come, for the most important part of his task was completed.

V

I T was some distance from the Poivriere to the Rue de Chevaleret, even by way of the plain, and fully four hours had been occupied by Lecoq and his colleague in collecting their elements of information.

All this while, the Widow Chupin's abode had remained open, accessible to any chance visitor. Still, when, on his return, the young police agent remembered this neglect of elementary precautions, he did not feel alarmed. Considering all the circumstances, it was very difficult to believe that any serious harm could have resulted from this carelessness.

For who would have been likely to visit this drinking-den after midnight? Its bad name served the purpose of a bulwark. The most daring vagrants did not drink there without some disquietude, fearing that if the liquor caused them to lose consciousness, they might be robbed or perhaps even murdered. Hence, if any one had been attracted to this notoriously dangerous drinking-shop by the light that streamed through the open door, it could only have been some very reckless person returning late at night from the ball at the

Rainbow, with a few sous left in his pocket. But, even then, a single glance inside would have sufficed to put the bravest to flight.

In less than a second the young police agent had weighed all these possibilities, concerning which he did not breathe a word to Father Absinthe. When, little by little, the excitement caused by his successive hopes and disappointments, and by the accomplishment of the experiment with the footprints had died away, and he had regained his usual calm of mind, he made a careful inspection of the abode, and was by no means satisfied with himself. He had experimented upon Father Absinthe with his new system of investigation, just as an aspiring orator tries his powers before his least gifted friends, not before the cleverest. He had certainly overwhelmed the old veteran by his superiority; he had literally crushed him. But what great merit, what wonderful victory was this? Why should he boast of having outwitted Father Absinthe, one of the least sagacious men in the service?

If he could only have given some startling proofs of his energy or of his penetration! But, after all, what had he accomplished? Was the mystery solved? Was his success more than problematical? When one thread is drawn out, the skein is not untangled. This night would undoubtedly decide his future as a detective, so he swore that if he could not conquer his vanity, he would, at least, compel himself to conceal it. Hence, it was in a very modest tone that he said to his companion: "We have done all that we can do outside, now, would it not be wise to busy ourselves with the inside of the house?"

Everything looked exactly in the same state as when the two men left the room. A candle, with a charred smoking wick, cast its flickering light upon the same scene of disorder, revealing to view the rigid features of the three victims. Without losing a moment, Lecoq began to pick up and study the various objects scattered over the floor. Some of these still remained intact. The Widow Chupin had recoiled from the expense of a tiled floor, judging the bare ground upon which the cabin was built quite good enough for the feet of her customers. This ground, which must originally have been well beaten down, had, by constant use and damp, become wellnigh as muddy as the soil outside.

The first fruits of Lecoq's·search were a large salad-bowl

and a big iron spoon, the latter so twisted and bent that it had evidently been used as a weapon during the conflict. On inspecting the bowl, it became evident that when the quarrel began the victims were regaling themselves with the familiar mixture of water, wine, and sugar, known round about the barrieres as *vin a la Française*. After the salad-bowl, the two men picked up five of the weighty glasses ordinarily used in wine-shops, and which, while looking as though they would contain half a bottle, are in point of fact so thick at the bottom that they hold next to nothing. Three of these glasses were broken, two were whole. All of them had contained wine—the same *vin a la Française*. This was plain, but for greater surety, Lecoq applied his tongue to the bluish mixture remaining in the bottom of each glass. "The deuce!" he muttered, with an astonished air.

Then he examined successively the surfaces of the three overturned tables. Upon one of these, the one nearest the fireplace and the window, the still wet marks of the five glasses, of the salad-bowl, and even of the spoons could be distinguished. Lecoq very properly regarded this circumstance as a matter of the greatest importance, for it proved clearly enough that five persons had emptied the salad-bowl in company. Who were these five persons?

"Oh! oh!" suddenly exclaimed Lecoq in two entirely different tones. "Then the two women could not have been with the murderer!"

A very simple mode of discovery had presented itself to his mind. It was to ascertain if there were any other glasses, and what they had contained. After a fresh search on the floor, a sixth glass was found, similar in form to the others, but much smaller. Its smell showed that it had contained brandy. Then these two women had not been with the murderer, and therefore he could not have fought because the other men had insulted them. This discovery proved the inaccuracy of Lecoq's original suppositions. It was an unexpected check, and he was mourning over it in silence, when Father Absinthe, who had not ceased ferreting about, uttered a cry of surprise.

The young man turned; he saw that his companion had become very pale. "What is it?" he asked.

"Some one has been here in our absence."

"Impossible!"

It was not impossible—it was true. When Gevrol had torn

the apron off Widow Chupin's head he had thrown it upon the steps of the stairs; neither of the police agents had since touched it. And yet the pockets of this apron were now turned inside out; this was a proof, this was evidence. At this discovery Lecoq was overcome with consternation, and the contraction of his features revealed the struggle going on in his mind. "Who could have been here?" he murmured. "Robbers? That is improbable."

Then, after a long silence which his companion took good care not to interrupt, he added: "The person who came here, who dared to penetrate into this abode and face the corpses of these murdered men—this person could have been none other than the accomplice. But it is not enough to suspect this, it is necessary to know it. I must—I will know it!"

They searched for a long time, and it was not until after an hour of earnest work that, in front of the door forced open by the police, they discovered in the mud, just inside the marks made by Gevrol's tread, a footprint that bore a close resemblance to those left by the man who had entered the garden. They compared the impressions and recognized the same designs formed by the nails upon the sole of the boot.

"It must have been the accomplice!" exclaimed Lecoq. "He watched us, he saw us go away, and then he entered. But why? What pressing, irresistible necessity made him decide to brave such imminent danger?" He seized his companion's hand, nearly crushing it in his excitement: "Ah! I know why!" continued he, violently. "I understand only too well. Some article that would have served to throw light on this horrible affair had been left or forgotten, or lost here, and to obtain it, to find it, he decided to run this terrible risk. And to think that it was my fault, my fault alone, that this convincing proof escaped us! And I thought myself so shrewd! What a lesson! The door should have been locked; any fool would have thought of it—" Here he checked himself, and remained with open mouth and distended eyes, pointing with his finger to one of the corners of the room.

"What is the matter?" asked his frightened companion.

Lecoq made no reply, but slowly, and with the stiff movements of a somnambulist, he approached the spot to which he had pointed, stooped, picked up something, and said: "My folly is not deserving of such luck."

The object he had found was an earring composed of a

single large diamond. The setting was of marvelous workmanship. "This diamond," declared Lecoq, after a moment's examination, "must be worth at least five or six thousand francs."

"Are you in earnest?"

"I think I could swear to it."

He would not have troubled about such a preamble as "I think" a few hours before, but the blunder he had made was a lesson that would not be forgotten so long as he lived.

"Perhaps it was that same diamond earring that the accomplice came to seek," ventured Father Absinthe.

"The supposition is scarcely admissible. In that case, he would not have sought for it in Mother Chupin's apron. No, he must have been seeking for something else—a letter, for example."

The older man was not listening; he had taken the earring, and was examining it in his turn. "And to think," he murmured, astonished by the brilliancy of the stone, "to think that a woman who had ten thousand francs' worth of jewels in her ears would have come to the Poivriere. Who would have believed it?"

Lecoq shook his head thoughtfully. "Yes, it is very strange, very improbable, very absurd. And yet we shall see many things quite as strange if we ever arrive—which I very much doubt—at a solution of this mysterious affair."

Day was breaking, cold, cheerless, and gloomy, when Lecoq and his colleague concluded their investigation. There was not an inch of space that had not been explored, carefully examined and studied, one might almost say, with a magnifying glass. There now only remained to draw up the report.

The younger man seated himself at the table, and, with the view of making his recital as intelligible as possible, he began by sketching a plan of the scene of the murder.

It will be seen that in the memoranda appended to this explanatory diagram, Lecoq had not once written his own name. In noting the things that he had imagined or discovered, he referred to himself simply as one of the police. This was not so much modesty as calculation. By hiding one's self on well-chosen occasions, one gains greater notoriety when one emerges from the shade. It was also through cunning that he gave Gevrol such a prominent position. These tactics, rather subtle, perhaps, but after all perfectly fair, could not fail to call atten-

A.—The point where the squad of police, under the command of Inspector Gevrol, heard the cries of the victims.

(The distance from this point to the wine-shop known as the Poivriere, is only one hundred and twenty-three yards; hence, it may reasonably be supposed that these cries were the first that were uttered, and consequently that the conflict had just commenced.)

B.—The window closed with shutters, through the cracks of which one of the police agents was able to see the scene within.

C.—The door forced open by Inspector Gevrol.

D.—The staircase upon which the Widow Chupin was seated, crying.

(It was upon the third step of this staircase that the Widow Chupin's apron was afterward found, the pockets turned inside out.)

F.—Fireplace.

HHH.—Tables.

(The remnants of the salad-bowl and of the five glasses were found scattered on the floor between the points F and B.)

T.—Door communicating with the back room of the hovel, before which the armed murderer was standing with the table H before him as a rampart.

K.—Back door of the hut, opening into the garden, by which the agent of police who thought of cutting off the murderer's retreat, entered and secured him.

L.—Gate of the garden, opening upon the unoccupied ground.

MM.—Footprints on the snow, discovered by the police agent remaining at the Poivriere, after the departure of Inspector Gevrol.

tion to the man who had shown himself so efficient when the efforts of his chief had been merely confined to breaking open the door.

The document Lecoq drew up was not a *proces-verbal*, a formal act reserved for the officers of judiciary police; it was a simple report, that would be admitted under the title of an inquiry, and yet the young detective composed it with quite as much care as a general would have displayed in drawing up the bulletin of his first victory.

While Lecoq was drawing and writing, Father Absinthe leaned over his shoulder to watch him. The plan amazed that worthy man. He had seen a great deal; but he had always supposed that it was necessary to be an engineer, an architect, or, at least, a carpenter, to execute such work. Not at all. With a tape-line with which to take some measurements, and a bit of board in place of a rule, his inexperienced colleague had soon accomplished the miracle. Father Absinthe's respect for Lecoq was thereby greatly augmented. It is true that the worthy veteran had not noticed the explosion of the young police agent's vanity, nor his return to his former modest demeanor. He had not observed his alarm, nor his perplexity, nor his lack of penetration.

After a few moments, Father Absinthe ceased watching his companion. He felt weary after the labors of the night, his head was burning, and he shivered and his knees trembled. Perhaps, though he was by no means sensitive, he felt the influence of the horrors that surrounded him, and which seemed more sinister than ever in the bleak light of morning. He began to ferret in the cupboards, and at last succeeded in discovering—oh, marvelous fortune!—a bottle of brandy, three parts full. He hesitated for an instant, then he poured out a glass, and drained it at a single draft.

"Will you have some?" he inquired of his companion. "It is not a very famous brand, to be sure; but it is just as good, it makes one's blood circulate and enlivens one."

Lecoq refused; he did not need to be enlivened. All his faculties were hard at work. He intended that, after a single perusal of his report, the investigating magistrate should say: "Let the officer who drew up this document be sent for." It must be remembered that Lecoq's future depended upon such an order. Accordingly, he took particular care to be brief, clear, and concise, to plainly indicate how his suspicions on the subject of the murder had been aroused, how they had increased, and how they had been confirmed. He explained by what series of deductions he had succeeded in establishing a theory which, if it was not the truth, was at least plausible enough to serve as the basis for further investigation.

Then he enumerated the articles of conviction ranged on the table before him. There were the flakes of brown wool collected upon the plank, the valuable earring, the models of the different footprints in the garden, and the Widow Chupin's apron with its pockets turned inside out. There was also the murderer's revolver, with two barrels discharged and three still loaded. This weapon, although not of an ornamental character, was still a specimen of highly finished workmanship. It bore the name of one Stephens, 14 Skinner Street, a well-known London gunsmith.

Lecoq felt convinced that by examining the bodies of the victims he would obtain other and perhaps very valuable information; but he did not dare venture upon such a course. Besides his own inexperience in such a matter, there was Gevrol to be thought of, and the inspector, furious at his own mistake, would not fail to declare that, by changing the attitude of the bodies, Lecoq had rendered a satisfactory examination by the physicians impossible.

The young detective accordingly tried to console himself for his forced inaction in this respect, and he was rereading his report, modifying a few expressions, when Father Absinthe, who was standing upon the threshold of the outer door, called to him.

"Is there anything new?" asked Lecoq.

"Yes," was the reply. "Here come Gevrol and two of our comrades with the commissary of police and two other gentlemen."

It was, indeed, the commissary who was approaching, interested but not disturbed by this triple murder which was sure to make his arrondissement the subject of Parisian conversation during the next few days. Why, indeed, should he be troubled about it? For Gevrol, whose opinion in such matters might be regarded as an authority, had taken care to reassure him when he went to arouse him from his slumbers.

"It was only a fight between some old offenders; former jail birds, habitues of the Poivriere," he had said, adding sententiously: "If all these ruffians would kill one another, we might have some little peace."

He added that as the murderer had been arrested and placed in confinement, there was nothing urgent about the case. Accordingly, the commissary thought there was no harm in taking another nap and waiting until morning before beginning the inquiry. He had seen the murderer, reported the case to the prefecture, and now he was coming—leisurely enough—accompanied by two physicians, appointed by the authorities to draw up a medico-legal report in all such cases. The party also comprised a sergeant-major of the 53d regiment of infantry of the line, who had been summoned by the commissary to identify, if possible, the murdered man who wore a uniform, for if one might believe the number engraved upon the buttons of his overcoat, he belonged to the 53d regiment, now stationed at the neighboring fort.

As the party approached it was evident that Inspector Gevrol was even less disturbed than the commissary. He whistled as he walked along, flourishing his cane, which never left his hand, and already laughing in his sleeve over the discomfiture of the presumptuous fool who had desired to remain to glean, where he, the experienced and skilful officer, had perceived nothing. As soon as he was within speaking distance, the inspector called to Father Absinthe, who, after warning Lecoq, remained on the threshold, leaning against the door-post, puffing his pipe, as immovable as a sphinx.

"Ah, well, old man!" cried Gevrol, "have you any great melodrama, very dark and very mysterious, to relate to us?"

"I have nothing to relate myself," replied the old detective, without even drawing his pipe from his lips, "I am too stupid, that is perfectly understood. But Monsieur Lecoq will tell you something that will astonish you."

The prefix, "monsieur," which the old police agent used in speaking of his colleague, displeased Gevrol so much that he pretended not to understand. "Who are you speaking of?" he asked abruptly.

"Of my colleague, of course, who is now busy finishing his report—of Monsieur Lecoq." Quite unintentionally, the worthy fellow had certainly become the young police agent's godfather. From that day forward, for his enemies as well as for his friends, he was and he remained "Monsieur" Lecoq.

"Ah! ah!" said the inspector, whose hearing was evidently impaired. "Ah, he has discovered—"

"The pot of roses which others did not scent, General." By this remark, Father Absinthe made an enemy of his superior officer. But he cared little for that: Lecoq had become his deity, and no matter what the future might reserve, the old veteran had resolved to follow his young colleague's fortunes.

"We'll see about that," murmured the inspector, mentally resolving to have an eye on this youth whom success might transform into a rival. He said no more, for the little party which he preceded had now overtaken him, and he stood aside to make way for the commissary of police.

This commissary was far from being a novice. He had served for many years, and yet he could not repress a gesture of horror as he entered the Poivriere. The sergeant-major of the 53d, who followed him, an old soldier, decorated and medaled —who had smelt powder many scores of times—was still more overcome. He grew as pale as the corpses lying on the ground, and was obliged to lean against the wall for support. The two physicians alone retained their stoical indifference.

Lecoq had risen, his report in his hand; he bowed, and assuming a respectful attitude, was waiting to be questioned.

"You must have passed a frightful night," said the commissary, kindly; "and quite unnecessarily, since any investigation was superfluous."

"I think, however," replied the young police agent, having recourse to all his diplomacy, "that my time has not been entirely lost. I have acted according to the instructions of my superior officer; I have searched the premises thoroughly, and I have ascertained many things. I have, for example, acquired the certainty that the murderer had a friend, possibly an accomplice, of whom I can give quite a close description. He must have been of middle age, and wore, if I am not mistaken, a soft cap and a brown woolen overcoat: as for his boots—"

"Zounds!" exclaimed Gevrol, "and I—" He stopped short, like a man whose impulse had exceeded his discretion, and who would have gladly recalled his words.

"And you?" inquired the commissary, "pray, what do you mean?"

The inspector had gone too far to draw back, and, unwittingly, was now obliged to act as his own executioner. "I was about to mention," he said, "that this morning, an hour or so ago, while I was waiting for you, sir, before the station-house, at the Barrière d'Italie, where the murderer is confined, I noticed close by an individual whose appearance was not unlike that of the man described by Lecoq. This man seemed to be very intoxicated, for he reeled and staggered against the walls. He tried to cross the street, but fell down in the middle of it, in such a position that he would inevitably have been crushed by the first passing vehicle."

Lecoq turned away his head; he did not wish them to read in his eyes how perfectly he understood the whole game.

"Seeing this," pursued Gevrol, "I called two men and asked them to aid me in raising the poor devil. We went up to him; he had apparently fallen asleep: we shook him—we made him sit up; we told him that he could not remain there, but he immediately flew into a furious rage. He swore at us, threatened us, and began fighting us. And, on my word, we had to take him to the station-house, and leave him there to recover from the effects of his drunken debauch."

"Did you shut him up in the same cell with the murderer?" inquired Lecoq.

"Naturally. You know very well that there are only two cages in the station-house at the barrière—one for men and the other for women; consequently—"

The commissary seemed thoughtful. "Ah! that's very unfortunate," he stammered; "and there is no remedy."

"Excuse me, there is one," observed Gevrol, "I can send one of my men to the station-house with an order to detain the drunken man—"

Lecoq interposed with a gesture: "Trouble lost," he said coldly. "If this individual is an accomplice, he has got sober by now—rest assured of that, and is already far away."

"Then what is to be done?" asked the inspector, with an ironical air. "May one be permitted to ask the advice of Monsieur Lecoq."

"I think chance offered us a splendid opportunity, and we did not know how to seize it; and that the best thing we can do now is to give over mourning, and prepare to profit by the next opportunity that presents itself."

Gevrol was, however, determined to send one of his men to the station-house; and it was not until the messenger had started that Lecoq commenced the reading of his report. He read it rapidly, refraining as much as possible from placing the decisive proofs in strong relief, reserving these for his own benefit; but so strong was the logic of his deductions that he was frequently interrupted by approving remarks from the commissary and the two physicians.

Gevrol, who alone represented the opposition, shrugged his shoulders till they were well-nigh dislocated, and grew literally green with jealousy.

"I think that you alone, young man, have judged correctly in this affair," said the commissary when Lecoq had finished reading. "I may be mistaken; but your explanations have made me alter my opinion concerning the murderer's attitude while I was questioning him (which was only for a moment). He refused, obstinately refused, to answer my questions, and wouldn't even give me his name."

The commissary was silent for a moment, reviewing the past circumstances in his mind, and it was in a serious tone that he eventually added: "We are, I feel convinced, in presence of one of those mysterious crimes the causes of which are beyond the reach of human sagacity—this strikes me as being one of those enigmatical cases which human justice never can reach."

Lecoq made no audible rejoinder; but he smiled to himself and thought: "We will see about that."

VI

N O consultation held at the bedside of a dying man ever took place in the presence of two physicians so utterly unlike each other as those who accompanied the commissary of police to the Poivriere.

One of them, a tall old man with a bald head, wearing a broad-brimmed hat, and an overcoat of antique cut, was evidently one of those modest *savants* encountered occasionally in the byways of Paris—one of those healers devoted to their art, who too often die in obscurity, after rendering immense services to mankind. He had the gracious calmness of a man who, having seen so much of human misery, has nothing left to learn, and no troubled conscience could have possibly sustained his searching glance, which was as keen as his lancet.

His colleague—young, fresh-looking, light-haired, and jovial —was somewhat foppishly attired; and his white hands were encased in handsome fur gloves. There was a soft self-satisfied smile on his face, and he had the manners of those practitioners who, for profit's sake, invariably recommend the infallible panaceas invented each month in chemical laboratories and advertised *ad nauseam* in the back pages of newspapers. He had probably written more than one article upon "Medicine for the use of the people"; puffing various mixtures, pills, ointments, and plasters for the benefit of their respective inventors.

"I will request you, gentlemen," said the commissary of police, "to begin your duties by examining the victim who wears a military costume. Here is a sergeant-major summoned to answer a question of identity, whom I must send back to his quarters as soon as possible."

The two physicians responded with a gesture of assent, and aided by Father Absinthe and another agent of police, they lifted the body and laid it upon two tables, which had previously been placed end to end. They were not obliged to make any note of the attitude in which they found the body, since the unfortunate man, who was still alive when the police entered the cabin, had been moved before he expired.

"Approach, sergeant," ordered the commissary, "and look carefully at this man."

It was with very evident repugnance that the old soldier obeyed.

"What is the uniform that he wears?"

"It is the uniform of the 2d battalion of the 53d regiment of the line."

"Do you recognize him?"

"Not at all."

"Are you sure that he does not belong to your regiment?"

"I can not say for certain: there are some conscripts at the depot whom I have never seen. But I am ready to swear that he had never formed part of the 2d battalion—which, by the way, is mine, and in which I am sergeant-major."

Lecoq, who had hitherto remained in the background, now stepped forward. "It might be as well," he suggested, "to note the numbers marked on the other articles of clothing."

"That is a very good idea," said the commissary, approvingly.

"Here is his shako," added the young police agent. "It bears the number 3,129."

The officials followed Lecoq's advice, and soon discovered that each article of clothing worn by the unfortunate man bore a different number.

"The deuce!" murmured the sergeant; "there is every indication— But it is very singular."

Invited to consider what he was going to say, the brave trooper evidently made an effort to collect his intellectual faculties. "I would stake my epaulets that this fellow never

was a soldier," he said at last. "He must have disguised himself to take part in the Shrove Sunday carnival."

"Why do you think that?"

"Oh, I know it better than I can explain it. I know it by
his hair, by his nails, by his whole appearance, by a certain
je ne sais quoi; in short, I know it by everything and by nothing.
Why look, the poor devil did not even know how to put on his
shoes; he has laced his gaiters wrong side outwards." Evidently
further doubt was impossible after this evidence, which confirmed the truth of Lecoq's first remark to Inspector Gevrol.

"Still, if this person was a civilian, how could he have
procured this clothing?" insisted the commissary. "Could he
have borrowed it from the men in your company?"

"Yes, that is possible; but it is difficult to believe."

"Is there no way by which you could ascertain?"

"Oh! very easily. I have only to run over to the fort and
order an inspection of clothing."

"Do so," approved the commissary; "it would be an excellent
way of getting at the truth."

But Lecoq had just thought of a method quite as convincing,
and much more prompt. "One word, sergeant," said he, "isn't
cast off military clothing sold by public auction?"

"Yes; at least once a year, after the inspection."

"And are not the articles thus sold marked in some way?"

"Assuredly."

"Then see if there isn't some mark of the kind on this poor
wretch's uniform."

The sergeant turned up the collar of the coat and examined
the waist-band of the pantaloons. "You are right," he said,
these are condemned garments."

The eyes of the young police agent sparkled. "We must
then believe that the poor devil purchased this costume," he
observed. "Where? Necessarily at the Temple, from one of
the dealers in military clothing. There are only five or six
of these establishments. I will go from one to another of them,
and the person who sold these clothes will certainly recognize
them by some trade mark."

"And that will assist us very much," growled Gevrol.

The sergeant-major, to his great relief, now received permission to retire, but not without having been warned that
very probably the commissary would require his deposition.

The moment had come to search the garments of the pretended soldier, and the commissary, who performed this duty himself, hoped that some clue as to the man's identity would be forthcoming. He proceeded with his task, at the same time dictating to one of the men a *proces-verbal* of the search; that is to say, a minute description of all the articles he found upon the dead man's person. In the right hand trousers pocket some tobacco, a pipe, and a few matches were found; in the left hand one, a linen handkerchief of good quality, but unmarked, and a soiled leather pocket-book, containing seven francs and sixty centimes.

There appeared to be nothing more, and the commissary was expressing his regret, when, on carefully examining the pocket-book he found a compartment which had at first escaped his notice, being hidden by a leather flap. This compartment contained a carefully folded paper. The commissary unfolded it and read the contents aloud:

*My dear Gustave,—To-morrow, Sunday evening, do not fail to come to the ball at the Rainbow, according to our agreement. If you have no money pass by my house, and I will leave some with the concierge, who will give it to you.

"Be at the ball by eight o'clock. If I am not already there, it will not be long before I make my appearance. Everything is going on satisfactorily.   "LACHENEUR."

Alas! what did this letter reveal? Only that the dead man's name was Gustave; that he had some connection with a man named Lacheneur, who had advanced him money for a certain object; and that they had met at the Rainbow some hours before the murder.

It was little—very little—but still it was something. It was a clue; and in this absolute darkness even the faintest gleam of light was eagerly welcomed.

"Lacheneur!" growled Gevrol; "the poor devil uttered that name in his last agony."

"Precisely," insisted Father Absinthe, "and he declared that he wished to revenge himself upon him. He accused him of having drawn him into a trap. Unfortunately, death cut his story short."

Lecoq was silent. The commissary of police had handed him the letter, and he was studying it with the closest attention. The paper on which it was written was of the ordinary kind; the ink was blue. In one of the corners was a half-effaced stamp, of which one could just distinguish the word—Beaumarchais.

This was enough for Lecoq. "This letter," he thought, "was certainly written in a café on the Boulevard Beaumarchais. In which one? I must ascertain that point, for this Lacheneur must be found."

While the agents of the prefecture were gathered around the commissary, holding council and deliberating, the physicians began their delicate and disagreeable task. With the assistance of Father Absinthe, they removed the clothing of the pretended soldier, and then, with sleeves rolled up, they bent over their "subject" like surgeons in the schools of anatomy, and examined, inspected, and appraised him physically. Very willingly would the younger doctor have dispensed with these formalities, which he considered very ridiculous, and entirely unnecessary; but the old physician had too high a regard for his profession, and for the duty he had been called upon to fulfil, to neglect the slightest detail. Minutely, and with the most scrupulous exactitude, he noted the height of the dead man, his supposed age, the nature of his temperament, the color and length of his hair, and the degree of development of his muscular system.

Then the doctors passed to an examination of the wound. Lecoq had judged correctly. The medical men declared it to be a fracture of the base of the skull. It could, they stated, only have been caused by some instrument with a very broad surface, or by a violent knock of the head against some hard substance of considerable magnitude.

But no weapon, other than the revolver, had been found; and it was evidently not heavy enough to produce such a wound. There must, then, necessarily, have been a hand-to-hand struggle between the pretended soldier and the murderer; and the latter, seizing his adversary by the throat, had dashed him violently against the wall. The presence of some very tiny but very numerous spots of extravasated blood about the neck made this theory extremely plausible.

No other wound, not even a bruise or a scratch, was to be found. Hence, it became evident that this terrible struggle must have been exceedingly short. The murder of the pretended soldier must have been consummated between the moment when the squad of police heard the shrieks of despair and the moment when Lecoq peered through the shutter and saw the victim fall.

The examination of the other murdered man required different but even greater precautions than those adopted by the doctors in their inspection of the pseudo soldier. The position of these two victims had been respected; they were still lying across the hearth as they had fallen, and their attitude was a matter of great importance, since it might have decisive bearing on the case. Now, this attitude was such that one could not fail to be impressed with the idea that with both these men death had been instantaneous. They were both stretched out upon their backs, their limbs extended, and their hands wide open.

No contraction or extension of the muscles, no trace of conflict could be perceived; it seemed evident that they had been taken unawares, the more so as their faces expressed the most intense terror.

"Thus," said the old doctor, "we may reasonably suppose that they were stupefied by some entirely unexpected, strange, and frightful spectacle. I have come across this terrified expression depicted upon the faces of dead people more than once. I recollect noticing it upon the features of a woman who died suddenly from the shock she experienced when one of her neighbors, with the view of playing her a trick, entered her house disguised as a ghost."

Lecoq followed the physician's explanations, and tried to make them agree with the vague hypotheses that were revolving in his own brain. But who could these individuals be? Would they, in death, guard the secret of their identity, as the other victim had done?

The first subject examined by the physicians was over fifty years of age. His hair was very thin and quite gray and his face was closely shaven, excepting a thick tuft of hair on his rather prominent chin. He was very poorly clad, wearing a soiled woolen blouse and a pair of dilapidated trousers hanging in rags over his boots, which were very much trodden down at the heels. The old doctor declared that this man must have been instantly killed by a bullet. The size of the circular wound, the absence of blood around its edge, and the blackened and burnt state of the flesh demonstrated this fact with almost mathematical precision.

The great difference that exists in wounds made by firearms, according to the distance from which the death-dealing missile comes, was seen when the physicians began to examine the last of the murdered men. The ball that had caused the latter's death had scarcely crossed a yard of space before reaching him, and his wound was not nearly so hideous in aspect as the other's. This individual, who was at least fifteen years younger than his companion, was short and remarkably ugly; his face, which was quite beardless, being pitted all over by the small-pox. His garb was such as is worn by the worst frequenters of the barrière. His trousers were of a gray checked material, and his blouse, turned back at the throat, was blue. It was noticed that his boots had been blackened quite recently. The smart glazed cap that lay on the floor beside him was in harmony with his carefully curled hair and gaudy necktie.

These were the only facts that the physicians' report set forth in technical terms, this was the only information obtained by the most careful investigation. The two men's pockets were explored and turned inside out; but they contained nothing that gave the slightest clue to their identity, either as regards name, social position, or profession. There was not even the slightest indication on any of these points, not a letter, nor an address, not a fragment of paper, nothing—not even such common articles of personal use, as a tobacco pouch, a knife, or a pipe which might be recognized, and thus establish the owner's identity. A little tobacco in a paper bag, a couple of pocket handkerchiefs that were unmarked, a packet of cigarettes—these were the only articles discovered beyond the money which the victims carried loose in their pockets. On this point, it should be mentioned that the elder man had sixty-seven francs about him, and the younger one, two louis.

Rarely had the police found themselves in the presence of so strange an affair, without the slightest clue to guide them. Of course, there was the fact itself, as evidenced by the bodies of the three victims; but the authorities were quite ignorant of the circumstances that had attended and of the motive that had inspired the crime. Certainly, they might hope with the powerful means of investigation at their disposal to finally arrive at the truth in the course of time, and after repeated efforts. But, in the mean while, all was mystery, and so strangely did the case present itself that it could not safely be said who was really responsible for the horrible tragedy at the Poivriere.

The murderer had certainly been arrested; but if he persisted in his obstinacy, how were they to ascertain his name? He protested that he had merely killed in self-defense. How could it be shown that such was not the case? Nothing was known concerning the victims; one of whom had with his dying breath accused himself. Then again. an inexplicable influence tied the Widow Chupin's tongue. Two women, one of whom had lost an earring valued at 5,000 francs, had witnessed the struggle—then disappeared. An accomplice, after two acts of unheard-of audacity, had also made his escape. And all these people—the women, the murderer, the keeper of the saloon, the accomplice, and the victims—were equally strange and mysterious, equally liable *not* to be what they seemed.

Perhaps the commissary of police thought he would spend a very unpleasant quarter of an hour at the prefecture when he reported the case. Certainly, he spoke of the crime in a very despondent tone.

"It will now be best," he said at last, "to transport these three bodies to the Morgue. There they will doubtless be identified." He reflected for a moment, and then added: "And to think that one of these dead men is perhaps Lacheneur himself!"

"That is scarcely possible," said Lecoq. "The spurious soldier, being the last to die, had seen his companions fall. If he had supposed Lacheneur to be dead, he would not have spoken of vengeance."

Gevrol, who for the past two hours had pretended to pay no attention to the proceedings, now approached. He was not the man to yield even to the strongest evidence. "If Monsieur, the Commissary, will listen to me, he shall hear my opinion, which is a trifle more definite than M. Lecoq's fancies."

Before he could say any more, the sound of a vehicle stopping before the door of the cabin interrupted him, and an instant afterward the investigating magistrate entered the room.

All the officials assembled at the Poivriere knew at least by sight the magistrate who now made his appearance, and Gevrol, an old habitue of the Palais de Justice, mechanically murmured his name: "M. Maurice d'Escorval."

He was the son of that famous Baron d'Escorval, who, in 1815, sealed his devotion to the empire with his blood, and upon whom Napoleon, in the Memorial of St. Helena, pronounced this magnificent eulogium: "Men as honest as he may, I believe, exist; but more honest, no, it is not possible."

Having entered upon his duties as magistrate early in life,

and being endowed with remarkable talents, it was at first supposed that the younger D'Escorval would rise to the most exalted rank in his profession. But he had disappointed all such prognostications by resolutely refusing the more elevated positions that were offered to him, in order to retain his modest but useful functions in the public prosecutor's offices at Paris. To explain his repeated refusals, he said that life in the capital had more charms for him than the most enviable advancement in provincial centres. But it was hard to understand this declaration, for in spite of his brilliant connections and large fortune, he had, ever since the death of his eldest brother, led a most retired life, his existence merely being revealed by his untiring labors and the good he did to those around him.

He was now about forty-two years of age, but appeared much younger, although a few furrows already crossed his brow. One would have admired his face, had it not been for the puzzling immobility that marred its beauty, the sarcastic curl of his thin lips, and the gloomy expression of his pale-blue eyes. To say that he was cold and grave, did not express the truth, it was saying too little. He was gravity and coldness personified, with a shade of *hauteur* added.

Impressed by the horror of the scene the instant he placed his foot upon the threshold, M. d'Escorval acknowledged the presence of the physicians and the commissary by a slight nod of the head. The others in the room had no existence so far as he was concerned. At once his faculties went to work. He studied the ground, and carefully noted all the surroundings with the attentive sagacity of a magistrate who realizes the immense weight of even the slightest detail, and who fully appreciates the eloquence of circumstantial evidence.

"This is a serious affair," he said gravely; "very serious."

The commissary's only response was to lift his eyes to heaven. A gesture that plainly implied, "I quite agree with you!" The fact is, that for the past two hours the worthy commissary's responsibility had weighed heavily upon him, and he secretly blessed the investigating magistrate for relieving him of it.

"The public prosecutor was unable to accompany me," resumed M. d'Escorval, "he has not the gift of omnipresence, and I doubt if it will be possible for him to join me here. Let us, therefore, begin operations at once."

The curiosity of those present had become intense; and the commissary only expressed the general feeling when he said: "You have undoubtedly questioned the murderer, sir, and have learnt—"

"I have learnt nothing," interrupted M. d'Escorval, apparently much astonished at the interruption.

He took a chair and sat himself down, and while his clerk was busy in authenticating the commissary's *proces-verbal,* he began to read the report prepared by Lecoq.

Pale, agitated, and nervous, the young police agent tried to read upon the magistrate's impassive face the impression produced by the document. His future depended upon the magistrate's approval or disapproval; and it was not with a fuddled mind like that of Father Absinthe that he had now to deal, but with a superior intelligence.

"If I could only plead my own cause," he thought. "What are cold written phrases in comparison with spoken, living words, palpitating with emotion and imbued with the convictions of the speaker."

However, he was soon reassured. The magistrate's face retained its immobility, but again and again did M. d'Escorval nod his head in token of approval, and occasionally some point more ingenious than the others extorted from his lips the exclamations: "Not bad—very good!"

When he had finished the perusal he turned to the commissary and remarked: "All this is very unlike your report of this morning, which represented the affair as a low broil between a party of miserable vagabonds."

The observation was only too just and fair; and the commissary deeply regretted that he had trusted to Gevrol's representations, and remained in bed. "This morning," he responded evasively, "I only gave you my first impressions. These have been modified by subsequent researches, so that—"

"Oh!" interrupted the magistrate, "I did not intend to reproach you; on the contrary, I must congratulate you. One could not have done better nor acted more promptly. The investigation that has been carried out shows great penetration and research, and the results are given with unusual clearness, and wonderful precision."

Lecoq's head whirled.

The commissary hesitated for an instant. At first he was

sorely tempted to confiscate this praise to his own profit. If he drove away the unworthy thought, it was because he was an honest man, and more than that, because he was not displeased to have the opportunity to do Gevrol a bad turn and punish him for his presumptuous folly."

"I must confess," he said with some embarrassment, "that the merit of this investigation does not belong to me."

"To whom, then, shall I attribute it—to the inspector?" thought M. d'Escorval, not without surprise, for having occasionally employed Gevrol, he did not expect from him such ingenuity and sagacity as was displayed in this report. "Is it you, then, who have conducted this investigation so ably?" he asked.

"Upon my word, no!" responded Inspector Gevrol. "I, myself, am not so clever as all that. I content myself with telling what I actually discover; and I only give proofs when I have them in hand. May I be hung if the grounds of this report have any existence save in the brains of the man who imagined them." Perhaps the inspector really believed what he said, being one of those persons who are blinded by vanity to such a degree that, with the most convincing evidence before their eyes, they obstinately deny it.

"And yet," insisted the magistrate, "these women whose footprints have been detected must have existed. The accomplice who left the flakes of wool adhering to the plank is a real being. This earring is a positive, palpable proof."

Gevrol had hard work to refrain from shrugging his shoulders. "All this can be satisfactorily explained," he said, "without a search of twelve or fourteen hours. That the murderer had an accomplice is possible. The presence of the women is very natural. Wherever there are male thieves, you will find female thieves as well. As for the diamond—what does that prove? That the scoundrels had just met with a stroke of good luck, that they had come here to divide their booty, and that the quarrel arose from the division."

This was an explanation, and such a plausible one, that M. d'Escorval was silent, reflecting before he announced his decision. "Decidedly," he declared at last, "decidedly, I adopt the hypothesis set forth in the report. Who prepared it?"

Gevrol's face turned red with anger. "One of my men," he replied, "a clever, adroit fellow, Monsieur Lecoq. Come forward, Lecoq, that the magistrate may see you."

The young man advanced, his lips tightly compressed so as to conceal a smile of satisfaction which almost betrayed itself.

"My report, sir, is only a summary," he began, "but I have certain ideas—"

"Which you will acquaint me with, when I ask for them," interrupted the magistrate. And oblivious of Lecoq's chagrin, he drew from his clerk's portfolio two forms, which he filled up and handed to Gevrol, saying: "Here are two orders; take them to the station, where the murderer and the landlady of this cabin are confined, and have them conducted to the prefecture, where they will be privately examined."

Having given these directions, M. d'Escorval was turning toward the physicians, when Lecoq, at the risk of a second rebuff, interposed. "May I venture, sir, to beg of you to confide this message to me?" he asked of the investigating magistrate.

"Impossible, I may have need of you here."

"I desired, sir, to collect certain evidence and an opportunity to do so may not present itself again."

The magistrate perhaps fathomed the young man's motive. "Then, let it be so," he replied, "but after your task is completed you must wait for me at the prefecture, where I shall proceed as soon as I have finished here. You may go."

Lecoq did not wait for the order to be repeated. He snatched up the papers, and hastened away.

He literally flew over the ground, and strange to say he no longer experienced any fatigue from the labors of the preceding night. Never had he felt so strong and alert, either in body or mind. He was very hopeful of success. He had every confidence in himself, and his happiness would indeed have been complete if he had had another judge to deal with. But M. d'Escorval overawed him to such a degree that he became almost paralyzed in his presence. With what a disdainful glance the magistrate had surveyed him! With what an imperious tone he had imposed silence upon him—and that, too, when he had found his work deserving of commendation.

"Still, never mind," the young detective mentally exclaimed, "no one ever tastes perfect happiness here below."

And concentrating all his thoughts on the task before him, he hurried on his way.

W HEN, after a rapid walk of twenty minutes, Lecoq reached the police station near the Barriere d'Italie, the door-keeper, with his pipe in his mouth, was pacing slowly to and fro before the guard-house. His thoughtful air, and the anxious glances he cast every now and then toward one of the little grated windows of the building sufficed to indicate that some very rare bird indeed had been entrusted to his keeping. As soon as he recognized Lecoq, his brow cleared, and he paused in his promenade.

"Ah, well!" he inquired, "what news do you bring?"

"I have an order to conduct the prisoners to the prefecture."

The keeper rubbed his hands, and his smile of satisfaction plainly implied that he felt a load the less on his shoulders.

"Capital! capital!" he exclaimed. "The Black Maria, the prison van, will pass here in less than an hour; we will throw them in, and hurry the driver off—"

Lecoq was obliged to interrupt the keeper's transports of satisfaction. "Are the prisoners alone?" he inquired.

"Quite alone: the woman in one cell, and the man in the other. This has been a remarkably quiet night, for Shrove Sunday! Quite surprising indeed! It is true your hunt was interrupted."

"You had a drunken man here, however."

"No—yes—that's true—this morning just at daybreak. A poor devil, who is under a great obligation to Gevrol."

The involuntary irony of this remark did not escape Lecoq. "Yes, under a great obligation, indeed!" he said with a derisive laugh.

"You may laugh as much as you like," retorted the keeper, "but such is really the case; if it hadn't been for Gevrol the man would certainly have been run over."

"And what has become of him?"

The keeper shrugged his shoulders. "You ask me too much," he responded. He was a worthy fellow who had been spending the night at a friend's house, and on coming out into the open air, the wine flew into his head. He told us all about it when he got sober, half an hour afterward. I never saw a man so vexed as he was. He wept, and stammered: "The father of a family, and at my age too! Oh! it is shameful! What shall I say to my wife? What will the children think?"

"Did he talk much about his wife?"

"He talked about nothing else. He mentioned her name—Eudosia Leocadie, or some name of that sort. He declared that he should be ruined if we kept him here. He begged us to send for the commissary to go to his house, and when we set him free, I thought he would go mad with joy; he kissed our hands, and thanked us again and again!"

"And did you place him in the same cage as the murderer?" inquired Lecoq.

"Of course."

"Then they talked with each other."

"Talked? Why, the drunkard was so 'gone,' I tell you, that he couldn't have said 'bread' distinctly. When he was placed in a cell, bang! He fell down like a log of wood. As soon as he recovered, we let him out. I'm sure, they didn't talk to each other."

The young police agent had grown very thoughtful. "I was evidently right," he murmured.

"What did you say?" inquired the keeper.

"Nothing," replied Lecoq, who was not inclined to communicate his reflections to the custodian of the guard-house. These reflections of his were by no means pleasant ones. "I was right," he thought; "this pretended drunkard was none other than the accomplice. He is evidently an adroit, audacious, cool-headed fellow. While we were tracking his footprints he was watching us. When we had got to some distance, he was bold enough to enter the hovel. Then he came here and compelled them to arrest him; and thanks to an assumption of childish simplicity, he succeeded in finding an opportunity to speak with the murderer. He played his part perfectly. Still, I know that he did play a part, and that is something. I know that one must believe exactly the opposite of what he said. He talked of his family, his wife and children—hence, he has neither children, wife, nor family."

Lecoq suddenly checked himself, remembering that he had no time to waste in conjectures. "What kind of fellow was this drunkard? he inquired.

"He was tall and stout, with full ruddy cheeks, a pair of white whiskers, small eyes, a broad flat nose, and a good-natured, jovial manner."

"How old would you suppose him to be?"

"Between forty and fifty."

"Did you form any idea of his profession?"

"It's my opinion, that what with his soft cap and his heavy brown overcoat, he must be either a clerk or the keeper of some little shop."

Having obtained this description, which agreed with the result of his investigations, Lecoq was about to enter the station house when a sudden thought brought him to a stand-still. "I hope this man has had no communication with this Widow Chupin!" he exclaimed.

The keeper laughed heartily. "How could he have had any?" he responded. "Isn't the old woman alone in her cell? Ah, the old wretch! She has been cursing and threatening ever since she arrived. Never in my whole life have I heard such language as she has used. It has been enough to make the very stones blush; even the drunken man was so shocked that he went to the grating in the door, and told her to be quiet."

Lecoq's glance and gesture were so expressive of impatience and wrath that the keeper paused in his recital much perturbed. "What is the matter?" he stammered. "Why are you angry?"

"Because," replied Lecoq, furiously, "because—" Not wishing to disclose the real cause of his anger, he entered the station house, saying that he wanted to see the prisoner.

Left alone, the keeper began to swear in his turn. "These police agents are all alike," he grumbled. "They question you, you tell them all they desire to know; and afterward, if you venture to ask them anything, they reply: 'nothing,' or 'because.' They have too much authority; it makes them proud."

Looking through the little latticed window in the door, by which the men on guard watch the prisoners, Lecoq eagerly examined the appearance of the assumed murderer. He was obliged to ask himself if this was really the same man he had seen some hours previously at the Poivriere, standing on the threshold of the inner door, and holding the whole squad of police agents in check by the intense fury of his attitude. Now, on the contrary, he seemed, as it were, the personification of weakness and despondency. He was seated on a bench opposite the grating in the door, his elbows resting on his knees, his chin upon his hand, his under lip hanging low and his eyes fixed upon vacancy.

"No," murmured Lecoq, "no, this man is not what he seems to be."

So saying he entered the cell, the culprit raised his head, gave the detective an indifferent glance, but did not utter a word.

"Well, how goes it?" asked Lecoq.

"I am innocent!" responded the prisoner, in a hoarse, discordant voice.

"I hope so, I am sure—but that is for the magistrate to decide. I came to see if you wanted anything."

"No," replied the murderer, but a second later he changed his mind. "All the same," he said, "I shouldn't mind a crust and a drink of wine."

"You shall have them," replied Lecoq, who at once went out to forage in the neighborhood for eatables of some sort. In his opinion, if the murderer had asked for a drink after at first refusing to partake of anything, it was solely with the view of conveying the idea that he was really the kind of man he pretended to be.

At all events, whoever he might be, the prisoner ate with an excellent appetite. He then took up the large glass of wine that had been brought him, drained it slowly, and remarked: "That's capital! There can be nothing to beat that!"

This seeming satisfaction greatly disappointed Lecoq, who had selected, as a test, one of those horribly thick, bluish, nauseous mixtures in vogue around the barrieres—hoping, nay, almost expecting, that the murderer would not drink it without some sign of repugnance. And yet the contrary proved the case. However, the young detective had no time to ponder over the circumstance, for a rumble of wheels now announced the approach of that lugubrious vehicle, the Black Maria.

When the Widow Chupin was removed from her cell she fought and scratched and cried "Murder!" at the top of her voice; and it was only by sheer force that she was at length got into the van. Then it was that the officials turned to the assassin. Lecoq certainly expected some sign of repugnance now, and he watched the prisoner closely. But he was again doomed to disappointment. The culprit entered the vehicle in the most unconcerned manner, and took possession of his compartment like one accustomed to it, knowing the most comfortable position to assume in such close quarters.

"Ah! what an unfortunate morning," murmured Lecoq, disconsolately. "Still I will lie in wait for him at the prefecture."

When the door of the prison-van had been securely closed, the driver cracked his whip, and the sturdy horses started off at a brisk trot. Lecoq had taken his seat in front, between the driver and the guard; but his mind was so engrossed with his own thoughts that he heard nothing of their conversation, which was very jovial, although frequently interrupted by the shrill voice of the Widow Chupin, who sang and yelled her imprecations alternately.

It is needless, however, to recapitulate her oaths; let us rather follow the train of Lecoq's meditation. By what means could he secure some clue to the murderer's identity? He was still convinced that the prisoner must belong to the higher ranks of society. After all, it was not so extraordinary that he should have succeeded in feigning an appetite, that he should have concealed his distaste for a nauseous beverage, and that he should have entered the Black Maria without hesitation. Such conduct was quite possible, indeed almost probable on the part of a man, endowed with considerable strength of will, and realizing the imminence of his peril. But granting this, would he be equally able to hide his feelings when he was obliged to submit to the humiliating formalities that awaited him—formalities which in certain cases can, and must, be pushed even to the verge of insult and outrage?

No; Lecoq could not believe that this would be possible. He felt sure that the disgraceful position in which the prisoner would find himself would cause him to revolt, to lose his self-control, to utter some word that might give the desired clue.

It was not until the gloomy vehicle had turned off the Pont Neuf on to the Quai de l'Horloge that the young detective became conscious of what was transpiring around him. Soon the van passed through an open gateway, and drew up in a small, damp courtyard.

Lecoq immediately alighted, and opened the door of the compartment in which the supposed murderer was confined, exclaiming as he did so: "Here we are, get out." There was no fear of the prisoner escaping. The iron gate had been closed, and at least a dozen agents were standing near at hand, waiting to have a look at the new arrivals.

The prisoner slowly stepped to the ground. His expression

of face remained unchanged, and each gesture evinced the perfect indifference of a man accustomed to such ordeals.

Lecoq scrutinized his demeanor as attentively as an anatomist might have watched the action of a muscle. He noted that the prisoner seemed to experience a sensation of satisfaction directly his foot touched the pavement of the courtyard, that he drew a long breath, and then stretched and shook himself, as if to regain the elasticity of his limbs, cramped by confinement in the narrow compartment from which he had just emerged. Then he glanced around him, and a scarcely perceptible smile played upon his lips. One might have sworn that the place was familiar to him, that he was well acquainted with these high grim walls, these grated windows, these heavy doors—in short, with all the sinister belongings of a prison.

"Good Lord!" murmured Lecoq, greatly chagrined, "does he indeed recognize the place?"

And his sense of disappointment and disquietude increased when, without waiting for a word, a motion, or a sign, the prisoner turned toward one of the five or six doors that opened into the courtyard. Without an instant's hesitation he walked straight toward the very doorway he was expected to enter —Lecoq asked himself was it chance? But his amazement and disappointment increased tenfold when, after entering the gloomy corridor, he saw the culprit proceed some little distance, resolutely turn to the left, pass by the keeper's room, and finally enter the registrar's office. An old offender could not have done better.

Big drops of perspiration stood on Lecoq's forehead. "This man," thought he, "has certainly been here before; he knows the ropes."

The registrar's office was a large room heated almost to suffocation by an immense stove, and badly lighted by three small windows, the panes of which were covered with a thick coating of dust. There sat the clerk reading a newspaper, spread out over the open register—that fatal book in which are inscribed the names of all those whom misconduct, crime, misfortune, madness, or error have brought to these grim portals.

Three or four attendants, who were awaiting the hour for entering upon their duties, reclined half asleep upon the wooden benches that lined three sides of the room. These benches, with a couple of tables, and some dilapidated chairs, constituted the entire furniture of the office, in one corner of which stood a measuring machine, under which each culprit was obliged to pass, the exact height of the prisoners being recorded in order that the description of their persons might be complete in every respect.

At the entrance of the culprit accompanied by Lecoq, the clerk raised his head. "Ah!" said he, "has the van arrived?"

"Yes," responded Lecoq. And showing the orders signed by M. d'Escorval, he added: "Here are this man's papers."

The registrar took the documents and read them. "Oh!" he exclaimed, "a triple assassination! Oh! oh!" The glance he gave the prisoner was positively deferential. This was no common culprit, no ordinary vagabond, no vulgar thief.

"The investigating magistrate orders a private examination," continued the clerk, "and I must get the prisoner other clothing, as the things he is wearing now will be used as evidence. Let some one go at once and tell the superintendent that the other occupants of the van must wait."

At this moment, the governor of the Depot entered the office. The clerk at once dipped his pen in the ink, and turning to the prisoner he asked: "What is your name?"

"May."

"Your Christian name?"

"I have none."

"What, have you no Christian name?"

The prisoner seemed to reflect for a moment, and then answered, sulkily: "I may as well tell you that you need not tire yourself by questioning me. I shan't answer any one else but the magistrate. You would like to make me cut my own throat, wouldn't you? A very clever trick, of course, but one that won't do for me."

"You must see that you only aggravate your situation," observed the governor.

"Not in the least. I am innocent; you wish to ruin me. I only defend myself. Get anything more out of me now, if you can. But you had better give me back what they took from me at the station-house. My hundred and thirty-six francs and eight sous. I shall need them when I get out of this place. I want you to make a note of them on the register. Where are they?"

The money had been given to Lecoq by the keeper of the station-house, who had found it upon the prisoner when he was placed in his custody. Lecoq now laid it upon the table.

"Here are your hundred and thirty-six francs and eight sous," said he, "and also your knife, your handkerchief, and four cigars."

An expression of lively contentment was discernible on the prisoner's features.

"Now," resumed the clerk, "will you answer?"

But the governor perceived the futility of further questioning; and silencing the clerk by a gesture, he told the prisoner to take off his boots.

Lecoq thought the assassin's glance wavered as he heard this order. Was it only a fancy?"

"Why must I do that?" asked the culprit.

"To pass under the beam," replied the clerk. "We must make a note of your exact height."

The prisoner made no reply, but sat down and drew off his heavy boots. The heel of the right one was worn down on the inside. It was, moreover, noticed that the prisoner wore no socks, and that his feet were coated with mud.

"You only wear boots on Sundays, then?" remarked Lecoq.

"Why do you think that?"

"By the mud with which your feet are covered, as high as the ankle-bone."

"What of that?" exclaimed the prisoner, in an insolent tone. "Is it a crime not to have a marchioness's feet?"

"It is a crime you are not guilty of, at all events," said the young detective slowly. "Do you think I can't see that if the mud were picked off your feet would be white and neat? The nails have been carefully cut and polished—"

He paused. A new idea inspired by his genius for investigation had just crossed Lecoq's mind. Pushing a chair in front of the prisoner, and spreading a newspaper over it, he said: "Will you place your foot there?"

The man did not comply with the request.

"It is useless to resist," exclaimed the governor, "we are in force."

The prisoner delayed no longer. He placed his foot on the chair, as he had been ordered, and Lecoq, with the aid of a knife, proceeded to remove the fragments of mud that adhered to the skin.

Anywhere else so strange and grotesque a proceeding would have excited laughter, but here, in this gloomy chamber, the anteroom of the assize court, an otherwise trivial act is fraught

with serious import. Nothing astonishes; and should a smile
threaten to curve one's lips, it is instantly repressed

All the spectators, from the governor of the prison to the
keepers, had witnessed many other incidents equally absurd;
and no one thought of inquiring the detective's motive. This
much was known already; that the prisoner was trying to conceal his identity. Now it was necessary to establish it, at any
cost, and Lecoq had probably discovered some means of attain-
ing this end.

The operation was soon concluded; and Lecoq swept the
dust off the paper into the palm of his hand. He divided it
into two parts, enclosing one portion in a scrap of paper, and
slipping it into his own pocket. With the remainder he
formed a package which he handed to the governor, saying:
"I beg you, sir, to take charge of this, and to seal it up
here, in presence of the prisoner. This formality is necessary, so that by and by he may not pretend that the dust has
been changed."

The governor complied with the request, and as he placed
this "bit of proof" (as he styled it) in a small satchel for safe
keeping, the prisoner shrugged his shoulders with a sneering
laugh. Still, beneath this cynical gaiety Lecoq thought he could
detect poignant anxiety. Chance owed him the compensation
of this slight triumph; for previous events had deceived all his
calculations.

The prisoner did not offer the slightest objection when he
was ordered to undress, and to exchange his soiled and blood-
stained garments for the clothing furnished by the Government.
Not a muscle of his face moved while he submitted his person
to one of those ignominious examinations which make the blood
rush to the forehead of the lowest criminal. It was with perfect indifference that he allowed an inspector to comb his hair
and beard, and to examine the inside of his mouth, so as to
make sure that he had not concealed either some fragment of
glass, by the aid of which captives can sever the strongest bars,
or one of those microscopical bits of lead with which prisoners
write the notes they exchange, rolled up in a morsel of bread,
and called "postilions."

These formalities having been concluded, the superintendent
rang for one of the keepers. "Conduct this man to No. 3 of
the secret cells," he ordered.

There was no need to drag the prisoner away. He walked

out, as he had entered, preceding the guard, like some old habitué, who knows where he is going.

"What a rascal!" exclaimed the clerk.

"Then you think—" began Lecoq, baffled but not convinced,

"Ah! there can be no doubt of it," declared the governor. "This man is certainly a dangerous criminal—an old offender —I think I have seen him before—I could almost swear to it."

Thus it was evident these people, with their long, varied experience, shared Gevrol's opinion; Lecoq stood alone. He did not discuss the matter—what good would it have done? Besides, the Widow Chupin was just being brought in.

The journey must have calmed her nerves, for she had become as gentle as a lamb. It was in a wheedling voice, and with tearful eyes, that she called upon these "good gentlemen" to witness the shameful injustice with which she was treated— she, an honest woman. Was she not the mainstay of her family (since her son Polyte was in custody, charged with pocket-picking), hence what would become of her daughter-in-law, and of her grandson Toto, who had no one to look after them but her?

Still, when her name had been taken, and a keeper was ordered to remove her, nature reasserted itself, and scarcely had she entered the corridor than she was heard quarreling with the guard.

"You are wrong not to be polite," she said; "you are losing a good fee, without counting many a good drink I would stand you when I get out of here."

Lecoq was now free until M. d'Escorval's arrival. He wandered through the gloomy corridors, from office to office, but finding himself assailed with questions by every one he came across, he eventually left the *depot,* and went and sat down on one of the benches beside the quay. Here he tried to collect his thoughts. His convictions were unchanged. He was more than ever convinced that the prisoner was concealing his real social standing, but, on the other hand, it was evident that he was well acquainted with the prison and its usages.

He had also proved himself to be endowed with far more cleverness than Lecoq had supposed. What self-control! What powers of dissimulation he had displayed! He had not so much as frowned while undergoing the severest ordeals, and he had managed to deceive the most experienced eyes in Paris.

The young detective had waited during nearly three hours,

as motionless as the bench on which he was seated, and so absorbed in studying his case that he had thought neither of the cold nor of the flight of time, when a carriage drew up before the entrance of the prison, and M. d'Escorval alighted, followed by his clerk.

Lecoq rose and hastened, well-nigh breathless with anxiety, toward the magistrate.

"My researches on the spot," said this functionary, "confirm me in the belief that you are right. Is there anything fresh?"

"Yes, sir; a fact that is apparently very trivial, though, in truth, it is of importance that—"

"Very well!" interrupted the magistrate. "You will explain it to me by and by. First of all, I must summarily examine the prisoners. A mere matter of form for to-day. Wait for me here."

Although the magistrate promised to make haste, Lecoq expected that at least an hour would elapse before he reappeared. In this he was mistaken. Twenty minutes later, M. d'Escorval emerged from the prison without his clerk.

He was walking very fast, and instead of approaching the young detective, he called to him at some little distance. "I must return home at once," he said, "instantly; I can not listen to you."

"But, sir—"

"Enough! the bodies of the victims have been taken to the Morgue. Keep a sharp lookout there. Then, this evening make —well—do whatever you think best."

"But, sir, I must—"

"To-morrow!—to-morrow, at nine o'clock, in my office in the Palais de Justice."

Lecoq wished to insist upon a hearing, but M. d'Escorval had entered, or rather thrown himself into, his carriage, and the coachman was already whipping up the horse.

"And to think that he's an investigating magistrate," panted Lecoq, left spellbound on the quay. "Has he gone mad?" As he spoke, an uncharitable thought took possession of his mind. "Can it be," he murmured, "that M. d'Escorval holds the key to the mystery? Perhaps he wishes to get rid of me."

This suspicion was so terrible that Lecoq hastened back to the prison, hoping that the prisoner's bearing might help to solve his doubts. On peering through the grated aperture in the door of the cell, he perceived the prisoner lying on the pallet that stood opposite the door. His face was turned toward the wall, and he was enveloped in the coverlid up to his eyes. He was not asleep, for Lecoq could detect a strange movement of the body, which puzzled and annoyed him. On applying his ear instead of his eye to the aperture, he distinguished a stifled moan. There could no longer be any doubt. The death rattle was sounding in the prisoner's throat.

"Help! help!" cried Lecoq, greatly excited. "The prisoner is killing himself!"

A dozen keepers hastened to the spot. The door was quickly opened, and it was then ascertained that the prisoner, having torn a strip of binding from his clothes, had fastened it round his neck and tried to strangle himself with the assistance of a spoon that had been left him with his food. He was already unconscious, and the prison doctor, who immediately bled him, declared that had another ten minutes elapsed, help would have arrived too late.

When the prisoner regained his senses, he gazed around him with a wild, puzzled stare. One might have supposed that he was amazed to find himself still alive. Suddenly a couple of big tears welled from his swollen eyelids, and rolled down his cheeks. He was pressed with questions, but did not vouchsafe so much as a single word in response. As he was in such a desperate frame of mind, and as the orders to keep him in solitary confinement prevented the governor giving him a companion, it was decided to put a straight waistcoat on him. Lecoq assisted at this operation, and then walked away, puzzled, thoughtful, and agitated. Intuition told him that these mysterious occurrences concealed some terrible drama.

"Still, what can have occurred since the prisoner's arrival here?" he murmured. "Has he confessed his guilt to the magistrate, or what is his reason for attempting so desperate an act?"

VIII

LECOQ did not sleep that night, although he had been on his feet for more than forty hours, and had scarcely paused either to eat or drink. Anxiety, hope, and even fatigue itself, had imparted to his body the fictitious strength of fever, and to his intellect the unhealthy acuteness which is so often the result of intense mental effort.

He no longer had to occupy himself with imaginary deductions, as in former times when in the employ of his patron, the astronomer. Once again did the fact prove stranger than fiction. Here was reality—a terrible reality personified by the corpses of three victims lying on the marble slabs at the Morgue. Still, if the catastrophe itself was a patent fact, its motive, its surroundings, could only be conjectured. Who could tell what circumstances had preceded and paved the way for this tragical dénouement?

It is true that all doubt might be dispelled by one discovery —the identity of the murderer. Who was he? Who was right, Gevrol or Lecoq? The former's views were shared by the officials at the prison; the latter stood alone. Again, the former's opinion was based upon formidable proof, the evidence of sight; while Lecoq's hypothesis rested only on a series of subtle observations and deductions, starting from a single sentence that had fallen from the prisoner's lips.

And yet Lecoq resolutely persisted in his theory, guided by the following reasons. He learnt from M. d'Escorval's clerk that when the magistrate had examined the prisoner, the latter not only refused to confess, but answered all the questions put to him in the most evasive fashion. In several instances, moreover, he had not replied at all. If the magistrate had not insisted, it was because this first examination was a mere formality, solely intended to justify the somewhat premature delivery of the order to imprison the accused.

Now, under these circumstances, how was one to explain the prisoner's attempt at self-destruction? Prison statistics show that habitual offenders do not commit suicide. When apprehended for a criminal act, they are sometimes seized with a wild frenzy and suffer repeated nervous attacks; at others they fall into a dull stupor, just as some glutted beast succumbs to sleep with the blood of his prey still dripping from his lips. However, such men never think of putting an end to their days. They hold fast to life, no matter how seriously they may be compromised. In truth, they are cowards.

On the other hand, the unfortunate fellow who, in a moment of frenzy, commits a crime, not unfrequently seeks to avoid the consequences of his act by self-destruction.

Hence, the prisoner's frustrated attempt at suicide was a

strong argument in favor of Lecoq's theory. This wretched man's secret must be a terrible one since he held it dearer than life, since he had tried to destroy himself that he might take it unrevealed to the grave.

Four o'clock was striking when Lecoq sprang from his bed on which he had thrown himself without undressing; and five minutes later he was walking down the Rue Montmartre. The weather was still cold and muggy; and a thick fog hung over the city. But the young detective was too engrossed with his own thoughts to pay attention to any atmospherical unpleasantness. Walking with a brisk stride, he had just reached the church of Saint Eustache, when a coarse, mocking voice accosted him with the exclamation: "Ah, ha! my fine fellow!"

He looked up and perceived Gevrol, who, with three of his men, had come to cast his nets round about the markets, whence the police generally return with a good haul of thieves and vagabonds.

"You are up very early this morning, Monsieur Lecoq," continued the inspector; "you are still trying to discover our man's identity, I suppose?"

"Still trying."

"Is he a prince in disguise, or only a marquis?"

"One or the other, I am quite certain."

"All right then. In that case you will not refuse us the opportunity to drink to your success."

Lecoq consented, and the party entered a wine-shop close by. When the glasses were filled, Lecoq turned to Gevrol and exclaimed: "Upon my word, General, our meeting will save me a long walk. I was going to the prefecture to request you, on M. d'Escorval's behalf, to send one of our comrades to the Morgue this morning. The affair at the Poivriere has been noised about, and all the world will be there, so he desires some officer to be present to watch the crowd and listen to the remarks of the visitors."

"All right; Father Absinthe shall be there when the doors open."

To send Father Absinthe where a shrewd and subtle agent was required was a mockery. Still Lecoq did not protest, for it was better to be badly served than to be betrayed; and he could at least trust Father Absinthe.

"It doesn't much matter," continued Gevrol; "but you should have informed me of this last evening. However, when I reached the prefecture you had gone."

"I had some work to do."

"Yes?"

"At the station-house near the Barriere d'Italie. I wanted to know whether the floor of the cell was paved or tiled." So saying, Lecoq paid the score, saluted his superior officer, and went out."

"Thunder!" exclaimed Gevrol, striking his glass violently upon the counter. "Thunder! how that fellow provokes me! He does not know the A B C of his profession. When he can't discover anything, he invents wonderful stories, and then misleads the magistrates with his high-sounding phrases, in the hope of gaining promotion. I'll give him advancement with a vengeance! I'll teach him to set himself above me!"

Lecoq had not been deceived. The evening before, he had visited the station-house where the prisoner had first been confined, and had compared the soil of the cell floor with the dust he had placed in his pocket; and he carried away with him, as he believed, one of those crushing proofs that often suffice to extort from the most obstinate criminal a complete confession.

If Lecoq was in haste to part company with Gevrol, it was because he was anxious to pursue his investigations still further, before appearing in M. d'Escorval's presence. He was determined to find the cab-driver who had been stopped by the two women in the Rue du Chevaleret; and with this object in view, he had obtained at the prefecture the names and addresses of all the cab-owners hiring between the road to Fontainebleau and the Seine.

His earlier efforts at investigation proved unsuccessful. At the first establishment he visited, the stable boys, who were not yet up, swore at him roundly. In the second, he found the grooms at work, but none of the drivers had as yet put in an appearance. Moreover, the owner refused to show him the books upon which are recorded—or should be recorded—each driver's daily engagements. Lecoq was beginning to despair, when at about half-past seven o'clock he reached an establishment just beyond the fortifications belonging to a man named Trigault. Here he learned that on Sunday night, or rather, early on Monday morning, one of the drivers had been accosted on his way home by some persons who succeeded in persuading him to drive them back into Paris.

This driver, who was then in the courtyard harnessing his horse, proved to be a little old man, with a ruddy complexion, and a pair of small eyes full of cunning. Lecoq walked up to him at once.

"Was it you," he asked, "who, on Sunday night or rather on Monday, between one and two in the morning, drove a couple of women from the Rue du Chevaleret into Paris?"

The driver looked up, and surveying Lecoq attentively, cautiously replied: "Perhaps."

"It is a positive answer that I want."

"Aha!" said the old man sneeringly, "you know two ladies who have lost something in a cab, and so—"

The young detective trembled with satisfaction. This man was certainly the one he was looking for. "Have you heard anything about a crime that has been committed in the neighborhood?" he interrupted.

"Yes; a murder in a low wine-shop."

"Well, then, I will tell you that these two women are mixed up in it; they fled when we entered the place. I am trying to find them. I am a detective; here is my card. Now, can you give me any information?"

The driver had grown very pale. "Ah! the wretches!" he exclaimed. "I am no longer surprised at the luck-money they gave me—a louis and two five-franc pieces for the fare—thirty francs in all. Cursed money! If I hadn't spent it, I'd throw it away!"

"And where did you drive them?"

"To the Rue de Bourgogne. I have forgotten the number, but I should recognize the house."

"Unfortunately, they would not have let you drive them to their own door."

"Who knows? I saw them ring the bell, and I think they went in just as I drove away. Shall I take you there?"

Lecoq's sole response was to spring on to the box, exclaiming: "Let us be off."

It was not to be supposed that the women who had escaped from the Widow Chupin's drinking-den at the moment of the murder were utterly devoid of intelligence. Nor was it at all likely that these two fugitives, conscious as they were of their perilous situation, had gone straight to their real home in a vehicle hired on the public highway. Hence, the driver's hope of finding them in the Rue de Bourgogne was purely chimerical. Lecoq was fully aware of this, and yet he did not hesitate to jump on to the box and give the signal for starting. In so doing, he obeyed a maxim which he had framed in his early days of meditation—a maxim intended to assure his after-fame, and which ran as follows: "Always suspect that which seems probable; and begin by believing what appears incredible."

As soon as the vehicle was well under way, the young detective proceeded to ingratiate himself into the driver's good graces, being anxious to obtain all the information that this worthy was able to impart.

In a tone that implied that all trifling would be useless the cabman cried: "Hey up, hey up, Cocotte!" and his mare pricked up her ears and quickened her pace, so that the Route de Choisy was speedily reached. Then it was that Lecoq resumed his inquiries.

"Well, my good fellow," he began, "you have told me the principal facts, now I should like the details. How did these two women attract your attention?"

"Oh, it was very simple. I had been having a most unfortunate day—six hours on a stand on the Boulevards, with the rain pouring all the time. It was simply awful. At midnight I had not made more than a franc and a half for myself, but I was so wet and miserable and the horse seemed so done up that I decided to go home. I *did* grumble, I can tell you. Well, I had just passed the corner of the Rue Picard, in the Rue du Chevaleret, when I saw two women standing under a lamp, some little distance off. I did not pay any attention to them; for when a man is as old as I am, women—"

"Go on!" said Lecoq, who could not restrain his impatience.

"I had already passed them, when they began to call after me. I pretended I did not hear them; but one of them ran after the cab, crying: 'A louis! a louis for yourself!' I hesitated for a moment, when the woman added: 'And ten francs for the fare!' I then drew up."

Lecoq was boiling over with impatience; but he felt that the wisest course was not to interrupt the driver with questions, but to listen to all he had to say.

"As you may suppose," continued the coachman, "I wasn't inclined to trust two such suspicious characters, alone at that hour and in that part of the city. So, just as they were about to get into the cab, I called to them: 'Wait a bit, my little friends, you have promised papa some sous; where are they?' The one who had called after the cab at once handed me thirty francs, saying: 'Above all, make haste!'"

"Your recital could not be more minute," exclaimed Lecoq, approvingly. "Now, how about these two women?"

"What do you mean?"

"I mean what kind of women did they seem to be; what did you take them for?"

"Oh, for nothing very good!" replied the driver, with a knowing smile.

"Ah! and how were they dressed?"

"Like most of the girls who go to dance at the Rainbow. One of them, however, was very neat and prim, while the other —well! she was a terrible dowdy."

"Which ran after you?"

"The girl who was neatly dressed, the one who—" The driver suddenly paused: some vivid remembrance passed through his brain, and, abruptly jerking the rains, he brought his horse to a standstill.

"Thunder!" he exclaimed. "Now I think of it, I did notice something strange. One of the two women called the other 'Madame' as large as life, while the other said 'thee' and 'thou,' and spoke as if she were somebody."

"Oh! oh! oh!" exclaimed the young detective, in three different keys. "And which was it that said 'thee' and 'thou'?"

"Why, the dowdy one. She with shabby dress and shoes as big as a gouty man's. You should have seen her shake the prim-looking girl, as if she had been a plum tree. 'You little fool!' said she, 'do you want to ruin us? You will have time to faint when we get home; now come along. And then she began to sob: 'Indeed, madame, indeed I can't!' she said, and really she seemed quite unable to move: in fact, she appeared to be so ill that I said to myself: 'Here is a young woman who has drunk more than is good for her!'"

These facts confirmed even if they corrected Lecoq's first suppositions. As he had suspected, the social position of the two women was not the same. He had been mistaken, however, in attributing the higher standing to the woman wearing the shoes with the high heels, the marks of which he had so particularly noticed in the snow, with all the attendant signs of precipitation, terror, and weakness. In reality, social pre-eminence belonged to the woman who had left the large, broad footprints behind her. And not merely was she of a superior rank, but she had also shown superior energy. Contrary to

Lecoq's original idea, it now seemed evident that she was the mistress, and her companion the servant.

"Is that all, my good fellow?" he asked the driver, who during the last few minutes had been busy with his horses.

"Yes," replied the cabman, "except that I noticed that the shabbily dressed woman who paid me had a hand as small as a child's, and in spite of her anger, her voice was as sweet as music."

"Did you see her face?"

"I just caught a glimpse of it."

"Could you tell if she were pretty, or whether she was a blonde or brunette?"

So many questions at a time confused the driver. "Stop a minute!" he replied. "In my opinion she wasn't pretty, and I don't believe she was young, but she certainly was a blonde, and with plenty of hair too."

"Was she tall or short, stout or slender?"

"Between the two."

This was very vague. "And the other," asked Lecoq, "the neatly dressed one?"

"The deuce! As for her, I did not notice her at all; all I know about her is that she was very small."

"Would you recognize her if you met her again?"

"Good heavens! no."

The vehicle was now rolling along the Rue de Bourgogne. Half-way down the street the driver pulled up, and, turning to Lecoq, exclaimed: "Here we are. That's the house the hussies went into."

To draw off the silk handkerchief that served him as a muffler, to fold it and slip it into his pocket, to spring to the ground and enter the house indicated, was only the work of an instant for the young detective.

In the concierge's little room he found an old woman knitting. Lecoq bowed to her politely, and, displaying the silk handkerchief, exclaimed: "Madame, I have come to return this article to one of your lodgers."

"To which one?"

"Really, I don't exactly know."

In a moment the worthy dame imagined that this polite young man was making fun of her. "You scamp—!" she began.

"Excuse me," interrupted Lecoq; "allow me to finish. I must tell you that at about three o'clock in the morning, of the day before yesterday, I was quietly returning home, when two ladies, who were seemingly in a great hurry, overtook me and passed on. One of them dropped this handkerchief, which I picked up. I hastened after her to restore it, but before I could overtake them they had rung the bell at your door and were already in the house. I did not like to ring at such an unearthly hour for fear of disturbing you. Yesterday I was so busy I couldn't come; however, here I am at last, and here's the handkerchief." So saying, Lecoq laid the handkerchief on the table, and turned as if to go, when the concierge detained him.

"Many thanks for your kindness," said she, "but you can keep it. We have no ladies in this house who are in the habit of coming home alone after midnight."

"Still I have eyes," insisted Lecoq, "and I certainly saw—"

"Ah! I had forgotten," exclaimed the old woman. "The night you speak of some one certainly did ring the bell here. I pulled the string that opens the door and listened, but not hearing any one close the door or come upstairs, I said to myself: 'Some mischievous fellow has been playing a trick on me.' I slipped on my dress and went out into the hall, where I saw two women hastening toward the door. Before I could reach them they slammed the door in my face. I opened it again as quickly as I could and looked out into the street. But they were hurrying away as fast as they could."

"In what direction?"

"Oh! they were running toward the Rue de Varennes."

Lecoq was baffled again; however, he bowed civilly to the concierge, whom he might possibly have need of at another time, and then went back to the cab. "As I had supposed, they do not live here," he remarked to the driver.

The latter shrugged his shoulders in evident vexation, which would inevitably have vent in a torrent of words, if Lecoq, who had consulted his watch, had not forestalled the outburst by saying: "Nine o'clock—I am an hour behind time already: still I shall have some news to tell. Now take me to the Morgue as quickly as possible."

When a mysterious crime has been perpetrated, or a great catastrophe has happened, and the identity of the victims has not been established, "a great day" invariably follows at the Morgue. The attendants are so accustomed to the horrors of the place that the most sickly sight fails to impress them; and even under the most distressing circumstances, they hasten gaily to and fro, exchanging jests well calculated to make an ordinary mortal's flesh creep. As a rule, they are far less interested in the corpses laid out for public view on the marble slabs in the principal hall than in the people of every age and station in life who congregate here all day long; at times coming in search of some lost relative or friend, but far more frequently impelled by idle curiosity.

As the vehicle conveying Lecoq reached the quay, the young detective perceived that a large, excited crowd was gathered outside the building. The newspapers had reported the tragedy at the Widow Chupin's drinking-den, of course, more or less correctly, and everybody wished to see the victims.

On drawing near the Pont Notre Dame, Lecoq told the driver to pull up. "I prefer to alight here, rather than in front of the Morgue," he said, springing to the ground. Then, producing first his watch, and next his purse, he added: "We have been an hour and forty minutes, my good fellow, consequently I owe you—"

"Nothing at all," replied the driver, decidedly.

"But—"

"No—not a sou. I am too worried already to think that I took the money these hussies offered me. It would only have served me right if the liquor I bought with it had given me the gripes. Don't be uneasy about the score, and if you need a trap use mine for nothing, till you have caught the jades."

As Lecoq's purse was low, he did not insist.

"You will, at least, take my name and address?" continued the driver.

"Certainly. The magistrate will want your evidence, and a summons will be sent you."

"All right, then. Address it to Papillon (Eugene), driver, care of M. Trigault. I lodge at his place, because I have some small interest in the business, you see."

The young detective was hastening away, when Papillon called him back. "When you leave the Morgue you will want to go somewhere else," he said, "you told me that you had another appointment, and that you were already late."

"Yes, I ought to be at the Palais de Justice; but it is only a few steps from here."

"No matter. I will wait for you at the corner of the bridge. It's useless to say 'no'; I've made up my mind, and I'm a

Breton, you know. I want you to ride out the thirty francs that those jades paid me."

It would have been cruel to refuse such a request. Accordingly, Lecoq made a gesture of assent, and then hurried toward the Morgue.

If there was a crowd on the roadway outside, it was because the gloomy building itself was crammed full of people. Indeed, the sightseers, most of whom could see nothing at all, were packed as closely as sardines, and it was only by dint of well-nigh superhuman efforts that Lecoq managed to effect an entrance. As usual, he found among the mob a large number of girls and women; for, strange to say, the Parisian fair sex is rather partial to the disgusting sights and horrible emotions that repay a visit to the Morgue.

The shop and work girls who reside in the neighborhood readily go out of their way to catch a glimpse of the corpses which crime, accident, and suicide bring to this horrible place. A few, the more sensitive among them, may come no further than the door, but the others enter, and after a long stare return and recount their impressions to their less courageous companions.

If there should be no corpse exhibited; if all the marble slabs are unoccupied, strange as it may seem, the visitors turn hastily away with an expression of disappointment or discontent. There was no fear of their doing so, however, on the morrow of the tragedy at Poivriere, for the mysterious murderer whose identity Lecoq was trying to establish had furnished three victims for their delectation. Panting with curiosity, they paid but little attention to the unhealthy atmosphere: and yet a damp chill came from beyond the iron railings, while from the crowd itself rose an infectious vapor, impregnated with the stench of the chloride of lime used as a disinfectant.

As a continuous accompaniment to the exclamations, sighs, and whispered comments of the bystanders came the murmur of the water trickling from a spigot at the head of each slab; a tiny stream that flowed forth only to fall in fine spray upon the marble. Through the small arched windows a gray light stole in on the exposed bodies, bringing each muscle into bold relief, revealing the ghastly tints of the lifeless flesh, and imparting a sinister aspect to the tattered clothing hung around the room to aid in the identification of the corpses. This clothing, after a certain time, is sold—for nothing is wasted at the Morgue.

However, Lecoq was too occupied with his own thoughts to remark the horrors of the scene. He scarcely bestowed a glance on the three victims. He was looking for Father Absinthe, whom he could not perceive. Had Gevrol intentionally or unintentionally failed to fulfil his promise, or had Father Absinthe forgotten his duty in his morning dram?

Unable to explain the cause of his comrade's absence, Lecoq addressed himself to the head keeper: "It would seem that no one has recognized the victims," he remarked.

"No one. And yet, ever since opening, we have had an immense crowd. If I were master here, on days like this, I would charge an admission fee of two sous a head, with half-price for children. It would bring in a round sum, more than enough to cover the expenses."

The keeper's reply seemed to offer an inducement to conversation, but Lecoq did not seize it. "Excuse me," he interrupted, "didn't a detective come here this morning?"

"Yes, there was one here."

"Has he gone away then? I don't see him anywhere?"

The keeper glanced suspiciously at his eager questioner, but after a moment's hesitation, he ventured to inquire: "Are you one of them?"

"Yes, I am," replied Lecoq, exhibiting his card in support of his assertion.

"And your name?"

"Is Lecoq."

The keeper's face brightened up. "In that case," said he, "I have a letter for you, written by your comrade, who was obliged to go away. Here it is."

The young detective at once tore open the envelope and read: "Monsieur Lecoq—"

"Monsieur?" This simple formula of politeness brought a faint smile to his lips. Was it not, on Father Absinthe's part, an evident recognition of his colleague's superiority. Indeed, our hero accepted it as a token of unquestioning devotion which it would be his duty to repay with a master's kind protection toward his first disciple. However, he had no time to waste in thought, and accordingly at once proceeded to peruse the note, which ran as follows:

"Monsieur Lecoq—I had been standing on duty since the opening of the Morgue, when at about nine o'clock three young men entered, arm-in-arm. From their manner and appearance, I judged them to be clerks in some store or warehouse. Suddenly I noticed that one of them turned as white as his shirt; and calling the attention of his companions to one of the unknown victims, he whispered: 'Gustave!'

"His comrades put their hands over his mouth, and one of them exclaimed: 'What are you about, you fool, to mix yourself up with this affair! Do you want to get us into trouble?'

"Thereupon they went out, and I followed them. But the person who had first spoken was so overcome that he could scarcely drag himself along; and his companions were obliged to take him to a little restaurant close by. I entered it myself, and it is there I write this letter, in the mean time watching them out of the corner of my eye. I send this note, explaining my absence, to the head keeper, who will give it you. You will understand that I am going to follow these men.   A. B. S."

The handwriting of this letter was almost illegible; and there were mistakes in spelling in well-nigh every line; still, its meaning was clear and exact, and could not fail to excite the most flattering hopes.

Lecoq's face was so radiant when he returned to the cab that, as the old coachman urged on his horse, he could not refrain from saying: "Things are going on to suit you."

A friendly "hush!" was the only response. It required all Lecoq's attention to classify this new information. When he alighted from the cab in front of the Palais de Justice, he experienced considerable difficulty in dismissing the old cabman, who insisted upon remaining at his orders. He succeeded at last, however, but even when he had reached the portico on the left side of the building, the worthy fellow, standing up, still shouted at the top of his voice: "At M. Trigault's house—don't forget—Father Papillon—No. 998—1,000 less 2—"

Lecoq had entered the left wing of the Palais. He climbed the stairs till he had reached the third floor, and was about to enter the long, narrow, badly-lighted corridor known as the Galerie de l'Instruction, when, finding a doorkeeper installed behind a heavy oaken desk, he remarked: "M. d'Escorval is, of course, in his office?"

The man shook his head. "No," said he, "M. d'Escorval is not here this morning, and he won't be here for several weeks."

"Why not! What do you mean?"

"Last night, as he was alighting from his carriage, at his own door, he had a most unfortunate fall, and broke his leg."

IX

SOME men are wealthy. They own a carriage drawn by a pair of high-stepping horses, and driven by a coachman in stylish livery; and as they pass by, leaning back on comfortable cushions, they become the object of many an envious glance. Sometimes, however, the coachman has taken a drop too much, and upsets the carriage; perhaps the horses run away and a general smash ensues; or, maybe, the hitherto fortunate owner, in a moment of absent-mindedness, misses the step, and fractures his leg on the curbstone. Such accidents occur every day; and their long list should make humble foot-passengers bless the lowly lot which preserves them from such peril.

On learning the misfortune that had befallen M. d'Escorval, Lecoq's face wore such an expression of consternation that the doorkeeper could not help laughing. "What is there so very extraordinary about that I've told you?" he asked.

"I—oh! nothing—"

The detective did not speak the truth. The fact is, he had just been struck by the strange coincidence of two events—the supposed murderer's attempted suicide, and the magistrate's fall. Still, he did not allow the vague presentiment that flitted through his mind to assume any definite form. For after all, what possible connection could there be between the two occurrences? Then again, he never allowed himself to be governed by prejudice, nor had he as yet enriched his formulary with an axiom he afterward professed: "Distrust all circumstances that seem to favor your secret wishes."

Of course, Lecoq did not rejoice at M. d'Escorval's accident; could he have prevented it, he would have gladly done so. Still, he could not help saying to himself that this stroke of misfortune would free him from all further connection with a man whose superciliousness and disdain had been painfully disagreeable to his feelings.

This thought caused a sensation of relief—almost one of light-heartedness. "In that case," said the young detective to the doorkeeper, "I shall have nothing to do here this morning."

"You must be joking," was the reply. "Does the world stop moving because one man is disabled? The news only arrived an hour ago; but all the urgent business that M. d'Escorval had in charge has already been divided among the other magistrates."

"I came here about that terrible affair that occurred the other night just beyond the Barrière de Fontainebleau."

"Eh! Why didn't you say so at once? A messenger has been sent to the prefecture after you already. M. Segmuller has charge of the case, and he's waiting for you."

Doubt and perplexity were plainly written on Lecoq's forehead. He was trying to remember the magistrate that bore this name, and wondered whether he was a likely man to espouse his views.

"Yes," resumed the doorkeeper, who seemed to be in a talkative mood, "M. Segmuller—you don't seem to know him. He is a worthy man, not quite so grim as most of our gentlemen. A prisoner he had examined said one day: 'That devil there has pumped me so well that I shall certainly have my head chopped off; but, nevertheless, he's a good fellow!'"

His heart somewhat lightened by these favorable reports, Lecoq went and tapped at a door that was indicated to him, and which bore the number—22.

"Come in!" called out a pleasant voice.

The young detective entered, and found himself face to face with a man of some forty years of age, tall and rather corpulent, who at once exclaimed: "Ah! you are Lecoq. Very well—take a seat. I am busy just now looking over the papers of the case, but I will attend to you in five minutes."

Lecoq obeyed, at the same time glancing furtively at the magistrate with whom he was about to work. M. Segmuller's appearance corresponded perfectly with the description given by the doorkeeper. His plump face wore an air of frankness and benevolence, and his blue eyes had a most pleasant expression. Nevertheless, Lecoq distrusted these appearances, and in so doing he was right.

Born near Strasbourg, M. Segmuller possessed that candid physiognomy common to most of the natives of blonde Alsace —a deceitful mask, which, behind seeming simplicity, not unfrequently conceals a Gascon cunning, rendered all the more dangerous since it is allied with extreme caution. He had a wonderfully alert, penetrating mind; but his system—every magistrate has his own—was mainly good-humor. Unlike most of his colleagues, who were as stiff and cutting in manner as the sword which the statue of Justice usually holds in her hand, he made simplicity and kindness of demeanor his leading trait, though, of course, without ever losing sight of his magisterial duties.

Still, the tone of his voice was so paternal, and the subtle purport of his questions so veiled by his seeming frankness, that most of those whom he examined forgot the necessity of protecting themselves, and unawares confessed their guilt. Thus, it frequently happened that while some unsuspecting culprit was complacently congratulating himself upon getting the best of the judge, the poor wretch was really being turned inside out like a glove.

By the side of such a man as M. Segmuller a grave and slender clerk would have excited distrust; so he had chosen one who was a caricature of himself. This clerk's name was Goguet. He was short but corpulent, and his broad, beardless face habitually wore a silly smile, not out of keeping with his intellect, which was none of the brightest.

As stated above, when Lecoq entered M. Segmuller's room the latter was busy studying the case which had so unexpectedly fallen into his hands. All the articles which the young detective had collected, from the flakes of wool to the diamond earring, were spread out upon the magistrate's desk. With the greatest attention, he perused the report prepared by Lecoq, and according to the different phases of the affair, he examined one or another of the objects before him, or else consulted the plan of the ground.

"A good half-hour elapsed before he had completed his inspection, when he threw himself back in his armchair. Monsieur Lecoq," he said, slowly, "Monsieur d'Escorval has informed me by a note on the margin of this file of papers that you are an intelligent man, and that we can trust you."

"I am willing, at all events."

"You speak too slightingly of yourself; this is the first time that an agent has brought me a report as complete as yours. You are young, and if you persevere, I think you will be able to accomplish great things in your profession."

Nervous with delight, Lecoq bowed and stammered his thanks.

"Your opinion in this matter coincides with mine," continued M. Segmuller, "and the public prosecutor informs me that M. d'Escorval shares the same views. An enigma is before us; and it ought to be solved."

"Oh!—we'll solve it, I am certain, sir," exclaimed Lecoq, who at this moment felt capable of the most extraordinary achievements. Indeed, he would have gone through fire and water for the magistrate who had received him so kindly, and his enthusiasm sparkled so plainly in his eyes that M. Segmuller could not restrain a smile.

"I have strong hopes of it myself," he responded; "but we are far from the end. Now, what have you been doing since yesterday? Did M. d'Escorval give you any orders? Have you obtained any fresh information?"

"I don't think I have wasted my time," replied Lecoq, who at once proceeded to relate the various facts that had come to his knowledge since his departure from the Poivriere.

With rare precision and that happiness of expression which seldom fails a man well acquainted with his subject, he recounted the daring feats of the presumed accomplice, the points he had noted in the supposed murderer's conduct, the latter's unsuccessful attempt at self-destruction. He repeated the testimony given by the cab-driver, and by the concierge in the Rue de Bourgogne, and then read the letter he had received from Father Absinthe.

In conclusion, he placed on the magistrate's desk some of the dirt he had scraped from the prisoner's feet; at the same time depositing beside it a similar parcel of dust collected on the floor of the cell in which the murderer was confined at the Barrière d'Italie.

When Lecoq had explained the reasons that had led him to collect this soil, and the conclusions that might be drawn from a comparison of the two parcels, M. Segmuller, who had been listening attentively, at once exclaimed: "You are right. It may be that you have discovered a means to confound all the prisoner's denials. At all events, this is certainly a proof of surprising sagacity on your part."

So it must have been, for Goguet, the clerk, nodded approvingly. "Capital!" he murmured. "I should never have thought of that."

While he was talking, M. Segmuller had carefully placed all the so-called "articles of conviction" in a large drawer, from which they would not emerge until the trial. "Now," said he, "I understand the case well enough to examine the Widow Chupin. We may gain some information from her."

He was laying his hand upon the bell, when Lecoq stopped him with an almost supplicating gesture. "I have one great favor to ask you, sir," he observed.

"What is it?—speak."

"I should very much like to be present at this examination. It takes so little, sometimes, to awaken a happy inspiration."

Although the law says that the accused shall first of all be privately examined by the investigating magistrate assisted by his clerk, it also allows the presence of police agents. Accordingly, M. Segmuller told Lecoq that he might remain. At the same time he rang his bell; which was speedily answered by a messenger.

"Has the Widow Chupin been brought here, in compliance with my orders?" asked M. Segmuller.

"Yes, sir; she is in the gallery outside."

"Let her come in then."

An instant later the hostess of the Poivriere entered the room, bowing to the right and to the left. This was not her first appearance before a magistrate, and she was not ignorant of the respect that is due to justice. Accordingly, she had arrayed herself for her examination with the utmost care. She had arranged her rebellious gray locks in smooth bandeaux, and her garments, although of common material, looked positively neat. She had even persuaded one of the prison warders to buy her—with the money she had about her at the time of her arrest—a black crape cap, and a couple of white pocket-handkerchiefs, intending to deluge the latter with her tears, should the situation call for a pathetic display.

She was indeed far too knowing to rely solely on the mere artifices of dress; hence, she had also drawn upon her *repertoire* of grimaces for an innocent, sad, and yet resigned expression, well fitted, in her opinion, to win the sympathy and indulgence of the magistrate upon whom her fate would depend.

Thus disguised, with downcast eyes and honeyed voice, she looked so unlike the terrible termagant of the Poivriere, that her customers would scarcely have recognized her. Indeed, an honest old bachelor might have offered her twenty francs a month to take charge of his chambers—solely on the strength of her good looks. But M. Segmuller had unmasked so many hypocrites that he was not deceived for a moment. "What an old actress!" he muttered to himself, and, glancing at Lecoq, he perceived the same thought sparkling in the young detective's eyes. It is true that the magistrate's penetration may have been due to some notes he had just perused—notes containing an abstract of the woman's former life, and furnished by the chief of police at the magistrate's request.

With a gesture of authority M. Segmuller warned Goguet, the clerk with the silly smile, to get his writing materials ready. He then turned toward the Widow Chupin. "Your name?" he asked in a sharp tone.

"Aspasie Claperdty, my maiden name," replied the old woman, "and to-day, the Widow Chupin, at your service, sir;" so saying, she made a low courtesy, and then added: "A lawful widow, you understand, sir; I have my marriage papers safe in my chest at home; and if you wish to send any one—"

"Your age?" interrupted the magistrate.

"Fifty-four."

"Your profession?"

"Dealer in wines and spirits outside of Paris, near the Rue du Château-des-Rentiers, just beyond the fortifications."

A prisoner's examination always begins with these questions as to individuality, which gives both the magistrate and the culprit time to study each other, to try, as it were, each other's strength, before joining in a serious struggle; just as two duelists, about to engage in mortal combat, first try a few passes with the foils.

"Now," resumed M. Segmuller, "we will note your antecedents. Have you not already been found guilty of several offenses?"

The Widow Chupin was too well versed in criminal procedure to be ignorant of those famous records which render the denial of identity such a difficult matter in France. "I have been unfortunate, my good judge," she whined.

"Yes, several times. First of all, you were arrested on a charge of receiving stolen goods."

"But it was proved that I was innocent, that my character was whiter than snow. My poor, dear husband had been deceived by his comrades; that was all."

"Possibly. But while your husband was undergoing his sentence, you were condemned, first to one month's and then to three months' imprisonment for stealing."

"Oh, I had some enemies who did their best to ruin me."

"Next you were imprisoned for having led some young girls astray."

"They were good-for-nothing hussies, my kind sir, heartless, unprincipled creatures. I did them many favors, and then they went and related a batch of falsehoods to ruin me. I have always been too kind and considerate toward others."

The list of the woman's offenses was not exhausted, but M. Segmuller thought it useless to continue. "Such is your past," he resumed. "At the present time your wine-shop is the resort of rogues and criminals. Your son is undergoing his fourth term of imprisonment; and it has been clearly proved that you abetted and assisted him in his evil deeds. Your daughter-in-law, by some miracle, has remained honest and industrious, hence you have tormented and abused her to such an extent that the authorities have been obliged to interfere. When she left your house you tried to keep her child—no doubt meaning to bring it up after the same fashion as its father."

"This," thought the Widow Chupin, "is the right moment to try and soften the magistrate's heart." Accordingly, she drew one of her new handkerchiefs from her pocket, and, by dint of rubbing her eyes, endeavored to extract a tear. "Oh, unhappy me," she groaned. "How can any one imagine that I would harm my grandson, my poor little Toto! Why, I should be worse than a wild beast to try and bring my own flesh and blood to perdition."

She soon perceived, however, that her lamentations did not much affect M. Segmuller, hence, suddenly changing both her tone and manner, she began her justification. She did not positively deny her past; but she threw all the blame on the injustice of destiny, which, while favoring a few, generally the less deserving, showed no mercy to others. Alas! she was one of those who had had no luck in life, having always been persecuted, despite her innocence. In this last affair, for instance, how was she to blame? A triple murder had stained her shop with blood; but the most respectable establishments are not exempt from similar catastrophes. During her solitary confinement, she had, said she, dived down into the deepest recesses of her conscience, and she was still unable to discover what blame could justly be laid at her door.

"I can tell you," interrupted the magistrate. "You are accused of impeding the action of the law."

"Good heavens! Is it possible?"

"And of seeking to defeat justice. This is equivalent to complicity, Widow Chupin; take care. When the police entered your cabin, after this crime had been committed, you refused to answer their questions."

"I told them all that I knew."

"Very well, then, you must repeat what you told them to me."

M. Segmuller had reason to feel satisfied. He had conducted the examination in such a way that the Widow Chupin would now have to initiate a narrative of the tragedy. This excellent point gained; for this shrewd old woman, possessed of all her coolness, would naturally have been on her guard against any direct questions. Now, it was essential that she should not suspect either what the magistrate knew of the affair, or what he was ignorant of. By leaving her to her own devices she might, in the course of the version which she proposed to substitute for the truth, not merely strengthen Lecoq's theories, but also let fall some remark calculated to facilitate the task of future investigation. Both M. Segmuller and Lecoq were of opinion that the version of the crime which they were about to hear had been concocted at the station-house of the Place d'Italie while the murderer and the spurious drunkard were left together, and that it had been transmitted by the accomplice to the widow during the brief conversation they were allowed to have through the wicket of the latter's cell.

Invited by the magistrate to recount the circumstances of the tragedy, Mother Chupin did not hesitate for a moment. "Oh, it was a very simple affair, my good sir," she began. "I was sitting by my fireside on Sunday evening, when suddenly the door opened, and three men and two women came in."

M. Segmuller and the young detective exchanged glances. The accomplice had evidently seen Lecoq and his comrade examining the footprints, and accordingly the presence of the two women was not to be denied.

"What time was this?" asked the magistrate.

"About eleven o'clock."

"Go on."

"As soon as they sat down they ordered a bowl of wine, *à la Française*. Without boasting, I may say that I haven't an equal in preparing that drink. Of course, I waited on them, and afterward, having a blouse to mend for my boy, I went upstairs to my room, which is just over the shop."

"Leaving the people alone?"

"Yes, my judge."

"That showed a great deal of confidence on your part."

The widow sadly shook her head. "People as poor as I am don't fear the thieves," she sighed.

"Go on—go on."

"Well, I had been upstairs about half an hour, when I heard some one below call out: 'Eh! old woman!' So I went down, and found a tall, big-bearded man, who had just come in. He asked for a glass of brandy, which I brought to a table where he had sat down by himself."

"And then did you go upstairs again?" interrupted the magistrate.

The exclamation was ironical, of course, but no one could have told from the Widow Chupin's placid countenance whether she was aware that such was the case.

"Precisely, my good sir," she replied in the most composed manner. "Only this time I had scarcely taken up my needle when I heard a terrible uproar in the shop. I hurried downstairs to put a stop to it—but heaven knows my interference would have been of little use. The three men who had come in first of all had fallen upon the newcomer, and they were beating him, my good sir, they were killing him. I screamed. Just then the man who had come in alone drew a revolver from his pocket; he fired and killed one of his assailants, who fell to the ground. I was so frightened that I crouched on the staircase and threw my apron over my head that I might not see the blood run. An instant later Monsieur Gevrol arrived with his men; they forced open the door, and behold—"

The Widow Chupin here stopped short. These wretched old women, who have trafficked in every sort of vice, and who have tasted every disgrace, at times attain a perfection of hypocrisy calculated to deceive the most subtle penetration. Any one unacquainted with the antecedents of the landlady of the Poivriere would certainly have been impressed by her apparent candor, so skilfully did she affect a display of frankness, surprise, and fear. Her expression would have been simply perfect, had it not been for her eyes, her small gray eyes, as restless as those of a caged animal, and gleaming at intervals with craftiness and cunning.

There she stood, mentally rejoicing at the success of her narrative, for she was convinced that the magistrate placed implicit confidence in her revelations, although during her recital, delivered, by the way, with conjurer-like volubility, not a muscle of M. Segmuller's face had betrayed what was passing in his mind. When she paused, out of breath, he rose from his seat, and without a word approached his clerk to inspect the notes taken during the earlier part of the examination.

From the corner where he was quietly seated, Lecoq did not cease watching the prisoner. "She thinks that it's all over," he muttered to himself; "she fancies that her deposition is accepted without question."

If such were, indeed, the widow's opinion, she was soon to be undeceived; for, after addressing a few low-spoken words to the smiling Goguet, M. Segmuller took a seat near the fireplace, convinced that the moment had now come to abandon defensive tactics, and open fire on the enemy's position.

"So, Widow Chupin," he began, "you tell us that you didn't remain for a single moment with the people who came into your shop that evening!"

"Not a moment."

"They came in and ordered what they wanted; you waited on them, and then left them to themselves?"

"Yes, my good sir."

"It seems to me impossible that you didn't overhear some words of their conversation. What were they talking about?"

"I am not in the habit of playing spy over my customers."

"Didn't you hear anything?"

"Nothing at all."

The magistrate shrugged his shoulders with an air of commiseration. "In other words," he remarked, "you refuse to inform justice—"

"Oh, my good sir!"

"Allow me to finish. All these improbable stories about leaving the shop and mending your son's clothes in your bedroom are so many inventions. You have concocted them so as to be able to say to me: 'I didn't see anything; I didn't hear anything.' If such is your system of defense, I warn you that it will be impossible for you to maintain it, and I may add that it would not be admitted by any tribunal."

"It is not a system of defense; it is the truth."

M. Segmuller seemed to reflect for a moment; then, suddenly, he exclaimed: "Then you have nothing to tell me about this miserable assassin?"

"But he is not an assassin, my good sir."

"What do you mean by such an assertion?"

"I mean that he only killed the others in protecting himself. They picked a quarrel with him; he was alone against three, and saw very plainly that he could expect no mercy from brigands who—"

The color rose to the Widow Chupin's cheeks, and she suddenly checked herself, greatly embarrassed, and evidently regretting that she had not bridled her tongue. It is true she might reasonably hope, that the magistrate had imperfectly heard her words, and had failed to seize their full purport, for two or three red-hot coals having fallen from the grate on the hearth, he had taken up the tongs, and seemed to be engrossed in the task of artistically arranging the fire.

"Who can tell me—who can prove to me that, on the contrary, it was not this man who first attacked the others?" he murmured, thoughtfully.

"I can," stoutly declared the widow, already forgetful of her prudent hesitation, "I can swear it."

M. Segmuller looked up, intense astonishment written upon his face. "How can you know that?" he said slowly. "How can you swear it? You were in your bedroom when the quarrel began."

Silent and motionless in his corner, Lecoq was inwardly jubilant. This was a most happy result, he thought, but a few questions more, and the old woman would be obliged to contradict herself. What she had already said sufficed to show that she must have a secret interest in the matter, or else she would never have been so imprudently earnest in defending the prisoner.

"However, you have probably been led to this conclusion by your knowledge of the murderer's character," remarked M. Segmuller, "you are apparently well acquainted with him."

"Oh, I had never set eyes on him before that evening."

"But he must have been in your establishment before?"

"Never in his life."

"Oh, oh! Then how do you explain that on entering the shop while you were upstairs, this unknown person—this stranger—should have called out: 'Here, old woman!' Did he merely *guess* that the establishment was kept by a woman; and that this woman was no longer young?"

"He did not say that."

"Reflect a moment; you, yourself just told me so."

"Oh, I didn't say that, I'm sure, my good sir."

"Yes, you did, and I will prove it by having your evidence read. Goguet, read the passage, if you please."

The smiling clerk looked back through his minutes and then, in his clearest voice, he read these words, taken down as they fell from the Widow Chupin's lips: "I had been upstairs about half an hour, when I heard some one below call out 'Eh! old woman.' So I went down," etc., etc.

"Are you convinced?" asked M. Segmuller.

The old offender's assurance was sensibly diminished by this proof of her prevarication. However, instead of discussing the subject any further, the magistrate glided over it as if he did not attach much importance to the incident.

"And the other men," he resumed, "those who were killed: did you know them?"

"No, good sir, no more than I knew Adam and Eve."

"And were you not surprised to see three men utterly unknown to you, and accompanied by two women, enter your establishment?"

"Sometimes chance—"

"Come! you do not think of what you are saying. It was not chance that brought these customers, in the middle of the night, to a wine-shop with a reputation like yours—an establishment situated far from any frequented route in the midst of a desolate waste."

"I'm not a sorceress; I say what I think."

"Then you did not even know the youngest of the victims, the man who was attired as a soldier, he who was named Gustave?"

"Not at all."

M. Segmuller noted the intonation of this response, and then slowly added: "But you must have heard of one of Gustave's friends, a man called Lacheneur?"

On hearing this name, the landlady of the Poivriere became visibly embarrassed, and it was in an altered voice that she stammered: "Lacheneur! Lacheneur! no, I have never heard that name mentioned."

Still despite her denial, the effect of M. Segmuller's remark was evident, and Lecoq secretly vowed that he would find this Lacheneur, at any cost. Did not the "articles of conviction" comprise a letter sent by this man to Gustave, and written, so Lecoq had reason to believe, in a café on the Boulevard Beaumarchais? With such a clue and a little patience, the mysterious Lacheneur might yet be discovered.

"Now," continued M. Segmuller, "let us speak of the women who accompanied these unfortunate men. What sort of women were they?"

"Oh! women of no account whatever!"

"Were they well dressed?"

"On the contrary, very miserably."

"Well, give me a description of them."

"They were tall and powerfully built, and indeed, as it was Shrove Sunday, I first of all took them for men in disguise. They had hands like shoulders of mutton, gruff voices, and very black hair. They were as dark as mulattoes—"

"Enough!" interrupted the magistrate, "I require no further proof of your mendacity. These women were short, and one of them was remarkably fair."

"I swear to you, my good sir—"

"Do not declare it upon oath. I shall be forced to confront you with an honest man, who will tell you to your face that you are a liar!"

The widow did not reply, and there was a moment's silence. M. Segmuller determined to deal a decisive blow. "Do you also affirm that you had nothing of a compromising character in the pocket of your apron?" he asked.

"Nothing—you may have it examined; it was left in the house."

"Then you still persist in your system," resumed M. Segmuller. "Believe me, you are wrong. Reflect—it rests with you to go to the Assize Court as a witness, or an accomplice."

Although the widow seemed crushed by this unexpected blow, the magistrate did not add another word. Her deposition was read over to her, she signed it, and was then led away.

M. Segmuller immediately seated himself at his desk, filled up a blank form and handed it to his clerk, saying: "This is an order for the governor of the Depot. Tell him to send the supposed murderer here at once."

IF it is difficult to extort a confession from a man interested in preserving silence and persuaded that no proofs can be produced against him, it is a yet more arduous task to make a woman, similarly situated, speak the truth. As they say at the Palais de Justice, one might as well try to make the devil confess.

The examination of the Widow Chupin had been conducted with the greatest possible care by M. Segmuller, who was as skilful in managing his questions as a tried general in maneuvring his troops.

However, all that he had discovered was that the landlady of the Poivriere was conniving with the murderer. The motive of her connivance was yet unknown, and the murderer's identity still a mystery. Both M. Segmuller and Lecoq were nevertheless of the opinion that the old hag knew everything. "It is almost certain," remarked the magistrate, "that she was acquainted with the people who came to her house—with the women, the victims, the murderer—with all of them, in fact. I am positive as regards that fellow Gustave—I read it in her eyes. I am also convinced that she knows Lacheneur—the man upon whom the dying soldier breathed vengeance—the mysterious personage who evidently possesses the key to the enigma. That man must be found."

"Ah!" replied Lecoq, "and I will find him even if I have to question every one of the eleven hundred thousand men who constantly walk the streets of Paris!"

This was promising so much that the magistrate, despite his preoccupation, could not repress a smile.

"If this old woman would only decide to make a clean breast of it at her next examination!" remarked Lecoq.

"Yes. But she won't."

The young detective shook his head despondingly. Such was his own opinion. He did not delude himself with false hopes, and he had noticed between the Widow Chupin's eyebrows those furrows which, according to physiognomists, indicate a senseless, brutish obstinacy.

"Women never confess," resumed the magistrate; "and even when they seemingly resign themselves to such a course they are not sincere. They fancy they have discovered some means of misleading their examiner. On the contrary, evidence will crush the most obstinate man; he gives up the struggle, and confesses. Now, a woman scoffs at evidence. Show her the sun; tell her it's daytime; at once she will close her eyes and say to you, 'No, it's night.' Male prisoners plan and combine different systems of defense according to their social positions; the women, on the contrary, have but one system, no matter what may be their condition in life. They deny everything, persist in their denials even when the proof against them is overwhelming, and then they cry. When I worry the Chupin with disagreeable questions, at her next examination, you may be sure she will turn her eyes into a fountain of tears."

In his impatience, M. Segmuller angrily stamped his foot. He had many weapons in his arsenal; but none strong enough to break a woman's dogged resistance.

"If I only understood the motive that guides this old hag!" he continued. "But not a clue! Who can tell me what powerful interest induces her to remain silent? Is it her own cause that she is defending? Is she an accomplice? Is it certain that she did not aid the murderer in planning an ambuscade?"

"Yes," responded Lecoq, slowly, "yes; this supposition very naturally presents itself to the mind. But think a moment, sir, such a theory would prove that the idea we entertained a short time since is altogether false. If the Widow Chupin is an accomplice, the murderer is not the person we have supposed him to be; he is simply the man he seems to be."

This argument apparently convinced M. Segmuller. "What is your opinion?" he asked.

The young detective had formed his opinion a long while ago. But how could he, a humble police agent, venture to express any decided views when the magistrate hesitated? He understood well enough that his position necessitated extreme reserve; hence, it was in the most modest tone that he replied: "Might not the pretended drunkard have dazzled Mother Chupin's eyes with the prospect of a brilliant reward? Might he not have promised her a considerable sum of money?"

He paused; Goguet, the smiling clerk, had just returned.

Behind him stood a private of the Garde de Paris who remained respectfully on the threshold, his heels in a straight line, his right hand raised to the peak of his shako, and his elbow on a level with his eyes, in accordance with the regulations.

"The governor of the Depot," said the soldier, "sends me to inquire if he is to keep the Widow Chupin in solitary confinement; she complains bitterly about it."

M. Segmuller reflected for a moment. "Certainly," he murmured, as if replying to an objection made by his own conscience; "certainly, it is an undoubted aggravation of suffering; but if I allow this woman to associate with the other prisoners, she will certainly find some opportunity to communicate with parties outside. This must not be; the interests of justice and truth must be considered first." The thought embodied in these last words decided him. "Despite her complaints the prisoner must be kept in solitary confinement until further orders," he said.

The soldier allowed his right hand to fall to his side, he carried his right foot three inches behind his left heel, and wheeled around. Goguet, the smiling clerk, then closed the door, and, drawing a large envelope from his pocket, handed it to the magistrate. "Here is a communication from the governor of the Depot," said he.

The magistrate broke the seal, and read aloud, as follows: "I feel compelled to advise M. Segmuller to take every precaution with the view of assuring his own safety before proceeding with the examination of the prisoner, May. Since his unsuccessful attempt at suicide, this prisoner has been in such a state of excitement that we have been obliged to keep him in a strait-waistcoat. He did not close his eyes all last night, and the guards who watched him expected every moment that he would become delirious. However, he did not utter a word. When food was offered him this morning, he resolutely rejected it, and I should not be surprised if it were his intention to starve himself to death. I have rarely seen a more determined criminal. I think him capable of any desperate act."

"Ah!" exclaimed the clerk, whose smile had disappeared, "If I were in your place, sir, I would only let him in here with an escort of soldiers."

"What! you—Goguet, you, an old clerk—make such a proposition! Can it be that you're frightened?"

"Frightened! No, certainly not; but—"

"Nonsense!" interrupted Lecoq, in a tone that betrayed superlative confidence in his own muscles; "Am I not here?"

If M. Segmuller had seated himself at his desk, that article of furniture would naturally have served as a rampart between the prisoner and himself. For purposes of convenience he usually did place himself behind it; but after Goguet's display of fear, he would have blushed to have taken the slightest measure of self-protection. Accordingly, he went and sat down by the fireplace—as he had done a few moments previously while questioning the Widow Chupin—and then ordered his door-keeper to admit the prisoner alone. He emphasized this word "alone."

A moment later the door was flung open with a violent jerk, and the prisoner entered, or rather precipitated himself into the room. Goguet turned pale behind his table, and Lecoq advanced a step forward, ready to spring upon the prisoner and pinion him should it be requisite. But when the latter reached the centre of the room, he paused and looked around him. "Where is the magistrate?" he inquired, in a hoarse voice.

"I am the magistrate," replied M. Segmuller.

"No, the other one."

"What other one?"

"The one who came to question me last evening."

"He has met with an accident. Yesterday, after leaving you, he fell down and broke his leg."

"Oh!"

"And I am to take his place."

The prisoner was apparently deaf to the explanation. Excitement had seemingly given way to stupor. His features, hitherto contracted with anger, now relaxed. He grew pale and tottered, as if about to fall.

"Compose yourself," said the magistrate in a benevolent tone; "if you are too weak to remain standing, take a seat."

Already, with a powerful effort, the man had recovered his self-possession. A momentary gleam flashed from his eyes. "Many thanks for your kindness," he replied, "but this is nothing. I felt a slight sensation of dizziness, but it is over now."

"Is it long since you have eaten anything?"

"I have eaten nothing since that man"—and so saying he pointed to Lecoq—"brought me some bread and wine at the station house."

"Wouldn't you like to take something?"

"No—and yet—if you would be so kind—I should like a glass of water."

"Will you not have some wine with it?"

"I should prefer pure water."

His request was at once complied with. He drained a first glassful at a single draft; the glass was then replenished and he drank again, this time, however, more slowly. One might have supposed that he was drinking in life itself. Certainly, when he laid down the empty glass, he seemed quite another man.

Eighteen out of every twenty criminals who appear before our investigating magistrates come prepared with a more or less complete plan of defense, which they have conceived during their preliminary confinement. Innocent or guilty, they have resolved on playing some part or other, which they begin to act as soon as they cross the threshold of the room where the magistrate awaits them.

The moment they enter his presence, the magistrate needs to bring all his powers of penetration into play; for such a culprit's first attitude as surely betrays his plan of defense as an index reveals a book's contents. In this case, however, M. Segmuller did not think that appearances were deceitful. It seemed evident to him that the prisoner was not feigning, but that the excited frenzy which marked his entrance was as real as his after stupor.

At all events, there seemed no fear of the danger the governor of the Depot had spoken of, and accordingly M. Segmuller seated himself at his desk. Here he felt stronger and more at ease for his back being turned to the window, his face was half hidden in shadow; and in case of need, he could, by bending over his papers, conceal any sign of surprise or discomfiture.

The prisoner, on the contrary, stood in the full light, and not a movement of his features, not the fluttering of an eyelid could escape the magistrate's attention. He seemed to have completely recovered from his indisposition; and his features assumed an expression which indicated either careless indifference, or complete resignation.

"Do you feel better?" asked M. Segmuller.

"I feel very well."

"I hope," continued the magistrate, paternally, "that in future you will know how to moderate your excitement. Yesterday you tried to destroy yourself. It would have been another great crime added to many others—a crime which—"

With a hasty movement of the hand, the prisoner interrupted him. "I have committed no crime," said he, in a rough, but no longer threatening voice. "I was attacked, and I defended myself. Any one has a right to do that. There were three men against me. It was a great misfortune; and I would give my right hand to repair it; but my conscience does not reproach me—that much!"

The prisoner's "that much," was a contemptuous snap of his finger and thumb.

"And yet I've been arrested and treated like an assassin," he continued. "When I saw myself interred in that living tomb which you call a secret cell, I grew afraid; I lost my senses. I said to myself: 'My boy, they've buried you alive; and it is better to die—to die quickly, if you don't wish to suffer.' So I tried to strangle myself. My death wouldn't have caused the slightest sorrow to any one. I have neither wife nor child depending upon me for support. However, my attempt was frustrated. I was bled; and then placed in a strait-waistcoat, as if I were a madman. Mad! I really believed I should become so. All night long the jailors sat around me, like children amusing themselves by tormenting a chained animal. They watched me, talked about me, and passed the candle to and fro before my eyes."

The prisoner talked forcibly, but without any attempt at oratorical display; there was bitterness but not anger in his tone; in short, he spoke with all the seeming sincerity of a man giving expression to some deep emotion or conviction. As the magistrate and the detective heard him speak, they were seized with the same idea. "This man," they thought, "is very clever; it won't be easy to get the better of him."

Then, after a moment's reflection, M. Segmuller added aloud: "This explains your first act of despair; but later on, for instance, even this morning, you refused to eat the food that was offered you."

As the prisoner heard this remark, his lowering face suddenly brightened, he gave a comical wink, and finally burst into a hearty laugh, gay, frank, and sonorous.

"That," said he, "is quite another matter. Certainly, I refused all they offered me, and now I will tell you why. As I had my hands confined in the strait-waistcoat, the jailor tried to feed me just as a nurse tries to feed a baby with pap. Now I wasn't going to submit to that, so I closed my lips as tightly as I could. Then he tried to force my mouth open and push the spoon in, just as one might force a sick dog's jaws apart and pour some medicine down its throat. The deuce take his impertinence! I tried to bite him: that's the truth, and if I had succeeded in getting his finger between my teeth, it would have stayed there. However, because I wouldn't be fed like a baby, all the prison officials raised their hands to heaven in holy horror, and pointed at me, saying: 'What a terrible man! What an awful rascal!' "

The prisoner seemed to thoroughly enjoy the recollection of the scene he had described, for he now burst into another hearty laugh, to the great amazement of Lecoq, and the scandal of Goguet, the smiling clerk.

M. Segmuller also found it difficult to conceal his surprise. "You are too reasonable, I hope," he said, at last, "to attach any blame to these men, who, in confining you in a strait-waistcoat, were merely obeying the orders of their superior officers with the view of protecting you from your own violent passions."

"Hum!" responded the prisoner, suddenly growing serious. "I do blame them, however, and if I had one of them in a corner— But, never mind, I shall get over it. If I know myself aright, I have no more spite in my composition than a chicken."

"Your treatment depends on your own conduct," rejoined M. Segmuller, "If you will only remain calm, you shan't be put in a strait-waistcoat again. But you must promise me that you will be quiet and conduct yourself properly."

The murderer sadly shook his head. "I shall be very prudent hereafter," said he, "but it is terribly hard to stay in prison with nothing to do. If I had some comrades with me, we could laugh and chat, and the time would slip by; but it is positively horrible to have to remain alone, entirely alone, in that cold, damp cell, where not a sound can be heard."

The magistrate bent over his desk to make a note. The word "comrades" had attracted his attention, and he proposed to ask the prisoner to explain it at a later stage of the inquiry.

"If you are innocent," he remarked, "you will soon be released: but it is necessary to prove your innocence."

"What must I do to prove it?"

"Tell the truth, the whole truth: answer my questions honestly without reserve."

"As for that, you may depend upon me." As he spoke the prisoner lifted his hand, as if to call upon God to witness his sincerity.

But M. Segmuller immediately intervened: "Prisoners do not take the oath," said he.

"Indeed!" ejaculated the man with an astonished air, "that's strange!"

Although the magistrate had apparently paid but little attention to the prisoner, he had in point of fact carefully noted his attitude, his tone of voice, his looks and gestures. M. Segmuller had, moreover, done his utmost to set the culprit's mind at ease, to quiet all possible suspicion of a trap, and his inspection of the prisoner's person led him to believe that this result had been attained.

"Now," said he, "you will give me your attention; and do not forget that your liberty depends upon your frankness. What is your name?"

"May."

"What is your Christian name?"

"I have none."

"That is impossible."

"I have been told that already three times since yesterday," rejoined the prisoner impatiently. "And yet it's the truth. If I were a liar, I could easily tell you that my name was Peter, James, or John. But lying is not in my line. Really, I have no Christian name. If it were a question of surnames, it would be quite another thing. I have had plenty of them."

"What were they?"

"Let me see—to commence with, when I was with Father Fougasse, I was called Affiloir, because you see—"

"Who was this Father Fougasse?"

"The great wild beast tamer, sir. Ah! he could boast of a menagerie and no mistake! Lions, tigers, and bears, serpents as big round as your thigh, parrakeets of every color under the sun. Ah! it was a wonderful collection. But unfortunately—"

Was the man jesting, or was he in earnest? It was so hard to decide, that M. Segmuller and Lecoq were equally in doubt. As for Goguet, the smiling clerk, he chuckled to himself as his pen ran over the paper.

"Enough," interrupted the magistrate. "How old are you?"

"Forty-four or forty-five years of age."

"Where were you born?"

"In Brittany, probably."

M. Segmuller thought he could detect a hidden vein of irony in this reply.

"I warn you," said he, severely, "that if you go on in this way your chances of recovering your liberty will be greatly compromised. Each of your answers is a breach of propriety."

As the supposed murderer heard these words, an expression of mingled distress and anxiety was apparent in his face. "Ah! I meant no offense, sir," he sighed. "You questioned me, and I replied. You will see that I have spoken the truth, if you will allow me to recount the history of the whole affair."

"When the prisoner speaks, the prosecution is enlightened," so runs an old proverb frequently quoted at the Palais de Justice. It does, indeed, seem almost impossible for a culprit to say more than a few words in an investigating magistrate's presence, without betraying his intentions or his thoughts; without, in short, revealing more or less of the secret he is endeavoring to conceal. All criminals, even the most simple-minded, understand this, and those who are shrewd prove remarkably reticent. Confining themselves to the few facts upon which they have founded their defense, they are careful not to travel any further unless absolutely compelled to do so, and even then they only speak with the utmost caution. When questioned, they reply, of course, but always briefly; and they are very sparing of details.

In the present instance, however, the prisoner was prodigal of words. He did not seem to think that there was any danger of his being the medium of accomplishing his own decapitation. He did not hesitate like those who are afraid of misplacing a word of the romance they are substituting for the truth. Under other circumstances, this fact would have been a strong argument in his favor.

"You may tell your own story, then," said M. Segmuller in answer to the prisoner's indirect request.

The presumed murderer did not try to hide the satisfaction he experienced at thus being allowed to plead his own cause, in his own way. His eyes sparkled and his nostrils dilated as if with pleasure. He sat himself down, threw his head back, passed his tongue over his lips as if to moisten them, and said: "Am I to understand that you wish to hear my history?"

"Yes."

"Then you must know that one day about forty-five years ago, Father Tringlot, the manager of a traveling acrobatic company, was going from Guingamp to Saint Brieuc, in Brittany. He had with him two large vehicles containing his wife, the necessary theatrical paraphernalia, and the members of the company. Well, soon after passing Chatelaudren, he perceived something white lying by the roadside, near the edge of a ditch. 'I must go and see what that is,' he said to his wife. He stopped the horses, alighted from the vehicle he was in, went to the ditch, picked up the object he had noticed, and uttered a cry of surprise. You will ask me what he had found? Ah! good heavens! A mere trifle. He had found your humble servant, then about six months old."

With these last words, the prisoner made a low bow to his audience.

"Naturally, Father Tringlot carried me to his wife. She was a kind-hearted woman. She took me, examined me, fed me, and said: 'He's a strong, healthy child; and we'll keep him since his mother has been so wicked as to abandon him by the roadside. I will teach him; and in five or six years he will be a credit to us.' They then asked each other what name they should give me, and as it happened to be the first day of May, they decided to call me after the month, and so it happens that May has been my name from that day to this."

The prisoner paused again and looked from one to another of his listeners, as if seeking some sign of approval. None being forthcoming, he proceeded with his story.

"Father Tringlot was an uneducated man, entirely ignorant of the law. He did not inform the authorities that he had found a child, and, for this reason, although I was living, I did not legally exist, for, to have a legal existence it is necessary that one's name, parentage, and birthplace should figure upon a municipal register.

"When I grew older, I rather congratulated myself on Father Tringlot's neglect. 'May, my boy,' said I, 'you are not put down on any government register, consequently there's no fear of your ever being drawn as a soldier.' I had a horror of military service, and a positive dread of bullets and cannon balls. Later on, when I had passed the proper age for the conscription, a lawyer told me that I should get into all kinds of trouble if I sought a place on the civil register so late in the day; and so I decided to exist surreptitiously. And this is why I have no Christian name, and why I can't exactly say where I was born."

If truth has any particular accent of its own, as moralists have asserted, the murderer had found that accent. Voice, gesture, glance, expression, all were in accord; not a word of his long story had rung false.

"Now," said M. Segmuller, coldly, "what are your means of subsistence?"

By the prisoner's discomfited mien one might have supposed that he had expected to see the prison doors fly open at the conclusion of his narrative. "I have a profession," he replied plaintively. "The one that Mother Tringlot taught me. I subsist by its practise; and I have lived by it in France and other countries."

The magistrate thought he had found a flaw in the prisoner's armor. "You say you have lived in foreign countries?" he inquired.

"Yes; during the seventeen years that I was with M. Simpson's company, I traveled most of the time in England and Germany."

"Then you are a gymnast and an athlete. How is it that your hands are so white and soft?"

Far from being embarrassed, the prisoner raised his hands from his lap and examined them with evident complacency. "It is true they are pretty," said he, "but this is because I take good care of them and scarcely use them."

"Do they pay you, then, for doing nothing?"

"Ah, no, indeed! But, sir, my duty consists in speaking to the public, in turning a compliment, in making things pass off pleasantly, as the saying is; and, without boasting, I flatter myself that I have a certain knack—"

M. Segmuller stroked his chin, according to his habit whenever he considered that a prisoner had committed some grave blunder. "In that case," said he, "will you give me a specimen of your talent?"

"Ah, ha!" laughed the prisoner, evidently supposing this to be a jest on the part of the magistrate. "Ah, ha!"

"Obey me, if you please," insisted M. Segmuller.

The supposed murderer made no objection. His face at once assumed a different expression, his features wearing a mingled air of impudence, conceit, and irony. He caught up a ruler that was lying on the magistrate's desk, and, flourishing it wildly, began as follows, in a shrill falsetto voice: "Silence, music! And you, big drum, hold your peace! Now is the hour, now is the moment, ladies and gentlemen, to witness the grand, unique performance of these great artists, unequaled in the world for their feats upon the trapeze and the tight-rope, and in innumerable other exercises of grace, suppleness, and strength!"

"That is sufficient," interrupted the magistrate. "You can speak like that in France; but what do you say in Germany?"

"Of course, I use the language of that country."

"Let me hear, then!" retorted M. Segmuller, whose mother tongue was German.

The prisoner ceased his mocking manner, assumed an air of comical importance, and without the slightest hesitation began to speak as follows, in very emphatic tones: "Mit Bewilligung der hochloeblichen Obrigkeit, wird heute, vor hiesiger ehrenwerthen Burgerschaft, zum erstenmal aufgefuhrt—Genovesa, oder—"

This opening of the prisoner's German harangue may be thus rendered: "With the permission of the local authorities there will now be presented before the honorable citizens, for the first time—Genevieve, or the—"

"Enough," said the magistrate, harshly. He rose, perhaps to conceal his chargin, and added: "We will send for an interpreter to tell us whether you speak English as fluently."

On hearing these words, Lecoq modestly stepped forward. "I understand English," said he.

"Very well. You hear, prisoner?"

But the man was already transformed. British gravity and apathy were written upon his features; his gestures were stiff and constrained, and in the most ponderous tones he exclaimed: "Walk up! ladies and gentlemen, walk up! Long life to the queen and to the honorable mayor of this town! No country, England excepted—our glorious England!—could produce such a marvel, such a paragon—" For a minute or two longer he continued in the same strain.

M. Segmuller was leaning upon his desk, his face hidden by his hands. Lecoq, standing in front of the prisoner, could not conceal his astonishment. Goguet, the smiling clerk, alone found the scene amusing.

THE governor of the depot, a functionary who had gained the reputation of an oracle by twenty years' experience in prisons and with prisoners—a man whom it was most difficult to deceive—had advised the magistrate to surround himself with every precaution before examining the prisoner, May.

And yet this man, characterized as a most dangerous criminal, and the very announcement of whose coming had made the clerk turn pale, had proved to be a practical, harmless, and jovial philosopher, vain of his eloquence, a bohemian whose existence depended upon his ability to turn a compliment; in short, a somewhat erratic genius.

This was certainly strange, but the seeming contradiction did not cause M. Segmuller to abandon the theory propounded by Lecoq. On the contrary, he was more than ever convinced of its truth. If he remained silent, with his elbows leaning on the desk, and his hands clasped over his eyes, it was only that he might gain time for reflection.

The prisoner's attitude and manner were remarkable. When his English harangue was finished, he remained standing in the centre of the room, a half-pleased, half-anxious expression on his face. Still, he was as much at ease as if he had been on the platform outside some stroller's booth, where, if one could believe his story, he had passed the greater part of his life. It was in vain that the magistrate sought for some indication of weakness on his features, which in their mobility were more enigmatical than the lineaments of the Sphinx.

Thus far, M. Segmuller had been worsted in the encounter. It is true, however, that he had not as yet ventured on any direct attack, nor had he made use of any of the weapons which Lecoq had forged for his use. Still he was none the less annoyed at his defeat, as it was easy to see by the sharp manner in which he raised his head after a few moments' silence. "I see that you speak three European languages correctly," said he. "It is a rare talent."

The prisoner bowed, and smiled complacently. "Still that does not establish your identity," continued the magistrate. "Have you any acquaintances in Paris? Can you indicate any respectable person who will vouch for the truth of this story?"

"Ah! sir, it is seventeen years since I left France."

"That is unfortunate, but the prosecution can not content itself with such an explanation. What about your last employer, M. Simpson? Who is he?"

"M. Simpson is a rich man," replied the prisoner, rather coldly, "worth more than two hundred thousand francs, and honest besides. In Germany he traveled with a show of marionettes, and in England with a collection of phenomena to suit the tastes of that country."

"Very well! Then this millionaire could testify in your favor; it would be easy to find him, I suppose?"

"Certainly," responded May, emphatically. "M. Simpson would willingly do me this favor. It would not be difficult for me to find him, only it would require considerable time."

"Why?"

"Because at the present moment he must be on his way to America. It was on account of this journey that I left his company—I detest the ocean."

A moment previously Lecoq's anxiety had been so intense that his heart almost stopped beating; on hearing these last words, however, he regained all his self-possession. As for the magistrate, he merely greeted the murderer's reply with a brief but significant ejaculation.

"When I say that he is on his way," resumed the prisoner, "I may be mistaken. He may not have started yet, though he had certainly made all his arrangements before we separated."

"What ship was he to sail by?"

"He did not tell me."

"Where was he when you left him?"

"At Leipsic."

"When was this?"

"Last Wednesday."

M. Segmuller shrugged his shoulders disdainfully. "So you say you were in Leipsic on Wednesday? How long have you been in Paris?"

"Since Sunday afternoon, at four o'clock."

"It will be necessary to prove that."

Judging by the murderer's contracted brow it might be conjectured that he was making a strenuous effort to remember something. He cast questioning glances first toward the ceiling and then toward the floor, scratching his head and tapping his foot in evident perplexity. "How *can* I prove it—how?" he murmured.

The magistrate did not appear disposed to wait. "Let me assist you," said he. "The people at the inn where you boarded while in Leipsic must remember you."

"We did not stop at an inn."

"Where did you eat and sleep, then?"

"In M. Simpson's large traveling-carriage; it had been sold, but he was not to give it up until he reached the port he was to sail from."

"What port was that?"

"I don't know."

At this reply Lecoq, who had less experience than the magistrate in the art of concealing one's impressions, could not help rubbing his hands with satisfaction. The prisoner was plainly convicted of falsehood, indeed driven into a corner.

"So you have only your own word to offer in support of this story?" inquired M. Segmuller.

"Wait a moment," said the prisoner, extending his arm as if to clutch at a still vague inspiration—"wait a moment. When I arrived in Paris I had with me a trunk containing my clothes. The linen is all marked with the first letter of my name, and besides some ordinary coats and trousers, there were a couple of costumes I used to wear when I appeared in public."

"Well, what have you done with all these things?"

"When I arrived in Paris, I took the trunk to a hotel, close by the Northern railway station—"

"Go on. Tell us the name of this hotel," said M. Segmuller, perceiving that the prisoner had stopped short, evidently embarrassed.

"That's just what I'm trying to recollect. I've forgotten it. But I haven't forgotten the house. I fancy I can see it now; and, if some one would only take me to the neighborhood, I should certainly recognize it. The people at the hotel would know me, and, besides, my trunk would prove the truth of what I've told you."

On hearing this statement, Lecoq mentally resolved to make a tour of investigation through the various hotels surrounding the Gare du Nord.

"Very well," retorted the magistrate. "Perhaps we will do as you request. Now, there are two questions I desire to ask. If you arrived in Paris at four o'clock in the afternoon, how did it happen that by midnight of the same day you had discovered the Poivriere, which is merely frequented by suspicious characters, and is situated in such a lonely spot that it would be impossible to find it at night-time, if one were not familiar with the surrounding localities? In the second place, how does it happen, if you possess such clothing as you describe, that you are so poorly dressed?"

The prisoner smiled at these questions. "I can easily explain that," he replied. "One's clothes are soon spoiled when one travels third-class, so on leaving Leipsic I put on the worst things I had. When I arrived here, and felt my feet on the pavements of Paris, I went literally wild with delight. I acted like a fool. I had some money in my pocket—it was Shrove Sunday—and my only thought was to make a night of it. I did not think of changing my clothes. As I had formerly been in the habit of amusing myself round about the Barrière d'Italie, I hastened there and entered a wine-shop. While I was eating a morsel, two men came in and began talking about spending the night at a ball at the Rainbow. I asked them to take me with them; they agreed, I paid their bills, and we started. But soon after our arrival there these young men left me and joined the dancers. It was not long before I grew weary of merely looking on. Rather disappointed, I left the inn, and being foolish enough not to ask my way, I wandered on till I lost myself, while traversing a tract of unoccupied land. I was about to go back, when I saw a light in the distance. I walked straight toward it, and reached that cursed hovel."

"What happened then?"

"Oh! I went in; called for some one. A woman came downstairs, and I asked her for a glass of brandy. When she brought it, I sat down and lighted a cigar. Then I looked about me. The interior was almost enough to frighten one Three men and two women were drinking and chatting in low tones at another table. My face did not seem to suit them. One of them got up, came toward me, and said: 'You are a police agent; you've come here to play the spy; that's very plain.' I answered that I wasn't a police agent. He replied that I was. I again declared that I wasn't. In short, he swore that he was sure of it, and that my beard was false. So saying, he caught hold of my beard and pulled it. This made me mad. I jumped up, and with a blow of my fist I felled him to the ground. In an instant all the others were upon me! I had my revolver—you know the rest."

"And while all this was going on what were the two women doing?"

"Ah! I was too busy to pay any attention to them. They disappeared!"

"But you saw them when you entered the place—what were they like?"

"Oh! they were big, ugly creatures, as tall as grenadiers, and as dark as moles!"

Between plausible falsehood, and improbable truth, justice —human justice, and therefore liable to error—is compelled to decide as best it can. For the past hour M. Segmuller had not been free from mental disquietude. But all his doubts vanished when he heard the prisoner declare that the two women were tall and dark. If he had said: "The women were fair," M. Segmuller would not have known what to believe, but in the magistrate's opinion the audacious falsehood he had just heard proved that there was a perfect understanding between the supposed murderer and Widow Chupin.

Certainly, M. Segmuller's satisfaction was great; but his face did not betray it. It was of the utmost importance that the prisoner should believe that he had succeeded in deceiving his examiner. "You must understand how necessary it is to find these women," said the magistrate kindly.

"If their testimony corresponds with your allegations, your innocence will be proved conclusively."

"Yes, I understand that; but how can I put my hand upon them?"

"The police can assist you—our agents are always at the service of prisoners who desire to make use of them in establishing their innocence. Did you make any observations which might aid in the discovery of these women?"

Lecoq, whose eyes never wandered from the prisoner's face, fancied that he saw the faint shadow of a smile on the man's lips.

"I remarked nothing," said the prisoner coldly.

M. Segmuller had opened the drawer of his desk a moment before. He now drew from it the earring which had been found on the scene of the tragedy, and handing it abruptly to the prisoner, he asked: "So you didn't notice this in the ear of one of the women?"

The prisoner's imperturbable coolness of demeanor did not forsake him. He took the jewel in his hand, examined it attentively, held it up to the light, admired its brilliant scintillations, and said: "It is a very handsome stone, but I didn't notice it."

"This stone," remarked the magistrate, "is a diamond."

"Ah!"

"Yes; and worth several thousand francs."

"So much as that!"

This exclamation may have been in accordance with the spirit of the part assumed by the prisoner; though, at the same time, its simplicity was undoubtedly far-fetched. It was strange that a nomad, such as the murderer pretended to have been, acquainted with most of the countries and capitals of Europe, should have displayed this astonishment on learning the value of a diamond. Still, M. Segmuller did not seem to notice the discrepancy.

"Another thing," said he. "When you threw down your pistol, crying, 'Come and take me,' what did you intend to do?"

"I intended to make my escape."

"In what way?"

"Why, of course, by the door, sir—by—"

"Yes, by the back door," retorted the magistrate, with freezing irony. "It remains for you to explain how you—you who had just entered that hovel for the first time—could have known of this door's existence."

For once, in the course of the examination, the prisoner seemed troubled. For an instant all his assurance forsook him. He evidently perceived the danger of his position, and after a considerable effort he contrived to burst out in a laugh. His laugh was a poor one, however; it rang false, and failed to conceal a sensation of deep anxiety. Growing gradually bolder, he at length exclaimed: "That's nonsense, I had just seen these two women go out by that very door."

"Excuse me, you declared a minute ago that you did not see these women leave: that you were too busy to watch their movements."

"Did I say that?"

"Word for word; the passage shall be shown you. Goguet, find it."

The clerk at once read the passage referred to, whereupon the prisoner undertook to show that the remark had been misunderstood. He had not said—at least, he did not intend to say —that; they had quite misinterpreted his words. With such remarks did he try to palliate the effect of his apparent blunders.

In the mean while, Lecoq was jubilant. "Ah, my fine fellow," thought he, "you are contradicting yourself—you are in deep water already—you are lost. There's no hope for you."

The prisoner's situation was indeed not unlike that of a bather, who, unable to swim, imprudently advances into the sea until the water rises above his chin. He may for a while have preserved his equilibrium, despite the buffeting of the waves, but now he totters, loses his footing—another second, and he will sink!

"Enough—enough!" said the magistrate, cutting the prisoner's embarrassed explanation short. "Now, if you started out merely with the intention of amusing yourself, how did it happen that you took your revolver with you?"

"I had it with me while I was traveling, and did not think of leaving it at the hotel any more than I thought of changing my clothes."

"Where did you purchase it?"

"It was given me by M. Simpson as a souvenir."

"Confess that this M. Simpson is a very convenient personage," said the magistrate coldly. "Still, go on with your story. Only two chambers of this murderous weapon were discharged, but three men were killed. You have not told me the end of the affair."

"What's the use?" exclaimed the prisoner, in saddened tones. "Two of my assailants had fallen; the struggle became an equal one. I seized the remaining man, the soldier, round the body, and threw him down. He fell against a corner of the table, and did not rise again."

M. Segmuller had unfolded upon his desk the plan of the Poivriere drawn by Lecoq. "Come here," he said, addressing the prisoner, "and show me on this paper the precise spot you and your adversaries occupied."

May obeyed, and with an assurance of manner a little surprising in a man in his position, he proceeded to explain the drama. "I entered," said he, "by this door, marked C; I seated myself at the table, H, to the left of the entrance: my assailants occupied the table between the fireplace, F, and the window, B."

"I must admit," said the magistrate, "that your assertions fully agree with the statements of the physicians, who say that one of the shots must have been fired about a yard off, and the other about two yards off."

This was a victory for the prisoner, but he only shrugged his shoulders and murmured: "That proves that the physicians knew their business."

Lecoq was delighted. This part of the prisoner's narrative not merely agreed with the doctor's statements, but also confirmed his own researches. The young detective felt that, had he been the examiner, he would have conducted the investigation in precisely the same way. Accordingly, he thanked heaven that M. Segmuller had supplied the place of M. d'Escorval.

"This admitted," resumed the magistrate, "it remains for you to explain a sentence you uttered when the agent you see here arrested you."

"What sentence?"

"You exclaimed: 'Ah, it's the Prussians who are coming; I'm lost!' What did you mean by that?"

A fleeting crimson tinge suffused the prisoner's cheek. It was evident that if he had anticipated the other questions, and had been prepared for them, this one, at least, was unexpected. "It's very strange," said he, with ill-disguised embarrassment, "that I should have said such a thing!"

"Five persons heard you," insisted the magistrate.

The prisoner did not immediately reply. He was evidently trying to gain time, ransacking in his mind for a plausible explanation. "After all," he ultimately said, "the thing's quite possible. When I was with M. Simpson, we had with us an old soldier who had belonged to Napoleon's body-guard and had fought at Waterloo. I recollect he was always repeating that phrase. I must have caught the habit from him."

This explanation, though rather slow in coming, was none the less ingenious. At least, M. Segmuller appeared to be perfectly satisfied. "That's very plausible," said he; "but there is one circumstance that passes my comprehension. Were you freed from your assailants before the police entered the place? Answer me, yes or no."

"Yes."

"Then why, instead of making your escape by the back door,

the existence of which you had divined, did you remain on the threshold of the door leading into the back room, with a table before you to serve as a barricade, and your revolver leveled at the police, as if to keep them at bay?"

The prisoner hung his head, and the magistrate had to wait for his answer. "I was a fool," he stammered at last. "I didn't know whether these men were police agents or friends of the fellows I had killed."

"In either case your own interest should have induced you to fly."

The prisoner remained silent.

"Ah, well!" resumed M. Segmuller, "let me tell you my opinion. I believe you designedly and voluntarily exposed yourself to the danger of being arrested in order to protect the retreat of the two women who had just left."

"Why should I have risked my own safety for two hussies I did not even know?"

"Excuse me. The prosecution is strongly inclined to believe that you know these two women very well."

"I should like to see any one prove that!" So saying, the prisoner smiled sneeringly, but at once changed countenance when the magistrate retorted in a tone of assurance: "I will prove it."

XII

MAGISTRATES are frequently nonplussed when dealing with these difficult and delicate questions of personal identity. Railroads, photography, and telegraphic communication have multiplied the means of investigation in vain. Every day it happens that criminals succeed in deceiving justice in regard to their true personality, and thus escape the consequences of former crimes. This is indeed so frequently the case that an eminent French public prosecutor once ventured to remark: "Uncertainty as regards a criminal's identity will only cease when the law prescribes the branding of a number on the shoulder of every child whose birth is reported to the mayor."

M. Segmuller certainly wished that a number had been branded upon the enigmatical prisoner before him. And yet he did not by any means despair, and his confidence, exaggerated though it might be, was not at all feigned. He was of opinion that the weakest point of the prisoner's defense so far was his pretended ignorance concerning the two women. He proposed to return to this subject later on. In the mean while, however, there were other matters to be dealt with.

When he felt that his threat as regards the women had had time to produce its full effect, the magistrate continued: "So, prisoner, you assert that you were acquainted with none of the persons you met at the Poivriere."

"I swear it."

"Have you never had occasion to meet a person called Lacheneur, an individual whose name is connected with this unfortunate affair?"

"I heard the name for the first time when it was pronounced by the dying soldier. Poor fellow! I had just dealt him his death blow; and yet his last words testified to my innocence."

This sentimental outburst produced no impression whatever upon the magistrate. "In that case," said he, "I suppose you are willing to accept this soldier's statement."

The man hesitated, as if conscious that he had fallen into a snare, and that he would be obliged to weigh each answer carefully. "I accept it," said he at last. "Of course I accept it."

"Very well, then. This soldier, as you must recollect, wished to revenge himself on Lacheneur, who, by promising him a sum of money, had inveigled him into a conspiracy. A conspiracy against whom? Evidently against you; and yet you pretend that you had only arrived in Paris that evening, and that mere chance brought you to the Poivriere. Can you reconcile such conflicting statements?"

The prisoner had the hardihood to shrug his shoulders disdainfully. "I see the matter in an entirely different light," said he. "These people were plotting mischief against I don't know whom—and it was because I was in their way that they sought a quarrel with me, without any cause whatever."

Skilfully as the magistrate had delivered this thrust, it had been as skilfully parried; so skilfully, indeed, that Goguet, the smiling clerk, could not conceal an approving grimace. Besides, on principle, he always took the prisoner's part, in a mild, Platonic way, of course.

"Let us consider the circumstances that followed your arrest," resumed M. Segmuller. "Why did you refuse to answer all the questions put to you?"

A gleam of real or assumed resentment shone in the prisoner's eyes.

"This examination," he growled, "will alone suffice to make a culprit out of an innocent man!"

"I advise you, in your own interest, to behave properly. Those who arrested you observed that you were conversant with all the prison formalities and rules."

"Ah! sir, haven't I told you that I have been arrested and put in prison several times—always on account of my papers? I told you the truth, and you shouldn't taunt me for having done so."

The prisoner had dropped his mask of careless gaiety, and had assumed a surly, discontented tone. But his troubles were by no means ended; in fact, the battle had only just begun. Laying a tiny linen bag on his desk, M. Segmuller asked him if he recognized it.

"Perfectly! It is the package that the governor of the Depot placed in his safe."

The magistrate opened the bag, and poured the dust that it contained on to a sheet of paper. "You are aware, prisoner," said he, "that this dust comes from the mud that was sticking to your feet. The police agent who collected it has been to the station-house where you spent the night of the murder, and has discovered that the composition of this dust is identical with that of the floor of the cell you occupied."

The prisoner listened with gaping mouth.

"Hence," continued the magistrate, "it was certainly at the station-house, and *designedly*, that you soiled your feet with that mud. In doing so you had an object."

"I wished—"

"Let me finish. Being determined to keep your identity secret, and to assume the character of a member of the lower classes—of a mountebank, if you please—you reflected that the care you bestow upon your person might betray you. You foresaw the impression that would be caused when the coarse, ill-fitting boots you wore were removed, and the officials perceived your trim, clean feet, which are as well kept as your hands. Accordingly, what did you do? You poured some of the water that was in the pitcher in your cell on to the ground and then dabbled your feet in the mud that had thus been formed."

During these remarks the prisoner's face wore, by turns, an expression of anxiety, astonishment, irony, and mirth. When the magistrate had finished, he burst into a hearty laugh.

"So that's the result of twelve or fourteen hours' research," he at length exclaimed, turning toward Lecoq. "Ah! Mr. Agent, it's good to be sharp, but not so sharp as that. The truth is, that when I was taken to the station-house, forty-eight hours—thirty-six of them spent in a railway carriage—had elapsed since I had taken off my boots. My feet were red and swollen, and they burned like fire. What did I do? I poured some water over them. As for your other suspicions, if I have a soft white skin, it is only because I take care of myself. Besides, as is usual with most men of my profession, I rarely wear anything but slippers on my feet. This is so true that, on leaving Leipsic, I only owned a single pair of boots, and that was an old cast-off pair given me by M. Simpson."

Lecoq struck his chest. "Fool, imbecile, idiot, that I am!" he thought. "He was waiting to be questioned about this circumstance. He is so wonderfully shrewd that, when he saw me take the dust, he divined my intentions; and since then he has managed to concoct this story—a plausible story enough— and one that any jury would believe."

M. Segmuller was saying the same thing to himself. But he was not so surprised nor so overcome by the skill the prisoner had displayed in fencing with this point. "Let us continue," said he. "Do you still persist in your statements, prisoner?"

"Yes."

"Very well; then I shall be forced to tell you that what you are saying is untrue."

The prisoner's lips trembled visibly, and it was with difficulty that he faltered: "May my first mouthful of bread strangle me, if I have uttered a single falsehood!"

"A single falsehood! Wait."

The magistrate drew from the drawer of his desk the molds of the footprints prepared by Lecoq, and showing them to the murderer, he said: "You told me a few minutes ago that the two women were as tall as grenadiers; now, just look at the footprints made by these female giants. They were as 'dark as moles,' you said; a witness will tell you that one of them was a small, delicate-featured blonde, with an exceedingly sweet voice." He sought the prisoner's eyes, gazed steadily into them, and added slowly: "And this witness is the driver whose cab was hired in the Rue de Chevaleret by the two fugitives, both short, fair-haired women."

This sentence fell like a thunderbolt upon the prisoner; he grew pale, tottered, and leaned against the wall for support.

"Ah! you have told me the truth!" scornfully continued the pitiless magistrate. "Then, who is this man who was waiting for you while you were at the Poivriere? Who is this accomplice who, after your arrest, dared to enter the Widow Chupin's den to regain possession of some compromising object—no doubt a letter—which he knew he would find in the pocket of the Widow Chupin's apron? Who is this devoted, courageous friend who feigned drunkenness so effectually that even the police were deceived, and thoughtlessly placed him in confinement with you? Dare you deny that you have not arranged your system of defense in concert with him? Can you affirm that he did not give the Widow Chupin counsel as to the course she should pursue?"

But already, thanks to his power of self-control, the prisoner had mastered his agitation. "All this," said he, in a harsh voice, "is a mere invention of the police!"

However faithfully one may describe an examination of this kind, a narrative can convey no more idea of the real scene than a heap of cold ashes can give the effect of a glowing fire. One can note down each word, each ejaculation, but phraseology is powerless to portray the repressed animation, the impassioned movements, the studied reticence, the varied tones of voice, the now bold, now faltering glances, full of hatred and suspicion, which follow each other in rapid succession, mostly on the prisoner's side, but not entirely so, for although the magistrate may be an adept in the art of concealing his feelings, at times nature can not be controlled.

When the prisoner reeled beneath the magistrate's last words, the latter could not control his feelings. "He yields," he thought, "he succumbs—he is mine!"

But all hope of immediate success vanished when M. Segmuller saw his redoubtable adversary struggle against his momentary weakness, and arm himself for the fight with renewed, and, if possible, even greater energy. The magistrate perceived that it would require more than one assault to overcome such a stubborn nature. So, in a voice rendered still more harsh by disappointment, he resumed: "It is plain that you are determined to deny evidence itself."

The prisoner had recovered all his self-possession. He must have bitterly regretted his weakness, for a fiendish spite glittered in his eyes. "What evidence!" he asked, frowning. "This romance invented by the police is very plausible, I don't deny it; but it seems to me that the truth is quite as probable. You talk to me about a cabman whose vehicle was hired by two short, fair-haired women: but who can prove that these women were the same that fled from the Poivriere?"

"The police agent you see here followed the tracks they left across the snow."

"Ah! at night-time—across fields intersected by ditches, and up a long street—a fine rain falling all the while, and a thaw already beginning! Oh, your story is very probable!"

As he spoke, the murderer extended his arm toward Lecoq, and then, in a tone of crushing scorn, he added: "A man must have great confidence in himself, or a wild longing for advancement, to try and get a man guillotined on such evidence as that!"

At these words, Goguet, the smiling clerk, whose pen was rapidly flying across the paper, could not help remarking to himself: "The arrow has entered the bull's-eye this time!"

The comment was not without foundation: for Lecoq was evidently cut to the quick. Indeed, he was so incensed that, forgetful of his subordinate position, he sprang to his feet, exclaiming: "This circumstance would be of slight importance if it were not one of a long chain—"

"Be good enough to keep silent," interrupted the magistrate, who, turning to the prisoner, added: "The court does not utilize the proofs and testimony collected by the police until it has examined and weighed them."

"No matter," murmured the prisoner. "I should like to see this cab-driver."

"Have no fear about that; he shall repeat his evidence in your presence."

"Very well. I am satisfied then. I will ask him how he can distinguish people's faces when it is as dark as—"

He checked himself, apparently enlightened by a sudden inspiration.

"How stupid I am!" he exclaimed. "I'm losing my temper

about these people when you know all the while who they are. For of course the cabmen drove them home."

M. Segmuller saw that the prisoner understood him. He perceived, moreover, that the latter was doing all he could to increase the mystery that enshrouded this essential point of the case—a point upon which the prosecution was particularly anxious to obtain information.

The prisoner was truly an incomparable comedian, for his last observation was made in a tone of remarkable candor, just tinged with sufficient irony to show that he felt he had nothing to fear in this direction.

"If you are consistent with yourself," remarked the magistrate, "you will also deny the existence of an accomplice, of a —comrade."

"What would be the use denying it, since you believe nothing that I say? Only a moment ago you insinuated that my former employer was an imaginary personage; so what need I say about my pretended accomplice? According to your agents, he's at all events a most faithful friend. Indeed, this wonderful being—invented by Monsieur" (with these words the prisoner pointed to Lecoq)—"was seemingly not satisfied at having once escaped the police, for, according to your account, he voluntarily placed himself in their clutches a second time. You gentlemen pretend that he conferred first of all with me, and next with the Widow Chupin. How did that happen? Perhaps after removing him from my cell, some of your agents obligingly shut him up with the old woman."

Goguet, the clerk, wrote all this down admiringly. "Here," thought he, "is a man of brain, who understands his case. He won't need any lawyer's eloquence to put his defense favorably before a jury."

"And after all," continued the prisoner, "what are the proofs against me? The name of Lacheneur faltered by a dying man; a few footprints on some melting snow; a sleepy cab-driver's declaration; and a vague doubt about a drunkard's identity. If that is all you have against me, it certainly doesn't amount to much—"

"Enough!" interrupted M. Segmuller. "Your assurance is perfect now; though a moment ago your embarrassment was most remarkable. What was the cause of it?"

"The cause!" indignantly exclaimed the prisoner, whom this query had seemingly enraged; "the cause! Can't you see, sir,

"Can't you see, sir, that you are torturing me frightfully, pitilessly!"

that you are torturing me frightfully, pitilessly! I am an innocent man, and you are trying to deprive me of my life. You have been turning me this way and that way for so many hours that I begin to feel as if I were standing on the guillotine. Each time I open my mouth to speak I ask myself, is it this answer that will send me to the scaffold? My anxiety and dismay surprise you, do they? Why, since this examination began, I've felt the cold knife graze my neck at least twenty times. I wouldn't like my worst enemy to be subjected to such torture as this."

The prisoner's description of his sufferings did not seem at all exaggerated. His hair was saturated with perspiration, and big drops of sweat rested on his pallid brow, or coursed down his cheeks on to his beard.

"I am not your enemy," said the magistrate more gently. "A magistrate is neither a prisoner's friend nor enemy, he is simply the friend of truth and the executor of the law. I am not seeking either for an innocent man or for a culprit; I merely wish to arrive at the truth. I must know who you are—and I do know—"

"Ah!—if the assertion costs me my life—I'm May and none other."

"No, you are not."

"Who am I then? Some great man in disguise? Ah! I wish I were! In that case, I should have satisfactory papers to show you; and then you would set me free, for you know very well, my good sir, that I am as innocent as you are."

The magistrate had left his desk, and taken a seat by the fireplace within a yard of the prisoner. "Do not insist," said he. Then, suddenly changing both manner and tone, he added with the urbanity that a man of the world displays when addressing an equal:

"Do me the honor, sir, to believe me gifted with sufficient perspicuity to recognize, under the difficult part you play to such perfection, a very superior gentleman—a man endowed with remarkable talents."

Lecoq perceived that this sudden change of manner had unnerved the prisoner. He tried to laugh, but his merriment partook somewhat of the nature of a sob, and big tears glistened in his eyes.

"I will not torture you any longer," continued the magistrate. "In subtle reasoning I confess that you have conquered me.

However, when I return to the charge I shall have proofs enough in my possession to crush you."

He reflected for a moment, then lingering over each word, he added: "Only do not then expect from me the consideration I have shown you to-day. Justice is human; that is, she is indulgent toward certain crimes. She has fathomed the depth of the abyss into which blind passion may hurl even an honest man. To-day I freely offer you any assistance that will not conflict with my duty. Speak. Shall I send this officer of police away? Would you like me to send my clerk out of the room, on an errand?" He said no more, but waited to see the effect of this last effort.

The prisoner darted upon him one of those searching glances that seem to pierce an adversary through. His lips moved; one might have supposed that he was about to make a revelation. But no; suddenly he crossed his arms over his chest, and murmured: "You are very frank, sir. Unfortunately for me, I'm only a poor devil, as I've already told you. My name is May, and I earn my living by speaking to the public and turning a compliment."

"I am forced to yield to your decision," said the magistrate sadly. "The clerk will now read the minutes of your examination—listen."

While Goguet read the evidence aloud, the prisoner listened without making any remark, but when asked to sign the document, he obstinately refused to do so, fearing, he said, "some hidden treachery."

A moment afterward the soldiers who had escorted him to the magistrate's room conducted him back to the Depot.

XIII

WHEN the prisoner had gone, M. Segmuller sank back in his armchair, literally exhausted. He was in that state of nervous prostration which so often follows protracted but fruitless efforts. He had scarcely strength enough to bathe his burning forehead and gleaming eyes with cool, refreshing water.

This frightful examination had lasted no less than seven consecutive hours.

The smiling clerk, who had kept his place at his desk busily writing the whole while, now rose to his feet, glad of an opportunity to stretch his limbs and snap his fingers, cramped by holding the pen. Still, he was not in the least degree bored. He invariably took a semi-theatrical interest in the dramas that were daily enacted in his presence; his excitement being all the greater owing to the uncertainty that shrouded the finish of the final act—a finish that only too often belied the ordinary rules and deductions of writers for the stage.

"What a knave!" he exclaimed after vainly waiting for the magistrate or the detective to express an opinion, "what a rascal!"

M. Segmuller ordinarily put considerable confidence in his clerk's long experience. He sometimes even went so far as to consult him, doubtless somewhat in the same style that Moliere consulted his servant. But, on this occasion he did not accept his opinion.

"No," said he in a thoughtful tone, "that man is not a knave. When I spoke to him kindly he was really touched; he wept, he hesitated. I could have sworn that he was about to tell me everything."

"Ah, he's a man of wonderful power!" observed Lecoq.

The detective was sincere in his praise. Although the prisoner had disappointed his plans, and had even insulted him, he could not help admiring his shrewdness and courage. He—Lecoq—had prepared himself for a strenuous struggle with this man, and he hoped to conquer in the end. Nevertheless in his secret soul he felt for his adversary, admiring that sympathy which a "foeman worthy of one's steel" always inspires.

"What coolness, what courage!" continued the young detective. "Ah! there's no denying it, his system of defense—of absolute denial—is a masterpiece. It is perfect. How well he played that difficult part of buffoon! At times I could scarcely restrain my admiration. What is a famous comedian beside that fellow? The greatest actors need the adjunct of stage scenery to support the illusion, whereas this man, entirely unaided, almost convinced me even against my reason."

"Do you know what your very appropriate criticism proves?" inquired the magistrate.

"I am listening, sir."

"Ah, well! I have arrived at this conclusion—either this man is really May, the stroller, earning his living by paying compliments, as he says—or else he belongs to the highest rank of society, and not to the middle classes. It is only in the lowest or in the highest ranks that you encounter such grim energy as he has displayed, such scorn of life, as well as such remarkable presence of mind and resolution. A vulgar tradesman attracted to the Poivriere by some shameful passion would have confessed it long ago."

"But, sir, this man is surely not the buffoon, May," replied the young detective.

"No, certainly not," responded M. Segmuller; "we must, therefore, decide upon some plan of action." He smiled kindly, and added, in a friendly voice: "It was unnecessary to tell you that, Monsieur Lecoq. Quite unnecessary, since to you belongs the honor of having detected this fraud. As for myself, I confess, that if I had not been warned in advance, I should have been the dupe of this clever artist's talent."

The young detective bowed; a blush of modesty tinged his cheeks, but a gleam of pleased vanity sparkled in his eyes. What a difference between this friendly, benevolent magistrate and M. d'Escorval, so taciturn and haughty. This man, at least, understood, appreciated, and encouraged him; and it was with a common theory and an equal ardor that they were about to devote themselves to a search for the truth. Scarcely had Lecoq allowed these thoughts to flit across his mind than he reflected that his satisfaction was, after all, a trifle premature, and that success was still extremely doubtful. With this chilling conclusion, presence of mind returned. Turning toward the magistrate, he exclaimed: "You will recollect, sir, that the Widow Chupin mentioned a son of hers, a certain Polyte—"

"Yes."

"Why not question him? He must know all the frequenters of the Poivriere, and might perhaps give us valuable information regarding Gustave, Lacheneur, and the murderer himself. As he is not in solitary confinement, he has probably heard of his mother's arrest; but it seems to me impossible that he should suspect our present perplexity."

"Ah! you are a hundred times right!" exclaimed the magistrate. I ought to have thought of that myself. In his position he can scarcely have been tampered with as yet, and I'll have him up here to-morrow morning; I will also question his wife."

Turning to his clerk, M. Segmuller added: "Quick, Goguet, prepare a summons in the name of the wife of Hippolyte Chupin, and address an order to the governor of the Depot to produce her husband!"

But night was coming on. It was already too dark to see to write, and accordingly the clerk rang the bell for lights. Just as the messenger who brought the lamps turned to leave the room, a rap was heard at the door. Immediately afterward the governor of the Depot entered.

During the past twenty-four hours this worthy functionary had been greatly perplexed concerning the mysterious prisoner he had placed in secret cell No. 3, and he now came to the magistrate for advice regarding him. "I come to ask," said he, "if I am still to retain the prisoner May in solitary confinement?"

"Yes."

"Although I fear fresh attacks of frenzy, I dislike to confine him in the strait-jacket again."

"Leave him free in his cell," replied M. Segmuller; "and tell the keepers to watch him well, but to treat him kindly."

By the provisions of Article 613 of the Code, accused parties are placed in the custody of the government, but the investigating magistrate is allowed to adopt such measures concerning them as he may deem necessary for the interest of the prosecution.

The governor bowed assent to M. Segmuller's instructions, and then added: "You have doubtless succeeded in establishing the prisoner's identity."

"Unfortunately, I have not."

The governor shook his head with a knowing air. "In that case," said he, "my conjectures were correct. It seems to me evident that this man is a criminal of the worst description— an old offender certainly, and one who has the strongest interest in concealing his identity. You will find that you have to deal with a man who has been sentenced to the galleys for life, and who has managed to escape from Cayenne."

"Perhaps you are mistaken."

"Hum! I shall be greatly surprised if such should prove the case. I must admit that my opinion in this matter is identical with that of M. Gevrol, the most experienced and the most skilful of our inspectors. I agree with him in thinking that young detectives are often overzealous, and run after fantoms originated in their own brains."

Lecoq, crimson with wrath, was about to make an angry response when M. Segmuller motioned to him to remain silent. Then with a smile on his face the magistrate replied to the governor. "Upon my word, my dear friend," he said, "the more I study this affair, the more convinced I am of the correctness of the theory advanced by the 'overzealous' detective. But, after all, I am not infallible, and I shall depend upon your counsel and assistance."

"Oh! I have means of verifying my assertion," interrupted the governor; "and I hope before the end of the next twenty-four hours that our man will have been identified, either by the police or by one of his fellow-prisoners."

With these words he took his leave. Scarcely had he done so than Lecoq sprang to his feet. The young detective was furious. "You see that Gevrol already speaks ill of me; he is jealous."

"Ah, well! what does that matter to you? If you succeed, you will have your revenge. If you are mistaken—then I am mistaken, too."

Then, as it was already late, M. Segmuller confided to Lecoq's keeping the various articles the latter had accumulated in support of his theory. He also placed in his hands the diamond earring, the owner of which must be discovered; and the letter signed "Lacheneur," which had been found in the pocket of the spurious soldier. Having given him full instructions, he asked him to make his appearance promptly on the morrow, and then dismissed him, saying: "Now go; and may good luck attend you!"

XIV

LONG, narrow, and low of ceiling, having on the one side a row of windows looking on to a small courtyard, and on the other a range of doors, each with a number on its central panel, thus reminding one of some corridor in a second-rate hotel, such is the Galerie d'Instruction at the Palais de Justice whereby admittance is gained into the various rooms occupied by the investigating magistrates. Even in the daytime, when it is thronged with prisoners, witnesses, and guards, it is a sad and gloomy place. But it is absolutely sinister of aspect at night-time, when deserted, and only dimly lighted by the smoky lamp of a solitary attendant, waiting for the departure of some magistrate whom business has detained later than usual.

Although Lecoq was not sensitive to such influences, he made haste to reach the staircase and thus escape the echo of his footsteps, which sounded most drearily in the silence and darkness pervading the gallery.

Finding an open window on the floor below, he looked out to ascertain the state of the weather. The temperature was much milder; the snow had altogether disappeared, and the pavement was almost dry. A slight haze, illumined by the ruddy glare of the street lamps, hung like a purple mantle over the city. The streets below were full of animation; vehicles were rolling rapidly to and fro, and the footways were too narrow for the bustling crowd, which, now that the labors of the day were ended, was hastening homeward or in search of pleasure.

The sight drew a sigh from the young detective. "And it is in this great city," he murmured, "in the midst of this world of people that I must discover the traces of a person I don't even know! Is it possible to accomplish such a feat?"

The feeling of despondency that had momentarily surprised him was not, however, of long duration. "Yes, it is possible," cried an inward voice. "Besides, it *must* be done; your future depends upon it. Where there's a will, there's a way." Ten seconds later he was in the street, more than ever inflamed with hope and courage.

Unfortunately, however, man can only place organs of limited power at the disposal of his boundless desires; and Lecoq had not taken twenty steps along the streets before he became aware that if the spirit was willing, the flesh was weak. His limbs trembled, and his head whirled. Nature was asserting her rights; during the last forty-eight hours, the young detective had taken scarcely a moment's rest, and he had, moreover, now passed an entire day without food.

"Am I going to be ill?" he thought, sinking on to a bench. And he groaned inwardly on recapitulating all that he wished to do that evening.

If he dealt only with the more important matters, must he

not at once ascertain the result of Father Absinthe's search after the man who had recognized one of the victims at the Morgue; test the prisoner's assertions regarding the box of clothes left at one of the hotels surrounding the Northern Railway Station; and last, but not the least, must he not procure the address of Polyte Chupin's wife, in order to serve her with the summons to appear before M. Segmuller?

Under the power of urgent necessity, he succeeded in triumphing over his attack of weakness, and rose, murmuring: "I will go first to the Prefecture and to the Morgue; then I will see."

But he did not find Father Absinthe at the Prefecture, and no one could give any tidings of him. He had not been there at all during the day. Nor could any one indicate, even vaguely, the abode of the Widow Chupin's daughter-in-law.

On the other hand, however, Lecoq met a number of his colleagues, who laughed and jeered at him unmercifully. "Ah! you are a shrewd fellow!" they said, "it seems that you have just made a wonderful discovery, and it's said you are going to be decorated with the Legion of Honor."

Gevrol's influence betrayed itself everywhere. The jealous inspector had taken pains to inform all his colleagues and subordinates that poor Lecoq, crazed by ambition, persisted in declaring that a low, vulgar murderer trying to escape justice was some great personage in disguise. However, the jeers and taunts of which Lecoq was the object had but little effect upon him, and he consoled himself with the reflection that, "He laughs best who laughs last."

If he were restless and anxious as he walked along the Quai des Orfevres, it was because he could not explain Father Absinthe's prolonged absence, and because he feared that Gevrol, mad with jealousy, might attempt, in some underhand way, to frustrate his, Lecoq's, efforts to arrive at a solution of the mystery.

At the Morgue the young detective met with no better success than at the Prefecture. After ringing three or four times, one of the keepers opened the door and informed him that the bodies had not been identified, and that the old police agent had not been seen since he went away early in the morning.

"This is a bad beginning," thought Lecoq. "I will go and get some dinner—that, perhaps, will change the luck; at all events, I have certainly earned the bottle of good wine to which I intend to treat myself."

It was a happy thought. A hearty meal washed down with a couple of glasses of Bordeaux sent new courage and energy coursing through his veins. If he still felt a trifle weary, the sensation of fatigue was at all events greatly diminished when he left the restaurant with a cigar between his lips.

Just at that moment he longed for Father Papillon's trap and sturdy steed. Fortunately, a cab was passing: he hired it, and as eight o'clock was striking, alighted at the corner of the square in front of the Northern Railway Station. After a brief glance round, he began his search for the hotel where the murderer pretended to have left a box of clothes.

It must be understood that he did not present himself in his official capacity. Hotel proprietors fight shy of detectives, and Lecoq was aware that if he proclaimed his calling he would probably learn nothing at all. By brushing back his hair and turning up his coat collar, he made, however, a very considerable alteration in his appearance; and it was with a marked English accent that he asked the landlords and servants of various hostelries surrounding the station for information concerning a "foreign workman named May."

He conducted his search with considerable address, but everywhere he received the same reply.

"We don't know such a person; we haven't seen any one answering the description you give of him."

Any other answer would have astonished Lecoq, so strongly persuaded was he that the prisoner had only mentioned the circumstances of a trunk left at one of these hotels in order to give a semblance of truth to his narrative. Nevertheless he continued his investigation. If he noted down in his memorandum book the names of all the hotels which he visited, it was with a view of making sure of the prisoner's discomfiture when he was conducted to the neighborhood and asked to prove the truth of his story.

Eventually, Lecoq reached the Hotel de Mariembourg, at the corner of the Rue St. Quentin. The house was of modest proportions; but seemed respectable and well kept. Lecoq pushed open the glass door leading into the vestibule, and entered the office—a neat, brightly lighted room, where he found a woman standing upon a chair, her face on a level with a large bird cage, covered with a piece of black silk. She was repeating three or four German words with great earnestness to the inmate of the cage, and was so engrossed in this occupation that Lecoq had to make considerable noise before he could attract her attention.

At length she turned her head, and the young detective exclaimed: "Ah! good evening, madame; you are much interested, I see, in teaching your parrot to talk."

"It isn't a parrot," replied the woman, who had not yet descended from her perch; "but a starling, and I am trying to teach it to say 'Have you breakfasted?' in German."

"What! can starlings talk?"

"Yes, sir, as well as you or I," rejoined the woman, jumping down from the chair.

Just then the bird, as if it had understood the question, cried very distinctly: "Camille! Where is Camille?"

But Lecoq was too preoccupied to pay any further attention to the incident. "Madame," he began, "I wish to speak to the proprietor of this hotel."

"I am the proprietor."

"Oh! very well. I was expecting a mechanic—from Leipsic —to meet me here in Paris. To my great surprise, he has not made his appearance; and I came to inquire if he was stopping here. His name is May."

"May!" repeated the hostess, thoughtfully. "May!"

"He ought to have arrived last Sunday evening."

The woman's face brightened. "Wait a moment," said she. "Was this friend of yours a middle-aged man, of medium size, of very dark complexion—wearing a full beard, and having very bright eyes?"

Lecoq could scarcely conceal his agitation. This was an exact description of the supposed murderer. "Yes," he stammered, "that is a very good portrait of the man."

"Ah, well! he came here on Shrove Sunday, in the afternoon. He asked for a cheap room, and I showed him one on the fifth floor. The office-boy was not here at the time, and he insisted upon taking his trunk upstairs himself. I offered him some refreshments; but he declined to take anything, saying that he was in a great hurry; and he went away after giving me ten francs as security for the rent."

"Where is he now?" inquired the young detective.

"Dear me! that reminds me," replied the woman. "He has never returned, and I have been rather anxious about him.

Lecoq pushed open the glass door . . . and entered the office.

Paris is such a dangerous place for strangers! It is true he spoke French as well as you or I; but what of that? Yesterday evening I gave orders that the commissary of police should be informed of the matter."

"Yesterday—the commissary?"

"Yes. Still, I don't know whether the boy obeyed me. I had forgotten all about it. Allow me to ring for the boy, and ask him."

A bucket of iced water falling upon Lecoq's head could not have astonished him more than did this announcement from the proprietress of the Hotel de Mariembourg. Had the prisoner indeed told the truth? Was it possible? Gevrol and the governor of the prison were right, then, and M. Segmuller and he, Lecoq, were senseless fools, pursuing a fantom. These ideas flashed rapidly through the young detective's brain. But he had no time for reflection. The boy who had been summoned now made his appearance, and proved to be a big overgrown lad with frank, chubby face.

"Fritz," asked his mistress, "did you go to the commissary's office?"

"Yes, madame."

"What did he say?"

"He was not in; but I spoke to his secretary, M. Casimir, who said you were not to worry yourself, as the man would no doubt return."

"But he has not returned."

The boy rejoined, with a movement of the shoulders that plainly implied: "How can I help that?"

"You hear, sir," said the hostess, apparently thinking the importunate questioner would now withdraw.

Such, however, was not Lecoq's intention, and he did not even move, though he had need of all his self-possession to retain his English accent. "This is very annoying," said he, "very! I am even more anxious and undecided than I was before, since I am not certain that this is the man I am seeking for."

"Unfortunately, sir, I can tell you nothing more," calmly replied the landlady.

Lecoq reflected for a moment, knitting his brows and biting his lips, as if he were trying to discover some means of solving the mystery. In point of fact, he was seeking for some adroit phrase which might lead this woman to show him the register in which all travelers are compelled to inscribe their full names, profession, and usual residence. At the same time, however, it was necessary that he should not arouse her suspicions.

"But, madame," said he at last, "can't you remember the name this man gave you? Was it May? Try to recollect if that was the name—May—May!"

"Ah! I have so many things to remember. But now I think of it, and the name must be entered in my book, which, if it would oblige you, I can show you. It is in the drawer of my writing-table. Whatever can I have done with my keys?"

And while the hostess, who seemed to possess about as much intelligence as her starling, was turning the whole office upside down looking for her keys, Lecoq scrutinized her closely. She was about forty years of age, with an abundance of light hair, and a very fair complexion. She was well preserved—that is to say, she was plump and healthy in appearance; her glance was frank and unembarrassed; her voice was clear and musical, and her manners were pleasing, and entirely free from affectation.

"Ah!" she eventually exclaimed, "I have found those wretched keys at last." So saying, she opened her desk, took out the register, laid it on the table, and began turning over the leaves. At last she found the desired page.

"Sunday, February 20th," said she. "Look, sir: here on the seventh line—May—no Christian name—foreign artist—coming from Leipsic—without papers."

While Lecoq was examining this record with a dazed air, the woman exclaimed: "Ah! now I can explain how it happened that I forgot the man's name and strange profession—'foreign artist.' I did not make the entry myself."

"Who made it, then?"

"The man himself, while I was finding ten francs to give him as change for the louis he handed me. You can see that the writing is not at all like that of other entries."

Lecoq had already noted this circumstance, which seemed to furnish an irrefutable argument in favor of the assertions made by the landlady and the prisoner. "Are you sure," he asked, "that this is the man's handwriting?"

In his anxiety he had forgotten his English accent. The woman noticed this at once, for she drew back, and cast a suspicious glance at the pretended foreigner. "I know what I am saying," she said, indignantly. "And now this is enough, isn't it?"

Knowing that he had betrayed himself, and thoroughly ashamed of his lack of coolness, Lecoq renounced his English accent altogether. "Excuse me," he said, "if I ask one more question. Have you this man's trunk in your possession?"

"Certainly."

"You would do me an immense service by showing it to me."

"Show it to you!" exclaimed the landlady, angrily. "What do you take me for? What do you want? and who are you?"

"You shall know in half an hour," replied the young detective, realizing that further persuasion would be useless.

He hastily left the room, ran to the Place de Roubaix, jumped into a cab, and giving the driver the address of the district commissary of police, promised him a hundred sous over and above the regular fare if he would only make haste. As might have been expected under such circumstances, the poor horse fairly flew over the ground.

Lecoq was fortunate enough to find the commissary at his office. Having given his name, he was immediately ushered into the magistrate's presence and told his story in a few words.

"It is really true that they came to inform me of this man's disappearance," said the commissary. "Casimir told me about it this morning."

"They—came—to inform—you—" faltered Lecoq.

"Yes, yesterday; but I have had so much to occupy my time. Now, my man, how can I serve you?"

"Come with me, sir; compel them to show us the trunk, and send for a locksmith to open it. Here is the authority—a search warrant given me by the investigating magistrate to use in case of necessity. Let us lose no time. I have a cab at the door."

"We will start at once," said the commissary.

The driver whipped up his horse once more, and they were soon rapidly rolling in the direction of the Rue St. Quentin.

"Now, sir," said the young detective, "permit me to ask if you know this woman who keeps the Hotel de Mariembourg?"

"Yes, indeed, I know her very well. When I was first appointed to this district, six years ago, I was a bachelor, and for a long while I took my meals at her table d'hote. Casimir, my secretary, boards there even now."

"And what kind of woman is she?"

"Why, upon my word, my young friend, Madame Milner—for such is her name—is a very respectable widow (highly esteemed by her neighbors) and having a very prosperous business. If she remains a widow, it is only from choice, for she is very prepossessing and has plenty of suitors."

"Then you don't think her capable of serving, for the sake of a good round sum, the interests of some wealthy culprit?"

"Have you gone mad?" interrupted the commissary. "What, Madame Milner perjure herself for the sake of money! Haven't I just told you that she is an honest woman, and that she is very well off! Besides, she informed me yesterday that this man was missing, so—"

Lecoq made no reply; the driver was pulling up; they had reached their destination.

On seeing her obstinate questioner reappear, accompanied by the commissary, Madame Milner seemed to understand everything.

"Good heavens!" she exclaimed, "a detective! I might have guessed it? Some crime has been committed; and now my hotel has lost its reputation forever!"

While a messenger was despatched for a locksmith, the commissary endeavored to reassure and console her, a task of no little difficulty, and which he was some time in accomplishing.

At last they all went up to the missing man's room, and Lecoq sprang toward the trunk. Ah! there was no denying it. It had, indeed, come from Leipsic; as the labels pasted upon it by the different railroad companies only too plainly proved. On being opened, it was, moreover, found to contain the various articles mentioned by the prisoner.

Lecoq was thunderstruck. When he had seen the commissary lock the trunk and its contents up in a cupboard and take possession of the key, he felt he could endure nothing more. He left the room with downcast head; and stumbled like a drunken man as he went down the stairs.

XV

MARDI GRAS, or Shrove Tuesday, was very gay that year; that is to say, all places of public resort were crowded. When Lecoq left the Hotel de Mariembourg about midnight, the streets were as full as if it had been noonday, and the cafés were thronged with customers.

But the young detective had no heart for pleasure. He mingled with the crowd without seemingly seeing it, and jostled against groups of people chatting at the corners, without hearing the imprecations occasioned by his awkwardness. Where was he going? He had no idea. He walked aimlessly, more disconsolate and desperate than the gambler who had staked his last hope with his last louis, and lost.

"I must yield," he murmured; "this evidence is conclusive. My presumptions were only chimeras; my deductions the playthings of chance! All I can now do is to withdraw, with the least possible damage and ridicule, from the false position I have assumed."

Just as he reached the boulevard, however, a new idea entered his brain, an idea of so startling a kind that he could scarcely restrain a loud exclamation of surprise. "What a fool I am!" cried he, striking his hand violently against his forehead. "Is it possible to be so strong in theory, and yet so ridiculously weak in practise? Ah! I am only a child, a mere novice, disheartened by the slightest obstacle. I meet with a difficulty, and at once I lose all my courage. Now, let me reflect calmly. What did I tell the judge about this murderer, whose plan of defense so puzzles us? Did I not tell him that we had to deal with a man of superior talent—with a man of consummate penetration and experience—a bold, courageous fellow of imperturbable coolness, who will do anything to insure the success of his plans? Yes; I told him all that, and yet I give up the game in despair as soon as I meet with a single circumstance that I can not instantly explain. It is evident that such a prisoner would not resort to old, hackneyed, commonplace expedients. Time, patience, and research are requisite to find a flaw in his defense. With such a man as he is, the more appearances are against my presumptions, and in favor of his narrative, the more certain it is that I am right —or else logic is no longer logic."

At this thought, Lecoq burst into a hearty laugh. "Still," continued he, "it would perhaps be premature to expose this theory at headquarters in Gevrol's presence. He would at once present me with a crtificate for admission into some lunatic asylum."

The young detective paused. While absorbed in thought,

his legs, obeying an instinctive impulse, had brought him to his lodgings. He rang the bell; the door opened, and he groped his way slowly up to the fourth floor. He had reached his room, and was about to enter, when some one, whom he could not distinguish in the dark, called out: "Is that you, Monsieur Lecoq?"

"Yes, it's I!" replied the young man, somewhat surprised; "but who are you?"

"I'm Father Absinthe."

"Oh! indeed! Well, you are welcome! I didn't recognize your voice—will you come in?"

They entered the room, and Lecoq lit a candle. Then the young man could see his colleague, and, good heavens! he found him in a most pitiable condition.

He was as dirty and as bespattered with mud as a lost dog that has been wandering about in the rain and the mire for a week at the very least. His overcoat bore the traces of frequent contact with damp walls; his hat had lost its form entirely. His eyes wore an anxious look, and his mustache drooped despondently. He spoke, moreover, so strangely that one might have supposed his mouth was full of sand.

"Do you bring me bad news?" inquired Lecoq, after a short examination of his companion.

"Yes, bad."

"The people you were following escaped you, then?"

The old man nodded his head affirmatively.

"It is unfortunate—very unfortunate!" said Lecoq. "But it is useless to distress ourselves about it. Don't be so cast down, Father Absinthe. To-morrow, between us, we will repair the damage."

This friendly encouragement only increased the old man's evident embarrassment. He blushed, this veteran, as if he had been a schoolgirl, and raising his hands toward heaven, he exclaimed: "Ah, you wretch! didn't I tell you so?"

"Why! what is the matter with you?" inquired Lecoq.

Father Absinthe made no reply. Approaching a looking-glass that hung against the wall, he surveyed himself reproachfully and began to heap cruel insults upon the reflection of his features.

"You old good-for-nothing!" he exclaimed. "You vile deserter! have you no shame left? You were entrusted with a mission, were you not? And how have you fulfilled it? You have got drunk, you old wretch, so drunk as to have lost your wits. Ah, you shan't escape punishment this time, for even if M. Lecoq is indulgent, you shan't taste another drop for a week. Yes, you old sot, you shall suffer for this escapade."

"Come, come," said Lecoq, "you can sermonize by and by. Now tell me your story."

"Ah! I am not proud of it, believe me. However, never mind. No doubt you received the letter in which I told you I was going to follow the young men who seemed to recognize Gustave?"

"Yes, yes—go on!"

"Well, as soon as they entered the café, into which I had followed them, they began drinking, probably to drive away their emotion. After that they apparently felt hungry. At all events they ordered breakfast. I followed their example. The mail, with coffee and beer afterward, took up no little time, and indeed a couple of hours had elapsed before they were ready to pay their bill and go. Good! I supposed they would now return home. Not at all. They walked down the Rue Dauphin; and I saw them enter another café. Five minutes later I glided in after them; and found them already engaged in a game of billiards."

At this point Father Absinthe hesitated; it is no easy task to recount one's blunders to the very person who has suffered by them.

"I seated myself at a little table," he eventually resumed, "and asked for a newspaper. I was reading with one eye and watching with the other, when a respectable-looking man entered, and took a seat beside me. As soon as he had seated himself he asked me to let him have the paper when I had finished with it. I handed it to him, and then we began talking about the weather. At last he proposed a game of bezique. I declined, but we afterward compromised the matter by having a game of piquet. The young men, you understand, were still knocking the balls about. We began by playing for a glass of brandy each. I won. My adversary asked for his revenge, and we played two games more. I still kept on winning. He insisted upon another game, and again I won, and still I drank—and drank again—"

"Go on, go on."

"Ah! here's the rub. After that I remember nothing—nothing either about the man I had been playing with or the young men. It seems to me, however, that I recollect falling asleep in the café, and that a long while afterward a waiter came and woke me and told me to go. Then I must have wandered about along the quays until I came to my senses, and decided to go to your lodgings and wait on the stairs until you returned."

To Father Absinthe's great surprise, Lecoq seemed rather thoughtful than angry. "What do you think about this chance acquaintance of yours, papa?" asked the young detective.

"I think he was following me while I was following the others, and that he entered the café with the view of making me drunk."

"What was he like?"

"Oh, he was a tall, stoutish man, with a broad, red face, and a flat nose; and he was very unpretending and affable in manner.

"It was he!" exclaimed Lecoq.

"He! Who?"

"Why, the accomplice—the man whose footprints we discovered—the pretended drunkard—a devil incarnate, who will get the best of us yet, if we don't keep our eyes open. Don't you forget him, papa; and if you ever meet him again—"

But Father Absinthe's confession was not ended. Like most devotees, he had reserved the worst sin for the last.

"But that's not all," he resumed; "and as it's best to make a clean breast of it, I will tell you that it seems to me this traitor talked about the affair at the Poivriere, and that I told him all we had discovered, and all we intended to do."

Lecoq made such a threatening gesture that the old tippler drew back in consternation. "You wretched man!" exclaimed the young detective, "to betray our plans to the enemy!"

But his calmness soon returned. If at first sight the evil seemed to be beyond remedy, on further thought it had a good side after all. It sufficed to dispel all the doubts that had assailed Lecoq's mind after his visit to the Hotel de Mariembourg.

"However," quoth our hero, "this is not the time for deliberation. I am overcome with fatigue; take a mattress from the bed for yourself, my friend, and let us get a little sleep."

Lecoq was a man of considerable forethought. Hence, before going to bed he took good care to wind up his alarm so that it might wake him at six o'clock. "With that to warn us," he remarked to his companion, as he blew out the candle, "there need be no fear of our missing the coach."

He had not, however, made allowance for his own extreme weariness or for the soporific effect of the alcoholic fumes with which his comrade's breath was redolent. When six o'clock struck at the church of St. Eustache, the young detective's alarm resounded faithfully enough, with a loud and protracted whir. Shrill and sonorous as was the sound, it failed, however, to break the heavy sleep of the two detectives. They would indeed, in all probability, have continued slumbering for several hours longer, if at half-past seven a sturdy fist had not begun to rap loudly at the door. With one bound Lecoq was out of bed, amazed at seeing the bright sunlight, and furious at the futility of his precautions.

"Come in!" he cried to his early visitor. He had no enemies to fear, and could, without danger, sleep with his door unlocked.

In response to his call, Father Papillon's shrewd face peered into the room.

"Ah! it is my worthy coachman!" exclaimed Lecoq. "Is there anything new?"

"Excuse me, but it's the old affair that brings me here," replied our eccentric friend the cabman. "You know—the thirty francs those wretched women paid me. Really, I shan't sleep in peace till you have worked off the amount by using my vehicle. Our drive yesterday lasted two hours and a half, which, according to the regular fare, would be worth a hundred sous; so you see I've still more than twelve hours at your disposal."

"That is all nonsense, my friend!"

"Possibly, but I am responsible for it, and if you won't use my cab, I've sworn to spend those twelve hours waiting outside your door. So now make up your mind." He gazed at Lecoq beseechingly, and it was evident that a refusal would wound him keenly.

"Very well," replied Lecoq, "I will take you for the morning, only I ought to warn you that we are starting on a long journey."

"Oh, Cocotte's legs may be relied upon."

"My companion and myself have business in your own neighborhood. It is absolutely necessary for us to find the Widow Chupin's daughter-in-law; and I hope we shall be able to obtain her address from the police commissary of the district where the Poivriere is situated."

"Very well, we will go wherever you wish; I am at your orders."

A few moments later they were on their way.

Papillon's features wore an air of self-satisfied pride as, sitting erect on his box, he cracked his whip, and encouraged the nimble Cocotte. The vehicle could not have got over the ground more rapidly if its driver had been promised a hundred sous' gratuity.

Father Absinthe alone was sad. He had been forgiven by Lecoq, but he could not forget that he, an old police agent, had been duped as easily as if he had been some ignorant provincial. The thought was humiliating, and then in addition he had been fool enough to reveal the secret plans of the prosecution! He knew but too well that this act of folly had doubled the difficulties of Lecoq's task.

The long drive in Father Papillon's cab was not a fruitless one. The secretary of the commissary of police for the thirteenth arrondissement informed Lecoq that Polyte Chupin's wife lived with her child, in the suburbs, in the Rue de la Butte-aux-Cailles. He could not indicate the precise number, but he described the house and gave them some information concerning its occupants.

The Widow Chupin's daughter-in-law, a native of Auvergne, had been bitterly punished for preferring a rakish Parisian ragamuffin to one of the grimy charcoal-burners of the Puy de Dome. She was hardly more than twelve years of age when she first came to Paris and obtained employment in a large factory. After ten years' privation and constant toil, she had managed to amass, sou by sou, the sum of three thousand francs. Then her evil genius threw Polyte Chupin across her path. She fell in love with this dissipated, selfish rascal; and he married her for the sake of her little hoard.

As long as the money lasted, that is, for some three or four months, matters went on pleasantly enough. But as soon as the last franc had been spent, Polyte left his wife, and complacently resumed his former life of idleness, thieving, and debauchery. When at times he returned home, it was merely with the view of robbing his wife of what little money she might have saved in the mean while; and periodically she uncomplainingly allowed him to despoil her of the last penny of her earnings.

Horrible to relate, this unworthy rascal even tried to trade on her good looks. Here, however, he met with a strenuous resistance—a resistance which excited not merely his own ire, but also the hatred of the villain's mother—that old hag, the Widow Chupin. The result was that Polyte's wife was subjected to such incessant cruelty and persecution that one night she was forced to fly with only the rags that covered her. The Chupins —mother and son—believed, perhaps, that starvation would effect what their horrible threats and insidious counsel had failed to accomplish. Their shameful expectations were not, however, gratified.

In mentioning these facts to Lecoq, the commissary's secretary added that they had become widely known, and that the unfortunate creature's force of character had won for her general respect. Among those she frequented, moreover, she was known by the nickname of "Toinon the Virtuous"—a rather vulgar but, at all events, sincere tribute to her worth.

Grateful for this information, Lecoq returned to the cab. The Rue de la Butte-aux-Cailles, whither Papillon was now directed to drive, proved to be very unlike the Boulevard Malesherbes, and one brief glance sufficed to show that opulence had not here fixed its abode. Luck seemed for the moment to have turned in Lecoq's favor. At all events, when he and Father Absinthe alighted at the corner of the street, it so happened that the very first person the young detective questioned concerning the virtuous Toinon was well acquainted with her whereabouts. The house in which she resided was pointed out, and Lecoq was instructed to go upstairs to the top floor, and knock at the door in front of him. With such precise directions the two detectives speedily reached Madame Polyte Chupin's abode.

This proved to be a cold and gloomy attic of medium size, windowless, but provided with a small skylight. A straw pallet, a broken table, two chairs, and a few plain kitchen utensils constituted the sole appointments of this miserable garret. But in spite of the occupant's evident poverty, everything was neat and clean, and to use a forcible expression that fell from Father Absinthe, one could have eaten off the floor.

The two detectives entered, and found a woman busily engaged in making a heavy linen sack. She was seated in the centre of the room, directly under the skylight, so that the sun's rays might fall upon her work. At the sight of two strangers, she half rose from her chair, surprised, and perhaps a little frightened; but when Lecoq had explained that they desired a few moments' conversation with her, she gave up her own seat, and drawing the second chair from a corner, invited both detectives to sit down. Lecoq complied, but Father Absinthe declared that he preferred to remain standing.

With a single glance Lecoq took an inventory of the humble abode, and, so to speak, appraised the woman. She was short, stout, and of commonplace appearance. Her forehead was extremely low, being crowned by a forest of coarse, black hair; while the expression of her large, black eyes, set very close together, recalled the look of patient resignation one so often detects in ill-treated and neglected animals. Possibly, in former days, she might have possessed that fleeting attraction called the *beaute du diable;* but now she looked almost as old as her wretched mother-in-law. Sorrow and privation, excessive toil and ill-treatment, had imparted to her face a livid hue, reddening her eyes and stamping deep furrows round about her temples. Still, there was an attribute of native honesty about her which even the foul atmosphere in which she had been compelled to live had not sufficed to taint.

Her little boy furnished a striking contrast. He was pale and puny; his eyes gleamed with a phosphorescent brilliancy; and his hair was of a faded flaxen tint. One little circumstance attracted both detectives' attention. If the mother was attired in an old, thin, faded calico dress, the child was warmly clad in stout woolen material.

"Madame, you have doubtless heard of a dreadful crime, committed in your mother-in-law's establishment," began Lecoq in a soft voice.

"Alas! yes, sir," replied Toinon the Virtuous, quickly adding: "But my husband could not have been implicated in it, since he is in prison."

Did not this objection, forestalling, as it were, suspicion, betray the most horrible apprehensions?

"Yes, I am aware of that," replied Lecoq. "Polyte was arrested a fortnight ago—"

"Yes, and very unjustly, sir," replied the neglected wife. "He was led astray by his companions, wicked, desperate men. He is so weak when he has taken a glass of wine that they can do whatever they like with him. If he were only left to himself he would not harm a child. You have only to look at him—"

As she spoke, the virtuous Toinon turned her red and swollen eyes to a miserable photograph hanging against the wall. This blotchy smudge portrayed an exceedingly ugly, dissipated-looking young man, afflicted with a terrible squint, and whose repulsive mouth was partially concealed by a faint mustache. This rake of the barrieres was Polyte Chupin. And yet despite his unprepossessing aspect there was no mistaking the fact that this unfortunate woman loved him—had always loved him; besides, he was her husband.

A moment's silence followed her indication of the portrait— an act which clearly revealed how deeply she worshiped her persecutor; and during this pause the attic door slowly and softly opened. Not of itself, however, for suddenly a man's head peered in. The intruder, whoever he was, instantly withdrew, uttering as he did so a low exclamation. The door was swiftly closed again; the key—which had been left on the outside—grated in the lock, and the occupants of the garret could hear hurried steps descending the stairs.

Lecoq was sitting with his back to the door, and could not, therefore, see the intruder's face. Quickly as he had turned, he had failed to see who it was: and yet he was far from being surprised at the incident. Intuition explained its meaning.

"That must have been the accomplice!" he cried.

Thanks to his position, Father Absinthe had seen the man's face. "Yes," said he, "yes, it was the same man who made me drink with him yesterday."

With a bound, both detectives threw themselves against the door, exhausting their strength in vain attempts to open it. It resisted all their efforts, for it was of solid oak, having been purchased by the landlord from some public building in process of demolition, and it was, moreover, furnished with a strong and massive fastening.

"Help us!" cried Father Absinthe to the woman, who stood petrified with astonishment; "give us a bar, a piece of iron, a nail—anything!"

The younger man was making frantic efforts to push back the bolt, or to force the lock from the wood. He was wild with rage. At last, having succeeded in forcing the door open, they dashed out in pursuit of their mysterious adversary. On reaching the street, they eagerly questioned the bystanders. Having described the man as best they could, they found two persons who had seen him enter the house of Toinon the Virtuous, and a third who had seen him as he left. Some children who were playing in the middle of the street added that he had run off in the direction of the Rue du Moulin-des-Pres as fast as his legs could carry him. It was in this street, near the corner of the Rue de la Butte-aux-Cailles, that Lecoq had left old Papillon waiting with the cab.

"Let us hasten there!" proposed Father Absinthe; "perhaps Papillon can give us some information."

But Lecoq shook his head despondingly. He would go no further. "It would be of no use," he said. "He had sufficient presence of mind to turn the key in the lock, and that saved him. He is at least ten minutes in advance of us, and we should never overtake him."

Father Absinthe could not restrain his anger. He looked upon this mysterious accomplice who had so cruelly duped him as a personal enemy, and he would willingly have given a month's pay to be able to lay his hand on his shoulder. Lecoq was quite as angry as his subordinate, and his vanity was likewise wounded; he felt, however, that coolness and deliberation were necessary.

"Yes," said he thoughtfully, "he's a shrewd and daring fellow—a perfect demon. He doesn't remain idle. If we are working, he's at work too. No matter what side I turn, I find him on the defensive. He foiled you, papa, in your effort to obtain a clue concerning Gustave's identity; and he made me appear a fool in arranging that little comedy at the Hotel de Mariembourg. His diligence has been wonderful. He has hitherto been in advance of us everywhere, and this fact explains the failures that have attended all my efforts. Here we arrive before him. But if he came here, it was because he scented danger. Hence, we may hope. Now let us get back and question Polyte's wife."

Alas! poor Toinon the Virtuous did not understand the affair at all. She had remained upstairs, holding her child by the hand, and leaning over the baluster; her mind in great perplexity and her eyes and ears on the alert. As soon as she perceived the two detectives coming up the stairs again, she hastened down to meet them. "In the name of heaven, what does this all mean?" she asked. "Whatever has happened?"

But Lecoq was not the man to tell his business on a landing, with inquisitive ears all around him, and before he answered Toinon he made her go up into her own garret, and securely close the door.

"We started in pursuit of a man who is implicated in the murders at the Poivriere," he said; "one who came here hoping to find you alone, who was frightened at seeing us."

"A murderer!" faltered Toinon, with clasped hands. "What could he want of me?"

"Who knows? It is very probable that he is one of your husband's friends."

"Oh! sir."

"Why, did you not tell me just now that Polyte had some very undesirable acquaintances? But don't be alarmed; this does not compromise him in the least. Besides, you can very easily clear him of all suspicion."

"How? In what way? Oh, tell me at once."

"Merely by answering me frankly, and by assisting me to find the guilty party. Now, among your husband's friends, don't you know any who might be capable of such a deed? Give me the names of his acquaintances."

The poor woman's hesitation was evident; undoubtedly she had been present at many sinister cabals, and had been threatened with terrible punishment if she dared to disclose the plans formed by Polyte or his associates.

"You have nothing to fear," said Lecoq, encouragingly, "and I promise you no one shall ever know that you have told me a word. Very probably you can tell me nothing more than I know already. I have heard a great deal about your former life, and the brutality with which Polyte and his mother have treated you."

"My husband has never treated me brutally," said the young woman, indignantly; "besides, that matter would only concern myself."

"And your mother-in-law?"

"She is, perhaps, a trifle quick-tempered; but in reality she has a good heart."

"Then, if you were so happy at the Widow Chupin's house, why did you fly from it?"

Toinon the Virtuous turned scarlet to the very roots of her hair. "I left for other reasons," she replied. "There were always a great many drunken men about the house; and, sometimes, when I was alone, some of them tried to carry their pleasantry too far. You may say that I have a solid fist of my own, and that I am quite capable of protecting myself. That's true. But while I was away one day some fellows were wicked enough to make this child drink to such an excess that when I came home I found him as stiff and cold as if he were dead. It was necessary to fetch a doctor or else—"

She suddenly paused; her eyes dilated. From red she turned livid, and in a hoarse, unnatural voice, she cried: "Toto! wretched child!"

Lecoq looked behind him, and shuddered. He understood everything. This child—not yet five years old—had stolen up behind him, and, ferreting in the pockets of his overcoat, had rifled them of their contents.

"Ah, well—yes!" exclaimed the unfortunate mother, bursting into tears. "That's how it was. Directly the child was out of my sight, they used to take him into town. They took him into the crowded streets, and taught him to pick people's pockets, and bring them everything he could lay his hands on. If the child was detected they were angry with him and beat him; and if he succeeded they gave him a sou to buy some sweets, and kept what he had taken."

The luckless Toinon hid her face in her hands, and sobbed in an almost unintelligible voice: "Ah, I did not wish my little one to be a thief."

But what this poor creature did not tell was that the man who had led the child out into the streets, to teach him to steal, was his own father, and her husband—the ruffian, Polyte Chupin. The two detectives plainly understood, however, that such was the case, and the father's crime was so horrible, and the woman's grief so great, that, familiar as they were with all the phases of crime, their very hearts were touched. Lecoq's main thought, however, was to shorten this painful scene. The poor mother's emotion was a sufficient guarantee of her sincerity.

"Listen," said he, with affected harshness. "Two questions only, and then I will leave you. Was there a man named Gustave among the frequenters of the Poivriere?"

"No, sir, I'm quite sure there wasn't."

"Very well. But Lacheneur—you must know Lacheneur!"

"Yes, sir; I know him."

The young police agent could not repress an exclamation of delight. "At last," thought he, "I have a clue that may lead me to the truth. What kind of man is he?" he asked with intense anxiety.

"Oh! he is not at all like the other men who come to drink

at my mother-in-law's shop. I have only seen him once; but I remember him perfectly. It was on a Sunday. He was in a cab. He stopped at the corner of the waste ground and spoke to Polyte. When he went away, my husband said to me: 'Do you see that old man there? he will make all our fortunes.' I thought him a very respectable-looking gentleman—"

"That's enough," interrupted Lecoq. "Now it is necessary for you to tell the investigating magistrate all you know about him. I have a cab downstairs. Take your child with you, if you like; but make haste; come, come quickly!"

XVI

M. SEGMULLER was one of those magistrates whose profession is their only love, and who devote to its duties all the energy, intelligence, and sagacity they possess. As an investigator, he displayed, in his constant searches after truth, the same tenacity and zeal that distinguishes a conscientious physician struggling against some unknown disease, the same enthusiasm that is shown by the artist, enamored of the beautiful, who seeks to realize the ideal of art. Hence, it is easy to understand how greatly this mysterious case attracted and interested him. The magnitude of the crime, the peculiar circumstances attending it, the mystery that enshrouded the identity of both the victims and the murderer, the strange attitude the latter had assumed, everything combined to make a profound impression on his mind. Even the romantic element was not lacking in this strange case; being represented by the two women who had disappeared.

The extreme uncertainty of the result was another attraction for M. Segmuller's investigating mind. Given the magnitude of the difficulties that were to be overcome, he rightly considered that if his efforts proved successful, he would have achieved a really wonderful victory. And, assisted by such a man as Lecoq, who had a positive genius for his calling, and in whom he recognized a most valuable auxiliary, he really felt confident of ultimate success.

Even on returning home after the fatiguing labors of the day he did not think of freeing himself from the burden of responsibility in relation to the business he had on hand, or of driving away care until the morrow. He dined in haste, and as soon as he had swallowed his coffee began to study the case with renewed ardor. He had brought from his office a copy of the prisoner's narrative, which he attentively perused, not once or twice, but several times, seeking for some weak point that might be attacked with a probability of success. He analyzed every answer, and weighed one expression after another, striving, as he did so, to find some flaw through which he might slip a question calculated to shatter the structure of defense. He worked thus, far into the night, and yet he was on his legs again at an early hour in the morning. By eight o'clock he was not merely dressed and shaved, he had not merely taken his matutinal chocolate and arranged his papers, but he was actually on his way to the Palais de Justice. He had quite forgotten that his own impatience was not shared by others.

In point of fact, the Palais de Justice was scarcely awake when he arrived there. The doors had barely opened. The attendants were busy sweeping and dusting; or changing their ordinary garments for their official costumes. Some of them standing in the windows of the long dressing room were shaking and brushing the judges' and advocates' gowns; while in the great hall several clerks stood in a group, chaffing each other while waiting for the arrival of the head registrar and the opening of the investigation offices.

M. Segmuller thought that he had better begin by consulting the public prosecutor, but he discovered that this functionary had not yet arrived. Angry and impatient, he proceeded to his own office; and with his eyes fixed on the clock, growled at the slowness of the minute hand. Just after nine o'clock, Goguet, the smiling clerk, put in an appearance and speedily learned the kind of humor his master was in.

"Ah, you've come at last," gruffly ejaculated M. Segmuller, momentarily oblivious of the fact that he himself scarcely ever arrived before ten, and that a quarter-past nine was certainly early for his clerk.

Goguet's curiosity had indeed prompted him to hurry to the Palais; still, although well aware that he did not deserve a reprimand, he endeavored to mumble an excuse—an excuse cut short by M. Segmuller in such unusually harsh tones that for once in a way Goguet's habitual smile faded from his face. "It's evident," thought he, "that the wind's blowing from a bad quarter this morning," with which reflection he philosophically put on his black sleeves and going to his table pretended to be absorbed in the task of mending his pens and preparing his paper.

In the mean while, M. Segmuller who was usually calmness personified, and dignity *par excellence,* paced restlessly to and fro. At times he would sit down and then suddenly spring to his feet again, gesticulating impatiently as he did so. Indeed, he seemed unable to remain quiet for a moment.

"The prosecution is evidently making no headway," thought the clerk. "May's prospects are encouraging." Owing to the magistrate's harsh reception the idea delighted him; and, indeed, letting his rancor have the upper hand, Goguet actually offered up a prayer that the prisoner might get the better of the fight.

From half-past nine till ten o'clock M. Segmuller rang for his messenger at least five times, and each time he asked him the same questions: "Are you sure that M. Lecoq has not been here this morning? Inquire! If he has not been here he must certainly have sent some one, or else have written to me."

Each time the astonished doorkeeper replied: "No one has been here, and there is no letter for you."

Five identical negative answers to the same inquiries only increased the magistrate's wrath and impatience. "It is inconceivable!" he exclaimed. "Here I am upon coals of fire, and that man dares to keep me waiting. Where can he be?"

At last he ordered a messenger to go and see if he could not find Lecoq somewhere in the neighborhood; perhaps in some restaurant or café. "At all events, he must be found and brought back immediately," said he.

When the man had started, M. Segmuller began to recover his composure. "We must not lose valuable time," he said to his clerk. "I was to examine the widow Chupin's son. I had better do so now. Go and tell them to bring him to me. Lecoq left the order at the prison."

In less than a quarter of an hour Polyte entered the room. From head to foot, from his lofty silk cap to his gaudy colored carpet slippers, he was indeed the original of the portrait upon which poor Toinon the Virtuous had lavished such loving glances. And yet the photograph was flattering. The lens had failed to convey the expression of low cunning that distinguished the man's features, the impudence of his leering smile, and the mingled cowardice and ferocity of his eyes, which never looked another person in the face. Nor could the portrait depict the unwholesome, livid pallor of his skin, the restless blinking of his eyelids, and the constant movement of his thin lips as he drew them tightly over his short, sharp teeth. There was no mistaking his nature; one glance and he was estimated at his worth.

When he had answered the preliminary questions, telling the magistrate that he was thirty years of age, and that he had been born in Paris, he assumed a pretentious attitude and waited to see what else was coming.

But before proceeding with the real matter in hand, M. Segmuller wished to relieve the complacent scoundrel of some of his insulting assurance. Accordingly, he reminded Polyte, in forcible terms, that his sentence in the affair in which he was now implicated would depend very much upon his behavior and answers during the present examination.

Polyte listened with a nonchalant and even ironical air. In fact, this indirect threat scarcely touched him. Having previously made inquiries he had ascertained that he could not be condemned to more than six months' imprisonment for the offense for which he had been arrested; and what did a month more or less matter to him?

The magistrate, who read this thought in Polyte's eyes, cut his preamble short. "Justice," said he, "now requires some information from you concerning the frequenters of your mother's establishment."

"There are a great many of them, sir," answered Polyte in a harsh voice.

"Do you know one of them named Gustave?"

"No, sir."

To insist would probably awaken suspicion in Polyte's mind; accordingly, M. Segmuller continued: "You must, however, remember Lacheneur?"

"Lacheneur? No, this is the first time I've heard that name."

"Take care. The police have means of finding out a great many things."

The scapegrace did not flinch. "I am telling the truth, sir," he retorted. "What interest could I possibly have in deceiving you?"

Scarcely had he finished speaking than the door suddenly opened and Toinon the Virtuous entered the room, carrying her child in her arms. On perceiving her husband, she uttered a joyful exclamation, and sprang toward him. But Polyte, stepping back, gave her such a threatening glance that she remained rooted to the spot.

"It must be an enemy who pretends that I know any one named Lacheneur!" cried the barriere bully. "I should like to kill the person who uttered such a falsehood. Yes, kill him; I will never forgive it."

The messenger whom M. Segmuller had instructed to go in search of Lecoq was not at all displeased with the errand; for it enabled him to leave his post and take a pleasant little stroll through the neighborhood. He first of all proceeded to the Prefecture of Police, going the longest way round as a matter of course, but, on reaching his destination, he could find no one who had seen the young detective.

Accordingly, M. Segmuller's envoy retraced his steps, and leisurely sauntered through the restaurants, cafés, and wine shops installed in the vicinity of the Palais de Justice, and dependent on the customers it brought them. Being of a conscientious turn of mind, he entered each establishment in succession and meeting now and again various acquaintances, he felt compelled to proffer and accept numerous glasses of the favorite morning beverage—white wine. Turn which way he would, however, loiter as long as he might, there were still no signs of Lecoq. He was returning in haste, a trifle uneasy on account of the length of his absence, when he perceived a cab pull up in front of the Palais gateway. A second glance, and oh, great good fortune, he saw Lecoq, Father Absinthe, and the virtuous Toinon alight from this very vehicle. His peace of mind at once returned; and it was in a very important and somewhat husky tone that he delivered the order for Lecoq to follow him without a minute's delay. "M. Segmuller has asked for you a number of times," said he, "He has been extremely impatient, and he is in a very bad humor, so you may expect to have your head snapped off in the most expeditious manner."

Lecoq smiled as he went up the stairs. Was he not bringing with him the most potent of justifications? He thought of the agreeable surprise he had in store for the magistrate, and fancied he could picture the sudden brightening of that functionary's gloomy face.

And yet, fate so willed it that the doorkeeper's message and his urgent appeal that Lecoq should not loiter on the way, produced the most unfortunate results. Believing that M. Segmuller was anxiously waiting for him, Lecoq saw nothing wrong in opening the door of the magistrate's room without previously knocking; and being anxious to justify his absence, he yielded, moreover, to the impulse that led him to push forward the poor woman whose testimony might prove so decisive. When he saw, however, that the magistrate was not alone, and when he recognized Polyte Chupin—the original of the photograph—in the man M. Segmuller was examining, his stupefaction became intense. He instantly perceived his mistake and understood its consequences.

There was only one thing to be done: He must prevent any exchange of words between the two. Accordingly, springing toward Toinon and seizing her roughly by the arm, he ordered her to leave the room at once. But the poor creature was quite overcome, and trembled like a leaf. Her eyes were fixed upon her unworthy husband, and the happiness she felt at seeing him again shone plainly in her anxious gaze. Just for one second; and then she caught his withering glance and heard his words of menace. Terror-stricken, she staggered back, and then Lecoq seized her around the waist, and, lifting her with his strong arms, carried her out into the passage. The whole scene had been so brief that M. Segmuller was still forming the order for Toinon to be removed from the room, when he found the door closed again, and himself and Goguet alone with Polyte.

"Ah, ah!" thought the smiling clerk, in a flutter of delight, "this is something new." But as these little diversions never made him forget his duties, he leaned toward the magistrate and asked: "Shall I take down the last words the witness uttered?"

"Certainly," replied M. Segmuller, "and word for word, if you please."

He paused; the door opened again, this time to admit the magistrate's messenger, who timidly, and with a rather guilty air, handed his master a note, and then withdrew. This note, scribbled in pencil by Lecoq on a leaf torn from his memorandum book, gave the magistrate the name of the woman who had just entered his room, and recapitulated briefly but clearly the information obtained in the Rue de la Butte-aux-Cailles.

"That young fellow thinks of everything!" murmured M.

Segmuller. The meaning of the scene that had just occurred was now explained to him. He understood everything.

He bitterly regretted this unfortunate meeting; at the same time casting the blame on his own impatience and lack of caution, which, as soon as the messenger had started in search of Lecoq, had induced him to summon Polyte Chupin. Although he could not conceal from himself the enormous influence this seemingly trivial incident might have, still he would not allow himself to be cast down, but prepared to resume his examination of Polyte Chupin in hopes of yet obtaining the information he desired.

"Let us proceed," he said to Polyte, who had not moved since his wife had been taken from the room, being to all appearances sublimely indifferent to everything passing around him. To the magistrate's proposal he carelessly nodded assent.

"Was that your wife who came in just now?" asked M. Segmuller.

"Yes."

"She wished to embrace you, and you repulsed her."

"I didn't repulse her."

"You kept her at a distance at all events. If you had a spark of affection in your nature, you would at least have looked at your child, which she held out to you. Why did you behave in that manner?"

"It wasn't the time for sentiment."

"You are not telling the truth. You simply desired to attract her attention, to influence her evidence."

"I—I influence her evidence! I don't understand you."

"But for that supposition, your words would have been meaningless?"

"What words?"

The magistrate turned to his clerk: "Goguet," said he, "read the last remark you took down."

In a monotonous voice, the smiling clerk repeated: "I should like to kill the person who dared to say that I knew Lacheneur."

"Well, then!" insisted M. Segmuller, "what did you mean by that?"

"It's very easy to understand, sir."

M. Segmuller rose. "Don't prevaricate any longer," he said. "You certainly ordered your wife not to say anything about Lacheneur. That's evident. Why did you do so? What are you afraid of her telling us? Do you suppose the police are ignorant of your acquaintance with Lacheneur—of your conversation with him when he came in a cab to the corner of the waste ground near your mother's wine-shop; and of the hopes of fortune you based upon his promises? Be guided by me; confess everything, while there is yet time; and abandon the present course which may lead you into serious danger. One may be an accomplice in more ways than one."

As these words fell on Polyte's ears, it was evident his impudence and indifference had received a severe shock. He seemed confounded, and hung his head as if thoroughly abashed. Still, he preserved an obstinate silence; and the magistrate finding that this last thrust had failed to produce any effect, gave up the fight in despair. He rang the bell, and ordered the guard to conduct the witness back to prison, and to take every precaution to prevent him seeing his wife again.

When Polyte had departed, Lecoq reentered the room. "Ah, sir," said he, despondently, "to think that I didn't draw out of this woman everything she knew, when I might have done so easily. But I thought you would be waiting for me, and made haste to bring her here. I thought I was acting for the best—"

"Never mind, the misfortune can be repaired."

"No, sir, no. Since she has seen her husband, it is quite impossible to get her to speak. She loves that rascal intensely, and he has a wonderful influence over her. You heard what he said. He threatened her with death if she breathed a word about Lacheneur, and she is so terrified that there is no hope of making her speak."

Lecoq's apprehension was based on fact, as M. Segmuller himself perceived the instant Toinon the Virtuous again set foot in his office. The poor creature seemed nearly heartbroken, and it was evident she would have given her life to retract the words that had escaped her when first questioned by Lecoq. Polyte's threat had aroused the most sinister apprehensions in her mind. Not understanding his connection with the affair, she asked herself if her testimony might not prove his death-warrant. Accordingly, she answered all M. Segmuller's questions with "no" or "I don't know"; and retracted everything she had previously stated to Lecoq. She swore that she had been misunderstood, that her words had been misconstrued; and vowed on her mother's memory, that she had never heard the name of Lacheneur before. At last, she burst into wild, despairing sobs, and pressed her frightened child against her breast.

What could be done to overcome this foolish obstinacy, as blind and unreasoning as a brute's? M. Segmuller hesitated. "You may retire, my good woman," said he kindly, after a moment's pause, "but remember that your strange silence injures your husband far more than anything you could say."

She left the room—or rather she rushed wildly from it as though only too eager to escape—and the magistrate and the detective exchanged glances of dismay and consternation.

"I said so before," thought Goguet, "the prisoner knows what he's about. I would be willing to bet a hundred to one in his favor."

A French investigating magistrate is possessed of almost unlimited powers. No one can hamper him, no one can give him orders. The entire police force is at his disposal. One word from him and twenty agents, or a hundred if need be, search Paris, ransack France, or explore Europe. If there be any one whom he believes able to throw light upon an obscure point, he simply sends an order to that person to appear before him, and the man must come even if he lives a hundred leagues away.

Such is the magistrate, such are his powers. On the other hand, the prisoner charged with a crime, but as yet unconvicted, is confined, unless his offense be of a trivial description, in what is called a "secret cell." He is, so to say, cut off from the number of the living. He knows nothing of what may be going on in the world outside. He can not tell what witnesses may have been called, or what they may have said, and in his uncertainty he asks himself again and again how far the prosecution has been able to establish the charges against him.

Such is the prisoner's position, and yet despite the fact that the two adversaries are so unequally armed, the man in the secret cell not unfrequently wins the victory. If he is sure that he has left behind him no proof of his having committed the crime; if he has no guilty antecedents to be afraid of, he can—impregnable in a defense of absolute denial—brave all the attacks of justice.

Such was, at this moment, the situation of May, the mysterious murderer; as both M. Segmuller and Lecoq were forced to admit, with mingled grief and anger. They had hoped to arrive at a solution of the problem by examining Polyte Chupin and his wife, and they had been disappointed; for the prisoner's identity remained as problematical as ever.

"And yet," exclaimed the magistrate impatiently, "these people know something about this matter, and if they would only speak—"

"But they won't."

"What motive is it that keeps them silent? This is what we must discover. Who will tell us the price that has been promised Polyte Chupin for his silence? What recompense can he count upon? It must be a great one, for he is braving real danger!"

Lecoq did not immediately reply to the magistrate's successive queries, but it was easy to see from his knit brows that his mind was hard at work. "You ask me, sir," he eventually remarked, "*what* reward has been promised Chupin? I ask on my part *who* can have promised him this reward?"

"Who has promised it? Why, plainly the accomplice who has beaten us on every point."

"Yes," rejoined Lecoq, "I suppose it must have been he. It certainly looks like his handiwork—now, what artifice can he have used? We know how he managed to have an interview with the Widow Chupin, but how has he succeeded in getting at Polyte, who is in prison, closely watched?"

The young detective's insinuation, vague as it was, did not escape M. Segmuller. "What do you mean?" asked the latter, with an air of mingled surprise and indignation. "You can't suppose that one of the keepers has been bribed?"

Lecoq shook his head, in a somewhat equivocal manner. "I mean nothing," he replied, "I don't suspect any one. All I want is information. Has Chupin been forewarned or not?"

"Yes, of course he has."

"Then if that point is admitted it can only be explained in two ways. Either there are informers in the prison, or else Chupin has been allowed to see some visitor."

These suppositions evidently worried M. Segmuller, who for a moment seemed to hesitate between the two opinions; then, suddenly making up his mind, he rose from his chair, took up his hat, and said: "This matter must be cleared up. Come with me, Monsieur Lecoq."

A couple of minutes later, the magistrate and the detective

had reached the Depot, which is connected with the Palais de Justice by a narrow passage, especially reserved for official use. The prisoners' morning rations had just been served to them, and the governor was walking up and down the courtyard, in the company of Inspector Gevrol. As soon as he perceived M. Segmuller he hastened toward him and asked if he had not come about the prisoner May.

As the magistrate nodded assent, the governor at once added: "Well I was only just now telling Inspector Gevrol that I was very well satisfied with May's behavior. It has not only been quite unnecessary to place him in the strait-waistcoat again, but his mood seems to have changed entirely. He eats with a good appetite; he is as gay as a lark, and he constantly laughs and jests with his keeper."

Gevrol had pricked up his ears when he heard himself named by the governor, and considering this mention to be a sufficient introduction, he thought there would be no impropriety in his listening to the conversation. Accordingly, he approached the others, and noted with some satisfaction the troubled glances which Lecoq and the magistrate exchanged.

M. Segmuller was plainly perplexed. May's gay manner to which the governor of the Depot alluded might perhaps have been assumed for the purpose of sustaining his character as a jester and buffoon, it might be due to a certainty of defeating the judicial inquiry, or, who knows? the prisoner had perhaps received some favorable news from outside.

With Lecoq's last words still ringing in his ears, it is no wonder that the magistrate should have dwelt on this last supposition. "Are you quite sure," he asked, "that no communication from outside can reach the inmates of the secret cells?"

The governor of the Depot was cut to the quick by M. Segmuller's implied doubt. What! were his subordinates suspected? Was his own professional honesty impugned? He could not help lifting his hands to heaven in mute protest against such an unjust charge.

"Am I sure?" he exclaimed. "Then you can never have visited the secret cells. You have no idea, then, of their situation; you are unacquainted with the triple bolts that secure the doors; the grating that shuts out the sunlight, to say nothing of the guard who walks beneath the windows day and night. Why, a bird couldn't even reach the prisoners in those cells."

Such a description was bound to reassure the most skeptical mind, and M. Segmuller breathed again: "Now that I am easy on that score," said he, "I should like some information about another prisoner—a fellow named Chupin, who isn't in the secret cells. I want to know if any visitor came for him yesterday."

"I must speak to the registrar," replied the governor, "before I can answer you with certainty. Wait a moment though, here comes a man who can perhaps tell us. He is usually on guard at the entrance. Here, Ferraud, this way!"

The man to whom the governor called hastened to obey the summons.

"Do you know whether any one asked to see the prisoner Chupin yesterday?"

"Yes, sir, I went to fetch Chupin to the parlor myself."

"And who was his visitor?" eagerly asked Lecoq, "wasn't he a tall man; very red in the face—"

"Excuse me, sir, the visitor was a lady—his aunt, at least so Chupin told me."

Neither M. Segmuller nor Lecoq could restrain an exclamation of surprise. "What was she like?" they both asked at the same time.

"She was short," replied the attendant, "with a very fair complexion and light hair; she seemed to be a very respectable woman."

"It must have been one of the female fugitives who escaped from the Widow Chupin's hovel," exclaimed Lecoq.

Gevrol, hitherto an attentive listener, burst into a loud laugh. "Still that Russian princess," said he.

Neither the magistrate nor the young detective relished this unseasonable jest. "You forget yourself, sir," said M. Segmuller severely. "You forget that the sneers you address to your comrade also apply to me!"

The General saw that he had gone too far; and while glancing hatefully at Lecoq, he mumbled an apology to the magistrate. The latter did not apparently hear him, for, bowing to the governor, he motioned Lecoq to follow him away.

"Run to the Prefecture of Police," he said as soon as they were out of hearing, "and ascertain how and under what pretext this woman obtained permission to see Polyte Chupin."

XVII

ON his way back to his office, M. Segmuller mentally reviewed the position of affairs; and came to the conclusion that as he had failed to take the citadel of defense by storm, he must resign himself to a regular protracted siege. He was exceedingly annoyed at the constant failures that had attended all Lecoq's efforts; for time was on the wing, and he knew that in a criminal investigation delay only increased the uncertainty of success. The more promptly a crime is followed by judicial action the easier it is to find the culprit, and prove his guilt. The longer investigation is delayed the more difficult it becomes to adduce conclusive evidence.

In the present instance there were various matters that M. Segmuller might at once attend to. With which should he begin? Ought he not to confront May, the Widow Chupin, and Polyte with the bodies of their victims? Such horrible meetings have at times the most momentous results, and more than one murderer when unsuspectedly brought into the presence of his victim's lifeless corpse has changed color and lost his assurance.

Then there were other witnesses whom M. Segmuller might examine. Papillon, the cab-driver; the concierge of the house in the Rue de Bourgogne—where the two women flying from the Poivriere had momentarily taken refuge; as well as a certain Madame Milner, landlady of the Hotel de Mariembourg. In addition, it would also be advisable to summon, with the least possible delay, some of the people residing in the vicinity of the Poivriere; together with some of Polyte's habitual companions, and the landlord of the Rainbow, where the victims and the murderer had apparently passed the evening of the crime. Of course, there was no reason to expect any great revelations from any of these witnesses, still they might know something, they might have an opinion to express, and in the present darkness one single ray of light, however faint, might mean salvation.

Obeying the magistrate's orders, Goguet, the smiling clerk, had just finished drawing up at least a dozen summonses, when Lecoq returned from the Prefecture. M. Segmuller at once asked him the result of his errand.

"Ah, sir," replied the young detective, "I have a fresh proof of that mysterious accomplice's skill. The permit that was used yesterday to see young Chupin was in the name of his mother's sister, a woman named Rose Pitard. A visiting card was given her more than a week ago, in compliance with a request indorsed by the commissary of police of her district."

The magistrate's surprise was so intense that it imparted to his face an almost ludicrous expression. "Is this aunt also in the plot?" he murmured.

"I don't think so," replied Lecoq, shaking his head. "At all events, it wasn't she who went to the prison parlor yesterday. The clerks at the Prefecture remember the widow's sister very well, and gave me a full description of her. She's a woman over five feet high, with a very dark complexion; and very wrinkled and weatherbeaten about the face. She's quite sixty years old; whereas, yesterday's visitor was short and fair, and not more than forty-five."

"If that's the case," interrupted M. Segmuller, "this visitor must be one of our fugitives."

"I don't think so."

"Who do you suppose she was, then?"

"Why, the landlady of the Hotel de Mariembourg—that clever woman who succeeded so well in deceiving me. But she had better take care! There are means of verifying my suspicions."

The magistrate scarcely heard Lecoq's last words, so enraged was he at the inconceivable audacity and devotion displayed by so many people: all of whom were apparently willing to run the greatest risks so long as they could only assure the murderer's incognito.

"But how could the accomplice have known of the existence of this permit?" he asked after a pause.

"Oh, nothing could be easier, sir," replied Lecoq. "When the Widow Chupin and the accomplice had that interview at the station-house near the Barriere d'Italie, they both realized the necessity of warning Polyte. While trying to devise some means of getting to him, the old woman remembered her sister's visiting card, and the man made some excuse to borrow it."

"Yes, such must be the case," said M. Segmuller, approvingly. "It will be necessary to ascertain, however—"

"And I *will* ascertain," interrupted Lecoq, with a resolute air, "if you will only intrust the matter to me, sir. If you will authorize me I will have two spies on the watch before to-night, one in the Rue de la Butte-aux-Cailles, and the other at the door of the Hotel de Mariembourg. If the accomplice ventured to visit Toinon or Madame Milner he would be arrested; and then we should have our turn!"

However, there was no time to waste in vain words and idle boasting. Lecoq therefore checked himself, and took up his hat preparatory to departure. "Now," said he, "I must ask you, sir, for my liberty; if you have any orders, you will find a trusty messenger in the corridor, Father Absinthe, one of my colleagues. I want to find out something about Lacheneur's letter and the diamond earring."

"Go, then," replied M. Segmuller, "and good luck to you!"

Good luck! Yes, indeed, Lecoq looked for it. If up to the present moment he had taken his successive defeats good-humoredly, it was because he believed that he had a talisman in his pocket which was bound to insure ultimate victory.

"I shall be very stupid if I can't discover the owner of such a valuable jewel," he soliloquized, referring to the diamond earring. "And when I find the owner I shall at the same time discover our mysterious prisoner's identity."

The first step to be taken was to ascertain whom the earring had been bought from. It would naturally be a tedious process to go from jeweler to jeweler and ask: "Do you know this jewel, was it set by you, and if so whom did you sell it to?" But fortunately Lecoq was acquainted with a man whose knowledge of the trade might at once throw light on the matter. This individual was an old Hollander, named Van Numen, who, as a connoisseur in precious stones, was probably without his rival in Paris. He was employed by the Prefecture of Police as an expert in all such matters. He was considered rich. Despite his shabby appearance, he was rightly considered rich, and, in point of fact, he was indeed far more wealthy than people generally supposed. Diamonds were his especial passion, and he always had several in his pocket, in a little box which he would pull out and open at least a dozen times an hour, just as a snuff-taker continually produces his snuff-box.

This worthy man greeted Lecoq very affably. He put on his glasses, examined the jewel with a grimace of satisfaction, and, in the tone of an oracle, remarked: "That stone is worth eight thousand francs, and it was set by Doisty, in the Rue de la Paix."

Twenty minutes later Lecoq entered this well-known jeweler's establishment. Van Numen had not been mistaken. Doisty immediately recognized the earring, which had, indeed, come from his shop. But whom had he sold it to? He could not recollect, for it had passed out of his hands three or four years before.

"Wait a moment though," said he, "I will just ask my wife, who has a wonderful memory."

Madame Doisty truly deserved this eulogium. A single glance at the jewel enabled her to say that she had seen this earring before, and that the pair had been purchased from them by the Marchioness d'Arlange.

"You must recollect," she added, turning to her husband, "that the Marchioness only gave us nine thousand francs on account, and that we had all the trouble in the world to make her pay the balance."

Her husband did remember this circumstance; and in recording his recollection, he exchanged a significant glance with his wife.

"Now," said the detective, "I should like to have this marchioness's address."

"She lives in the Faubourg St. Germain," replied Madame Doisty, "near the Esplanade des Invalides."

Lecoq had refrained from any sign of satisfaction while he was in the jeweler's presence. But directly he had left the shop he evinced such delirious joy that the passers-by asked themselves in amazement if he were not mad. He did not walk, but fairly danced over the stones, gesticulating in the most ridiculous fashion as he addressed this triumphant monologue to the empty air: "At last," said he, "this affair emerges from the mystery that has enshrouded it. At last I reach the veritable actors in the drama, the exalted personages whose existence I had suspected. Ah! Gevrol, my illustrious General! you talked about a Russian princess, but you will be obliged to content yourself with a simple marchioness."

But the vertigo that had seized the young detective gradually disappeared. His good sense reasserted itself, and, looking calmly at the situation, he felt that he should need all his presence of mind, penetration, and sagacity to bring the expedition to a successful finish. What course should he pursue, on entering the marchioness's presence, in order to draw from her a full confession and to obtain full particulars of the murder, as well as the murderer's name!

"It will be best to threaten her, to frighten her into confession," he soliloquized. "If I give her time for reflection, I shall learn nothing."

He paused in his cogitations, for he had reached the residence of the Marchioness d'Arlange—a charming mansion with a courtyard in front and garden in the rear. Before entering, he deemed it advisable to obtain some information concerning the inmates.

"It is here, then," he murmured, "that I am to find the solution of the enigma! Here, behind these embroidered curtains, dwells the frightened fugitive of the other night. What agony of fear must torture her since she has discovered the loss of her earring!"

For more than an hour, standing under a neighbor's *porte cochere*, Lecoq remained watching the house. He would have liked to see the face of any one; but the time passed by and not even a shadow could be detected behind the curtain; not even a servant passed across the courtyard. At last, losing patience, the young detective determined to make inquiries in the neighborhood, for he could not take a decisive step without obtaining some knowledge of the people he was to encounter. While wondering where he could obtain the information he required, he perceived, on the opposite side of the street, the keeper of a wine-shop smoking on his doorstep.

At once approaching and pretending that he had forgotten an address, Lecoq politely asked for the house where Marchioness d'Arlange resided. Without a word, and without condescending to take his pipe from his mouth, the man pointed to the mansion which Lecoq had previously watched.

There was a way, however, to make him more communicative, namely, to enter the shop, call for something to drink, and invite the landlord to drink as well. This was what Lecoq did, and the sight of two well-filled glasses unbound, as by enchantment, the man's hitherto silent tongue. The young detective could not have found a better person to question, for this same individual had been established in the neighborhood for ten years, and enjoyed among the servants of the aristocratic families here residing a certain amount of confidence.

"I pity you if you are going to the marchioness's house to collect a bill," he remarked to Lecoq. "You will have plenty of time to learn the way here before you see your money. You will only be another of the many creditors who never let her bell alone."

"The deuce! Is she as poor as that?"

"Poor! Why, every one knows that she has a comfortable income, without counting this house. But when one spends double one's income every year, you know—"

The landlord stopped short, to call Lecoq's attention to two ladies who were passing along the street, one of them, a woman of forty, dressed in black; the other, a girl half-way through her teens. "There," quoth the wine-seller, "goes the marchioness's granddaughter, Mademoiselle Claire, with her governess, Mademoiselle Smith."

Lecoq's head whirled. "Her granddaughter!" he stammered.

"Yes—the daughter of her deceased son, if you prefer it."

"How old is the marchioness, then?"

"At least sixty: but one would never suspect it. She is one of those persons who live a hundred years. And what an old wretch she is too. She would think no more of knocking me over the head than I would of emptying this glass of wine—"

"Excuse me," interrupted Lecoq, "but does she live alone in that great house?"

"Yes—that is—with her granddaughter, the governess, and two servants. But what is the matter with you?"

This last question was not uncalled for; for Lecoq had turned deadly white. The magic edifice of his hopes had crumbled beneath the weight of this man's words as completely as if it were some frail house of cards erected by a child. He had only sufficient strength to murmur: "Nothing—nothing at all."

Then, as he could endure this torture of uncertainty no longer, he went toward the marchioness's house and rang the bell. The servant who came to open the door examined him attentively, and then announced that Madame d'Arlange was in the country. He evidently fancied that Lecoq was a creditor.

But the young detective insisted so adroitly, giving the lackey to understand so explicitly that he did not come to collect money, and speaking so earnestly of urgent business, that the servant finally admitted him to the hall, saying that he would go and see if madame had really gone out.

Fortunately for Lecoq, she happened to be at home, and an instant afterward the valet returned requesting the young detective to follow him. After passing through a large and magnificently furnished drawing-room, they reached a charming boudoir, hung with rose-colored curtains, where, sitting by the fireside, in a large easy-chair, Lecoq found an old woman, tall, bony, and terrible of aspect, her face loaded with paint, and her person covered with ornaments. This aged coquette was Madame, the Marchioness, who, for the time being, was engaged in knitting a stripe of green wool. She turned toward her visitor just enough to show him the rouge on one cheek, and then, as he seemed rather frightened—a fact flattering to her vanity—she spoke in an affable tone. "Ah, well! young man," said she, "what brings you here?"

In point of fact, Lecoq was not frightened, but he was intensely disappointed to find that Madame d'Arlange could not possibly be one of the women who had escaped from the Widow Chupin's hovel on the night of the murder. There was nothing about her appearance that corresponded in the least degree with the descriptions given by Papillon.

Remembering the small footprints left in the snow by the two fugitives, the young detective glanced, moreover, at the marchioness's feet, just perceivable beneath her skirt, and his disappointment reached its climax when he found that they were truly colossal in size.

"Well, are you dumb?" inquired the old lady, raising her voice.

Without making a direct reply, Lecoq produced the precious earring, and, placing it upon the table beside the marchioness, remarked: "I bring you this jewel, madame, which I have found, and which, I am told, belongs to you."

Madame de'Arlange laid down her knitting and proceeded to examine the earring. "It is true," she said, after a moment, "that this ornament formerly belonged to me. It was a fancy I had, about four years ago, and it cost me dear—at least twenty thousand francs. Ah! Doisty, the man who sold me those diamonds, must make a handsome income. But I had a granddaughter to educate! and pressing need of money compelled me to sell them."

"To whom?" asked Lecoq, eagerly.

"Eh?" exclaimed the old lady, evidently shocked at his audacity, "you are very inquisitive upon my word!"

"Excuse me, madame, but I am anxious to find the owner of this valuable ornament."

Madame d'Arlange regarded her visitor with an air of mingled curiosity and surprise. "Such honesty!" said she. "Oh, oh! And of course you don't hope for a sou by way of reward—"

"Madame!"

"Good, good! There is not the least need for you to turn as red as a poppy, young man. I sold these diamonds to a great Austrian lady—the Baroness de Watchau."

"And where does this lady reside?"

"At the Pere la Chaise, probably, since she died about a year ago. Ah! these women of the present day—an extra waltz, or the merest draft, and it's all over with them! In my time, after each gallop, we girls used to swallow a tumbler of sweetened wine, and sit down between two open doors. And we did very well, as you see."

"But, madame," insisted Lecoq, "the Baroness de Watchau must have left some one behind her—a husband, or children—"

"No one but a brother, who holds a court position at Vienna: and who could not leave even to attend the funeral. He sent orders that all his sister's personal property should be sold—not even excepting her wardrobe—and the money sent to him."

Lecoq could not repress an exclamation of disappointment. "How unfortunate!" he murmured.

"Why?" asked the old lady. "Under these circumstances, the diamond will probably remain in your hands, and I am rejoiced that it should be so. It will be a fitting reward for your honesty."

Madame d'Arlange was naturally not aware that her remark implied the most exquisite torture for Lecoq. Ah! if it should be as she said, if he should *never* find the lady who had lost this costly jewel! Smarting under the marchioness's unintended irony, he would have liked to apostrophize her in angry terms; but it could not be, for it was advisable if not absolutely necessary that he should conceal his true identity. Accordingly, he contrived to smile, and even stammered an acknowledgment of Madame d'Arlange's good wishes. Then, as if he had no more to expect, he made her a low bow and withdrew.

This new misfortune well-nigh overwhelmed him. One by

one all the threads upon which he had relied to guide him out of this intricate labyrinth were breaking in his hands. In the present instance he could scarcely be the dupe of some fresh comedy, for if the murderer's accomplice had taken Doisty, the jeweler, into his confidence he would have instructed him to say that the earring had never come from his establishment, and that he could not consequently tell whom it had been sold to. On the contrary, however, Doisty and his wife had readily given Madame d'Arlange's name, and all the circumstances pointed in favor of their sincerity. Then, again, there was good reason to believe in the veracity of the marchioness's assertions. They were sufficiently authenticated by a significant glance which Lecoq had detected between the jeweler and his wife. The meaning of this glance could not be doubted. It implied plainly that both husband and wife were of opinion that in buying these earrings the marchioness engaged in one of those little speculations which are more common than many people might suppose among ladies moving in high-class society. Being in urgent want of ready money, she had bought on credit at a high price to sell for cash at a loss.

As Lecoq was anxious to investigate the matter as far as possible, he returned to Doisty's establishment, and, by a plausible pretext, succeeded in gaining a sight of the books in which the jeweler recorded his transactions. He soon found the sale of the earrings duly recorded—specified by Madame Doisty at the date—both in the day-book and the ledger. Madame d'Arlange first paid 9,000 francs on account and the balance of the purchase money (an equivalent sum) had been received in instalments at long intervals subsequently. Now, if it had been easy for Madame Milner to make a false entry in her traveler's registry at the Hotel de Mariembourg, it was absurd to suppose that the jeweler had falsified all his accounts for four years. Hence, the facts were indisputable; and yet, the young detective was not satisfied.

He hurried to the Faubourg Saint Honore, to the house formerly occupied by the Baroness de Watchau, and there found a good-natured concierge, who at once informed him that after the Baroness's death her furniture and personal effects had been taken to the great auction mart in the Rue Drouot; the sale being conducted by M. Petit, the eminent auctioneer.

Without losing a minute, Lecoq hastened to this individual's office. M. Petit remembered the Watchau sale very well; it had made quite a sensation at the time, and on searching among his papers he soon found a long catalogue of the various articles sold. Several lots of jewelry were mentioned, with the sums paid, and the names of the purchasers; but there was not the slightest allusion to these particular earrings. When Lecoq produced the diamond he had in his pocket, the auctioneer could not remember that he had ever seen it; though of course this was no evidence to the contrary, for, as he himself remarked,—so many articles passed through his hands! However, this much he could declare upon oath; the baroness's brother, her only heir, had preserved nothing—not so much as a pin's worth of his sister's effects: although he had been in a great hurry to receive the proceeds, which amounted to the pleasant sum of one hundred and sixty-seven thousand five hundred and thirty francs, all expenses deducted.

"Everything this lady possessed was sold?" inquired Lecoq.

"Everything."

"And what is the name of this brother of hers?"

"Watchau, also. The baroness had probably married one of her relatives. Until last year her brother occupied a very prominent diplomatic position. I think he now resides at Berlin."

Certainly this information would not seem to indicate that the auctioneer had been tampered with; and yet Lecoq was not satisfied. "It is very strange," he thought, as he walked toward his lodgings, "that whichever side I turn, in this affair, I find mention of Germany. The murderer comes from Leipsic, Madame Milner must be a Bavarian, and now here is an Austrian baroness."

It was too late to make any further inquiries that evening, and Lecoq went to bed; but the next morning, at an early hour, he resumed his investigations with fresh ardor. There now seemed only one remaining clue to success: the letter signed "Lacheneur," which had been found in the pocket of the murdered soldier. This letter, judging from the half-effaced heading at the top of the note-paper, must have been written in some café on the Boulevard Beaumarchais. To discover which precise cafe would be mere child's play; and indeed the fourth landlord to whom Lecoq exhibited the letter recognized the paper as his. But neither he, nor his wife, nor the young lady at the counter, nor the waiters, nor any of the customers present at the time, had ever once heard mention made of this singular name—Lacheneur.

And now what was Lecoq to do? Was the case utterly hopeless? Not yet. Had not the spurious soldier declared that this Lacheneur was an old comedian? Seizing upon this frail clue, as a drowning man clutches at the merest fragment of the floating wreck, Lecoq turned his steps in another direction, and hurried from theatre to theatre, asking every one, from doorkeeper to manager: "Don't you know an actor named Lacheneur?"

Alas! one and all gave a negative reply, at times indulging in some rough joke at the oddity of the name. And when any one asked the young detective what the man he was seeking was like, what could he reply? His answer was necessarily limited to the virtuous Toinon's phrase: "I thought him a very respectable-looking gentleman." This was not a very graphic description, however, and, besides, it was rather doubtful what a woman like Polyte Chupin's wife might mean by the word "respectable." Did she apply it to the man's age, to his personal aspect, or to his apparent fortune.

Sometimes those whom Lecoq questioned would ask what parts this comedian of his was in the habit of playing; and then the young detective could make no reply whatever. He kept for himself the harassing thought that the rôle now being performed by the unknown Lacheneur was driving him—Lecoq —wild with despair.

Eventually our hero had recourse to a method of investigation which, strange to say, the police seldom employ, save in extreme cases, although it is at once sensible and simple, and generally fraught with success. It consists in examining all the hotel and lodging-house registers, in which the landlords are compelled to record the names of their tenants, even should the latter merely sojourn under their roofs for a single night.

Rising long before daybreak and going to bed late at night, Lecoq spent all his time in visiting the countless hotels and furnished lodgings in Paris. But still and ever his search was vain. He never once came across the name of Lacheneur; and at last he began to ask himself if such a name really existed, or if it were not some pseudonym invented for convenience. He had not found it even in Didot's directory, the so-called "Almanach Boitin," where one finds all the most singular and absurd names in France—those which are formed of the most fantastic mingling of syllables.

Still, nothing could daunt him or turn him from the almost

impossible task he had undertaken, and his obstinate perseverance well-nigh developed into monomania. He was no longer subject to occasional outbursts of anger, quickly repressed; but lived in a state of constant exasperation, which soon impaired the clearness of his mind. No more theories, or ingenious deductions, no more subtle reasoning. He pursued his search without method and without order—much as Father Absinthe might have done when under the influence of alcohol. Perhaps he had come to rely less upon his own shrewdness than upon chance to reveal to him the substance of the mystery, of which he had as yet only detected the shadow.

XVIII

WHEN a heavy stone is thrown into a lake a considerable commotion ensues, the water spouts and seethes and bubbles and frequently a tall jet leaps into the air. But all this agitation only lasts for a moment; the bubbling subsides as the circles of the passing whirlpool grow larger and larger; the surface regains at last its customary smoothness; and soon no trace remains of the passage of the stone, now buried in the depths below.

So it is with the events of our daily life, however momentous they may appear at the hour of their occurrence. It seems as if their impressions would last for years; but no, they speedily sink into the depths of the past, and time obliterates their passage—just as the water of the lake closes over and hides the stone, for an instant the cause of such commotion. Thus it was that at the end of a fortnight the frightful crime committed in the Widow Chupin's drinking-den, the triple murder which had made all Paris shudder, which had furnished the material for so many newspaper articles, and the topic for such indignant comments, was completely forgotten. Indeed, had the tragedy at the Poivriere occurred in the times of Charlemagne, it could not have passed more thoroughly out of people's minds. It was remembered only in three places, at the Depot, at the Prefecture de Police, and at the Palais de Justice.

M. Segmuller's repeated efforts had proved as unsuccessful as Lecoq's. Skilful questioning, ingenious insinuations, forcible threats, and seductive promises had proved powerless to overcome the dogged spirit of absolute denial which persistently animated, not merely the prisoner May, but also the Widow Chupin, her son Polyte, Toinon the Virtuous, and Madame Milner. The evidence of these various witnesses showed plainly enough that they were all in league with the mysterious accomplice; but what did this knowledge avail? Their attitude never varied! And, even if at times their looks gave the lie to their denials, one could always read in their eyes an unshaken determination to conceal the truth.

There were moments when the magistrate, overpowered by a sense of the insufficiency of the purely moral weapons at his disposal, almost regretted that the Inquisition was suppressed. Yes, in presence of the lies that were told him, lies so impudent that they were almost insults, he no longer wondered at the judicial cruelties of the Middle Ages, or at the use of the muscle-breaking rack, the flesh-burning, red-hot pincers, and other horrible instruments, which, by the physical torture they inflicted, forced the most obstinate culprit to confess. The prisoner May's manner was virtually unaltered; and far from showing any signs of weakness, his assurance had, if anything, increased, as though he were confident of ultimate victory and as though he had in some way learned that the prosecution had failed to make the slightest progress.

On one occasion, when summoned before M. Segmuller, he ventured to remark in a tone of covert irony: "Why do you keep me confined so long in a secret cell? Am I never to be set at liberty or sent to the assizes. Am I to suffer much longer on account of your fantastic idea that I am some great personage in disguise?"

"I shall keep you until you have confessed," was M. Segmuller's answer.

"Confessed what?"

"Oh! you know very well."

The prisoner shrugged his shoulders at these last words, and then in a tone of mingled despondency and mockery retorted: "In that case there is no hope of my ever leaving this cursed prison!"

It was probably this conviction that induced him to make all seeming preparations for an indefinite stay. He applied for and obtained a portion of the contents of the trunk found at the Hotel de Mariembourg, and evinced great joy when the various knickknacks and articles of clothing were handed over to him. Thanks to the money found upon his person when arrested, and deposited with the prison registrar, he was, moreover, able to procure many little luxuries, which are never denied to unconvicted prisoners, no matter what may be the charges against them, for they have a right to be considered as innocent until a jury has decided to the contrary. To while away the time, May next asked for a volume of Beranger's songs, and his request being granted, he spent most of the day in learning several of the ditties by heart, singing them in a loud voice and with considerable taste. This fancy having excited some comment, he pretended that he was cultivating a talent which might be useful to him when he was set at liberty. For he had no doubt of his acquittal; at least, so he declared; and if he were anxious about the date of his trial, he did not show the slightest apprehension concerning its result.

He was never despondent save when he spoke of his profession. To all appearance he pined for the stage, and, in fact, he almost wept when he recalled the fantastic, many-colored costumes, clad in which he had once appeared before crowded audiences—audiences that had been convulsed with laughter by his sallies of wit, delivered between bursts of noisy music. He seemed to have become altogether a better fellow; more frank, communicative, and submissive. He eagerly embraced every opportunity to babble about his past, and over and over again did he recount the adventures of the roving life he had led while in the employ of M. Simpson, the showman. He had, of course, traveled a great deal; and he remembered everything he had seen; possessing, moreover, an inexhaustible fund of amusing stories, with which he entertained his custodians. His manner and his words were so natural that head keepers and subordinate turnkeys alike were quite willing to give credit to his assertions.

The governor of the Depot alone remained unconvinced. He had declared that this pretended buffoon must be some dangerous criminal who had escaped from Cayenne, and who for this reason was determined to conceal his antecedents. Such being this functionary's opinion, he tried every means to substantiate it. Accordingly, during an entire fortnight,

May was submitted to the scrutiny of innumerable members of the police force, to whom were added all the more notable private detectives of the capital. No one recognized him, however, and although his photograph was sent to all the prisons and police stations of the empire, not one of the officials could recognize his features.

Other circumstances occurred, each of which had its influence, and one and all of them speaking in the prisoner's favor. For instance, the second bureau of the Prefecture de Police found positive traces of the existence of a strolling artist, named Tringlot, who was probably the man referred to in May's story. This Tringlot had been dead several years. Then again, inquiries made in Germany revealed the fact that a certain M. Simpson was very well known in that country, where he had achieved great celebrity as a circus manager.

In presence of this information and the negative result of the scrutiny to which May had been subjected, the governor of the Depot abandoned his views and openly confessed that he had been mistaken. "The prisoner, May," he wrote to the magistrate, "is really and truly what he pretends to be. There can be no further doubt on the subject." This message, it may be added, was sent at Gevrol's instigation.

So thus it was that M. Segmuller and Lecoq alone remained of their opinion. This opinion was at least worthy of consideration, as they alone knew all the details of the investigation which had been conducted with such strict secrecy; and yet this fact was of little import. It is not merely unpleasant, but often extremely dangerous to struggle on against all the world, and unfortunately for truth and logic one man's opinion, correct though it may be, is nothing in the balance of daily life against the faulty views of a thousand adversaries.

The "May affair" had soon become notorious among the members of the police force; and whenever Lecoq appeared at the Prefecture he had to brave his colleagues' sarcastic pleasantry. Nor did M. Segmuller escape scot free; for more than one fellow magistrate, meeting him on the stairs or in the corridor, inquired, with a smile, what he was doing with his Caspar-Hauser, his man in the Iron Mask, in a word, with his mysterious mountebank. When thus assailed, both M. Segmuller and Lecoq could scarcely restrain those movements of angry impatience which come naturally to a person who feels certain he is in the right and yet can not prove it.

"Ah, me!" sometimes exclaimed the magistrate, "why did D'Escorval break his leg? Had it not been for that cursed mishap, he would have been obliged to endure all these perplexities, and I—I should be enjoying myself like other people."

"And I thought myself so shrewd!" murmured the young detective by his side.

Little by little anxiety did its work. Magistrate and detective both lost their appetites and looked haggard; and yet the idea of yielding never once occurred to them. Although of very different natures, they were both determined to persevere in the task they had set themselves—that of solving this tantalizing enigma. Lecoq, indeed, had resolved to renounce all other claims upon his time, and to devote himself entirely to the study of the case. "Henceforth," he said to M. Segmuller, "I also will constitute myself a prisoner; and although the suspected murderer will be unable to see *me*, I shall not lose sight of *him!*"

It so happened that there was a loft between the cell occupied by May and the roof of the prison, a loft of such diminutive proportions that a man of average height could not stand upright in it. This loft had neither window nor skylight, and the gloom would have been intense, had not a few faint sunrays struggled through the interstices of some ill-adjusted tiles. In this unattractive garret Lecoq established himself one fine morning, just at the hour when May was taking his daily walk in the courtyard of the prison accompanied by a couple of keepers. Under these circumstances there was no fear of Lecoq's movements attracting the prisoner's notice or suspicion. The garret had a paved floor, and first of all the young detective removed one of the stones with a pickax he had brought for the purpose. Beneath this stone he found a timber beam, through which he next proceeded to bore a hole of funnel shape, large at the top and gradually dwindling until on piercing the ceiling of the cell it was no more than two-thirds of an inch in diameter. Prior to commencing his operations, Lecoq had visited the prisoner's quarters and had skilfully chosen the place of the projected aperture, so that the stains and graining of the beam would hide it from the view of any one below. He was yet at work when the governor of the Depot and his rival Gevrol appeared upon the threshold of the loft.

"So this is to be your observatory, Monsieur Lecoq!" remarked Gevrol, with a sneering laugh.

"Yes, sir."

"You will not be very comfortable here."

"I shall be less uncomfortable than you suppose; I have brought a large blanket with me, and I shall stretch myself out on the floor and manage to sleep here.

"So that, night and day, you will have your eye on the prisoner?"

"Yes, night and day."

"Without giving yourself time to eat or drink?" inquired Gevrol.

"Excuse me! Father Absinthe will bring me my meals, execute any errand I may have, and relieve me at times if necessary."

The jealous General laughed; but his laugh, loud as it was, was yet a trifle constrained. "Well, I pity you," he said.

"Very possibly."

"Do you know what you will look like, with your eye glued to that hole?"

"Like what? Tell me, we needn't stand on ceremony."

"Ah, well! you will look just like one of those silly naturalists who put all sorts of little insects under a magnifying glass, and spend their lives in watching them."

Lecoq had finished his work; and rose from his kneeling position. "You couldn't have found a better comparison, General," said he. "I owe my idea to those very naturalists you speak about so slightingly. By dint of studying those little creatures—as you say—under a microscope, these patient, gifted men discover the habits and instincts of the insect world. Very well, then. What they can do with an insect, I will do with a man!"

"Oh, ho!" said the governor of the prison, considerably astonished.

"Yes; that's my plan," continued Lecoq. "I want to learn this prisoner's secret; and I will do so. That I've sworn; and success must be mine, for, however strong his courage may be, he will have his moments of weakness, and then I shall be present at them. I shall be present if ever his will fails him, if, believing himself alone, he lets his mask fall, or forgets his part for an instant, if an indiscreet word escapes him in his sleep, if his despair elicits a groan, a gesture, or a look —I shall be there to take note of it."

The tone of resolution with which the young detective spoke

made a deep impression upon the governor's mind. For an instant he was a believer in Lecoq's theory; and he was impressed by the strangeness of this conflict between a prisoner, determined to preserve the secret of his identity, and the agent for the prosecution, equally determined to wrest it from him. "Upon my word, my boy, you are not wanting in courage and energy," said he.

"Misdirected as it may be," growled Gevrol, who, although he spoke very slowly and deliberately, was in his secret soul by no means convinced of what he said. Faith is contagious, and he was troubled in spite of himself by Lecoq's imperturbable assurance. What if this debutant in the profession should be right, and he, Gevrol, the oracle of the Prefecture, wrong! What shame and ridicule would be his portion, then! But once again he inwardly swore that this inexperienced youngster could be no match for an old veteran like himself, and then added aloud: "The prefect of police must have more money than he knows what to do with, to pay two men for such a nonsensical job as this."

Lecoq disdained to reply to this slighting remark. For more than a fortnight the General had profited of every opportunity to make himself as disagreeable as possible, and the young detective feared he would be unable to control his temper if the discussion continued. It would be better to remain silent, and to work and wait for success. To succeed would be revenge enough! Moreover, he was impatient to see these unwelcome visitors depart; believing, perhaps, that Gevrol was quite capable of attracting the prisoner's attention by some unusual sound.

As soon as they went away, Lecoq hastily spread his blanket over the stones and stretched himself out upon it in such a position that he could alternately apply his eye and his ear to the aperture. In this position he had an admirable view of the cell below. He could see the door, the bed, the table, and the chair; only the small space near the window and the window itself were beyond his range of observation. He had scarcely completed his survey, when he heard the bolts rattle: the prisoner was returning from his walk. He seemed in excellent spirits, and was just completing what was, undoubtedly, a very interesting story, since the keeper who accompanied him lingered for a moment to hear the finish. Lecoq was delighted with the success of his experiment. He could hear as easily as he could see. Each syllable reached his ear distinctly, and he had not lost a single word of the recital, which was amusing, though rather coarse.

The turnkey soon left the cell; the bolts rattled once more, and the key grated in the lock. After walking once or twice across his cell, May took up his volume of Beranger and for an hour or more seemed completely engrossed in its contents. Finally, he threw himself down upon his bed. Here he remained until meal-time in the evening, when he rose and ate with an excellent appetite. He next resumed the study of his book, and did not go to bed until the lights were extinguished.

Lecoq knew well enough that during the night his eyes would not serve him, but he trusted that his ears might prove of use, hoping that some telltale word might escape the prisoner's lips during his restless slumber. In this expectation he was disappointed. May tossed to and fro upon his pallet; he sighed, and one might have thought he was sobbing, but not a syllable escaped his lips. He remained in bed until very late the next morning; but on hearing the bell sound the hour of breakfast, eleven o'clock, he sprang from his couch with a bound, and after capering about his cell for a few moments, began to sing, in a loud and cheerful voice, the old ditty:

> "Diogene!
> Sous ton manteau, libre et content,
> Je ris, je bois, sans gene—"

The prisoner did not stop singing until a keeper entered his cell carrying his breakfast. The day now beginning differed in no respect from the one that had preceded it, neither did the night. The same might be said of the next day, and of those which followed. To sing, to eat, to sleep, to attend to his hands and nails—such was the life led by this so-called buffoon. His manner, which never varied, was that of a naturally cheerful man terribly bored.

Such was the perfection of his acting that, after six days and nights of constant surveillance, Lecoq had detected nothing decisive, nor even surprising. And yet he did not despair. He had noticed that every morning, while the employees of the prison were busy distributing the prisoner's food, May invariably began to sing the same ditty.

"Evidently this song is a signal," thought Lecoq. "What

can be going on there by the window I can't see? I must know to-morrow."

Accordingly on the following morning he arranged that May should be taken on his walk at half-past ten o'clock, and he then insisted that the governor should accompany him to the prisoner's cell. That worthy functionary was not very well pleased. with the change in the usual order of things. "What do you wish to show me?" he asked. "What is there so very curious to see?"

"Perhaps nothing," replied Lecoq, "but perhaps something of great importance."

Eleven o'clock sounding soon after, he began singing the prisoner's song, and he had scarcely finished the second line, when a bit of bread, no larger than a bullet, adroitly thrown through the window, dropped at his feet.

A thunderbolt falling in May's cell would not have terrified the governor as much as did this inoffensive projectile. He stood in silent dismay; his mouth wide open, his eyes starting from their sockets, as if he distrusted the evidence of his own senses. What a disgrace! An instant before he would have staked his life upon the inviolability of the secret cells; and now he beheld his prison dishonored.

"A communication! a communication!" he repeated, with a horrified air.

Quick as lightning, Lecoq picked up the missile. "Ah," murmured he, "I guessed that this man was in communication with his friends."

The young detective's evident delight changed the governor's stupor into fury. "Ah! my prisoners are writing!" he exclaimed, wild with passion. "My warders are acting as postmen! By my faith, this matter shall be looked into."

So saying, he was about to rush to the door when Lecoq stopped him. "What are you going to do, sir?" he asked.

"I am going to call all the employees of this prison together, and inform them that there is a traitor among them, and that I must know who he is, as I wish to make an example of him. And if, in twenty-four hours from now, the culprit has not been discovered, every man connected with this prison shall be removed."

Again he started to leave the room, and Lecoq, this time, had almost to use force to detain him. "Be calm, sir; be calm," he entreated.

"I *will* punish—"

"Yes, yes—I understand that—but wait until you have regained your self-possession. It is quite possible that the guilty party may be one of the prisoners who assist in the distribution of food every morning."

"What does that matter?"

"Excuse me, but it matters a great deal. If you noise this discovery abroad, we shall never discover the truth. The traitor will not be fool enough to confess his guilt. We must be silent and wait. We will keep a close watch and detect the culprit in the very act."

These objections were so sensible that the governor yielded. "So be it," he sighed, "I will try and be patient. But let me see the missive that was enclosed in this bit of bread."

Lecoq could not consent to this proposal. "I warned M. Segmuller," said he, "that there would probably be something new this morning; and he will be waiting for me in his office. We must only examine the letter in his presence."

This remark was so correct that the governor assented; and they at once started for the Palais de Justice. On their way, Lecoq endeavored to convince his companion that it was wrong to deplore a circumstance which might be of incalculable benefit to the prosecution. "It was an illusion," said he, "to imagine that the governor of a prison could be more cunning than the prisoners entrusted to him. A prisoner is almost always a match in ingenuity for his custodians."

The young detective had not finished speaking when they reached the magistrate's office. Scarcely had Lecoq opened the door than M. Segmuller and his clerk rose from their seats. They both read important intelligence in our hero's troubled face. "What is it?" eagerly asked the magistrate. Lecoq's sole response was to lay the pellet of bread upon M. Segmuller's desk. In an instant the magistrate had opened it, extracting from the centre a tiny slip of the thinnest tissue paper. This he unfolded, and smoothed upon the palm of his hand. As soon as he glanced at it, his brow contracted. "Ah! this note is written in cipher," he exclaimed, with a disappointed air.

"We must not lose patience," said Lecoq quietly. He took the slip of paper from the magistrate and read the numbers inscribed upon it. They ran as follows: "235, 15, 3, 8, 25, 2, 16, 208, 5, 360, 4, 36, 19, 7, 14, 118, 84, 23, 9, 40, 11, 99."

"And so we shall learn nothing from this note," murmured the governor.

"Why not?" the smiling clerk ventured to remark. "There is no system of cipher which can not be read with a little skill and patience; there are some people who make it their business."

"You are right," said Lecoq, approvingly. "And I, myself, once had the knack of it."

"What!" exclaimed the magistrate; "do you hope to find the key to this cipher?"

"With time, yes."

Lecoq was about to place the paper in his breast-pocket, when the magistrate begged him to examine it a little further. He did so; and after a while his face suddenly brightened. Striking his forehead with his open palm, he cried: "I've found it!"

An exclamation of incredulous surprise simultaneously escaped the magistrate, the governor, and the clerk.

"At least I think so," added Lecoq, more cautiously. "If I am not mistaken, the prisoner and his accomplice have adopted a very simple system called the double book-cipher. The correspondents first agree upon some particular book; and both obtain a copy of the same edition. When one desires to communicate with the other, he opens the book haphazard, and begins by writing the number of the page. Then he must find on the same page the words that will express his thoughts. If the first word he wishes to write is the twentieth on the page, he places number 20 after the number of the page; then he begins to count one, two, three, and so on, until he finds the next word he wishes to use. If this word happens to be the sixth, he writes the figure 6; and he continues so on till he has finished his letter. You see, now, how the correspondent who receives the note must begin. He finds the page indicated, and then each figure represents a word."

"Nothing could be clearer," said the magistrate, approvingly.

"If this note," pursued Lecoq, "had been exchanged between two persons at liberty, it would be folly to attempt its translation. This simple system is the only one which has completely baffled inquisitive efforts, simply because there is no way of ascertaining the book agreed upon. But in this instance such is not the case; May is a prisoner, and he has only one book in his possession, 'The Songs of Beranger.' Let this book be sent for—"

The governor of the Depot was actually enthusiastic. "I will run and fetch it myself," he interrupted.

But Lecoq, with a gesture, detained him. "Above all, sir," said he, "take care that May doesn't discover his book has been tampered with. If he has returned from his promenade, make some excuse to have him sent out of his cell again; and don't allow him to return there while we are using his book."

"Oh, trust me!" replied the governor, hastily leaving the room.

Less than a quarter of an hour afterward he returned, carrying in triumph a little volume in 32mo. With a trembling hand Lecoq turned to page 235, and began to count. The fifteenth word on the page was *'I'*; the third afterward, *'have'*; the eighth following, *'told'*; the twenty-fifth, *'her'*; the second, *'your'*; the sixteenth, *'wishes.'* Hence, the meaning of those six numbers was: "I have told her your wishes."

The three persons who had witnessed this display of shrewdness could not restrain their admiration. "Bravo! Lecoq," exclaimed the magistrate. "I will no longer bet a hundred to one on May," thought the smiling clerk.

But Lecoq was still busily engaged in deciphering the missive, and soon, in a voice trembling with gratified vanity, he read the entire note aloud. It ran as follows: "I have told her your wishes; she submits. Our safety is assured; we are waiting your orders to act. Hope! Courage!"

XIX

YET what a disappointment it produced after the fever of anxiety and expectation that had seized hold of everybody present. This strange epistle furnished no clue whatever to the mystery; and the ray of hope that had sparkled for an instant in M. Segmuller's eyes speedily faded away. As for the versatile Goguet he returned with increased conviction to his former opinion, that the prisoner had the advantage over his accusers.

"How unfortunate," remarked the governor of the Depot, with a shade of sarcasm in his voice, "that so much trouble, and such marvelous penetration, should be wasted!"

"So you think, sir, that I have wasted my time!" rejoined Lecoq in a tone of angry banter, a scarlet flush mantling at the same time over his features. "Such is not my opinion. This scrap of paper undeniably proves that if any one has been mistaken as regards the prisoner's identity, it is certainly not I."

"Very well," was the reply. "M. Gevrol and myself may have been mistaken: no one is infallible. But have you learned anything more than you knew before? Have you made any progress?"

"Why, yes. Now that people know the prisoner is not what he pretends to be, instead of annoying and hampering me, perhaps they will assist us to discover who he really is."

Lecoq's tone, and his allusion to the difficulties he had encountered, cut the governor to the quick. The knowledge that the reproof was not altogether undeserved increased his resentment and determined him to bring this discussion with an inferior to an abrupt close. "You are right," said he, sarcastically. "This May must be a very great and illustrious personage. Only, my dear Monsieur Lecoq (for there is an only), do me the favor to explain how such an important personage could disappear, and the police not be advised of it? A man of rank, such as you suppose this prisoner to be, usually has a family, friends, relatives, proteges, and numerous connections; and yet not a single person has made any inquiry during the three weeks that this fellow May has been under my charge! Come, admit you never thought of that."

The governor had just advanced the only serious objection that could be found to the theory adopted by the prosecution. He was wrong, however, in supposing that Lecoq had failed to foresee it; for it had never once been out of the young detective's mind; and he had racked his brain again and again to find some satisfactory explanation. At the present moment he would undoubtedly have made some angry retort to the governor's sneering criticism, as people are wont to do when their antagonists discover the weak spot in their armor, had not M. Segmuller opportunely intervened.

"All these recriminations do no good," he remarked, calmly; "we can make no progress while they continue. It would be much wiser to decide upon the course that is now to be pursued."

Thus reminded of the present situation of affairs, the young detective smiled; all his rancor was forgotten. "There is, I think, but one course to pursue," he replied in a modest tone; "and I believe it will be successful by reason of its simplicity. We must substitute a communication of our own composition for this one. That will not be at all difficult, since I have the key to the cipher. I shall only be obliged to purchase a similar volume of Beranger's songs; and May, believing that he is addressing his accomplice, will reply in all sincerity—will reveal everything perhaps—"

"Excuse me!" interrupted the governor, "but how will you obtain possession of his reply?"

"Ah! you ask me too much. I know the way in which his letters have reached him. For the rest, I will watch and find a way—never fear!"

Goguet, the smiling clerk, could not conceal an approving grin. If he had happened to have ten francs in his pocket just then he would have risked them all on Lecoq without a moment's hesitation.

"First," resumed the young detective, "I will replace this missive by one of my own composition. To-morrow, at breakfast time, if the prisoner gives the signal, Father Absinthe shall throw the morsel of bread enclosing my note through the window while I watch the effect through the hole in the ceiling of the cell."

Lecoq was so delighted with this plan of his that he at once rang the bell, and when the magistrate's messenger appeared, he gave him half a franc and requested him to go at once and purchase some of the thinnest tissue paper. When this had been procured, Lecoq took his seat at the clerk's desk, and, provided with the volume of Beranger's songs, began to compose a fresh note, copying as closely as possible the forms of the figures used by the unknown correspondent. The task did not occupy him more than ten minutes, for, fearing lest he might commit some blunder, he reproduced most of the words of the original letter, giving them, however, an entirely different meaning.

When completed, his note read as follows: "I have told her your wishes; she does not submit. Our safety is threatened. We are awaiting your orders. I tremble."

Having acquainted the magistrate with the purport of the note, Lecoq next rolled up the paper, and enclosing it in the

fragment of bread, remarked: "To-morrow we shall learn something new."

To-morrow! The twenty-four hours that separated the young
man from the decisive moment he looked forward to seemed as
it were a century; and he resorted to every possible expedient
to hasten the passing of the time. At length, after giving precise instructions to Father Absinthe, he retired to his loft for
the night. The hours seemed interminable, and such was his
nervous excitement that he found it quite impossible to sleep.
On rising at daybreak he discovered that the prisoner was
already awake. May was sitting on the foot of his bed, apparently plunged in thought. Suddenly he sprang to his feet and
paced restlessly to and fro. He was evidently in an unusually
agitated frame of mind: for he gesticulated wildly, and at intervals repeated: "What misery! My God! what misery!"

"Ah! my fine fellow," thought Lecoq, "you are anxious about
the daily letter you failed to receive yesterday. Patience,
patience! One of my writing will soon arrive."

At last the young detective heard the stir usually preceding
the distribution of the food. People were running to and fro,
sabots clicked noisily in the corridors, and the keepers could be
heard engaged in loud conversation. By and by the prison bell
began to toll. It was eleven o'clock, and soon afterward the
prisoner commenced to sing his favorite song:

"Diogene!
Sous ton manteau, libre et content—"

Before he commenced the third line the slight sound caused
by the fragment of bread as it fell upon the stone floor caused
him to pause abruptly.

Lecoq, at the opening in the ceiling above, was holding his
breath and watching with both eyes. He did not miss one of
the prisoner's movements—not so much as the quiver of an eyelid. May looked first at the window, and then all round the
cell, as if it were impossible for him to explain the arrival of
this projectile. It was not until some little time had elapsed
that he decided to pick it up. He held it in the hollow of his
hand, and examined it with apparent curiosity. His features
expressed intense surprise, and any one would have sworn that
he was innocent of all complicity. Soon a smile gathered round
his lips, and after a slight shrug of the shoulders, which might
be interpreted, "Am I a fool?" he hastily broke the pellet in

half. The sight of the paper which it contained seemed to amaze him.

"What does all this mean?" wondered Lecoq.

The prisoner had opened the note, and was examining with knitted brows the figures which were apparently destitute of all meaning to him. Then, suddenly rushing to the door of his cell, and hammering upon it with clenched fists, he cried at the top of his voice: "Here! keeper! here!"

"What do you want?" shouted a turnkey, whose footsteps Lecoq could hear hastening along the adjoining passage.

"I wish to speak to the magistrate."

"Very well. He shall be informed."

"Immediately, if you please. I have a revelation to make."

"He shall be sent for immediately."

Lecoq waited to hear no more. He tore down the narrow staircase leading from the loft, and rushed to the Palais de Justice to acquaint M. Segmuller with what had happened.

"What can all this mean?" he wondered as he darted over the pavement. "Are we indeed approaching a denouement? This much is certain, the prisoner was not deceived by my note. He could only decipher it with the aid of his volume of Beranger, and he did not even touch the book; plainly, then, he hasn't read the letter."

M. Segmuller was no less amazed than the young detective. They both hastened to the prison, followed by the smiling clerk, who was the magistrate's inevitable shadow. On their way they encountered the governor of the Depot, arriving all in a flutter, having been greatly excited by that important word "revelation." The worthy official undoubtedly wished to express an opinion, but the magistrate checked him by the abrupt remark, "I know all about it, and I am coming."

When they had reached the narrow corridor leading to the secret cells, Lecoq passed on in advance of the rest of the party. He said to himself that by stealing upon the prisoner unawares he might possibly find him engaged in surreptitiously reading the note. In any case, he would have an opportunity to glance at the interior of the cell. May was seated beside the table, his head resting on his hands. At the grating of the bolt, drawn by the governor himself, the prisoner rose to his feet, smoothed his hair, and remained standing in a respectful attitude, apparently waiting for the visitors to address him.

"Did you send for me?" inquired the magistrate.

"Yes, sir."

"You have, I understand, some revelation to make to me."

"I have something of importance to tell you."

"Very well! these gentlemen will retire."

M. Segmuller had already turned to Lecoq and the governor to request them to withdraw, when the prisoner motioned him not to do so.

"It is not necessary," said May, "I am, on the contrary, very well pleased to speak before these gentlemen."

"Speak, then."

May did not wait for the injunction to be repeated. Throwing his chest forward, and his head back as had been his wont throughout his examinations, whenever he wished to make an oratorical display, he began as follows: "It shall be for you to say, gentlemen, whether I'm an honest man or not. The profession matters little. One may, perhaps, act as the clown of a traveling show, and yet be an honest man—a man of honor."

"Oh, spare us your reflections!"

"Very well, sir, that suits me exactly. To be brief, then here is a little paper which was thrown into my cell a few minutes ago. There are some numbers on it which may mean something; but I have examined them, and they are quite Greek to me."

He paused, and then handing Lecoq's missive to the magistrate, quietly added: "It was rolled up in a bit of bread."

This declaration was so unexpected, that it struck all the officials dumb with surprise, but the prisoner, without seeming to notice the effect he had produced, placidly continued: "I suppose the person who threw it, made a mistake in the window. I know very well that it's a mean piece of business to denounce a companion in prison. It's a cowardly act and one may get into trouble by doing so; still, a fellow must be prudent when he's charged with murder as I am, and with something very unpleasant, perhaps, in store for him."

A terribly significant gesture of severing the head from the body left no doubt whatever as to what May meant by the "something very unpleasant."

"And yet I am innocent," continued May, in a sorrowful, reproachful tone.

The magistrate had by this time recovered the full possession of his faculties. Fixing his eyes upon the prisoner and concentrating in one magnetic glance all his power of will, he slowly exclaimed: "You speak falsely! It was for you that this note was intended."

"For me! Then I must be the greatest of fools, or why should I have sent for you to show it you? For me? In that case, why didn't I keep it? Who knew, who could know that I had received it?"

These words were uttered with such a marvelous semblance of honesty, May's gaze was frank and open, his voice rang so true, and his reasoning was so specious, that all the governor's doubts returned.

"And what if I could prove that you are uttering a falsehood?" insisted M. Segmuller. "What if I could prove it—here and now?"

"You would have to lie to do so! Oh! pardon! Excuse me; I mean—"

But the magistrate was not in a frame of mind to stickle for nicety of expression. He motioned May to be silent; and, turning to Lecoq, exclaimed: "Show the prisoner that you have discovered the key to his secret correspondence."

A sudden change passed over May's features. "Ah! it is this agent of police who says the letter was for me," he remarked in an altered tone. "The same agent who asserts that I am a grand seigneur." Then, looking disdainfully at Lecoq, he added: "Under these circumstances there's no hope for me. When the police are absolutely determined that a man shall be found guilty, they contrive to prove his guilt; everybody knows that. And when a prisoner receives no letters, an agent, who wishes to show that he is corresponding knows well enough how to write to him."

May's features wore such an expression of marked contempt that Lecoq could scarcely refrain from making an angry reply. He restrained his impulse, however, in obedience to a warning gesture from the magistrate, and taking from the table the volume of Beranger's songs, he endeavored to prove to the prisoner that each number in the note which he had shown M. Segmuller corresponded with a word on the page indicated, and that these various words formed several intelligible phrases. This overpowering evidence did not seem to trouble May in the least. After expressing the same admiration for this novel system of correspondence that a child would show for a new toy, he declared his belief that no one could equal the police in such machinations.

What could have been done in the face of such obstinacy? M. Segmuller did not even attempt to argue the point, but quietly retired, followed by his companions. Until they reached the governor's office, he did not utter a word; then, sinking down into an armchair, he exclaimed: "We must confess ourselves beaten. This man will always remain what he is—an inexplicable enigma."

"But what is the meaning of the comedy he has just played? I do not understand it at all," remarked the governor.

"Why," replied Lecoq, "don't you see that he wished to persuade the magistrate that the first note, the one that fell into the cell while you and I were there yesterday, had been written by me in a mad desire to prove the truth of my theory at any cost? It was a hazardous project; but the importance of the result to be gained must have emboldened him to attempt it. Had he succeeded, I should have been disgraced; and he would have remained May—the stroller, without any further doubt as to his identity. But how could he know that I had discovered his secret correspondence, and that I was watching him from the loft overhead? That will probably never be explained."

The governor and the young detective exchanged glances of mutual distrust. "Eh! eh!" thought the former, "yes, indeed, that note which fell into the cell while I was there the other day might after all have been this crafty fellow's work. His Father Absinthe may have served him in the first instance just as he did subsequently."

While these reflections were flitting through the governor's mind, Lecoq suspiciously remarked to himself: "Who knows but what this fool of a governor confided everything to Gevrol? If he did so, the General, jealous as he is, would not have scrupled to play one such a damaging trick."

His thoughts had gone no further when Goguet, the smiling clerk, boldly broke the silence with the trite remark: "What a pity such a clever comedy didn't succeed."

These words startled the magistrate from his reverie. "Yes, a shameful farce," said he, "and one I would never have authorized, had I not been blinded by a mad longing to arrive at the truth. Such tricks only bring the sacred majesty of justice into contempt!"

At these bitter words, Lecoq turned white with anger. This was the second affront within an hour. The prisoner had first insulted him, and now it was the magistrate's turn. "I am defeated," thought he. "I must confess it. Fate is against me! Ah! if I had only succeeded!"

Disappointment alone had impelled M. Segmuller to utter these harsh words; they were both cruel and unjust, and the magistrate soon regretted them, and did everything in his power to drive them from Lecoq's recollection. They met every day after this unfortunate incident; and every morning, when the young detective came to give an account of his investigations, they had a long conference together. For Lecoq still continued his efforts; still labored on with an obstinacy intensified by constant sneers; still pursued his investigations with that cold and determined zeal which keeps one's faculties on the alert for years.

The magistrate, however, was utterly discouraged. "We must abandon this attempt," said he. "All the means of detection have been exhausted. I give it up. The prisoner will go to the Assizes, to be acquitted or condemned under the name of May. I will trouble myself no more about the matter."

He said this, but the anxiety and disappointment caused by defeat, sneering criticism, and perplexity, as to the best course to be pursued, so affected his health that he became really ill—so ill that he had to take to his bed.

He had been confined to his room for a week or so, when one morning Lecoq called to inquire after him.

"You see, my good fellow," quoth M. Segmuller, despondently, "that this mysterious murderer is fatal to us magistrates. Ah! he is too much for us; he will preserve the secret of his identity."

"Possibly," replied Lecoq. "At all events, there is now but one way left to discover his secret; we must allow him to escape—and then track him to his lair."

This expedient, although at first sight a very startling one, was not of Lecoq's own invention, nor was it by any means novel. At all times, in cases of necessity, have the police closed their eyes and opened the prison doors for the release of suspected criminals. And not a few, dazzled by liberty and ignorant of being watched, have foolishly betrayed themselves. All prisoners are not like the Marquis de Lavalette, protected by royal connivance; and one might enumerate many individuals who have been released, only to be rearrested after confessing their guilt to police spies or auxiliaries who have won their confidence.

Naturally, however, it is but seldom, and only in special cases, and as a last resort, that such a plan is adopted. Moreover, the authorities only consent to it when they hope to derive some important advantage, such as the capture of a whole band of criminals. For instance, the police perhaps arrest one of a band. Now, despite his criminal propensities the captured culprit often has a certain sense of honor—we all know that there is honor among thieves—which prompts him to refuse all information concerning his accomplices. In such a case what is to be done? Is he to be sent to the Assizes by himself, tried and convicted, while his comrades escape scot free? No; it is best to set him at liberty. The prison doors are opened, and he is told that he is free. But each after step he takes in the streets outside is dogged by skilful detectives; and soon, at the very moment when he is boasting of his good luck and audacity to the comrades he has rejoined, the whole gang find themselves caught in the snare.

M. Segmuller knew all this, and much more, and yet, on hearing Lecoq's proposition, he made an angry gesture and exclaimed: "Are you mad?"

"I think not, sir."

"At all events your scheme is a most foolish one!"

"Why so, sir? You will recollect the famous murder of the Chaboiseaus. The police soon succeeded in capturing the guilty parties; but a robbery of a hundred and sixty thousand francs in bank-notes and coin had been committed at the same time, and this large sum of money couldn't be found. The murderers obstinately refused to say where they had concealed it; for, of course, it would prove a fortune for them, if they ever escaped the gallows. In the mean while, however, the children of the victims were ruined. Now, M. Patrigent, the magistrate who investigated the affair, was the first to convince the authorities that it would be best to set one of the murderers at liberty. His advice was followed; and three days later the culprit was surprised unearthing the money from among a bed of mushrooms. Now, I believe that our prisoner—"

"Enough!" interrupted M. Segmuller. "I wish to hear no more on the matter. I have, it seems to me, forbidden you to broach the subject."

The young detective hung his head with a hypocritical air of submission. But all the while he watched the magistrate out of the corner of his eye and noted his agitation. "I can afford to be silent," he thought; "he will return to the subject of his own accord."

And in fact M. Segmuller did return to it only a moment afterward. "Suppose this man were released from prison," said he, "what would you do?"

"What would I do, sir! I would follow him like grim death; I would not once let him out of my sight; I would be his shadow."

"And do you suppose he wouldn't discover this surveillance?"

"I should take my precautions."

"But he would recognize you at a single glance."

"No, sir, he wouldn't, for I should disguise myself. A detective who can't equal the most skilful actor in the matter of make-up is no better than an ordinary policeman. I have only practised at it for a twelvemonth, but I can easily make myself look old or young, dark or light, or assume the manner of a man of the world, or of some frightful ruffian of the barrieres."

"I wasn't aware that you possessed this talent, Monsieur Lecoq."

"Oh! I'm very far from the perfection I hope to arrive at; though I may venture to say that in three days from now I could call on you and talk with you for half an hour without being recognized."

M. Segmuller made no rejoinder; and it was evident to Lecoq that the magistrate had offered this objection rather in the hope of its being overruled, than with the wish to see it prevail.

"I think, my poor fellow," he at length observed, "that you are strangely deceived. We have both been equally anxious to penetrate the mystery that enshrouds this strange man. We have both admired his wonderful acuteness—for his sagacity *is* wonderful; so marvelous, indeed, that it exceeds the limits of imagination. Do you believe that a man of his penetration would betray himself like an ordinary prisoner? He will understand at once, if he is set at liberty, that his freedom is only given him so that we may surprise his secret."

"I don't deceive myself, sir. May will guess the truth of course. I'm quite aware of that."

"Very well. Then, what would be the use of attempting what you propose?"

"I have come to this conclusion," replied Lecoq, "May will find himself strangely embarrassed, even when he's set free.

He won't have a sou in his pocket; we know he has no trade, so what will he do to earn a living? He may struggle along for a while; but he won't be willing to suffer long. Man must have food and shelter, and when he finds himself without a roof over his head, without even a crust of bread to break, he will remember that he is rich. Won't he then try to recover possession of his property? Yes, certainly he will. He will try to obtain money, endeavor to communicate with his friends, and I shall wait till that moment arrives. Months may elapse, before, seeing no signs of my surveillance, he may venture on some decisive step; and then I will spring forward with a warrant for his arrest in my hand."

"And what if he should leave Paris? What if he should go abroad?"

"Oh, I will follow him. One of my aunts has left me a little land in the provinces worth about twelve thousand francs. I will sell it, and spend the last sou, if necessary, so long as I only have my revenge. This man has outwitted me as if I were a child, and I must have my turn."

"And what if he should slip through your fingers?"

Lecoq laughed like a man that was sure of himself. "Let him try," he exclaimed; "I will answer for him with my life."

"Your idea is not a bad one," said M. Segmuller, eventually. "But you must understand that law and justice will take no part in such intrigues. All I can promise you is my tacit approval. Go, therefore, to the Prefecture; see your superiors—"

With a really despairing gesture, the young man interrupted M. Segmuller. "What good would it do for *me* to make such a proposition?" he exclaimed. "They would not only refuse my request, but they would dismiss me on the spot, if my name is not already erased from the roll."

"What, dismissed, after conducting this case so well?"

"Ah, sir, unfortunately every one is not of that opinion. Tongues have been wagging busily during your illness. Somehow or other, my enemies have heard of the last scene we had with May; and impudently declare that it was *I* who imagined all the romantic details of this affair, being eager for advancement. They pretend that the only reasons to doubt the prisoner's identity are those I have invented myself. To hear them talk at the Depot, one might suppose that I invented the scene in the Widow Chupin's cabin; imagined the accomplices; suborned the witnesses; manufactured the articles of conviction; wrote the first note in cipher as well as the second; duped Father Absinthe, and mystified the governor."

"The deuce!" exclaimed M. Segmuller; "in that case, what do they think of me?"

The wily detective's face assumed an expression of intense embarrassment.

"Ah! sir," he replied with a great show of reluctance, "they pretend that you have allowed yourself to be deceived by me, and that you haven't weighed at their proper worth the proofs I've furnished."

A fleeting flush mantled over M. Segmuller's forehead. "In a word," said he, "they think I'm your dupe—and a fool besides."

The recollection of certain sarcastic smiles he had often detected on the faces of colleagues and subordinates alike, the memory of numerous covert allusions to Casper Hauser, and the Man with the Iron Mask—allusions which had stung him to the quick—induced him to hesitate no longer.

"Very well! I will aid you, Monsieur Lecoq," he exclaimed. "I should like you to triumph over your enemies. I will get up at once and accompany you to the Palais de Justice. I will see the public prosecutor myself; I will speak to him, and plead your case for you."

Lecoq's joy was intense. Never, no never, had he dared to hope for such assistance. Ah! after this he would willingly go through fire on M. Segmuller's behalf. And yet, despite his inward exultation, he had sufficient control over his feelings to preserve a sober face. This victory must be concealed under penalty of forfeiting the benefits that might accrue from it. Certainly, the young detective had said nothing that was untrue; but there are different ways of presenting the truth, and he had, perhaps, exaggerated a trifle in order to excite the magistrate's rancor, and win his needful assistance.

"I suppose," remarked M. Segmuller, who was now quite calm again—no outward sign of wounded vanity being perceptible—"I suppose you have decided what stratagem must be employed to lull the prisoner's suspicions if he is permitted to escape."

"I must confess I haven't given it a thought," replied Lecoq. "Besides, what good would any such stratagem do? He knows too well that he is the object of suspicion not to remain on the alert. Still, there is one precaution which I believe absolutely necessary, indispensable indeed, if we wish to be successful."

"What precaution do you mean?" inquired the magistrate.

"Well, sir, I think an order should be given to have May transferred to another prison. It doesn't in the least matter which; you can select the one you please."

"Why should we do that?"

"Because, during the few days preceding his release, it is absolutely necessary he should hold no communication with his friends outside, and that he should be unable to warn his accomplice."

"Then you think he's badly guarded where he is?" inquired M. Segmuller with seeming amazement.

"No, sir, I did not say that. I am satisfied that since the affair of the cipher note the governor's vigilance has been unimpeachable. However, news from outside certainly reaches the suspected murderer at the Depot; we have had material evidence—full proof of that—and besides—"

The young detective paused in evident embarrassment. He plainly had some idea in his head to which he feared to give expression.

"And besides?" repeated the magistrate.

"Ah, well, sir! I will be perfectly frank with you. I find that Gevrol enjoys too much liberty at the Depot; he is perfectly at home there, he comes and goes as he likes, and no one ever thinks of asking what he is doing, where he is going, or what he wants. No pass is necessary for his admission, and he can influence the governor just as he likes. Now, to tell the truth, I distrust Gevrol."

"Oh! Monsieur Lecoq!"

"Yes, I know very well that it's a bold accusation, but a man is not master of his presentiments: so there it is, I distrust Gevrol. Did the prisoner know that I was watching him from the loft, and that I had discovered his secret correspondence, was he ignorant of it? To my mind he evidently knew everything, as the last scene we had with him proves."

"I must say that's my own opinion," interrupted M. Segmuller.

"But how could he have known it?" resumed Lecoq. "He could not have discovered it by himself. I endured tortures for a while in the hope of solving the problem. But all my trouble was wasted. Now the supposition of Gevrol's intervention would explain everything."

M. Segmuller had turned pale with anger. "Ah! if I could

really believe that!" he exclaimed; "if I were sure of it! Have you any proofs?"

The young man shook his head. "No," said he, "I haven't; but even if my hands were full of proofs I should not dare to show them. I should ruin my future. Ah, if ever I succeed, I must expect many such acts of treachery. There is hatred and rivalry in every profession. And, mark this, sir—I don't doubt Gevrol's honesty. If a hundred thousand francs were counted out upon the table and offered to him, he wouldn't even try to release a prisoner. But he would rob justice of a dozen criminals in the mere hope of injuring me, jealous as he is, and fearing lest I might obtain advancement."

How many things these simple words explained. Did they not give the key to many and many an enigma which justice has failed to solve, simply on account of the jealousy and rivalry that animate the detective force? Thus thought M. Segmuller, but he had no time for further reflection.

"That will do," said he, "go into the drawing-room for a moment. I will dress and join you there. I will send for a cab: for we must make haste if I am to see the public prosecutor to-day."

Less than a quarter of an hour afterward M. Segmuller, who usually spent considerable time over his toilet, was dressed and ready to start. He and Lecoq were just getting into the cab that had been summoned when a footman in a stylish livery was seen approaching.

"Ah! Jean," exclaimed the magistrate, "how's your master?"

"Improving, sir," was the reply. "He sent me to ask how you were, and to inquire how that affair was progressing?"

"There has been no change since I last wrote to him. Give him my compliments, and tell him that I am out again."

The servant bowed. Lecoq took a seat beside the magistrate and the cab started off.

"That fellow is one of D'Escorval's servants," remarked M. Segmuller. "He's richer than I, and can well afford to keep a footman."

"D'Escorval's," ejaculated Lecoq, "the magistrate who—"

"Precisely. He sent his man to me two or three days ago to ascertain what we were doing with our mysterious May."

"Then M. d'Escorval is interested in the case?"

"Prodigiously! I conclude it is because he opened the prosecution, and because the case rightfully belongs to him. Perhaps he regrets that it passed out of his hands, and thinks that he could have managed the investigation better himself. We would have done better with it if we could. I would give a good deal to see him in my place."

But this change would not have been at all to Lecoq's taste. "Ah," thought he, "such a fellow as D'Escorval would never have shown me such confidence as M. Segmuller." He had, indeed, good reason to congratulate himself: for that very day M. Segmuller, who was a man of his word, a man who never rested until he had carried his plan into execution, actually induced the authorities to allow May to be set at liberty; and the details of this measure only remained to be decided upon. As regards the proposed transfer of the suspected murderer to another prison, this was immediately carried into effect, and May was removed to Mazas, where Lecoq had no fear of Gevrol's interference.

That same afternoon, moreover, the Widow Chupin received her conditional release. There was no difficulty as regards her son, Polyte. He had, in the mean time, been brought before the correctional court on a charge of theft; and, to his great astonishment, had heard himself sentenced to thirteen months' imprisonment. After this, M. Segmuller had nothing to do but to wait, and this was the easier as the advent of the Easter holidays gave him an opportunity to seek a little rest and recreation with his family in the provinces.

On the day he returned to Paris—the last of the recess, and by chance a Sunday—he was sitting alone in his library when his cook came to tell him that there was a man in the vestibule who had been sent from a neighboring register office to take the place of a servant he had recently dismissed. The newcomer was ushered into the magistrate's presence and proved to be a man of forty or thereabouts, very red in the face and with carroty hair and whiskers. He was, moreover, strongly inclined to corpulence, and was clad in clumsy, ill-fitting garments. In a complacent tone, and with a strong Norman accent, he informed the magistrate that during the past twenty years he had been in the employment of various literary men, as well as of a physician, and notary; that he was familiar with the duties that would be required of him at the Palais de Justice, and that he knew how to dust papers without disarranging them. In short, he produced such a favorable impression that, although M. Segmuller reserved twenty-four hours in which to make further inquiries, he drew a twenty-franc piece from his pocket on the spot and tendered it to the Norman valet as the first instalment of his wages.

But instead of pocketing the proffered coin, the man, with a sudden change of voice and attitude, burst into a hearty laugh, exclaiming: "Do you think, sir, that May will recognize me?"

"Monsieur Lecoq!" cried the astonished magistrate.

"The same, sir; and I have come to tell you that if you are ready to release May, all my arrangements are now completed."

XX

WHEN one of the investigating magistrates of the Tribunal of the Seine wishes to examine a person confined in one of the Paris prisons, he sends by his messenger to the governor of that particular jail a so-called "order of extraction," a concise, imperative formula, which reads as follows: "The keeper of —— prison will give into the custody of the bearer of this order the prisoner known as ——, in order that he may be brought before us in our cabinet at the Palais de Justice." No more, no less, a signature, a seal, and everybody is bound to obey.

But from the moment of receiving this order until the prisoner is again incarcerated, the governor of the prison is relieved of all responsibility. Whatever may happen, his hands are clear. Minute precautions are taken, however, so that a prisoner may not escape during his journey from the prison to the Palais. He is carefully locked up in a compartment of one of the lugubrious vehicles that may be often seen waiting on the Quai de l'Horloge, or in the courtyard of the Sainte-Chapelle. This van conveys him to the Palais, and while he is awaiting examination, he is immured in one of the cells of the gloomy jail, familiarly known as "la Souriciere" or the "mouse-trap." On entering and leaving the van the prisoner is surrounded by guards: and on the road, in addition to the mounted troopers who always accompany these vehicles, there are prison warders or linesmen of the Gard de Paris installed

in the passage between the compartments of the van and seated
on the box with the driver. Hence, the boldest criminals ordinarily realize the impossibility of escaping from this ambula-
tory prison.

Indeed, statistics record only thirty attempts at escape in a
period of ten years. Of these thirty attempts, twenty-five were
ridiculous failures; four were discovered before their authors
had conceived any serious hope of success: and only one man
actually succeeded in alighting from the vehicle, and even he
had not taken fifty steps before he was recaptured.

Lecoq was well acquainted with all these facts, and in preparing everything for May's escape, his only fear was lest the
murderer might decline to profit of the opportunity. Hence,
it was necessary to offer every possible inducement for flight.
The plan the young detective had eventually decided on con-
sisted in sending an order to Mazas for May to be despatched
to the Palais de Justice. He could be placed in one of the
prison vans, and at the moment of starting the door of his
compartment would not be perfectly secured. When the van
reached the Palais de Justice and discharged its load of criminals at the door of the "mouse-trap" May would purposely be
forgotten and left in the vehicle, while the latter waited on the
Quai de l'Horloge until the hour of returning to Mazas. It
was scarcely possible that the prisoner would fail to embrace
this apparently favorable opportunity to make his escape.

Everything was, therefore, prepared and arranged according
to Lecoq's directions on the Monday following the close of
the Easter holidays; the requisite "order of extraction" being
entrusted to an intelligent man with the most minute instructions.

Now, although the van in which May would journey was not
to be expected at the Palais de Justice before noon, it so happened that at nine o'clock that same morning a queer-looking
"loafer" having the aspect of an overgrown, overaged "gamin
de Paris" might have been seen hanging about the Prefecture
de Police. He wore a tattered black woolen blouse and a pair
of wide, ill-fitting trousers, fastened about his waist by a leather
strap. His boots betrayed a familiar acquaintance with the
puddles of the barrieres, and his cap was shabby and dirty,
though, on the other hand, his necktie, a pretentious silk scarf
of flaming hue, was evidently quite fresh from some haber-
dasher's shop. No doubt it was a present from his sweetheart.

This uncomely being had the unhealthy complexion, hollow eyes, slouching mien, and straggling beard common to his tribe. His yellow hair, cut closely at the back of the head, as if to save the trouble of brushing, was long in front and at the sides; being plastered down over his forehead and advancing above his ears in extravagant corkscrew ringlets.

What with his attire, his affected jaunty step, his alternate raising of either shoulder, and his way of holding his cigarette and of ejecting a stream of saliva from between his teeth, Polyte Chupin, had he been at liberty, would undoubtedly have proffered a paw, and greeted this barrière beauty as a "pal."

It was the 14th of April; the weather was lovely, and, on the horizon, the youthful foliage of the chestnut trees in the Tuileries gardens stood out against a bright blue sky. The "ethereal mildness" of "gentle spring" seemed to have a positive charm for the tattered "loafer" who lazily loitered in the sunlight, dividing his attention between the passers-by and some men who were hauling sand from the banks of the Seine. Occasionally, however, he crossed the roadway, and, strange to say, exchanged a few remarks with a neatly dressed, long-bearded gentleman, who wore gold-rimmed spectacles over his nose and drab silk gloves on his hands. This individual exhibited all the outward characteristics of eminent respectability, and seemed to take a remarkable interest in the contents of an optician's shop window.

Every now and then a policeman or an agent of the detective corps passed by on his way to the Prefecture, and the elderly gentleman or the "loafer" would at times run after these officials to ask for some trifling information. The person addressed replied and passed on; and then the "loafer" and the gentleman would join each other and laughingly exclaim: "Good!—there's another who doesn't recognize us."

And in truth the pair had just cause for exultation, good reason to be proud, for of some twelve or fifteen comrades they accosted, not one recognized the two detectives, Lecoq and Father Absinthe. For the "loafer" was none other than our hero, and the gentleman of such eminent respectability his faithful lieutenant.

"Ah!" quoth the latter with admiration, "I am not surprised they don't recognize me, since I can't recognize myself. No one but you, Monsieur Lecoq, could have so transformed me."

Unfortunately for Lecoq's vanity, the good fellow spoke at

a moment when the time for idle conversation had passed. The prison van was just crossing the bridge at a brisk trot.

"Attention!" exclaimed the young detective, "there comes our friend! Quick!—to your post; remember my directions, and keep your eyes open!"

Near them, on the quay, was a large pile of timber, behind which Father Absinthe immediately concealed himself, while Lecoq, seizing a spade that was lying idle, hurried to a little distance and began digging in the sand. They did well to make haste. The van came onward and turned the corner. It passed the two detectives, and with a noisy clang rolled under the heavy arch leading to "la Souriciere." May was inside, as Lecoq assured himself on recognizing the keeper sitting beside the driver.

The van remained in the courtyard for more than a quarter of an hour. When it reappeared, the driver had left his perch and the quay opposite the Palais de Justice, threw a covering over his horses, lighted his pipe, and quietly walked away. The moment for action was now swiftly approaching.

For a few minutes the anxiety of the two watchers amounted to actual agony; nothing stirred—nothing moved. But at last the door of the van was opened with infinite caution, and a pale, frightened face became visible. It was the face of May. The prisoner cast a rapid glance around him. No one was in sight. Then as swiftly and as stealthily as a cat he sprang to the ground, noiselessly closed the door of the vehicle, and walked quietly toward the bridge.

Lecoq breathed again. He had been asking himself if some trifling circumstance could have been forgotten or neglected, thus disarranging all his plans. He had been wondering if this strange man would refuse the dangerous liberty which had been offered him. But he had been anxious without cause. May had fled; not thoughtlessly, but with premeditation.

From the moment when he was left alone, apparently forgotten, in the insecurely locked compartment, until he opened the door and glanced around him, sufficient time had elapsed for a man of his intellect and discernment to analyze and calculate all the chances of so grave a step. Hence, if he had stepped into the snare laid for him, it must be with a full knowledge of the risks he had to run. He and Lecoq were alone together, free in the streets of Paris, armed with mutual distrust, equally obliged to resort to strategy, and forced to

hide from each other. Lecoq, it is true, had an auxiliary—
Father Absinthe. But who could say that May would not be
aided by his redoubtable accomplice? Hence, it was a veritable
duel, the result of which depended entirely upon the courage,
skill, and coolness of the antagonists.

All these thoughts flashed through the young detective's brain
with the quickness of lightning. Throwing down his spade,
and running toward a sergeant de ville, who was just coming
out of the Palais de Justice, he gave him a letter which was
ready in his pocket. "Take this to M. Segmuller at once; it
is a matter of importance," said he.

The policeman attempted to question this "loafer" who was
in correspondence with the magistrates; but Lecoq had already
darted off on the prisoner's trail.

May had covered but a short distance. He was sauntering
along with his hands in his pockets; his head high in the air,
his manner composed and full of assurance. Had he reflected
that it would be dangerous to run while so near the prison
from which he had just escaped? Or was he of opinion that
as an opportunity of flight had been willingly furnished him,
there was no danger of immediate rearrest? This was a point
Lecoq could not decide. At all events, May showed no signs
of quickening his pace even after crossing the bridge; and it
was with the same tranquil manner that he next crossed the
Quai aux Fleurs and turned into the Rue de la Cite.

Nothing in his bearing or appearance proclaimed him to
be an escaped prisoner. Since his trunk—that famous trunk
which he pretended to have left at the Hotel de Mariembourg
—had been returned to him, he had been well supplied with
clothing: and he never failed, when summoned before the magistrate, to array himself in his best apparel. The garments
he wore that day were black cloth, and their cut, combined
with his manner, gave him the appearance of a working man
of the better class taking a holiday.

His tread, hitherto firm and decided, suddenly became uncertain when, after crossing the Seine, he reached the Rue St.
Jacques. He walked more slowly, frequently hesitated, and
glanced continually at the shops on either side of the way.

"Evidently he is seeking something," thought Lecoq: "but
what?"

It was not long before he ascertained. Seeing a second-hand-
clothes shop close by, May entered in evident haste. Lecoq at

once stationed himself under a gateway on the opposite side of the street, and pretended to be busily engaged lighting a cigarette. The criminal being momentarily out of sight, Father Absinthe thought he could approach without danger.

"Ah, well," said he, "there's our man changing his fine clothes for coarser garments. He will ask for the difference in money; and they will give it him. You told me this morning: 'May without a sou'—that's the trump card in our game!"

"Nonsense! Before we begin to lament, let us wait and see what happens. It is not likely that shopkeeper will give him any money. He won't buy clothing of the first passer-by."

Father Absinthe withdrew to a little distance. He distrusted these reasons, but not Lecoq who gave them.

In the mean while, in his secret soul, Lecoq was cursing himself. Another blunder, thought he, another weapon left in the hands of the enemy. How was it that he, who fancied himself so shrewd, had not foreseen this emergency? Calmness of mind returned, however, a moment afterward when he saw May emerge from the shop attired as when he entered it. Luck had for once been in the young detective's favor.

May actually staggered when he stepped out on the pavement. His bitter disappointment could be read in his countenance, which disclosed the anguish of a drowning man who sees the frail plank which was his only hope of salvation snatched from his grasp by the ruthless waves.

What could have taken place? This Lecoq must know without a moment's delay. He gave a peculiar whistle, to warn his companion that he momentarily abandoned the pursuit of him; and having received a similar signal in response, he entered the shop. The owner was still standing behind the counter. Lecoq wasted no time in parleying. He merely showed his card to acquaint the man with his profession, and curtly asked: "What did the fellow want who was just in here?"

The shopkeeper seemed embarrassed. "It's a long story," he stammered.

"Then tell it!" said Lecoq, surprised at the man's hesitation.

"Oh, it's very simple. About twelve days ago a man entered my shop with a bundle under his arm. He claimed to be a countryman of mine."

"Are you an Alsatian?"

"Yes, sir. Well, I went with this man to the wine-shop at

the corner, where he ordered a bottle of good wine; and while we drank together, he asked me if I would consent to keep the package he had with him until one of his cousins came to claim it. To prevent any mistake, this cousin was to say certain words—a countersign, as it were. I refused, shortly and decidedly, for the very month before I had got into trouble and had been charged with receiving stolen goods, all by obliging a person in this way. Well, you never saw a man so vexed and so surprised. What made me all the more determined in my refusal was that he offered me a good round sum in payment for my trouble. This only increased my suspicion, and I persisted in my refusal."

The shopkeeper paused to take breath; but Lecoq was on fire with impatience. "And what then?" he insisted.

"Well, he paid for the wine and went away. I had forgotten all about the matter until that man came in here just now, and after asking me if I hadn't a package for him, which had been left by one of his cousins, began to say some peculiar words— the countersign, no doubt. When I replied that I had nothing at all he turned as white as his shirt; and I thought he was going to faint. All my suspicions came back to me. So when he afterward proposed that I should buy his clothes, I told him I couldn't think of it."

All this was plain enough to Lecoq. "And this cousin who was here a fortnight ago, what was he like?" asked he.

"He was a tall, rather corpulent man, with a ruddy complexion, and white whiskers. Ah! I should recognize him in an instant!"

"The accomplice!" exclaimed Lecoq.

"What did you say?"

"Nothing that would interest you. Thank you. I am in a hurry. You will see me again: good morning."

Lecoq had not remained five minutes in the shop: and yet, when he emerged, May and Father Absinthe were nowhere in sight. Still, the young detective was not at all uneasy on that score. In making arrangements with his old colleague for this pursuit Lecoq had foreseen such a situation, and it had been agreed that if one of them were obliged to remain behind, the other, who was closely following May, should from time to time make chalk marks on the walls, shutters, and facings of the shops, so as to indicate the route, and enable his companion to rejoin him. Hence, in order to know which way to go, Lecoq had only to glance at the buildings around him. The task was neither long nor difficult, for on the front of the third shop beyond that of the second-hand-clothes dealer a superb dash of the crayon instructed him to turn into the Rue Saint-Jacques.

On he rushed in that direction, his mind busy at work with the incident that had just occurred. What a terrible warning that old-clothes dealer's declaration had been! Ah! that mysterious accomplice was a man of foresight. He had even done his utmost to insure his comrade's salvation in the event of his being allowed to escape. What did the package the shopkeeper had spoken of contain? Clothes, no doubt. Everything necessary for a complete disguise—money, papers, a forged passport most likely.

While these thoughts were rushing through Lecoq's mind, he had reached the Rue Soufflot, where he paused for an instant to learn his way from the walls. This was the work of a second. A long chalk mark on a watchmaker's shop pointed to the Boulevard Saint-Michel, whither the young detective at once directed his steps. "The accomplice," said he to himself, resuming his meditation, "didn't succeed with that old-clothes dealer; but he isn't a man to be disheartened by one rebuff. He has certainly taken other measures. How shall I divine what they are in order to defeat them?"

The supposed murderer had crossed the Boulevard Saint-Michel, and had then taken to the Rue Monsieur-le-Prince, as Father Absinthe's dashes of the crayon proclaimed with many eloquent flourishes.

"One circumstance reassures me," the young detective murmured, "May's going to this shop, and his consternation on finding that there was nothing for him there. The accomplice had informed him of his plans, but had *not* been able to inform him of their failure. Hence, from this hour, the prisoner is left to his own resources. The chain that bound him to his accomplice is broken; there is no longer an understanding between them. Everything depends now upon keeping them apart. Yes, everything lies in that!"

Ah! how Lecoq rejoiced that he had succeeded in having May transferred to another prison; for he was convinced that the accomplice had warned May of the attempt he was going to make with the old-clothes dealer on the very evening before May's removal to Mazas. Hence, it had not been possible to acquaint him with the failure of this scheme or the substitution of another.

Still following the chalk marks, Lecoq now reached the Odeon theatre. Here were fresh signs, and what was more, Father Absinthe could be perceived under the colonnade, standing in front of one of the book-stalls, and apparently engrossed in the contemplation of a print.

Assuming the nonchalant manner of the loafer whose garb he wore, Lecoq took his stand beside his colleague. "Where is he?" asked the young detective.

"There," replied his companion, with a slight movement of his head in the direction of the steps.

The fugitive was, indeed, seated on one of the steps at the side of the theatre, his elbows resting on his knees and his face hidden in his hands, as if he felt the necessity of concealing the expression of his face from the passers-by. Undoubtedly, at that moment, he gave himself up for lost. Alone in the midst of Paris, without a penny, what was to become of him? He knew beyond the shadow of a doubt that he was being watched; that his steps were being dogged, that the first attempt he made to inform his accomplice of his whereabouts would cost him his secret—the secret which he plainly held as more precious than life itself, and which, by immense sacrifices, he had so far been able to preserve.

Having for some short time contemplated in silence this unfortunate man whom after all he could but esteem and admire, Lecoq turned to his old companion: "What did he do on the way?" he asked.

"He went into the shops of five dealers in second-hand clothing without success. Then he addressed a man who was passing with a lot of old rubbish on his shoulder: but the man wouldn't even answer him."

Lecoq nodded his head thoughtfully. "The moral of this is, that there's a vast difference between theory and practise," he remarked. "Here's a fellow who has made some most discerning men believe that he's only a poor devil, a low buffoon. Well, now he's free; and this so-called Bohemian doesn't even know how to go to work to sell the clothes on his back. The comedian who could play his part so well on the stage has disappeared; while the man remains—the man who has always been rich, and knows nothing of the vicissitudes of life."

The young detective suddenly ceased moralizing, for May

had risen from his seat. Lecoq was only ten yards distant, and could see that his face was pallid. His attitude expressed profound dejection and one could read his indecision in his eyes. Perhaps he was wondering if it would not be best to return and place himself again in the hands of his jailers, since he was without the resources upon which he had depended.

After a little, however, he shook off the torpor that had for a time overpowered him; his eyes brightened, and, with a gesture of defiance, he left the steps, crossed the open square and walked down the Rue de l'Ancienne-Comedie. He strode onward now with the brisk, determined step of a man who has a definite aim in view.

"Who knows where he is going now?" murmured Father Absinthe, as he trotted along by Lecoq's side.

"I do," replied the young detective. "And the proof is, that I am going to leave you, and run on in advance, to prepare for his reception. I may be mistaken, however, and as we must be prepared for any emergency, leave me the chalk-marks as you go along. If our man doesn't come to the Hotel de Mariembourg, as I think he will, I shall come back here to start in pursuit of you again."

Just then an empty cab chanced to be passing, and Lecoq hastily got into it, telling the driver to take him to the Northern Railway Station by the shortest route and as quickly as possible. As time was precious, he handed the cabman his fare while on the road, and then began to search his pocket-book, among the various documents confided to him by M. Segmuller, for a particular paper he would now require.

Scarcely had the cab stopped at the Place de Roubaix than the young detective alighted and ran toward the Hotel de Mariembourg, where, as on the occasion of his first visit, he found Madame Milner standing on a chair in front of her bird-cage, obstinately trying to teach her starling German, while the bird with equal obstinacy repeated: "Camille! where is Camille?"

On perceiving the individual of questionable mien who had presumed to cross her threshold, the pretty widow did not deign to change her position.

"What do you want?" she asked in a curt, sharp voice.

"I am the nephew of a messenger at the Palais de Justice," replied Lecoq with an awkward bow, in perfect keeping with his attire. "On going to see my uncle this morning, I found him laid up with rheumatism; and he asked me to bring you this paper in his stead. It is a summons for you to appear at once before the investigating magistrate."

This reply induced Madame Milner to abandon her perch. "Very well," she replied after glancing at the summons; "give me time to throw a shawl over my shoulder, and I'll start."

Lecoq withdrew with another awkward bow; but he had not reached the street before a significant grimace betrayed his inward satisfaction. She had duped him once, and now he had repaid her. On looking round him he perceived a half-built house at the corner of the Rue St. Quentin, and being momentarily in want of a hiding-place he concluded that he had best conceal himself there. The pretty widow had only asked for sufficient time to slip on a shawl before starting; but then it so happened that she was rather particular as to her personal appearance—and such a plump, attractive little body as herself, having an eye perhaps to renewed wedlock, could not possibly be expected to tie her bonnet strings in less than a quarter of an hour. Hence, Lecoq's sojourn behind the scaffolding of the half-built house proved rather longer than he had expected, and at the thought that May might arrive at any moment he fairly trembled with anxiety. How much was he in advance of the fugitive? Half an hour, perhaps! And he had accomplished only half his task.

At last, however, the coquettish landlady made her appearance as radiant as a spring morning. She probably wished to make up for the time she had spent over her toilet, for as she turned the corner she began to run. Lecoq waited till she was out of sight, and then bounding from his place of concealment, he burst into the Hotel de Mariembourg like a bombshell.

Fritz, the Bavarian lad, must have been warned that the house was to be left in his sole charge for some hours; for having comfortably installed himself in his mistress's own particular armchair, with his legs resting on another one, he had already commenced to fall asleep.

"Wake up!" shouted Lecoq; "wake up!"

At the sound of this voice, which rang like a trumpet blast, Fritz sprang to his feet, frightened half out of his wits.

"You see that I am an agent of the Prefecture of Police," said the visitor, showing his card. "Now, if you wish to avoid all sorts of disagreeable things, the least of which will be a sojourn in prison, you must obey me."

The boy trembled in every limb. "Yes, mein Herr—Monsieur, I mean—I will obey you," he stammered. "But what am I to do?"

"Oh, very little. A man is coming here in a moment: you will know him by his black clothes and his long beard. You must answer him word for word as I tell you. And remember, if you make any mistake, you will suffer for it."

"You may rely upon me, sir," replied Fritz. "I have an excellent memory."

The prospect of imprisonment had terrified him into abject submission. He spoke the truth; he would have been willing to say or do anything just then. Lecoq profited by this disposition; and then clearly and concisely gave the lad his instructions. "And now," added he, "I must see and hear you. Where can I hide myself?"

Fritz pointed to a glass door. "In the dark room there, sir. By leaving the door ajar you can hear and you can see everything through the glass."

Without another word Lecoq darted into the room in question. Not a moment too soon, however, for the spring bell of the outer door announced the arrival of a visitor. It was May. "I wish to speak to the landlady," he said.

"What landlady?" replied the lad.

"The person who received me when I came here six weeks ago—"

"Oh, I understand," interrupted Fritz; "it's Madame Milner you want to see; but you have come too late; she sold the house about a month ago, and has gone back to Alsace."

May stamped his foot and uttered a terrible oath. "I have come to claim something from her," he insisted.

"Do you want me to call her successor?"

Concealed behind the glass door, Lecoq could not help admiring Fritz, who was uttering these glaring falsehoods with that air of perfect candor which gives the Germans such a vast advantage over the Latin races, who seem to be lying even when they are telling the truth.

"Her successor would order me off," exclaimed May. "I came to reclaim the money I paid for a room I never occupied."

"Such money is never refunded."

May uttered some incoherent threat, in which such words as "downright robbery" and "justice" could be distinguished, and then abruptly walked back into the street, slamming the door behind him.

"Well! did I answer properly?" asked Fritz triumphantly as Lecoq emerged from his hiding-place.

"Yes, perfectly," replied the detective. And then pushing aside the boy, who was standing in his way, he dashed after May.

A vague fear almost suffocated him. It had struck him that the fugitive had not been either surprised or deeply affected by the news he had heard. He had come to the hotel depending upon Madame Milner's assistance, and the news of this woman's departure would naturally have alarmed him, for was she not the mysterious accomplice's confidential friend? Had May, then, guessed the trick that had been played upon him? And if so, how?

Lecoq's good sense told him plainly that the fugitive must have been put on his guard, and on rejoining Father Absinthe, he immediately exclaimed: "May spoke to some one on his way to the hotel."

"Why, how could you know that?" exclaimed the worthy man, greatly astonished.

"Ah! I was sure of it!"

"Who did he speak to?"

"To a very pretty woman, upon my word!—fair and plump as a partridge!"

"Ah! fate is against us!" exclaimed Lecoq with an oath. "I run on in advance to Madame Milner's house, so that May shan't see her. I invent an excuse to send her out of the hotel, and yet they meet each other."

Father Absinthe gave a despairing gesture. "Ah! if I had known!" he murmured; "but you did not tell me to prevent May from speaking to the passers-by."

"Never mind, my old friend," said Lecoq, consolingly; "it couldn't have been helped."

While this conversation was going on, the fugitive had reached the Faubourg Montmartre, and his pursuers were obliged to hasten forward and get closer to their man, so that they might not lose him in the crowd.

"Now," resumed Lecoq when they had overtaken him, "give me the particulars. Where did they meet?"

"In the Rue Saint-Quentin."

"Which saw the other first?"

"May."

"What did the woman say? Did you hear any cry of surprise?"

"I heard nothing, for I was quite fifty yards off; but by the woman's manner I could see she was stupefied."

Ah! if Lecoq could have witnessed the scene, what valuable deductions he might have drawn from it. "Did they talk for a long time?" he asked.

"For less than a quarter of an hour."

"Do you know whether Madame Milner gave May money or not?"

"I can't say. They gesticulated like mad—so violently, indeed, that I thought they were quarreling."

"They knew they were being watched, and were endeavoring to divert suspicion."

"If they would only arrest this woman and question her," suggested Father Absinthe.

"What good would it do? Hasn't M. Segmuller examined and cross-examined her a dozen times without drawing anything from her! Ah! she's a cunning one. She would declare that May met her and insisted that she should refund the ten francs he paid her for his room. We must do our best, however. If the accomplice has not been warned already, he will soon be told; so we must try to keep the two men apart. What ruse they will employ, I can't divine. But I know that it will be nothing hackneyed."

Lecoq's presumptions made Father Absinthe nervous. "The surest way, perhaps," ventured the latter, "would be to lock him up again!"

"No!" replied the young detective. "I want his secret, and I'll have it. What will be said of us if we two allow this man to escape us? He can't be visible and invisible by turns, like the devil. We'll see what he is going to do now that he's got some money and a plan—for he has both at the present moment. I would stake my right hand upon it."

At that same instant, as if May intended to convince Lecoq of the truth of his suspicion, he entered a tobacconist's shop and emerged an instant afterward with a cigar in his mouth.

SO the landlady of the Hotel de Mariembourg had given May money. There could be no further doubt on that point after the purchase of this cigar. But had they agreed upon any plan? Had they had sufficient time to decide on the method that May was to employ with the view of baffling his pursuit?

It would seem so, since the fugitive's manner had now changed in more respects than one. If hitherto he had seemed to care little for the danger of pursuit and capture, at present he was evidently uneasy and agitated. After walking so long in the full sunlight, with his head high in the air, he now slunk along in the shadow of the houses, hiding himself as much as possible.

"It is evident that his fears have increased in proportion with his hopes," said Lecoq to his companion. "He was quite unnerved when we saw him at the Odeon, and the merest trifle would have decided him to surrender; now, however, he thinks he has a chance to escape with his secret."

The fugitive was following the boulevards, but suddenly he turned into a side street and made his way toward the Temple, where, soon afterward, Father Absinthe and Lecoq found him conversing with one of those importunate dealers in cast-off garments who consider every passer-by their lawful prey. The vender and May were evidently debating a question of price; but the latter was plainly no skilful bargainer, for with a somewhat disappointed air he soon gave up the discussion and entered the shop.

"Ah, so now he has some coin he has determined on a costume," remarked Lecoq. "Isn't that always an escaped prisoner's first impulse?"

Soon afterward May emerged into the street. His appearance was decidedly changed, for he wore a pair of dark blue linen trousers, of the type French "navvies" habitually affect, and a loosely fitting coat of rough woolen material. A gay silk 'kerchief was knotted about his throat, and a black silk

cap was set on one side of his head.   Thus attired, he was
scarcely more prepossessing in appearance than Lecoq, and one
would have hesitated before deciding which of the two it would
be preferable to meet at night on a deserted highway.

May seemed very well pleased with his transformation, and
was evidently more at ease in his new attire.   On leaving the
shop, however, he glanced suspiciously around him, as if to
ascertain which of the passers-by were watching his movements.   He had not parted with his broadcloth suit, but was
carrying it under his arm, wrapped up in a handkerchief.   The
only thing he had left behind him was his tall chimney-pot hat.

Lecoq would have liked to enter the shop and make some
inquiries, but he felt that it would be imprudent to do so, for
May had settled his cap on his head with a gesture that left no
doubt as to his intentions.   A second later he turned into the
Rue du Temple, and now the chase began in earnest; for the
fugitive proved as swift and agile as a stag, and it was no
small task to keep him well in sight.   He had no doubt lived
in England and Germany, since he spoke the language of these
countries like a native; but one thing was certain—he knew
Paris as thoroughly as the most expert Parisian.

This was shown by the way in which he dashed into the
Rue des Gravelliers, and by the precision of his course through
the many winding streets that lie between the Rue du Temple
and the Rue Beaubourg.   He seemed to know this quarter of
the capital by heart; as well, indeed, as if he had spent half his
life there.   He knew all the wine-shops communicating with
two streets—all the byways, passages, and tortuous alleys.
Twice he almost escaped his pursuers, and once his salvation
hung upon a thread.   If he had remained in an obscure corner,
where he was completely hidden, only an instant longer, the
two detectives would have passed him by and his safety would
have been assured.

The pursuit presented immense difficulties.   Night was coming
on, and with it that light fog which almost invariably accom-
panies a spring sunset.   Soon the street-lamps glimmered luridly
in the mist, and then it required a keen eyesight indeed to see
even for a moderate distance.   And, to add to this drawback,
the streets were now thronged with workmen returning home
after their daily toil, and with housewives intent on purchasing
provisions for the evening meal, while round about each dwelling there congregated its numerous denizens swarming like

He glanced suspiciously around him.

bees around a hive. May, however, took advantage of every opportunity to mislead the persons who might be following him. Groups collected around some cheap-jack's stall, street accidents, a block of vehicles—everything was utilized by him with such marvelous presence of mind that he often glided through the crowd without leaving any sign of his passage.

At last he left the neighborhood of the Rue des Gravelliers and made for a broader street. Reaching the Boulevard de Sebastopol, he turned to the left, and took a fresh start. He darted on with marvelous rapidity, with his elbows pressed close to his body—husbanding his breath and timing his steps with the precision of a dancing-master. Never pausing, and without once turning his head, he ever hurried on. And it was at the same regular but rapid pace that he covered the Boulevard de Sebastopol, crossed the Place du Chatelet, and proceeded to mount the Boulevard Saint-Michel.

Here he suddenly halted before a cab-stand. He spoke to one of the drivers, opened the door of his vehicle, and jumped in. The cab started off at a rapid pace. But May was not inside. He had merely passed through the vehicle, getting out at the other door, and just as the driver was departing for an imaginary destination May slipped into an adjacent cab which left the stand at a gallop. Perhaps, after so many ruses, after such formidable efforts after this last stratagem—perhaps May believed that he was free.

He was mistaken. Behind the cab which bore him onward, and while he leaned back against the cushions to rest, a man was running; and this man was Lecoq. Poor Father Absinthe had fallen by the way. In front of the Palais de Justice he paused, exhausted and breathless, and Lecoq had little hope of seeing him again, since he had all he could do to keep his man in sight without stopping to make the chalk-marks agreed upon.

May had instructed his driver to take him to the Place d'Italie: requesting him, moreover, to stop exactly in the middle of the square. This was about a hundred paces from the police station in which he had been temporarily confined with the Widow Chupin. When the vehicle halted, he sprang to the ground and cast a rapid glance around him, as if looking for some dreaded shadow. He could see nothing, however, for although surprised by the sudden stoppage, Lecoq had yet had time to fling himself flat on his stomach under the body of the cab, regardless of all danger of being crushed by the wheels.

May was apparently reassured. He paid the cabman and then retraced his course toward the Rue Mouffetard.

With a bound, Lecoq was on his feet again, and started after the fugitive as eagerly as a ravenous dog might follow a bone. He had reached the shadow cast by the large trees in the outer boulevards when a faint whistle resounded in his ears. "Father Absinthe!" he exclaimed in a tone of delighted surprise.

"The same," replied the old detective, "and quite rested, thanks to a passing cabman who picked me up and brought me here—"

"Oh, enough!" interrupted Lecoq. "Let us keep our eyes open."

May was now walking quite leisurely. He stopped first before one and then before another of the numerous wine-shops and eating-houses that abound in this neighborhood. He was apparently looking for some one or something, which of the two Lecoq could not, of course, divine. However, after peering through the glass doors of three of these establishments and then turning away, the fugitive at last entered the fourth. The two detectives, who were enabled to obtain a good view of the shop inside, saw the supposed murderer cross the room and seat himself at a table where a man of unusually stalwart build, ruddy-faced and gray-whiskered, was already seated.

"The accomplice!" murmured Father Absinthe.

Was this really the redoubtable accomplice? Under other circumstances Lecoq would have hesitated to place dependence on a vague similarity in personal appearance; but here probabilities were so strongly in favor of Father Absinthe's assertion that the young detective at once admitted its truth. Was not this meeting the logical sequence of May and Madame Milner's chance interview a few hours before?

"May," thought Lecoq, "began by taking all the money Madame Milner had about her, and then instructed her to tell his accomplice to come and wait for him in some cheap restaurant near here. If he hesitated and looked inside the different establishments, it was only because he hadn't been able to specify any particular one. Now, if they don't throw aside the mask, it will be because May is not sure he has eluded pursuit and because the accomplice fears that Madame Milner may have been followed."

The accomplice, if this new personage was really the accomplice, had resorted to a disguise not unlike that which May and

Lecoq had both adopted. He wore a dirty blue blouse and a hideous old slouch hat, which was well-nigh in tatters. He had, in fact, rather exaggerated his make-up, for his sinister physiognomy attracted especial attention even beside the depraved and ferocious faces of the other customers in the shop. For this low eating-house was a regular den of thieves and cut-throats. Among those present there were not four workmen really worthy of that name. The others occupied in eating and drinking there were all more or less familiar with prison life. The least to be dreaded were the barriere loafers, easily recognized by their glazed caps and their loosely-knotted neckerchiefs. The majority of the company appeared to consist of this class.

And yet May, that man who was so strongly suspected of belonging to the highest social sphere, seemed to be perfectly at home. He called for the regular "ordinary" and a "chopine" of wine, and then, after gulping down his soup, bolted great pieces of beef, pausing every now and then to wipe his mouth on the back of his sleeve. But was he conversing with his neighbor? This it was impossible to discern through the glass door, all obscured by smoke and steam.

"I must go in," said Lecoq, resolutely. "I must get a place near them, and listen."

"Don't think of such a thing," said Father Absinthe. "What if they recognized you?"

"They won't recognize me."

"If they do, they'll kill you."

Lecoq made a careless gesture.

"I certainly think that they wouldn't hesitate to rid themselves of me at any cost. But, nonsense! A detective who is afraid to risk his life is no better than a low spy. Why! you never saw even Gevrol flinch."

Perhaps Father Absinthe had wished to ascertain if his companion's courage was equal to his shrewdness and sagacity. If such were the case he was satisfied on this score now.

"You, my friend, will remain here to follow them if they leave hurriedly," resumed Lecoq, who in the mean while had already turned the handle of the door. Entering with a careless air and taking a seat at a table near that occupied by the fugitive and the man in the slouch hat, he called for a plate of meat and a "chopine" of wine in a guttural voice.

The fugitive and the ruffian opposite him *were* talking, but like strangers who had met by chance, and not at all after the fashion of friends who have met at a rendezvous. They spoke in the jargon of their pretended rank in life, not that puerile slang met with in romances descriptive of low life, but that obscene, vulgar dialect which it is impossible to render, so changeable and diverse is the signification of its words.

"What wonderful actors!" thought Lecoq; "what perfection! what method! How I should be deceived if I were not absolutely certain!"

For the moment the man in the slouch hat was giving a detailed account of the different prisons in France. He described the governors of the principal houses of detention; explained the divergencies of discipline in different establishments; and recounted that the food at Poissy was ten times better than that at Fontevrault.

Lecoq, having finished his repast, ordered a small glass of brandy, and, leaning his back against the wall and closing his eyes, pretended to fall asleep. His ears were wide open, however, and he carefully listened to the conversation.

Soon May began talking in his turn; and he narrated his story exactly as he had related it to the magistrate, from the murder up to his escape, without forgetting to mention the suspicions attached to his identity—suspicions which afforded him great amusement, he said. He added that he would be perfectly happy if he had money enough to take him back to Germany; but unfortunately he only had a few sous and didn't know where or how to procure any more. He had not even succeeded in selling some clothing which belonged to him, and which he had with him in a bundle.

At these words the man in the tattered felt hat declared that he had too good a heart to leave a comrade in such embarrassment. He knew, in the very same street, an obliging dealer in such articles, and he offered to take May to his place at once. May's only response was to rise, saying: "Let us start." And they did start, with Lecoq at their heels.

They walked rapidly on until passing the Rue Fer-a-Moulin, when they turned into a narrow, dimly lighted alley, and entered a dingy dwelling.

"Run and ask the concierge if there are not two doors by which any one can leave this house," said Lecoq, addressing Father Absinthe.

The latter instantly obeyed. He learned, however, that the

house had only one street door, and accordingly the two detectives waited. "We are discovered!" murmured Lecoq. "I am sure of it. May must have recognized me, or the boy at the Hotel de Mariembourg has described me to the accomplice."

Father Absinthe made no response, for just then the two men came out of the house. May was jingling some coins in his hand, and seemed to be in a very bad temper. "What infernal rascals these receivers are!" he grumbled.

However, although he had only received a small sum for his clothing, he probably felt that his companion's kindness deserved some reward; for immediately afterward he proposed they should take a drink together, and with that object in view they entered a wine-shop close by. They remained here for more than an hour, drinking together; and only left this establishment to enter one a hundred paces distant. Turned out by the landlord, who was anxious to shut up, the two friends now took refuge in the next one they found open. Here again they were soon turned out and then they hurried to another boozing-den—and yet again to a fifth. And so, after drinking innumerable bottles of wine, they contrived to reach the Place Saint-Michel at about one o'clock in the morning. Here, however, they found nothing to drink; for all the wine-shops were closed.

The two men then held a consultation together, and, after a short discussion, they walked arm-in-arm toward the Faubourg Saint-Germain, like a pair of friends. The liquor they had imbibed was seemingly producing its effect, for they often staggered in their walk, and talked not merely loudly but both at the same time. In spite of the danger, Lecoq advanced near enough to catch some fragments of their conversation; and the words "a good stroke," and "money enough to satisfy one," reached his ears.

Father Absinthe's confidence wavered. "All this will end badly," he murmured.

"Don't be alarmed," replied his friend. "I frankly confess that I don't understand the maneuvres of these wily confederates, but what does that matter after all; now the two men are together, I feel sure of success—sure. If one runs away, the other will remain, and Gevrol shall soon see which is right, he or I."

Meanwhile the two drunkards had slackened their pace. By the manner in which they examined the magnificent mansions of the Faubourg Saint-German, one might have suspected them of the very worst intentions. In the Rue de Varrennes, at only a few steps from the Rue de la Chaise, they suddenly paused before a wall of moderate height surrounding an immense garden. The man in the slouch hat now did the talking, and explained to May—as the detectives could tell by his gestures—that the mansion to which the garden belonged had its front entrance in the Rue de Grenelle.

"Bah!" growled Lecoq, "how much further will they carry this nonsense?"

They carried it farther than the young detective had ever imagined. May suddenly sprang on to his companion's shoulders, and raised himself to a level with the summit of the wall. An instant afterward a heavy thud might have been heard. He had let himself drop into the garden. The man in the slouch hat remained in the street to watch.

The enigmatical fugitive had accomplished this strange, inconceivable design so swiftly that Lecoq had neither the time nor the desire to oppose him. His amazement at this unexpected misfortune was so great that for an instant he could neither think nor move. But he quickly regained his self-possession, and at once decided what was to be done. With a sure eye he measured the distance separating him from May's accomplice, and with three bounds he was upon him. The man in the slouched hat attempted to shout, but an iron hand stifled the cry in his throat. He tried to escape, and to beat off his assailant, but a vigorous kick stretched him on the ground as if he had been a child. Before he had time to think of further resistance he was bound, gagged, and carried, half-suffocated, to the corner of the Rue de la Chaise. No sound had been heard; not a word, not an ejaculation, not even a noise of shuffling—nothing. Any suspicious sound might have reached May, on the other side of the wall, and warned him of what was going on.

"How strange," murmured Father Absinthe, too much amazed to lend a helping hand to his younger colleague. "How strange! Who would have supposed—"

"Enough! enough!" interrupted Lecoq, in that harsh, imperious voice, which imminent peril always gives to energetic men. "Enough!—we will talk to-morrow. I must run away for a minute, and you will remain here. If May shows himself, capture him; don't allow him to escape."

"I understand; but what is to be done with the man who is lying there?"

"Leave him where he is. I have bound him securely, so there is nothing to fear. When the night-police pass, we will give him into charge—"

He paused and listened. A short way down the street, heavy, measured footsteps could be heard approaching.

"There they come," said Father Absinthe.

"Ah! I dared not hope it! I shall have a good chance now."

At the same moment, two sergeants de ville, whose attention had been attracted by this group at the street corner, hastened toward them. In a few words, Lecoq explained the situation, and it was decided that one of the sergeants should take the accomplice to the station-house, while the other remained with Father Absinthe to cut off May's retreat.

"And now," said Lecoq, "I will run round to the Rue de Grenelle and give the alarm. To whose house does this garden belong?"

"What!" replied one of the sergeants in surprise, "don't you know the gardens of the Duke de Sairmeuse, the famous duke who is a millionaire ten times over, and who was formerly the friend—"

"Ah, yes, I know, I know!" said Lecoq.

"The thief," resumed the sergeant, "walked into a pretty trap when he got over that wall. There was a reception at the mansion this evening, as there is every Monday, and every one in the house is still up. The guests are only just leaving, for there were five or six carriages still at the door as we passed by."

Lecoq darted off extremely troubled by what he had just heard. It now seemed to him that if May had got into this garden, it was not for the purpose of committing a robbery, but in the hope of throwing his pursuers off the track, and making his escape by way of the Rue de Grenelle, which he hoped to do unnoticed, in the bustle and confusion attending the departure of the guests.

On reaching the Hotel de Sairmeuse, a princely dwelling, the long façade of which was brilliantly illuminated, Lecoq found a last carriage just coming from the courtyard, while several footmen were extinguishing the lights, and an imposing "Suisse," dazzling to behold in his gorgeous livery, prepared to close the heavy double doors of the grand entrance.

The young detective advanced toward this important personage: "Is this the Hotel de Sairmeuse?" he inquired.

The Suisse suspended his work to survey the audacious vagabond who ventured to question him, and then in a harsh voice replied: "I advise you to pass on. I want none of your jesting."

Lecoq had forgotten that he was clad as a barriere loafer. "Ah," he rejoined, "I'm not what I seem to be. I'm an agent of the secret service; by name Lecoq. Here is my card, and I came to tell you that an escaped criminal has just scaled the garden wall in the rear of the Hotel de Sairmeuse."

"A crim-in-al?"

The young detective thought a little exaggeration could do no harm, and might perhaps insure him more ready aid. "Yes," he replied; "and one of the most dangerous kind—a man who has the blood of three victims already on his hands. We have just arrested his accomplice, who helped him over the wall."

The flunky's ruby nose paled perceptibly. "I will summon the servants," he faltered, and suiting the action to the word, he was raising his hand to the bell-chain, employed to announce the arrival of visitors, when Lecoq hastily stopped him.

"A word first!" said he. "Might not the fugitive have passed through the house and escaped by this door, without being seen? In that case he would be far away by this time."

"Impossible!"

"But why?"

"Excuse me, but I know what I am saying. First, the door opening into the garden is closed; it is only open during grand receptions, not for our ordinary Monday drawing-rooms. Secondly, Monseigneur requires me to stand on the threshold of the street door when he is receiving. To-day he repeated this order, and you may be sure that I haven't disobeyed him."

"Since that's the case," said Lecoq, slightly reassured, "we shall perhaps succeed in finding our man. Warn the servants, but without ringing the bell. The less noise we make, the greater will be our chance of success."

In a moment the fifty servants who peopled the ante-rooms, stables, and kitchens of the Hotel de Sairmeuse were gathered together. The great lanterns in the coach houses and stables were lighted, and the entire garden was illuminated as by enchantment.

"If May is concealed here," thought Lecoq, delighted to see so many auxiliaries, "it will be impossible for him to escape."

But it was in vain that the gardens were thoroughly explored over and over again; no one could be found. The sheds where gardening tools were kept, the conservatories, the summer houses, the two rustic pavilions at the foot of the garden, even the dog kennels, were scrupulously visited, but all in vain. The trees, with the exception of some horse-chestnuts at the rear of the garden, were almost destitute of leaves, but they were not neglected on that account. An agile boy, armed with a lantern, climbed each tree, and explored even the topmost branches.

"The murderer must have left by the way he came," obstinately repeated the Suisse who had armed himself with a huge pistol, and who would not let go his hold on Lecoq, fearing an accident perhaps.

To convince the Suisse of his error it was necessary for the young detective to place himself in communication with Father Absinthe and the sergeant de ville on the other side of the wall. As Lecoq had expected, the latter both replied that they had not once taken their eyes off the wall, and that not even a mouse had crossed into the street.

The exploration had hitherto been conducted after a somewhat haphazard fashion, each of the servants obeying his own inspiration; but the necessity of a methodically conducted search was now recognized. Accordingly, Lecoq took such measures that not a corner, not a recess, could possibly escape scrutiny; and he was dividing the task between his willing assistants, when a new-comer appeared upon the scene. This was a grave, smooth-faced individual in the attire of a notary.

"Monsieur Otto, Monseigneur's· first valet de chambre," the Suisse murmured in Lecoq's ear.

This important personage came on behalf of Monsieur le Duc (*he* did not say "Monseigneur") to inquire the meaning of all this uproar. When he had received an explanation, M. Otto condescended to compliment Lecoq on his efficiency, and to recommend that the house should be searched from garret to cellar. These precautions alone would allay the fears of Madame la Duchesse.

He then departed, and the search began again with renewed ardor. A mouse concealed in the gardens of the Hotel de Sairmeuse could not have escaped discovery, so minute were the

investigations. Not a single object of any size was left undis-
turbed. The trees were examined leaf by leaf, one might almost
say. Occasionally the discouraged servants proposed to abandon
the search; but Lecoq urged them on. He ran from one to the
other, entreating and threatening by turns, swearing that he
asked only one more effort, and that this effort would assuredly
be crowned with success. Vain promises! The fugitive could
not be found.

The evidence was now conclusive. To persist in searching
the garden any longer would be worse than folly. Accordingly,
the young detective decided to recall his auxiliaries. "That's
enough," he said, in a despondent voice. "It is now certain
that the criminal is no longer in the garden."

Was he cowering in some corner of the great house, white
with fear, and trembling at the noise made by his pursuers?
One might reasonably suppose this to be the case; and such
was the opinion of the servants. Above all, such was the
opinion of the Suisse who renewed with growing assurance
his affirmations of a few moments before.

"I have not moved from the threshold of the house to-night,"
he said, "and I should certainly have seen any person who
passed out."

"Let us go into the house, then," said Lecoq. "But first
let me ask my companion, who is waiting for me in the street,
to join me. It is unnecessary for him to remain any longer
where he is."

When Father Absinthe had responded to the summons all
the lower doors were carefully closed and guarded, and the
search recommenced inside the house, one of the largest and
most magnificent residences of the Faubourg Saint-Germain.
But at this moment all the treasures of the universe could
not have won a single glance or a second's attention from Lecoq.
All his thoughts were occupied with the fugitive. He passed
through several superb drawing-rooms, along an unrivaled
picture gallery, across a magnificent dining-room, with sideboards groaning beneath their load of massive plate, without
paying the slightest attention to the marvels of art and uphols-
tery that were offered to his view. He hurried on, accompanied by
the servants who were guiding and lighting him. He lifted heavy
articles of furniture as easily as he would have lifted a feather;
he moved each chair and sofa from its place, he explored each
cupboard and wardrobe, and drew back in turns all the wall-

hangings, window-curtains, and *portieres*. A more complete search would have been impossible. In each of the rooms and passages that Lecoq entered not a nook was left unexplored, not a corner was forgotten. At length, after two hours' continuous work, Lecoq returned to the first floor. Only five or six servants had accompanied him on his tour of inspection. The others had dropped off one by one, weary of this adventure, which had at first possessed the attractions of a pleasure party.

"You have seen everything, gentlemen," declared an old footman.

"Everything!" interrupted the Suisse, "everything! Certainly not. There are the private apartments of Monseigneur and those of Madame la Duchesse still to be explored."

"Alas!" murmured Lecoq, "What good would it be?"

But the Suisse had already gone to rap gently at one of the doors opening into the hall. His interest equaled that of the detectives. They had seen the murderer enter; he had not seen him go out; therefore the man was in the house and he wished him to be found.

The door at which he had knocked soon opened, and the grave, clean-shaven face of Otto, the duke's first valet de chambre, showed itself. "What the deuce do you want?" he asked in surly tones.

"To enter Monseigneur's room," replied the Suisse, "in order to see if the fugitive has not taken refuge there."

"Are you crazy?" exclaimed the head valet de chambre. "How could any one have entered here? Besides, I can't suffer Monsieur le Duc to be disturbed. He has been at work all night, and he is just going to take a bath before going to bed."

The Suisse seemed very vexed at this rebuff; and Lecoq was presenting his excuses, when another voice was heard exclaiming. "Let these worthy men do their duty, Otto."

"Ah! do you hear that!" exclaimed the Suisse triumphantly.

"Very well, since Monsieur le Duc permits it. Come in, I will light you through the apartments."

Lecoq entered, but it was only for form's sake that he walked through the different apartments; a library, an admirable study, and a charming smoking-room. As he was passing through the bed-chamber, he had the honor of seeing the Duc de Sairmeuse through the half-open door of a small, white, marble bath-room.

"Ah, well!" cried the duke, affably, "is the fugitive still invisible?"

"Still invisible, monsieur," Lecoq respectfully replied.

The valet de chambre did not share his master's good humor. "I think, gentlemen," said he, "that you may spare yourselves the trouble of visiting the apartments of the duchess. It is a duty we have taken upon ourselves—the women and I—and we have looked even in the bureau drawers."

Upon the landing the old footman, who had not ventured to enter his master's apartments, was awaiting the detectives. He had doubtless received his orders, for he politely inquired if they desired anything, and if, after such a fatiguing night, they would not find some cold meat and a glass of wine acceptable. Father Absinthe's eyes sparkled. He probably thought that in this *quasi*-royal abode they must have delicious things to eat and drink—such viands, indeed, as he had never tasted in his life. But Lecoq civilly refused, and left the Hotel de Sairmeuse, reluctantly followed by his old companion.

He was eager to be alone. For several hours he had been making immense efforts to conceal his rage and despair. May escaped! vanished! evaporated! The thought drove him almost mad. What he had declared to be impossible had nevertheless occurred. In his confidence and pride, he had sworn to answer for the prisoner's head with his own life; and yet he had allowed him to slip between his fingers.

When he was once more in the street, he paused in front of Father Absinthe, and crossing his arms, inquired: "Well, my friend, what do you think of all this?"

The old detective shook his head, and in serene unconsciousness of his want of tact, responded: "I think that Gevrol will chuckle with delight."

At this mention of his most cruel enemy, Lecoq bounded from the ground like a wounded bull. "Oh!" he exclaimed. "Gevrol has not won the battle yet. We have lost May; it is a great misfortune; but his accomplice remains in our hands. We hold the crafty man who has hitherto defeated all our plans, no matter how carefully arranged. He is certainly shrewd and devoted to his friend; but we will see if his devotion will withstand the prospect of hard labor in the penitentiary. And that is what awaits him, if he is silent, and if he thus accepts the responsibility of aiding and abetting the fugitive's escape. Oh! I've no fears—M. Segmuller will know how to draw the truth out of him."

So speaking, Lecoq brandished his clinched fist with a threatening air and then, in calmer tones, he added: "But we must go to the station-house where the accomplice was removed. I wish to question him a little."

XXII

I T was six o'clock, and the dawn was just breaking when Father Absinthe and his companion reached the station-house, where they found the superintendent seated at a small table, making out his report. He did not move when they entered, failing to recognize them under their disguises. But when they mentioned their names, he rose with evident cordiality, and held out his hand.

"Upon my word!" said he, "I congratulate you on your capture last night."

Father Absinthe and Lecoq exchanged an anxious look. "What capture?" they both asked in a breath.

"Why, that individual you sent me last night so carefully bound."

"Well, what about him?"

The superintendent burst into a hearty laugh. "So you are ignorant of your good fortune," said he. "Ah! luck has favored you, and you will receive a handsome reward."

"Pray tell us what we've captured?" asked Father Absinthe, impatiently.

"A scoundrel of the deepest dye, an escaped convict, who has been missing for three months. You must have a description of him in your pocket—Joseph Couturier, in short."

On hearing these words, Lecoq became so frightfully pale that Father Absinthe, fearing he was going to faint, raised his arms to prevent his falling. A chair stood close by, however, and on this Lecoq allowed himself to drop. "Joseph Couturier," he faltered, evidently unconscious of what he was saying. "Joseph Couturier! an escaped convict!"

The superintendent certainly did not understand Lecoq's agitation any better than Father Absinthe's discomfited air.

"You have reason to be proud of your work; your success will make a sensation this morning," he repeated. "You have captured a famous prize. I can see Gevrol's nose now when he hears the news. Only yesterday he was boasting that he alone was capable of securing this dangerous rascal."

After such an irreparable failure as that which had overtaken Lecoq, the unintended irony of these compliments was bitter in the extreme. The superintendent's words of praise fell on his ears like so many blows from a sledge hammer.

"You must be mistaken," he eventually remarked, rising from his seat and summoning all his energy to his assistance. "That man is not Couturier."

"Oh, I'm not mistaken; you may be quite sure of that. He fully answers the description appended to the circular ordering his capture, and even the little finger of his left hand is lacking, as is mentioned."

"Ah! that's a proof indeed!" groaned Father Absinthe.

"It is indeed. And I know another one more conclusive still. Couturier is an old acquaintance of mine. I have had him in custody before; and he recognized *me* last night just as I recognized him."

After this further argument was impossible; hence it was in an entirely different tone that Lecoq remarked: "At least, my friend, you will allow me to address a few questions to your prisoner."

"Oh! as many as you like. But first of all, let us bar the door and place two of my men before it. This Couturier has a fondness for the open air, and he wouldn't hesitate to dash out our brains if he only saw a chance of escape."

After taking these precautions, the man was removed from the cage in which he had been confined. He stepped forward with a smile on his face, having already recovered that nonchalant manner common to old offenders who, when in custody, seem to lose all feeling of anger against the police. They are not unlike those gamblers who, after losing their last halfpenny, nevertheless willingly shake hands with their adversary.

Couturier at once recognized Lecoq. "Ah!" said he, "It was you who did that business last night. You can boast of having a solid fist! You fell upon me very unexpectedly; and the back of my neck is still the worse for your clutch."

"Then, if I were to ask a favor of you, you wouldn't be disposed to grant it?"

"Oh, yes! all the same. I have no more malice in my composition than a chicken; and I rather like your face. What do you want of me?"

"I should like to have some information about the man who accompanied you last night."

Couturier's face darkened. "I am really unable to give you any," he replied.

"Why?"

"Because I don't know him. I never saw him before last night."

"It's hard to believe that. A fellow doesn't enlist the first-comer for an expedition like yours last evening. Before undertaking such a job with a man, one finds out something about him."

"I don't say I haven't been guilty of a stupid blunder," replied Couturier. "Indeed I could murder myself for it, but there was nothing about the man to make me suspect that he belonged to the secret-service. He spread a net for me, and I jumped into it. It was made for me, of course; but it wasn't necessary for me to put my foot into it."

"You are mistaken, my man," said Lecoq. "The individual in question didn't belong to the police force. I pledge you my word of honor, he didn't."

For a moment Couturier surveyed Lecoq with a knowing air, as if he hoped to discover whether he were speaking the truth or attempting to deceive him. "I believe you," he said at last. "And to prove it I'll tell you how it happened. I was dining alone last evening in a restaurant in the Rue Mouffetard, when that man came in and took a seat beside me. Naturally we began to talk; and I thought him a very good sort of a fellow. I forget how it began, but somehow or other he mentioned that he had some clothes he wanted to sell; and being glad to oblige him, I took him to a friend, who bought them from him. It was doing him a good turn, wasn't it? Well, he offered me something to drink, and I returned the compliment. We had a number of glasses together, and by midnight I began to see double. He then began to propose a plan, which, he swore, would make us both rich. It was to steal the plate from a superb mansion. There would be no risk for me; he would take charge of the whole affair.

I had only to help him over the wall, and keep watch. The proposal was tempting—was it not? You would have thought so, if you had been in my place, and yet I hesitated. But the fellow insisted. He swore that he was acquainted with the habits of the house; that Monday evening was a grand gala night there, and that on these occasions the servants didn't lock up the plate. After a little while I consented."

A fleeting flush tinged Lecoq's pale cheeks. "Are you sure he told you that the Duc de Sairmeuse received every Monday evening?" he asked, eagerly.

"Certainly; how else could I have known it! He even mentioned the name you uttered just now, a name ending in 'euse.'"

A strange thought had just flitted through Lecoq's mind. "What if May and the Duc de Sairmeuse should be one and the same person?" But the notion seemed so thoroughly absurd, so utterly inadmissible that he quickly dismissed it, despising himself even for having entertained it for a single instant. He cursed his inveterate inclination always to look at events from a romantic impossible side, instead of considering them as natural commonplace incidents. After all there was nothing surprising in the fact that a man of the world, such as he supposed May to be, should know the day set aside by the Duc de Sairmeuse for the reception of his friends.

The young detective had nothing more to expect from Couturier. He thanked him, and after shaking hands with the superintendent, walked away, leaning on Father Absinthe's arm. For he really had need of support. His legs trembled, his head whirled, and he felt sick both in body and in mind. He had failed miserably, disgracefully. He had flattered himself that he possessed a genius for his calling, and yet he had been easily outwitted.

To rid himself of pursuit, May had only had to invent a pretended accomplice, and this simple stratagem had sufficed to nonplus those who were on his trail.

Father Absinthe was rendered uneasy by his colleague's evident dejection. "Where are we going?" he inquired; "to the Palais de Justice, or to the Prefecture de Police?"

Lecoq shuddered on hearing this question, which brought him face to face with the horrible reality of his situation. "To the Prefecture!" he responded. "Why should I go there? To expose myself to Gevrol's insults, perhaps? I haven't courage enough for that. Nor do I feel that I have strength to go to M. Segmuller and say: 'Forgive me: you have judged me too favorably. I am a fool!'"

"What are we to do?"

"Ah! I don't know. Perhaps I shall embark for America—perhaps I shall throw myself into the river."

He had walked about a hundred yards when suddenly he stopped short. "No!" he exclaimed, with a furious stamp of his foot. "No, this affair shan't end like this. I have sworn to have the solution of the enigma—and I will have it!" For a moment he reflected; then, in a calmer voice, he added: "There is one man who can save us, a man who will see what I haven't been able to discern, who will understand things that I couldn't. Let us go and ask his advice, my course will depend on his reply—come!"

After such a day and such a night, it might have been expected that these two men would have felt an irresistible desire to sleep and rest. But Lecoq was sustained by wounded vanity, intense disappointment, and yet unextinguished hope of revenge: while poor Father Absinthe was not unlike some luckless cab-horse, which, having forgotten there is such a thing as repose, is no longer conscious of fatigue, but travels on until he falls down dead. The old detective felt that his limbs were failing him; but Lecoq said: "It is necessary," and so he walked on.

They both went to Lecoq's lodgings, where they laid aside their disguises and made themselves trim. Then after breakfasting they hastily betook themselves to the Rue St. Lazare, where, entering one of the most stylish houses in the street, Lecoq inquired of the concierge: "Is M. Tabaret at home?"

"Yes, but he's ill," was the reply.

"Very ill?" asked Lecoq anxiously.

"It is hard to tell," replied the man: "it is his old complaint—gout." And with an air of hypocritical commiseration, he added: "M. Tabaret is not wise to lead the life he does. Women are very well in a way, but at his age—"

The two detectives exchanged a meaning glance, and as soon as they were out of hearing burst out laughing. Their hilarity had scarcely ceased when they reached the first floor, and rang the bell at the door of one of the apartments. The buxom-looking woman who appeared in answer to his summons, informed them that her master would receive them, although he was confined to his bed. "However, the doctor is with him now," she added. "But perhaps the gentlemen would not mind waiting until he has gone?" The gentlemen replying in the affirmative, she then conducted them into a handsome library, and invited them to sit down.

The person whom Lecoq had come to consult was a man celebrated for wonderful shrewdness and penetration, well-nigh exceeding the bounds of possibility. For five-and-forty years he had held a petty post in one of the offices of the Mont de Piete, just managing to exist upon the meagre stipend he received. Suddenly enriched by the death of a relative, of whom he had scarcely ever heard, he immediately resigned his functions, and the very next day began to long for the same employment he had so often anathematized. In his endeavors to divert his mind, he began to collect old books, and heaped up mountains of tattered, worm-eaten volumes in immense oak bookcases. But despite this pastime to many so attractive, he could not shake off his weariness. He grew thin and yellow, and his income of forty thousand francs was literally killing him, when a sudden inspiration came to his relief. It came to him one evening after reading the memoirs of a celebrated detective, one of those men of subtle penetration, soft as silk, and supple as steel, whom justice sometimes sets upon the trail of crime.

"And I also am a detective!" he exclaimed.

This, however, he must prove. From that day forward he perused with feverish interest every book he could find that had any connection with the organization of the police service and the investigation of crime. Reports and pamphlets, letters and memoirs, he eagerly turned from one to the other, in his desire to master his subject. Such learning as he might find in books did not suffice, however, to perfect his education. Hence, whenever a crime came to his knowledge he started out in quest of the particulars and worked up the case by himself.

Soon these platonic investigations did not suffice, and one evening, at dusk, he summoned all his resolution, and, going on foot to the Prefecture de Police, humbly begged employment from the officials there. He was not very favorably received, for applicants were numerous. But he pleaded his cause so adroitly that at last he was charged with some trifling commissions. He performed them admirably. The great difficulty was then overcome. Other matters were entrusted to him, and he soon displayed a wonderful aptitude for his chosen work.

The case of Madame B——, the rich banker's wife, made him virtually famous. Consulted at a moment when the police had abandoned all hope of solving the mystery, he proved by A plus B—by a mathematical deduction, so to speak—that the dear lady must have stolen her own property; and events soon proved that he had told the truth. After this success he was always called upon to advise in obscure and difficult cases.

It would be difficult to tell his exact status at the Prefecture. When a person is employed, salary or compensation of some kind is understood, but this strange man had never consented to receive a penny. What he did he did for his own pleasure —for the gratification of a passion which had become his very life. When the funds allowed him for expenses seemed insufficient, he at once opened his private purse; and the men who worked with him never went away without some substantial token of his liberality. Of course, such a man had many enemies. He did as much work—and far better work than any two inspectors of police; and he didn't receive a sou of salary. Hence, in calling him "spoil-trade," his rivals were not far from right.

Whenever any one ventured to mention his name favorably in Gevrol's presence, the jealous inspector could scarcely control himself, and retorted by denouncing an unfortunate mistake which this remarkable man once made. Inclined to obstinacy, like all enthusiastic men, he had indeed once effected the conviction of an innocent prisoner—a poor little tailor, who was accused of killing his wife. This single error (a grievous one no doubt), in a career of some duration, had the effect of cooling his ardor perceptibly; and subsequently he seldom visited the Prefecture. But yet he remained "the oracle," after the fashion of those great advocates who, tired of practise at the bar, still win great and glorious triumphs in their consulting rooms, lending to others the weapons they no longer care to wield themselves.

When the authorities were undecided what course to pursue in some great case, they invariably said: "Let us go and consult Tirauclair." For this was the name by which he was most generally known: a sobriquet derived from a phrase which was always on his lips. He was constantly saying: "Il faut que cela se tire au clair: That must be brought to light." Hence, the not altogether inappropriate appellation of "Pere Tirauclair," or "Father Bring-to-Light."

Perhaps this sobriquet assisted him in keeping his occupation secret from his friends among the general public. At all events they never suspected them. His disturbed life when he was working up a case, the strange visitors he received, his frequent and prolonged absences from home, were all imputed to a very unreasonable inclination to gallantry. His concierge was deceived as well as his friends, and laughing at his supposed infatuation, disrespectfully called him an old libertine. It was only the officials of the detective force who knew that Tirauclair and Tabaret were one and the same person.

Lecoq was trying to gain hope and courage by reflecting on the career of this eccentric man, when the buxom housekeeper reentered the library and announced that the physician had left. At the same time she opened a door and exclaimed: "This is the room; you gentlemen can enter now."

XXIII

O N a large canopied bed, sweating and panting beneath the weight of numerous blankets, lay the two-faced oracle—Tirauclair, of the Prefecture—Tabaret, of the Rue Saint Lazare. It was impossible to believe that the owner of such a face, in which a look of stupidity was mingled with one of perpetual astonishment, could possess superior talent, or even an average amount of intelligence. With his retreating forehead, and his immense ears, his odious turned-up nose, tiny eyes, and coarse, thick lips, M. Tabaret seemed an excellent type of the ignorant, pennywise, petty *rentier* class. Whenever he took his walks abroad, the juvenile street Arabs would impudently shout after him or try to mimic his favorite grimace. And yet his ungainliness did not seem to worry him in the least, while he appeared to take real pleasure in increasing his appearance of stupidity, solacing himself with the reflection that "he is not really a genius who seems to be one."

At the sight of the two detectives, whom he knew very well, his eyes sparkled with pleasure. "Good morning, Lecoq, my boy," said he. "Good morning, my old Absinthe. So you think enough down there of poor Papa Tirauclair to come and see him?"

"We need your advice, Monsieur Tabaret."

"Ah, ah!"

"We have just been as completely outwitted as if we were babies in long clothes."

"What! was your man such a very cunning fellow?"

Lecoq heaved a sigh. "So cunning," he replied, "that, if I were superstitious, I should say he was the devil himself."

The sick man's face wore a comical expression of envy. "What! you have found a treasure like that," said he, "and you complain! Why, it is a magnificent opportunity—a chance to be proud of! You see, my boys, everything has degenerated in these days. The race of great criminals is dying out—those who've succeeded the old stock are like counterfeit coins. There's scarcely anything left outside a crowd of low offenders who are not worth the shoe leather expended in pursuing them. It is enough to disgust a detective, upon my word. No more trouble, emotion, anxiety, or excitement. When a crime is committed nowadays, the criminal is in jail the next morning, you've only to take the omnibus, and go to the culprit's house and arrest him. He's always found, the more the pity. But what has your fellow been up to?"

"He has killed three men."

"Oh! oh! oh!" said old Tabaret, in three different tones, plainly implying that this criminal was evidently superior to others of his species. "And where did this happen?"

"In a wine-shop near the barriere."

"Oh, yes, I recollect: a man named May. The murders were committed in the Widow Chupin's cabin. I saw the case mentioned in the 'Gazette des Tribunaux,' and your comrade, Fanferlot l'Ecureuil, who comes to see me, told me you were strangely puzzled about the prisoner's identity. So you are charged with investigating the affair? So much the better. Tell me all about it, and I will assist you as well as I can."

Suddenly checking himself, and lowering his voice, Tirauclair added: "But first of all, just do me the favor to get up. Now, wait a moment, and when I motion you, open that door there, on the left, very suddenly. Mariette, my housekeeper, who is curiosity incarnate, is standing there listening. I hear her hair rubbing against the lock. Now!"

The young detective immediately obeyed, and Mariette, caught in the act, hastened away, pursued by her master's sarcasms. "You might have known that you couldn't succeed at that!" he shouted after her.

Although Lecoq and Father Absinthe were much nearer the door than old Tirauclair, neither of them had heard the slightest sound; and they looked at each other in astonishment, wondering whether their host had been playing a little farce for their benefit, or whether his sense of hearing was really so acute as this incident would seem to indicate.

"Now," said Tabaret, settling himself more comfortably upon his pillows—"now I will listen to you, my boy. Mariette will not come back again."

On his way to Tabaret's, Lecoq had busied himself in preparing his story; and it was in the clearest possible manner that he related all the particulars, from the moment when Gevrol opened the door of the Poivriere to the instant when May leaped over the garden wall in the rear of the Hotel de Sairmeuse.

While the young detective was telling his story, old Tabaret seemed completely transformed. His gout was entirely forgotten. According to the different phases of the recital, he either turned and twisted on his bed, uttering little cries of delight or disappointment, or else lay motionless, plunged in the same kind of ecstatic reverie which enthusiastic admirers of classical music yield themselves up to while listening to one of the great Beethoven's divine sonatas.

"If I had been there! If only I had been there!" he murmured regretfully every now and then through his set teeth, though when Lecoq's story was finished, enthusiasm seemed decidedly to have gained the upper hand. "It is beautiful! it is grand!" he exclaimed. "And with just that one phrase: 'It is the Prussians who are coming,' for a starting point! Lecoq, my boy, I must say that you have conducted this affair like an angel!"

"Don't you mean to say like a fool?" asked the discouraged detective.

"No, my friend, certainly not. You have rejoiced my old heart. I can die; I shall have a successor. Ah! that Gevrol who betrayed you—for he did betray you, there's no doubt about it—that obtuse, obstinate 'General' is not worthy to blacken your shoes!"

"You overpower me, Monsieur Tabaret!" interrupted Lecoq,

as yet uncertain whether his host was poking fun at him or not. "But it is none the less true that May has disappeared, and I have lost my reputation before I had begun to make it."

"Don't be in such a hurry to reject my compliments," replied old Tabaret, with a horrible grimace. "I say that you have conducted this investigation very well; but it could have been done much better, very much better. You have a talent for your work, that's evident; but you lack experience; you become elated by a trifling advantage, or discouraged by a mere nothing; you fail, and yet persist in holding fast to a fixed idea, as a moth flutters about a candle. Then, you are young. But never mind that, it's a fault you will outgrow only too soon. And now, to speak frankly, I must tell you that you have made a great many blunders."

Lecoq hung his head like a schoolboy receiving a reprimand from his teacher. After all was he not a scholar, and was not this old man his master?

"I will now enumerate your mistakes," continued old Tabaret, "and I will show you how, on at least three occasions, you allowed an opportunity for solving this mystery to escape you."

"But—"

"Pooh! pooh! my boy, let me talk a little while now. What axiom did you start with? You said: 'Always distrust appearances; believe precisely the contrary of what appears true, or even probable.'"

"Yes, that is exactly what I said to myself."

"And it was a very wise conclusion. With that idea in your lantern to light your path, you ought to have gone straight to the truth. But you are young, as I said before; and the very first circumstance you find that seems at all probable you quite forget the rule which, as you yourself admit, should have governed your conduct. As soon as you meet a fact that seems even *more* than probable, you swallow it as eagerly as a gudgeon swallows an angler's bait."

This comparison could but pique the young detective. "I don't think I've been so simple as that," protested he.

"Bah! What did you think, then, when you heard that M. d'Escorval had broken his leg in getting out of his carriage?"

"Believe! I believed what they told me, because—"

He paused, and Tirauclair burst into a hearty fit of laughter. "You believed it," he said, "because it was a very plausible story."

"What would you have believed had you been in my place?"

"Exactly the opposite of what they told me. I might have been mistaken; but it would be the logical conclusion as my first course of reasoning."

This conclusion was so bold that Lecoq was disconcerted. "What!" he exclaimed; "do you suppose that M. d'Escorval's fall was only a fiction? that he didn't break his leg?"

Old Tabaret's face suddenly assumed a serious expression. "I don't suppose it," he replied; "I'm sure of it."

XXIV

LECOQ'S confidence in the oracle he was consulting was very great; but even old Tirauclair might be mistaken, and what he had just said seemed such an enormity, so completely beyond the bounds of possibility, that the young man could not conceal a gesture of incredulous surprise.

"So, Monsieur Tabaret, you are ready to affirm that M. d'Escorval is in quite as good health as Father Absinthe or myself; and that he has confined himself to his room for a couple of months to give a semblance of truth to a falsehood?"

"I would be willing to swear it."

"But what could possibly have been his object?"

Tabaret lifted his hands to heaven, as if imploring forgiveness for the young man's stupidity. "And it was in you," he exclaimed, "in you that I saw a successor, a disciple to whom I might transmit my method of induction; and now, you ask me such a question as that! Reflect a moment. Must I give you an example to assist you? Very well. Let it be so. Suppose yourself a magistrate. A crime is committed; you are charged with the duty of investigating it, and you visit the prisoner to question him. Very well. This prisoner has, hitherto, succeeded in concealing his identity—this was the case in the present instance, was it not? Very well. Now, what would you do if, at the very first glance, you recognized under the prisoner's disguise your best friend, or your worst enemy? What would you do, I ask?"

"I should say to myself that a magistrate who is obliged to hesitate between his duty and his inclinations, is placed in a very trying position, and I should endeavor to avoid the responsibility."

"I understand that; but would you reveal this prisoner's identity—remember, he might be your friend or your enemy?"

The question was so delicate that Lecoq remained silent for a moment, reflecting before he replied.

The pause was interrupted by Father Absinthe. "I should reveal nothing whatever!" he exclaimed. "I should remain absolutely neutral. I should say to myself others are trying to discover this man's identity. Let them do so if they can; but let my conscience be clear."

This was the cry of honesty; not the counsel of a casuist.

"I also should be silent," Lecoq at last replied; "and it seems to me that, in holding my tongue, I should not fail in my duty as a magistrate."

On hearing these words, Tabaret rubbed his hands together, as he always did when he was about to present some overwhelming argument. "Such being the case," said he, "do me the favor to tell me what pretext you would invent in order to withdraw from the case without exciting suspicion?"

"I don't know; I can't say now. But if I were placed in such a position I should find some excuse—invent something—"

"And if you could find nothing better," interrupted Tabaret, "you would adopt M. d'Escorval's expedient; you would pretend you had broken a limb. Only, as you are a clever fellow, you would sacrifice your arm; it would be less inconvenient than your leg; and you wouldn't be condemned to seclusion for several months."

"So, Monsieur Tabaret, you are convinced that M. d'Escorval knows who May really is."

Old Tirauclair turned so suddenly in his bed that his forgotten gout drew from him a terrible groan. "Can you doubt?" he exclaimed. "Can you possibly doubt it? What proofs do you want then? What connection do you see between the magistrate's fall and the prisoner's attempt at suicide? I wasn't there as you were; I only know the story as you have told it to me. I can't look at the facts with my own eyes, but according to your statements, which are I suppose correct, this is what I understand. When M. d'Escorval has completed his task at the Widow Chupin's house, he comes to the prison to examine the supposed murderer. The two men recognize each other. Had they been alone, mutual explanations might have ensued, and affairs taken quite a different turn. But they were not alone; a third party was present—M. d'Escorval's clerk. So they could say nothing. The magistrate asked a few common-place questions, in a troubled voice, and the prisoner, terribly agitated, replied as best he could. Now, after leaving the cell, M. d'Escorval no doubt said to himself: 'I can't investigate the offenses of a man I hate!' He was certainly terribly perplexed. When you tried to speak to him, as he was leaving the prison, he harshly told you to wait till the next day; and a quarter of an hour later he pretended to fall down and break his leg."

"Then you think that M. d'Escorval and May are enemies?" inquired Lecoq.

"Don't the facts prove that beyond a doubt?" retorted Tabaret. "If they had been friends, the magistrate might have acted in the same manner; but then the prisoner wouldn't have attempted to strangle himself. But thanks to you; his life was saved; for he owes his life to you. During the night, confined in a straight-waistcoat, he was powerless to injure himself. Ah! how he must have suffered that night! What agony! So, in the morning, when he was conducted to the magistrate's room for examination, it was with a sort of frenzy that he dashed into the dreaded presence of his enemy. He expected to find M. d'Escorval there, ready to triumph over his misfortunes; and he intended to say: 'Yes, it's I. There is a fatality in it. I have killed three men, and I am in your power. But there is a mortal feud between us, and for that very reason you haven't the right to prolong my tortures! It would be infamous cowardice if you did so.' However, instead of M. d'Escorval, he sees M. Segmuller. Then what happens? He is surprised, and his eyes betray the astonishment he feels when he realizes the generosity of his enemy—an enemy from whom he had expected no indulgence. Then a smile comes to his lips—a smile of hope; for he thinks, since M. d'Escorval has not betrayed his secret, that he may be able to keep it, and emerge, perhaps, from this shadow of shame and crime with his name and honor still untarnished."

Old Tabaret paused, and then, with a sudden change of tone and an ironical gesture, he added: "And that—is my explanation."

Father Absinthe had risen, frantic with delight. "Cristi!" he exclaimed, "that's it! that's it!"

Lecoq's approbation was none the less evident although unspoken. He could appreciate this rapid and wonderful work of induction far better than his companion.

For a moment or two old Tabaret reclined upon his pillows enjoying the sweets of admiration; then he continued: "Do you wish for further proofs, my boy? Recollect the perseverance M. d'Escorval displayed in sending to M. Segmuller for information. I admit that a man may have a passion for his profession; but not to such an extent as that. You believed that his leg was broken. Then were you not surprised to find a magistrate, with a broken limb, suffering mortal anguish, taking such wonderful interest in a miserable murderer? I haven't any broken bones, I've only got the gout; but I know very well that when I'm suffering, half the world might be judging the other half, and yet the idea of sending Mariette for information would never occur to me. Ah! a moment's reflection would have enabled you to understand the reason of his solicitude, and would probably have given you the key to the whole mystery."

Lecoq, who was such a brilliant casuist in the Widow Chupin's hovel, who was so full of confidence in himself, and so earnest in expounding his theories to simple Father Absinthe —Lecoq hung his head abashed and did not utter a word. But he felt neither anger nor impatience.

He had come to ask advice, and was glad that it should be given him. He had made many mistakes, as he now saw only too plainly; and when they were pointed out to him he neither fumed nor fretted, nor tried to prove that he had been right when he had been wrong. This was certainly an excellent trait in his character.

Meanwhile, M. Tabaret had poured out a great glass of some cooling drink and drained it. He now resumed: "I need not remind you of the mistake you made in not compelling Toinon Chupin to tell you all she knew about this affair while she was in your power. 'A bird in the hand'—you know the proverb."

"Be assured, Monsieur Tabaret, that this mistake has cost me enough to make me realize the danger of allowing a well-disposed witness's zeal to cool down."

"We will say no more about that, then. But I must tell you

that three or four times, at least, it has been in your power to clear up this mystery."

The oracle paused, awaiting some protestation from his disciple. None came, however. "If he says this," thought the young detective, "it must indeed be so."

This discretion made a great impression on old Tabaret, and increased the esteem he had conceived for Lecoq. "The first time that you were lacking in discretion," said he, "was when you tried to discover the owner of the diamond earring found at the Poivriere."

"I made every effort to discover the last owner."

"You tried very hard, I don't deny it; but as for making every effort—that's quite another thing. For instance, when you heard that the Baroness de Watchau was dead, and that all her property had been sold, what did you do?"

"You know; I went immediately to the person who had charge of the sale."

"Very well! and afterwards?"

"I examined the catalogue; and as, among the jewels mentioned, I could find none that answered the description of these diamonds, I knew that the clue was quite lost."

"There is precisely where you are mistaken!" exclaimed old Tirauclair, exultantly. "If such valuable jewels are not mentioned in the catalogue of the sale, the Baroness de Watchau could not have possessed them at the time of her death. And if she no longer possessed them she must have given them away or sold them. And who could she have sold them to? To one of her lady friends, very probably. For this reason, had I been in your place, I should have found out the names of her intimate friends; this would have been a very easy task; and then, I should have tried to win the favor of all the lady's-maids in the service of these friends. This would have only been a pastime for a good-looking young fellow like you. Then, I should have shown this earring to each maid in succession until I found one who said: 'That diamond belongs to my mistress,' or one who was seized with a nervous trembling."

"And to think that this idea did not once occur to me!" ejaculated Lecoq.

"Wait, wait, I am coming to the second mistake you made," retorted the oracle. "What did you do when you obtained possession of the trunk which May pretended was his? Why you played directly into this cunning adversary's hand. How could you fail to see that this trunk was only an accessory article; a bit of 'property' got ready in 'mounting' the 'comedy'? You should have known that it could only have been deposited with Madame Milner by the accomplice, and that all its contents must have been purchased for the occasion."

"I knew this, of course; but even under these circumstances, what could I do?"

"What could you do, my boy? Well, I am only a poor old man, but I should have interviewed every clothier in Paris; and at last some one would have exclaimed: 'Those articles! Why, I sold them to an individual like this or that—who purchased them for one of his friends whose measure he brought with him.'"

Angry with himself, Lecoq struck his clenched hand violently upon the table beside him. "*Sacrebleu!*" he exclaimed, "that method was infallible, and so simple too! Ah! I shall never forgive myself for my stupidity as long as I live!"

"Gently, gently!" interrupted old Tirauclair. "You are going too far, my dear boy. Stupidity is not the proper word at all; you should say carelessness, thoughtlessness. You are young—what else could one expect? What is far less inexcusable is the manner in which you conducted the chase, after the prisoner was allowed to escape."

"Alas!" murmured the young man, now completely discouraged; "did I blunder in that?"

"Terribly, my son; and here is where I really blame you. What diabolical influence induced you to follow May, step by step, like a common policeman?"

This time Lecoq was stupefied. "Ought I to have allowed him to escape me?" he inquired.

"No; but if I had been by your side in the gallery of the Odeon, when you so clearly divined the prisoner's intentions, I should have said to you: 'This fellow, friend Lecoq, will hasten to Madame Milner's house to inform her of his escape. Let us run after him.' I shouldn't have tried to prevent his seeing her, mind. But when he had left the Hotel de Mariembourg, I should have added: 'Now, let him go where he chooses; but attach yourself to Madame Milner; don't lose sight of her; cling to her as closely as her own shadow, for she will lead you to the accomplice—that is to say—to the solution of the mystery.'"

"That's the truth; I see it now."

"But instead of that, what did you do? You ran to the hotel, you terrified the boy! When a fisherman has cast his bait and the fish are swimming near, he doesn't sound a gong to frighten them all away!"

Thus it was that old Tabaret reviewed the entire course of investigation and pursuit, remodeling it in accordance with his own method of induction. Lecoq had originally had a magnificent inspiration. In his first investigations he had displayed remarkable talent; and yet he had not succeeded. Why? Simply because he had neglected the axiom with which he started: "Always distrust what seems probable!"

But the young man listened to the oracle's "summing up" with divided attention. A thousand projects were darting through his brain, and at length he could no longer restrain himself. "You have saved me from despair," he exclaimed, "I thought everything was lost; but I see that my blunders can be repaired. What I neglected to do, I can do now; there is still time. Haven't I the diamond earring, as well as various effects belonging to the prisoner, still in my possession? Madame Milner still owns the Hotel de Mariembourg, and I will watch her."

"And what for, my boy?"

"What for? Why, to find my fugitive, to be sure!"

Had the young detective been less engrossed with his idea, he would have detected a slight smile that curved Papa Tirauclair's thick lips.

"Ah, my son! is it possible that you don't suspect the real name of this pretended buffoon?" inquired the oracle somewhat despondently.

Lecoq trembled and averted his face. He did not wish Tabaret to see his eyes. "No," he replied, "I don't suspect—"

"You are uttering a falsehood!" interrupted the sick man. "You know as well as I do, that May resides in the Rue de Grenelle-Saint-Germain, and that he is known as the Duc de Sairmeuse."

On hearing these words, Father Absinthe indulged in a hearty laugh: "Ah! that's a good joke!" he exclaimed. "Ah, ha!"

Such was not Lecoq's opinion, however. "Well, yes, Monsieur Tabaret," said he, "the idea *did* occur to me; but I drove it away."

"And why, if you please?"

"Because—because—"

"Because you would not believe in the logical sequence of your premises; but I am consistent, and I say that it seems impossible the murderer arrested in the Widow Chupin's drinking den should be the Duc de Sairmeuse. Hence, the murderer arrested there, May, the pretended buffoon, *is* the Duc de Sairmeuse!"

XXV

HOW this idea had entered old Tabaret's head, Lecoq could not understand. A vague suspicion had, it is true, flitted through his own mind; but it was in a moment of despair when he was distracted at having lost May, and when certain of Couturier's remarks furnished the excuse for any ridiculous suppostition. And yet now Father Tirauclair calmly proclaimed this suspicion—which Lecoq had not dared seriously to entertain, even for an instant—to be an undoubted fact.

"You look as if you had suddenly fallen from the clouds," exclaimed the oracle, noticing his visitor's amazement. "Do you suppose that I spoke at random like a parrot?"

"No, certainly not, but—"

"Tush! You are surprised because you know nothing of contemporary history. If you don't wish to remain all your life a common detective, like your friend Gevrol, you must read, and make yourself familiar with all the leading events of the century."

"I must confess that I don't see the connection."

M. Tabaret did not deign to reply. Turning to Father Absinthe, he requested the old detective, in the most affable tones, to go to the library and fetch two large volumes entitled: "General Biography of the Men of the Present Age," which he would find in the bookcase on the right. Father Absinthe hastened to obey; and as soon as the books were brought, M. Tabaret began turning the pages with an eager hand, like a person seeking some word in a dictionary.

"Esbayron," he muttered, "Escars, Escayrac, Escher, Escodica —at last we have it—Escorval! Listen attentively, my boy, and you will be enlightened."

This injunction was entirely unnecessary. Never had the young detective's faculties been more keenly on the alert. It was in an emphatic voice that the sick man then read: "Escorval (Louis-Guillaume, baron d').—Diplomatist and politician, born at Montaignac, December 3d, 1769; of an old family of lawyers. He was completing his studies in Paris at the outbreak of the Revolution and embraced the popular cause with all the ardor of youth. But, soon disapproving the excesses committed in the name of Liberty, he sided with the Reactionists, advised, perhaps, by Roederer, who was one of his relatives. Commended to the favor of the First Counsel by M. de Talleyrand, he began his diplomatic career with a mission to Switzerland; and during the existence of the First Empire he was entrusted with many important negotiations. Devoted to the Emperor, he found himself gravely compromised at the advent of the Second Restoration. At the time of the celebrated rising at Montaignac, he was arrested on the double charge of high treason and conspiracy. He was tried by a military commission, and condemned to death. The sentence was not executed, however. He owed his life to the noble devotion and heroic energy of a priest, one of his friends, the Abbe Midon, cure of the little village of Sairmeuse. The baron d'Escorval had only one son, who embraced the judicial profession at a very early age."

Lecoq was intensely disappointed. "I understand," he remarked. "This is the biography of our magistrate's father. Only I don't see that it teaches us anything."

An ironical smile curved old Tirauclair's lips. "It teaches us that M. d'Escorval's father was condemned to death," he replied. "That's something, I assure you. A little patience, and you will soon know everything."

Having found a new leaf, he recommenced to read: "Sairmeuse (Anne-Marie-Victor de Tingry, Duc de).—A French general and politician, born at the chateau de Sairmeuse, near Montaignac, in 1758. The Sairmeuse family is one of the oldest and most illustrious in France. It must not be confounded with the ducal family of Sermeuse, whose name is written with an 'e.' Leaving France at the beginning of the Revolution, Anne de Sairmeuse began by serving in the army

of Conde. Some years later he offered his sword to Russia;
and it is asserted by some of his biographers that he was fighting
in the Russian ranks at the time of the disastrous retreat from
Moscow. Returning to France with the Bourbons, he became
notorious by the intensity of his ultra-royalist opinions. It is
certain that he had the good fortune to regain possession of
his immense family estates; and the rank and dignities which
he had gained in foreign lands were confirmed. Appointed by
the king to preside at the military commission charged with
arresting and trying the conspirators of Montaignac his zeal
and severity resulted in the capture and conviction of·all the
parties implicated."

Lecoq sprang up with sparkling eyes. "I see it clearly
now," he exclaimed. "The father of the present Duc de Sairmeuse tried to have the father of the present M. d'Escorval
beheaded."

M. Tabaret was the picture of complacency. "You see the
assistance history gives," said he. "But I have not finished,
my boy; the present Duc de Sairmeuse also has his article
which will be of interest to us. So listen: Sairmeuse (Anne-
Marie-Martial)—Son of the preceding, was born in London
toward the close of the last century; received his early education in England, and completed it at the Court of Austria,
which he subsequently visited on several confidential missions.
Heir to the opinions, prejudices, and animosities of his father,
he placed at the service of his party a highly cultivated intellect,
unusual penetration, and extraordinary abilities. A leader at
a time when political passion was raging highest, he had the
courage to assume the sole responsibility of the most unpopular
measures. The hostility he encountered, however eventually
obliged him to retire from office, leaving behind him animosities likely to terminate only with his life."

The sick man closed the book, and with assumed modesty,
he asked: "Ah, well! What do you think of my little method
of induction?"

But Lecoq was too much engrossed with his own thoughts
to reply to this question. "I think," he remarked, "that if the
Duc de Sairmeuse had disappeared for two months—the
period of May's imprisonment, all Paris would have known
of it—and so—"

"You are dreaming," interrupted Tabaret. "Why with his
wife and his valet de chambre for accomplices, the duke could

absent himself for a year if he liked, and yet all his servants would believe him to be in the house."

"I admit that," said Lecoq, at last; "but unfortunately, there is one circumstance which completely upsets the theory we have built up so laboriously."

"And what is that if you please?"

"If the man who took part in the broil at the Poivriere had been the Duc de Sairmeuse, he would have disclosed his name—he would have declared that, having been attacked, he had only defended himself—and his name alone would have opened the prison doors. Instead of that, what did the prisoner do? He attempted to kill himself. Would a grand seigneur, like the Duc de Sairmeuse, to whom life must be a perpetual enchantment, have thought of committing suicide?"

A mocking whistle from the old Tabaret interrupted the speaker. "You seem to have forgotten the last sentence in his biography: 'M. Sairmeuse leaves behind him ill-will and hatred.' Do you know the price he might have been compelled to pay for his liberty! No—no more do I. To explain his presence at the Poivriere, and the presence of a woman, who was perhaps his wife, who knows what disgraceful secrets he would have been obliged to reveal? Between shame and suicide, he chose suicide. He wished to save his name and honor intact."

Old Tirauclair spoke with such vehemence that even Father Absinthe was deeply impressed, although, to tell the truth, he had understood but little of the conversation.

As for Lecoq, he rose very pale, his lips trembling a little. "You will excuse my hypocrisy, Monsieur Tabaret," he said in an agitated voice. "I only offered these last objections for form's sake. I had thought of what you now say, but I distrusted myself, and I wanted to hear you say it yourself." Then with an imperious gesture, he added: "Now, I know what I have to do."

Old Tabaret raised his hands toward heaven with every sign of intense dismay. "Unhappy man!" he exclaimed; "do you think of going to arrest the Duc de Sairmeuse! Poor Lecoq! Free, this man is almost omnipotent, and you, an infinitesimal agent of police, would be shattered as easily as glass. Take care, my boy, don't attack the duke. I wouldn't be responsible for the consequences. You might imperil your life."

The young detective shook his head. "Oh! I don't deceive myself," said he. "I know that the duke is far beyond my reach—at least for the present. But he will be in my power again, the day I learn his secret. I don't fear danger; but I know, that if I am to succeed, I must conceal myself, and so I will. Yes, I will remain in the shade until I can unveil this mystery; but then I shall reappear in my true character. And if May be really the Duc de Sairmeuse, I shall have my revenge."

EDITORIAL NOTE

Monsieur Lecoq was originally published as a two-volume set in France, but in both England and the United States it has usually been broken into separate volumes, most frequently entitled *Monsieur Lecoq* and *The Honor of the Name*. This division fits the structure of the work well, since *The Honor of the Name* is really a separate work that has very little to do with the contest between Lecoq and the Duc de Sairmeuse. It is a long historical novel set around 1815, for the most part, and the modern reader is likely to have the suspicion that Gaboriau either planned the total work badly or simply made use of a novel "from the trunk." *The Honor of the Name* does not fit the chronology of the first part of *Monsieur Lecoq*; the characterizations do not agree at all with those of the detective story; and most of the novel is simply irrelevant. Most damning of all, however, is the poor quality of *The Honor of the Name*, which is almost universally considered to be Gaboriau's weakest mature work. It is inconsistent, confused, and unbelievable. Valentine Williams aptly characterized it as one extended yawn.

Nevertheless, the reader, at the end of the first part of *Monsieur Lecoq*, has a right to know whether Lecoq ever evened the score against the evasive duke, and we have included in this volume a brief summary of the novel, as a springboard, and those portions (pages 618 through the end, page 639, of the Caldwell edition) of *The Honor of the Name* that are relevant.

I I

The motivation of *The Honor of the Name* is a complex feud among three families in Southern France: (1) the Duc de Sairmeuse and his son Martial de Sairmeuse, who is the present Duc de Sairmeuse in the first part of *Monsieur Lecoq*; (2) the Baron d'Escorval and his son Maurice, who is the magistrate in *Monsieur Lecoq*; (3) Lacheneur, a family retainer of the Sairmeuses, and his daughter Marie-Anne and his son Jean. In 1815 the Sairmeuses return from exile, and the arrogant older Sairmeuse affronts Lacheneur, who had served the Sairmeuses well during the Revolutionary and Napoleonic periods, guarding their estates. Lacheneur, thirsting for revenge, leads an unsuccessful peasant insurrection. During the following trials the elder Sairmeuse, out of vengefulness, tries to implicate the Baron d'Escorval, who is innocent, and the Escorvals barely manage to escape to Italy. Both young Martial de Sairmeuse and Maurice d'Escorval are in love with Marie-Anne Lacheneur, but Maurice d'Escorval secretly marries her and has a son by her. Years later when Martial de Sairmeuse's wife (Blanche) learns that Marie-Anne had born a child, she believes, wrongly, that it is Sairmeuse's, and she poisons Marie-Anne. Her guilt is known to the Chupin family, who are blackmailing her. Sairmeuse does not know of his wife's crime.

Shortly before *Monsieur Lecoq* begins, Jean Lacheneur, the brother of the murdered girl, returns from abroad, and while trying to trace his sister's fate, stumbles on the secret that Blanche had murdered her. Half-crazed with a desire for revenge, he plots to destroy both Blanche and Martial de Sairmeuse, and using the Chupins as tools he sets his trap at the Poivrière.

A FEW lines of the article consecrated to Martial in the "General Biography of Men of the Time," fittingly epitomize the history of his public life. "Martial de Sairmeuse," says the writer, "placed at the service of his party a highly cultivated intellect, unusual penetration, and extraordinary abilities. A leader at the time when political passion was raging highest, he had the courage to assume the sole responsibility of the most unpopular measures. But the hostility he encountered, the danger in which he placed the throne, compelled him to retire from office, leaving behind him animosities which will only be extinguished with his life." In thus summing up Martial's public career, his biographer omits to say that if the Duc de Sairmeuse was wrong in his policy —and that depends entirely on the point of view from which his conduct is regarded—he was doubly wrong, since he was not possessed of that ardent conviction verging on fanaticism which makes men fools, heroes, and martyrs. He was not even truly ambitious. When those associated with him witnessed his passionate struggles and unceasing activity, they thought him actuated by an insatiable thirst for power. But, in reality, he cared little or nothing for it. He considered its burdens heavy; its compensations slight. His pride was too lofty to feel any satisfaction in applause; and flattery disgusted him. Often, during some brilliant fete, his acquaintances and subordinates, finding him thoughtful and preoccupied, respectfully refrained from disturbing him. "His mind is occupied with momentous questions," they fancied. "Who can tell what important decisions may result from his reverie?" But in this surmise they were mistaken. And indeed, at that very moment when royal favor filled his rivals' hearts with envy, when occupying the highest position a subject can aspire to, and it seemed he could have nothing left to wish for in this world, Martial was saying to himself: "What an empty life! What weariness and vexation of spirit! To live for others—what a mockery!"

He looked at his wife, radiant in her beauty, worshiped like a queen, and sighed. He thought of her who was dead—Marie-Anne—the only woman he had ever loved. She was never absent from his mind, and after all these years he saw her yet, stretched cold, rigid, lifeless, on the canopied bedstead, in that luxurious room at the Borderie. Time, far from effacing from his heart the image of the fair girl whose beauty unwittingly had wrought such wo—had only intensified youthful impressions, endowing the lost idol with almost superhuman grace of person and character. Ah! if fate had but given him Marie-Anne for his wife! Thus said Martial, again and again, picturing the happiness which then would have been his. They would have remained at Sairmeuse. They would have had children playing round them! And he would not be condemned to this continual warfare—to this hollow, unsatisfying, restless life. The truly happy are not those who parade their dignities and opulence before the eyes of the multitude. They rather hide themselves from the curious gaze, and they are right; for here on earth happiness is almost a crime. So thought Martial; and he, the envied statesman, often said to himself, with a feeling of vexation: "To love, and to be loved—that is everything! All else is vanity."

He had really tried to love his wife; he had done his best to resuscitate the feeling of admiration with which she had inspired him at their first meeting; but he had not succeeded. It seemed as if there was between them a wall of ice which nothing could melt, and which only grew and expanded as time went on. "Why is it?" he wondered, again and again. "It is incomprehensible. There are days when I could swear she loves me. Her character, formerly so irritable, is entirely changed; she is gentleness itself." But still he could not conquer his aversion; it was stronger than his own will.

These unavailing regrets, the disappointment and sorrow that preyed upon his mind, undoubtedly aggravated the bitterness and severity of Martial's policy. At least he knew how to fall nobly. He passed, even without a change of countenance, from all but omnipotence to a position so compromising that his very life was endangered. On perceiving his antechambers, formerly thronged with flatterers and place-hunters, now empty and deserted, he laughed—naturally, sincerely, without the least affectation. "The ship is sinking," said he; "the rats have deserted it." He did not even turn pale when the mob gathered outside his house, hurling stones at his windows, and hooting and cursing the fallen statesman; and when Otto, his faithful valet de chambre, entreated him to assume a disguise, and make his escape through the gardens, he quietly replied: "By no means! I am simply odious; I don't wish to become ridiculous!" They could not even dissuade him from going to a window and looking down on the rabble in the street below. A singular idea had just occurred to him. "If Jean Lacheneur is still alive," he thought, "how much he would enjoy this! And if he is alive, no doubt he is there in the foremost rank, urging on the crowd." And he wished to see. But Jean Lacheneur was in Russia at that epoch.

The excitement eventually subsided; and the Hotel de Sairmeuse was not seriously threatened. However, Martial realized that it would be better for him to go away for a while, and allow people to forget him. He did not ask the duchess to accompany him. "The fault has been mine entirely," he said to her, "and it would be most unjust to make you suffer for it by condemning you to exile. Remain here; I think it will be much better for you to remain." She did not offer to go with him, although she longed to do so, but then she dared not leave Paris. She knew that she must remain in order to secure her persecutor's silence. On the two occasions when she had left Paris before, everything was near being discovered, and yet then she had had Aunt Medea to take her place. Martial went away, accompanied only by his servant, Otto. In intelligence, this man was decidedly superior to his position; he was indeed decently well-off, and he had a hundred reasons—one, by the way, was a very pretty one—for desiring to remain in Paris; but his master was in trouble, and so he did not hesitate. During four years the Duc de Sairmeuse wandered through Europe, always chafing beneath the burden of a life no longer animated by interest or sustained by hope. He remained for a time in London, then he went to Vienna, and afterward to Venice. One day he was seized by an irresistible desire to see Paris again, and he returned. It was not a very prudent step, perhaps, for his bitterest enemies—personal enemies, whom he had mortally offended and persecuted—were in power; but still he did not hesitate. Besides, how could they injure him, since he had no favors to ask, no cravings of ambition to satisfy?

The exile which had weighed so heavily on him, the loneliness he had endured, had softened his nature and inclined his heart to tenderness; and he returned firmly resolved to overcome his aversion to his wife, and seek a reconciliation. "Old age is coming," he thought. "If I have not the love of youth by my fireside, I may at least have a friend." Blanche was astonished by his manner toward her when he returned. She almost believed she had found again the Martial of the old days at Courtornieu, but the realization of the dream, so fondly cherished and so long deferred, now proved only another torture added to all the others. Still, Martial was striving to carry his plan into execution, when one day the following brief note came to him through the post: "Monsieur le Duc—If I were in your place, I would watch my wife."

It was only an anonymous letter, and yet on perusing it Martial's blood mounted to his forehead. "Can she have a lover?" he thought. Then reflecting on his own conduct toward his wife since their marriage, he said to himself: "And if she has, what right have I to complain? Did I not tacitly give her back her liberty?" However, he was greatly troubled; and yet he did not once think of playing the spy.

A few mornings afterward, at about eleven o'clock, he was returning from a ride on horseback, and was not thirty paces from the Hotel de Sairmeuse when he suddenly perceived a lady hurriedly emerge from the house. She was very plainly dressed—entirely in black—but her whole appearance recalled that of the duchess in a striking fashion. "That's certainly my wife," thought Martial, "but why is she dressed in that fashion?" Then, yielding to a sudden impulse, he walked his horse up the Rue de Grenelle behind the woman in black. Blanche it was. She was tripping swiftly over the pavement, keeping her face shrouded by a thick veil, and she never once turned her head. On reaching the Rue Taranne, she spoke hurriedly to a cab-driver on the stand, and then sprang into his vehicle. The Jehu was already on his box, and he at once gave his bony horse such a vigorous cut of the whip that it was evident he had just been promised a princely gratuity. The cab had already turned into the Rue du Dragon, and Martial, ashamed of what he had already done and irresolute as to what he should do now, was still tarrying at the corner of the Rue des Saint-Peres, where he had originally stopped his horse. Scarcely daring to entertain the suspicions that flitted across his mind, he tried to deceive himself. "After all," he muttered, "it is of no use advancing. The cab's a long way off by now, and I couldn't overtake it." Still he mechanically gave his horse the rein, and when he reached the Croix Rouge he espied Blanche's vehicle among a crowd of others. He recognized it by its green body and wheels striped with white. This decided him. The cab-driver had just managed to extricate himself from the block which traffic so frequently causes hereabout, and whipping up his horse once more turned literally at a gallop up the Rue du Vieux Colombier— leading into the Place St. Sulpice. Thence he took the shortest cut to gain the outer boulevards.

Martial's thoughts were busy as he trotted along a hundred yards or so behind the vehicle. "She's in a terrible hurry," he said to himself. "But this is scarcely the quarter for a lover's rendezvous." The cab had indeed now reached the squalid region extending beyond the Place d'Italie. It turned into the Rue du Chateau des Rentiers and soon drew up before a tract of waste ground. The Duchesse de Sairmeuse then hastily alighted, and, without stopping to look to the right or to the left, hurried across the open space. Martial had prudently paused in the rear. Not far from him he espied a man sitting on a block of stone and apparently immersed in the task of coloring a clay pipe. "Will you hold my horse a moment?" inquired Martial.

"Certainly," answered the man, rising to his feet. He wore a workman's blouse and a long beard, and his aspect altogether was scarcely prepossessing. Had Martial been less preoccupied, his suspicions might have been aroused by the malicious smile that curved the fellow's lips; and had he scrutinized him closely, he would perhaps have recognized him. For the seeming vagrant was Jean Lacheneur. Since forwarding that anonymous letter to the Duc de Sairmeuse, he had compelled the duchess to multiply her visits to the Widow Chupin's den, and on each occasion he had watched for her arrival. "So, if her husband decides to follow her I shall know it," he thought. It was indispensable for the success of his plans that Blanche should be watched by her husband. For from among a thousand schemes of revenge, Jean had chosen the most frightful his fevered brain could conceive. He longed to see the haughty Duchesse de Sairmeuse subjected to the vilest ignominy, and Martial in the hands of the lowest of the low. He pictured a bloody struggle in this miserable den; the sudden arrival of the police, summoned by himself, and the indiscriminate arrest of all the parties present. He gloated over the thought of a trial in which the crime committed at the Borderie would be brought to light; he saw the duke and the duchess in prison, and the great names of Sairmeuse and Courtornieu shrouded in eternal disgrace. And he believed that nothing was wanting to insure the success of his plans. He had two miserable wretches who were capable of any crime at his disposal; and an unfortunate youth named Gustave, whom poverty and cowardice had made his willing slave, was intended to play the part of Marie-Anne's son. These three accomplices had no suspicions of Lacheneur's real intentions, while, as for the Widow Chupin and her son, if they suspected some infamous plot, all they really knew in regard to it was the duchess's name. Moreover, Jean held Polyte and his mother completely under his control by the wealth he had promised them if they served him faithfully. If Martial decided to follow his wife into the Poivriere the first time he watched her, Jean had, moreover, so arranged matters that the duke would at first suppose that Blanche had been led there by charity. "But he will not go in," thought the seeming vagrant, as, holding Martial's horse some little distance off, he looked in the direction of the hovel. "Monsieur le Duc it too cunning for that."

And Martial did not go in. Though he was horrified when

he saw his wife enter so vile a den, as if she were at home there, he said to himself that he should learn nothing by following her. He, therefore, contented himself by making a thorough examination of the hovel from outside, and then remounting his horse, and throwing Lacheneur a silver coin, he started back home at a gallop. He was completely mystified: he did not know what to think, what to imagine, what to believe. But, at the same time, he was fully resolved to fathom the mystery; and as soon as he returned home he sent Otto out in search of information. He could confide everything to this devoted servant from whom he had no secrets. At four o'clock in the afternoon the faithful valet de chambre returned with an expression of consternation on his face. "What is it?" asked Martial, divining some great misfortune.

"Ah, sir, the mistress of that wretched den is the widow of Chupin's son—"

Martial's face turned ghastly pale. He knew life well enough to understand that since the duchess had been compelled to submit to these people's power, they must be masters of some secret which she was anxious at any price to keep unrevealed. But what secret could it be? The years which had furrowed Martial's brow had not cooled the ardor of his blood. He was, as he had always been, a man of impulse, and so, without pausing, he rushed to his wife's apartments.

"Madame has just gone downstairs to receive the Comtesse de Mussidan and the Marquise d'Arlange," said the maid whom he met on the landing.

"Very well; I will wait for her here. You may retire."

So saying, Martial entered Blanche's dressing-room. It was in disorder, for, after returning from the Poivriere, the duchess was still engaged at her toilet when visitors were announced. The wardrobe doors stood open, two or three chairs were encumbered with wearing apparel, and Blanche's watch, her purse, and several bunches of keys were lying on the dressing table and the mantelpiece. Martial did not sit down. His self-possession was returning. "I will commit no act of folly," he thought; "if I question her, I shall learn nothing. I must be silent and watchful."

He was about to retire, when, on glancing round the room, he noticed a large casket, inlaid with silver, which had belonged to his wife ever since she was a girl, and which accompanied her everywhere. "That, no doubt, contains the solution of the mystery," he said to himself. This was one of those moments when a man obeys the dictates of passion without pausing to reflect. Seeing the keys on the mantelpiece, he seized them, and endeavored to find one that would fit the lock of the casket. The fourth key opened it. It was full of papers. With feverish haste, Martial examined their contents. He had thrown aside several unimportant letters, when he came to a bill that read as follows: "Search made for Madame de Sairmeuse's child. Expenses for the third quarter of the year 18—." Martial's brain reeled. A child! His wife had a child! But he read on: "For the services of two agents at Sairmeuse, ——. For expenses attending my own journey, ——. Divers gratuities, ——. Etc., etc." The total amounted to six thousand francs; and it was receipted "Chefteux." With a sort of cold rage, Martial continued his examination of the casket's contents, and found a miserably written note, which said: "Two thousand francs this evening, or I will tell the duke the history of the affair at the Borderie." Then there were several more of Chefteux's bills; next, a letter from Aunt Medea, in which she spoke of prison and remorse; and, finally, at the bottom of the casket, he found the marriage certificate of Marie-Anne Lacheneur and Maurice d'Escorval, drawn up by the cure of Vigano and signed by the old physician and Corporal Bavois.

The truth was as clear as daylight. Stunned, frozen with horror, Martial scarcely had strength enough to place the letters in the casket again and restore it to its place. Then he tottered back to his own room, clinging to the walls for support. "It was she who murdered Marie-Anne," he murmured. He was confounded, terror-stricken, by the perfidy of this woman who was his wife—by her criminal audacity, cool calculation and assurance, and her marvelous powers of dissimulation.

Still he swore he would discover everything, either through the duchess or through the Widow Chupin; and he ordered Otto to procure him a costume such as was generally worn by the frequenters of the Poivriere. He did not know how soon he might have need of it. This happened early in February, and from that moment Blanche did not take a single step without being watched. Not a letter reached her that her husband had not previously read. And she had not the slightest suspicion of the constant supervision to which she was subjected. Martial did not leave his room; he pretended to be ill.

He felt he could not meet his wife and remain silent. He remembered the oath of vengeance which he had sworn over Marie-Anne's lifeless form only too well. However, the watch which Otto kept over the duchess, and the perusal of the letters addressed to her, did not yield any fresh information, and for this reason: Polyte Chupin had been arrested on a charge of theft, and this accident caused a delay in the execution of Lacheneur's plans.

But at last the latter prepared everything for Shrove Sunday, the 20th of February. On the previous day, in accordance with her instructions, the Widow Chupin wrote to the duchess that she must come to the Poivriere on Sunday night at eleven o'clock. On that same evening Jean was to meet his accomplices at a ball at the Rainbow—a wine-shop bearing a very unenviable reputation—and give them their final instructions. These accomplices were to open the scene; he was only to appear at the *denouement*. "All is well arranged; the mechanism will work of its own accord," he said to himself. But, as is already known, the "mechanism," as he styled it, failed to act.

On receiving the Widow Chupin's summons, Blanche revolted for a moment. The lateness of the hour, the distance, the isolation of the appointed meeting-place, frightened her. Still, she was obliged to submit, and on Sunday evening she furtively left the house, accompanied by Camille, the same maid who had been present when Aunt Medea died. The duchess and Camille were attired like women of the lowest order, and felt no fear of being recognized. And yet a man was watching who quickly followed them. This was Martial. He had perused the note appointing this rendezvous even before his wife, and had disguised himself in the costume Otto had procured for him—that of a laborer about the quays. Then, in hope of making himself absolutely unrecognizable, he had soiled and matted his hair and beard; his hands were grimed with dirt; and he really seemed to belong to the class of which he wore the attire. Otto had begged to be allowed to accompany his master; but the duke refused, remarking that his revolver would prove quite sufficient protection. He knew Otto well enough, however, to feel certain he would disobey him.

Ten o'clock was striking when Blanche and Camille left the house, and it did not take them five minutes to reach the Rue Taranne. There was only one cab on the stand, which they at once hired. This circumstance drew from Martial an oath worthy of his costume. But he reflected that, since he knew where to find his wife, a slight delay in obtaining a vehicle would not matter. He soon found one, and, thanks to a gratuity of ten francs, the driver started off to the Rue du Chateau-des-Rentiers as fast as his horse could go. However, the duke had scarcely alighted before he heard the rumbling of another vehicle, which pulled up abruptly a little distance behind. "Otto is evidently following me," he thought. And he then started across the open space in the direction of the Poivriere. The prevailing silence and absence of life were rendered still more oppressive by a chill fog which heralded an approaching thaw. Martial stumbled and slipped at almost every step he took over the rough, snow-covered ground; but at last through the mist he distinguished a building in the distance. This was the Poivriere. The light burning inside filtered through the heart-shaped apertures cut in the upper part of the shutters, and it almost seemed as if a pair of lurid eyes were striving to peer through the fog.

Could it really be possible that the Duchesse de Sairmeuse was there! Martial cautiously approached the window, and, clinging to the hinges of the shutters, raised himself up so that he could glance through one of the apertures. Yes, there was no mistake. His wife and Camille were seated at a table before a large punch-bowl, in the company of two ragged, leering scoundrels, and a soldier of youthful appearance. In the centre of the room stood the Widow Chupin, with a small glass in her hand. She was talking with great volubility, and punctuating her sentences with occasional sips of brandy. The impression this scene produced on Martial was so acute that his hold relaxed and he dropped to the ground. A ray of pity stole into his soul, for he vaguely realized the frightful suffering which had been the murderess's chastisement. But he wished for another glance, and so once more he lifted himself up to the opening and looked in. The old woman had disappeared; the young soldier had risen from the table, and was talking and gesticulating earnestly. Blanche and Camille were listening to him with the closest attention. The two men who were sitting face to face, with their elbows on the table, were looking at each other; and Martial saw them exchange a significant glance. He was not wrong. The scoundrels were plotting "a rich haul." Blanche, who had dressed herself with much care, and to render her disguise perfect had encased her feet in large, coarse shoes, that were causing her well-nigh intolerable agony—Blanche had neglected to remove her superb diamond earrings. She had forgotten them, but Lacheneur's accomplices had noticed them, and were now glancing at them with eyes that glittered more brilliantly than the diamonds themselves. While awaiting Lacheneur's coming, these wretches, as had been agreed upon, were playing the part which he had imposed upon them. For this and their assistance afterward they were to receive a certain sum of money. But they were thinking that this sum did not represent a quarter of the value of these jewels, and their looks only too plainly said: "What if we could secure them and go off before Lacheneur comes!" The temptation was too strong to be resisted. One of the scoundrels suddenly rose, and seizing the duchess by the back of the neck, forced her head down on the table. The diamonds would have been at once torn from her ears if it had not been for Camille, who bravely came to her mistress's assistance. Martial could endure no more. He sprang to the door of the hovel, opened it, and entered, bolting it behind him.

"Martial!" "Monsieur le Duc!" cried Blanche and Camille in the same breath, for, despite his disguise, they had both recognized him. Their exclamations turned the momentary stupor of their assailants into fury; and both ruffians precipitated themselves on Martial, determined to kill him. But, springing to one side, the duke avoided them. He had his revolver in his hand; he fired twice, and both the scoundrels fell. However, he was not yet safe, for the young soldier rushed forward and attempted to disarm him. Then began a furious struggle, in the midst of which Martial did not leave off crying, in a panting voice, "Fly! Blanche, fly! Otto is not far off. The name—save the honor of the name!"

The two women obeyed him, making their escape through the back door, which opened into the garden; and they had scarcely done so before a violent knocking was heard at the front entry. The police were coming! This increased Martial's frenzy; and in a supreme effort to free himself from his assailant, he hurled him backward so violently that, striking his head against a corner of the table, the young soldier fell on to the floor, and lay there to all appearance dead. In the mean while, the Widow Chupin, who had hastened from the room above on hearing the uproar, was shrieking on the staircase, while at the front door a voice was crying: "Open in the name of the law!" Martial might have fled; but if he fled the duchess might be captured, for he would certainly be pursued. · He saw the peril at a glance, and determined to remain. Shaking the Widow Chupin by the arm, he said to her in an imperious voice: "If you know how to hold your tongue you shall have a hundred thousand francs." Then, drawing a table before the door opening into the back room, he intrenched himself behind it as a rampart, and awaited the enemy's approach.

The next moment the door was forced open, and a squad of police agents, headed by Inspector Gevrol, entered the room. "Surrender!" cried the inspector.

Martial did not move; his revolver was turned toward the intruders. "If I can parley with them and hold them in check only two minutes, all may yet be saved," he thought. He obtained the required delay; then throwing his weapon to the ground, he was about to bound through the back door when a police agent, who had gone round to the rear of the house, seized him about the body and threw him to the floor. From this side he expected only assistance, hence he exclaimed: "Lost! It is the Prussians who are coming!"

In the twinkling of an eye he was bound; and two hours later he was an inmate of the station-house at the Place d'Italie. He had played his part so perfectly that he had deceived even Gevrol. His assailants were dead, and he could rely upon the Widow Chupin. But he knew that the trap had been set for him by Jean Lacheneur; and he read a whole volume of suspicion in the eyes of the young officer who had cut off his retreat, and who was called Lecoq by his companions.

THE Duc de Sairmeuse was one of those men who remain superior to circumstances. He was possessed of vast experience and great natural shrewdness. His mind was quick to act and fertile in resources. But when he found himself immured in the damp and loathsome station-house at the Place d'Italie, after the terrible scene we have just recalled, he felt inclined to relinquish all hope. He knew that justice does not trust to appearances, and that when an investigating magistrate finds himself in the presence of a mystery, he does not rest until he has fathomed it. He knew only too well, moreover, that if his identity were established the authorities would endeavor to discover the reason that had led him to the Poivriere; now he could scarcely doubt but what this reason would soon be discovered, and in that case the crime at the Borderie, and the duchess's guilt, would undoubtedly be made public. This meant the Assize Court for the woman who bore his name—imprisonment, perhaps execution; at all events, a frightful scandal, dishonor, eternal disgrace! And the power he had wielded in former days was a positive disadvantage to him now, when his past position was filled by his political adversaries. Among them were two personal enemies, whose vanity he once had wounded, and who had never forgiven him. They would certainly not neglect the present opportunity for revenge. At the thought of such an ineffaceable stain on the great name of Sairmeuse, which was his pride and glory, reason almost forsook him. "My God, inspire me," he murmured. "How shall I save the honor of the name?"

He saw but one chance of salvation—death. They now believed him to be one of the miserable loafers who haunt the suburbs of Paris; if he were dead they would not trouble themselves about his identity. "It is the only way!" he thought, and he was indeed endeavoring to find some means of committing suicide when suddenly he heard a bustle outside his cell. A few moments afterward the door was opened and a man was thrust in—a man who staggered a few steps, fell heavily on to the floor, and then began to snore. The new arrival was apparently only some vulgar drunkard.

A minute or so elapsed, and then a vague, strange hope touched Martial's heart—no, he must be mistaken—and yet—yes, certainly this drunkard was Otto—Otto in disguise, and almost unrecognizable! It was a bold ruse and no time must be lost in profiting by it. Martial stretched himself on a bench, as if to sleep, and in such a way that his head was close to Otto's. "The duchess is out of danger," murmured the faithful servant.

"For to-day, perhaps. But to-morrow, through me, everything will be discovered."

"Have you told them who you are?"

"No; all the police agents but one took me for a vagabond."

"You must continue to personate that character."

"What good will it do? Jean Lacheneur will betray me."
But Martial, though he little knew it, had no need to fear
Lacheneur for the present, at least. A few hours previously,
on his way in the dark from the Rainbow to the Poivriere,
Jean had fallen to the bottom of a stone quarry, and fractured
his skull. The laborers, on returning to their work early in the
morning, found him lying there senseless; and that very moment they were carrying him to the hospital.

Although Otto also was ignorant of this circumstance, he
did not seem discouraged. "There will be some way of getting
rid of Lacheneur," said he, "if you will only sustain your present character. An escape is an easy matter when a man has
millions at his command."

"They will ask me who I am, where I've come from, and how
I've lived."

"You speak English and German, don't you? Tell them that
you have just returned from foreign parts; that you were a
foundling, and that you have always lived a roving life."

"How can I prove that?"

Otto drew a little nearer his master, and said, impressively:
"We must agree on our plans, for success depends on a perfect
understanding between us. I have a sweetheart in Paris—and
no one knows of our connection. She is as sharp as steel. Her
name is Milner, and she keeps the Hotel de Mariembourg, in
the Rue Saint-Quentin. You can say that you arrived here
from Leipsic on Sunday; that you went to that hotel, that you
left your trunk there, and that it has a card nailed to the top
with your name—say May, foreign artist."

"Capital!" said Martial, approvingly. And then, with extraordinary quickness and precision, they agreed, point by point,
on their plan of defense. When everything had been arranged,
Otto pretended to awake from the heavy sleep of intoxication;
he clamored to be released, and the keeper finally opened the
door and set him at liberty. Before leaving the station-house,
however, he succeeded in throwing a note to the Widow Chupin, who was imprisoned in the opposite cell. So, when Lecoq,
after his skilful investigations at the Poivriere, rushed to the
Place d'Italie, panting with hope and ambition, he found himself outwitted by these men, who were inferior to him in penetration, but whose tact was superior to his own.

Martial's plans being fully formed, he intended to carry them out with absolute perfection of detail, and, after his removal to the Depot, he was preparing himself for the investigating magistrate's visit, when Maurice d'Escorval entered his cell. They recognized each other. They were both terribly agitated, and the examination was an examination only in name. After Maurice's departure Martial attempted to destroy himself; for he had no faith in his former enemy's generosity. But when he found M. Segmuller occupying Maurice's place the next morning, he really believed that he was saved.

Then began that struggle between the magistrate and Lecoq on one side, and the prisoner on the other—a struggle in which neither conquered. Martial knew that Lecoq was the only person he had to fear, still he bore him no ill-will. Faithful to his nature, which compelled him to be just even to his enemies, he could not help admiring the astonishing penetration and perseverance of this young police agent, who, undismayed by the obstacles surrounding him, struggled on, unassisted, to reach the truth. But Lecoq was always outwitted by Otto, the mysterious accomplice, who seemed to know his every movement in advance. At the Morgue, at the Hotel de Mariembourg, with Toinon, the wife of Polyte Chupin, as well as with Polyte himself, Lecoq was always just a little too late. He detected the secret correspondence between the prisoner and his accomplice, and he was even ingenious enough to discover the key to it, but this served no purpose. A man, who had seen a rival, or rather a future master, in Lecoq—in short, Gevrol —had betrayed him. If his efforts to arrive at the truth through the jeweler and the Marquise d'Arlange had failed, it was only because Blanche had not purchased the diamond earrings she wore at the Poivriere at any shop, but from one of her friends, the Baroness de Watchau. And finally, if no one in Paris had missed the Duc de Sairmeuse, it was because—thanks to an understanding between the duchess, Otto, and Camille— no other inmates of the Hotel de Sairmeuse suspected his absence. All the servants supposed that the duke was confined to his room by illness. His breakfast and dinner were taken up to his private apartments every day; and soups and tisanes were prepared ostensibly for his benefit.

So the weeks went by, and Martial was expecting to be summoned before the Assize Court and condemned under the name of May, when he was afforded an opportunity to escape. Too shrewd not to discern the trap that had been set for him, it was only after horrible hesitation that he decided to alight from the prison-van, determined to run the risk, and commending himself for protection to his lucky star. And he decided wisely, for that same night he leaped over his own garden wall, leaving an escaped convict, Joseph Couturier by name, whom he had picked up in a low eating-house, as a hostage in Lecoq's hands. Warned by Madame Milner, thanks to a blunder which Lecoq committed, Otto was waiting for his master. In the twinkling of an eye Martial's beard fell under the razor; he plunged into the bath which was already prepared, and his clothes were burned. And he it was who, during the search a few minutes later, had the hardihood to call out: "Otto, by all means allow these men to do their duty." But he did not breathe freely until the police agents had departed. "At last," he exclaimed, "honor is saved! We have outwitted Lecoq!"

He had just left his bath, and assumed a dressing-gown, when Otto handed him a letter from the duchess. He hastily opened the envelope and read: "You are safe. You know everything. I am dying. Farewell. I loved you."

With two bounds he reached his wife's apartments. The outer door was locked: he burst it open; but he came too late. Blanche was dead—poisoned, like Marie-Anne; but she had procured a drug having an instantaneous effect, and extended on her couch, clad in her wonted apparel, her hands folded over her breast, she seemed only asleep. A tear glistened in Martial's eye. "Poor, unhappy woman!" he murmured; "may God forgive you as I forgive you—you whose crime has been so frightfully expiated here below!"

SAFE, in his own princely mansion, and surrounded by an army of retainers, the Duc de Sairmeuse had triumphantly exclaimed: "We have outwitted Lecoq!"

In this he was right; for the young detective was certainly nonplused for the time being; but when his grace fancied himself forever beyond this wily, keen-witted, aspiring agent's reach, he was most decidedly wrong. Lecoq was not the man to sit down with folded hands and brood over the humiliation of defeat. Before he went to old Tabaret, he was beginning to recover from his despondency; and when he left that experienced detective's presence, he had regained his courage, energy, and command over his faculties. "Well, my worthy friend," he remarked to Father Absinthe, who was trotting along by his side, "you heard what the great Monsieur Tabaret said, didn't you? So, you see, I was right."

But his companion evinced no enthusiasm. "Yes, you were right," he responded, in wobegone tones.

"Do you think we are ruined by two or three mistakes? Nonsense! I will soon turn to-day's defeat into a glorious victory."

"Ah! you might do so perhaps, if—they don't dismiss us from the force."

This doleful remark recalled Lecoq to a sense of his present position. He and Absinthe had allowed a prisoner to slip through their fingers. That was vexatious, it is true; but, on the other hand, they had captured a most notorious criminal— Joseph Couturier. Surely there was some comfort in that. Still, of course, they both might be dismissed—and yet Lecoq could have borne the prospect, dismal as it was, if it had not been for the thought that dismissal would forever prevent him from following up the Poivriere affair. What would his superiors say when he told them that May and the Duc de Sairmeuse were one and the same person. They would, no doubt, shrug their shoulders and turn up their noses. "Still, M. Segmuller will believe me," he thought. "But will he dare to take any action in the matter without plain evidence before him?"

This was very unlikely, as Lecoq fully realized, and for a moment he asked himself if he and his fellows could not make a descent on the Hotel de Sairmeuse, and, on some pretext or other, compel the duke to show himself. It would then be easy to identify him as the prisoner May. However, after a little thought he dismissed the idea. "It would be a stupid expedient!" he exclaimed. "Two such men as the duke and his accomplice are not likely to be caught napping. They are prepared for such a visit, and we should only have our labor for our pains."

He made these reflections in a low tone of voice; and Father

Absinthe's curiosity was aroused. "Excuse me," said the old veteran, "I don't quite understand you."

"I say that we must find some tangible proof before asking permission to proceed further—" Lecoq paused with knitted brows. An idea had occurred to him. He fancied he could prove complicity between at least one of the witnesses summoned to give evidence, and some member of the duke's household. He was indeed thinking of Madame Milner, the landlady of the Hotel de Mariembourg, and of his first meeting with her. He saw her again, in his mind's eye, standing on a chair, her face on a level with a cage, covered with a large piece of black silk, while she persistently repeated three or four German words to a starling, who with equal persistency retorted: "Camille! Where is Camille?" "One thing is certain," exclaimed Lecoq aloud, "if Madame Milner—who is a German, and who speaks French with the strongest possible German accent—had reared this bird, it would either have spoken in German or else in French, and in the latter case with the same accent as its mistress. So it can't have been in her possession long; but then who can have given it to her?"

"Father Absinthe was beginning to grow impatient. "In sober earnest, what are you talking about?" he asked, petulantly.

"I say that if there is any one at the Hotel de Sairmeuse named Camille, I have the proof I wish for. Come, Papa Absinthe, let us hurry on." And without another word of explanation, he dragged his companion rapidly toward the Seine.

When they reached the Rue de Grenelle, Lecoq perceived a commissionaire leaning against the door of a wine-shop. He walked straight toward him. "Come, my good fellow," said he. "I want you to go to the Hotel de Sairmeuse and ask for Camille. Tell her that her uncle is waiting for her here."

"But, sir—"

"What, you haven't gone yet?"

The messenger started off, and the two police agents entered the wine-shop, Father Absinthe scarcely having time to swallow a glass of brandy before the envoy returned. "I was unable to see Mademoiselle Camille," said he. "The house is closed from top to bottom. The duchess died very suddenly this morning."

"Ah! the wretch!" exclaimed the young police agent. Then controlling himself, he mentally added: "He must have killed his wife on returning home, but his fate is sealed. Now, I shall be allowed to continue my investigations."

In less than twenty minutes they arrived at the Palais de Justice. M. Segmuller did not seem to be immoderately surprised by Lecoq's revelations, though he listened with evident doubt to the young police agent's ingenious deductions; it was the circumstance of the starling which at last decided him. "Perhaps you are right, my dear Lecoq," he said, "and to tell the truth, I quite agree with you. But I can take no further action in the matter until you can furnish proof so convincing in its nature that the Duc de Sairmeuse will be unable to think of denying it."

"Ah! my superiors won't allow me—"

"On the contrary," interrupted the magistrate, "they will allow you the fullest liberty after I have spoken to them." Such action on M. Segmuller's part required no little courage; for in official circles there had been considerable merriment over the magistrate's mysterious man with the iron mask, disguised as a mountebank; and the former by his persistent support of the young detective's theories had almost become an object of ridicule.

"And when will you speak to them?" timidly inquired Lecoq.

"At once."

The magistrate had already turned toward the door when the young police agent stopped him. "I have one more favor to ask you, sir," he said, entreatingly. "You are so kind, you are the first person who has given me any encouragement—who has had any faith in me."

"Speak, my good fellow."

"Ah! sir, will you give me a message for M. d'Escorval? Any insignificant message—inform him of the prisoner's escape. I will take it myself, and then— Oh! fear nothing, sir; I will be very prudent."

"Very well!" replied the magistrate, "I will write him a note."

When he finally left the office, Lecoq was fully authorized to proceed with his investigations, and he carried in his pocket M. Segmuller's letter to M. d'Escorval. His satisfaction was so intense that he did not deign to notice the sneers bestowed upon him as he passed along the corridors; but on the threshold downstairs he encountered Gevrol, the general, who was evidently watching for him. "Ah, ha!" laughed the inspector, as Lecoq passed out, "here's one of those simpletons who fish for whales and don't even catch a gudgeon."

For an instant Lecoq felt angry. He turned round abruptly and looked Gevrol full in the face. "At all events," retorted he in the tone of a man who knows what he's saying, "that's better than assisting prisoners to carry on a surreptitious correspondence with people outside."

In his surprise, Gevrol almost lost countenance, and his blush was equivalent to a confession. But Lecoq did not add another word. What did it matter to him now if Gevrol had betrayed him! Was he not about to win a glorious revenge!

He spent the remainder of the day in preparing his plan of action; and in thinking what he should say when he took M. Segmuller's note to Maurice d'Escorval. The next morning, at about eleven o'clock, he presented himself at the latter's house. "M. d'Escorval is in his study with a young man," replied the servant to the young detective's inquiry, "but, as he gave me no orders to the contrary, you may go in."

Lecoq entered, but found the study unoccupied. From the adjoining room, however, only separated from the study by velvet hangings, came a sound of stifled exclamations, of sobs mingled with kisses. Not knowing whether to remain or to retire, the young police agent stood for a moment undecided; when suddenly he perceived an open letter lying on the carpet. Impelled by an impulse stronger than his will, Lecoq picked the letter up, and his eyes meeting the signature, he started back in surprise. He could not now refrain from reading this missive, which ran as follows:

"The bearer of this letter is Marie-Anne's son—your son, Maurice. I have given him all the proofs necessary to establish his identity. It was to his education that I consecrated poor Marie-Anne's inheritance. Those to whose care I confided him have made a noble man of him. If I restore him to you, it is only because the life I lead is not a fitting life for him. Yesterday, the miserable woman who murdered my sister died from poison administered by her own hand. Poor Marie-Anne! she would have been far more terribly avenged had not an accident which happened to me saved the Duc and the Duchesse de Sairmeuse from the snare into which I had drawn them. JEAN LACHENEUR."

Lecoq stood as if petrified. Now he understood the terrible drama enacted in the Widow Chupin's cabin. "I must go to Sairmeuse at once," he said to himself; "there I can discover everything." He left the room without seeing M. d'Escorval, and even successfully resisted the temptation to take Lacheneur's letter with him.

Exactly a month had transpired since Blanche's death. His grace the Duc de Sairmeuse was reclining on a divan in his library, reading one of his favorite authors, when Otto, his valet de chambre, came in to inform him that a messenger was below, charged with delivering into his grace's own hands a letter from M. d'Escorval.

Martial sprang to his feet. "It is impossible," he exclaimed; and then he quickly added: "Let the messenger come up."

A tall man, with florid complexion, and red hair and beard, timidly handed the duke a letter. Martial instantly broke the seal, and read:

"I saved you, monsieur, by not recognizing the prisoner, May. In your turn assist me. By noon on the day after to-morrow, I must have two hundred and sixty thousand francs. I have sufficient confidence in your honor to apply to you.

"MAURICE D'ESCORVAL."

For a moment Martial stood bewildered, then springing to a table he began writing, without noticing that the messenger was looking over his shoulder: "Monsieur—Not the day after to-morrow, but this evening, what you ask will be at your service. My fortune and my life are at your disposal. It is but a slight return for the generosity shown by you in withdrawing, when, under the rags of May, you recognized your former enemy, but now your devoted friend.

"MARTIAL DE SAIRMEUSE."

The duke folded this letter with a feverish hand, and giving it to the messenger with a louis, he said: "Here is the answer, make haste!"

But the messenger did not stir. He slipped the letter into his pocket, and then hastily cast his red beard and wig on the floor.

"Lecoq!" exclaimed Martial, paler than death.

"Lecoq, yes, sir," replied the young detective. "I was obliged to take my revenge; my future depended on it, and so I ventured to imitate M. d'Escorval's writing." And as Martial offered no remark: "I must also say to Monsieur le Duc," he continued, "that if your grace will transmit a confession of your presence at the Poivriere in your own handwriting to the investigating magistrate I can and will at the same time furnish proofs of your grace's innocence—that you were dragged into a snare, and that you only acted in self-defense."

Martial looked up in fair astonishment, but to show that he was acquainted with everything, Lecoq slowly added: "As madame is dead, there will be nothing said concerning what took place at the Borderie."

A week later a private report setting forth that there were no grounds to proceed against the Duc de Sairmeuse was forwarded by M. Segmuller to the public prosecutor.

Appointed to the position of inspector, which he coveted, Lecoq had the good taste, or perhaps, the shrewdness, to wear his honors modestly. But on the day of his promotion, he ordered a seal, on which was engraved the exultant rooster, his chosen armorial design, with a motto to which he ever remained faithful: *"Semper Vigilans."*

A CATALOGUE OF SELECTED DOVER BOOKS
IN ALL FIELDS OF INTEREST

A CATALOGUE OF SELECTED DOVER BOOKS
IN ALL FIELDS OF INTEREST

AMERICA'S OLD MASTERS, James T. Flexner. Four men emerged unexpectedly from provincial 18th century America to leadership in European art: Benjamin West, J. S. Copley, C. R. Peale, Gilbert Stuart. Brilliant coverage of lives and contributions. Revised, 1967 edition. 69 plates. 365pp. of text.

21806-6 Paperbound $3.00

FIRST FLOWERS OF OUR WILDERNESS: AMERICAN PAINTING, THE COLONIAL PERIOD, James T. Flexner. Painters, and regional painting traditions from earliest Colonial times up to the emergence of Copley, West and Peale Sr., Foster, Gustavus Hesselius, Feke, John Smibert and many anonymous painters in the primitive manner. Engaging presentation, with 162 illustrations. xxii + 368pp.

22180-6 Paperbound $3.50

THE LIGHT OF DISTANT SKIES: AMERICAN PAINTING, 1760-1835, James T. Flexner. The great generation of early American painters goes to Europe to learn and to teach: West, Copley, Gilbert Stuart and others. Allston, Trumbull, Morse; also contemporary American painters—primitives, derivatives, academics—who remained in America. 102 illustrations. xiii + 306pp.

22179-2 Paperbound $3.50

A HISTORY OF THE RISE AND PROGRESS OF THE ARTS OF DESIGN IN THE UNITED STATES, William Dunlap. Much the richest mine of information on early American painters, sculptors, architects, engravers, miniaturists, etc. The only source of information for scores of artists, the major primary source for many others. Unabridged reprint of rare original 1834 edition, with new introduction by James T. Flexner, and 394 new illustrations. Edited by Rita Weiss. 6⅝ x 9⅝.

21695-0, 21696-9, 21697-7 Three volumes, Paperbound $15.00

EPOCHS OF CHINESE AND JAPANESE ART, Ernest F. Fenollosa. From primitive Chinese art to the 20th century, thorough history, explanation of every important art period and form, including Japanese woodcuts; main stress on China and Japan, but Tibet, Korea also included. Still unexcelled for its detailed, rich coverage of cultural background, aesthetic elements, diffusion studies, particularly of the historical period. 2nd, 1913 edition. 242 illustrations. lii + 439pp. of text.

20364-6, 20365-4 Two volumes, Paperbound $6.00

THE GENTLE ART OF MAKING ENEMIES, James A. M. Whistler. Greatest wit of his day deflates Oscar Wilde, Ruskin, Swinburne; strikes back at inane critics, exhibitions, art journalism; aesthetics of impressionist revolution in most striking form. Highly readable classic by great painter. Reproduction of edition designed by Whistler. Introduction by Alfred Werner. xxxvi + 334pp.

21875-9 Paperbound $3.00

VISUAL ILLUSIONS: THEIR CAUSES, CHARACTERISTICS, AND APPLICATIONS, Matthew Luckiesh. Thorough description and discussion of optical illusion, geometric and perspective, particularly; size and shape distortions, illusions of color, of motion; natural illusions; use of illusion in art and magic, industry, etc. Most useful today with op art, also for classical art. Scores of effects illustrated. Introduction by William H. Ittleson. 100 illustrations. xxi + 252pp.

21530-X Paperbound $2.00

A HANDBOOK OF ANATOMY FOR ART STUDENTS, Arthur Thomson. Thorough, virtually exhaustive coverage of skeletal structure, musculature, etc. Full text, supplemented by anatomical diagrams and drawings and by photographs of undraped figures. Unique in its comparison of male and female forms, pointing out differences of contour, texture, form. 211 figures, 40 drawings, 86 photographs. xx + 459pp. 5⅜ x 8⅜.

21163-0 Paperbound $3.50

150 MASTERPIECES OF DRAWING, Selected by Anthony Toney. Full page reproductions of drawings from the early 16th to the end of the 18th century, all beautifully reproduced: Rembrandt, Michelangelo, Dürer, Fragonard, Urs, Graf, Wouwerman, many others. First-rate browsing book, model book for artists. xviii + 150pp. 8⅜ x 11¼.

21032-4 Paperbound $3.50

THE LATER WORK OF AUBREY BEARDSLEY, Aubrey Beardsley. Exotic, erotic, ironic masterpieces in full maturity: Comedy Ballet, Venus and Tannhauser, Pierrot, Lysistrata, Rape of the Lock, Savoy material, Ali Baba, Volpone, etc. This material revolutionized the art world, and is still powerful, fresh, brilliant. With *The Early Work,* all Beardsley's finest work. 174 plates, 2 in color. xiv + 176pp. 8⅛ x 11.

21817-1 Paperbound $3.75

DRAWINGS OF REMBRANDT, Rembrandt van Rijn. Complete reproduction of fabulously rare edition by Lippmann and Hofstede de Groot, completely reedited, updated, improved by Prof. Seymour Slive, Fogg Museum. Portraits, Biblical sketches, landscapes, Oriental types, nudes, episodes from classical mythology—All Rembrandt's fertile genius. Also selection of drawings by his pupils and followers. "Stunning volumes," *Saturday Review.* 550 illustrations. lxxviii + 552pp. 9⅛ x 12¼.

21485-0, 21486-9 Two volumes, Paperbound $10.00

THE DISASTERS OF WAR, Francisco Goya. One of the masterpieces of Western civilization—83 etchings that record Goya's shattering, bitter reaction to the Napoleonic war that swept through Spain after the insurrection of 1808 and to war in general. Reprint of the first edition, with three additional plates from Boston's Museum of Fine Arts. All plates facsimile size. Introduction by Philip Hofer, Fogg Museum. v + 97pp. 9⅜ x 8¼.

21872-4 Paperbound $2.50

GRAPHIC WORKS OF ODILON REDON. Largest collection of Redon's graphic works ever assembled: 172 lithographs, 28 etchings and engravings, 9 drawings. These include some of his most famous works. All the plates from *Odilon Redon: oeuvre graphique complet,* plus additional plates. New introduction and caption translations by Alfred Werner. 209 illustrations. xxvii + 209pp. 9⅛ x 12¼.

21966-8 Paperbound $5.00

DESIGN BY ACCIDENT; A BOOK OF "ACCIDENTAL EFFECTS" FOR ARTISTS AND DESIGNERS, James F. O'Brien. Create your own unique, striking, imaginative effects by "controlled accident" interaction of materials: paints and lacquers, oil and water based paints, splatter, crackling materials, shatter, similar items. Everything you do will be different; first book on this limitless art, so useful to both fine artist and commercial artist. Full instructions. 192 plates showing "accidents," 8 in color. viii + 215pp. 8⅜ x 11¼. 21942-9 Paperbound $3.75

THE BOOK OF SIGNS, Rudolf Koch. Famed German type designer draws 493 beautiful symbols: religious, mystical, alchemical, imperial, property marks, runes, etc. Remarkable fusion of traditional and modern. Good for suggestions of timelessness, smartness, modernity. Text. vi + 104pp. 6⅛ x 9¼. 20162-7 Paperbound $1.25

HISTORY OF INDIAN AND INDONESIAN ART, Ananda K. Coomaraswamy. An unabridged republication of one of the finest books by a great scholar in Eastern art. Rich in descriptive material, history, social backgrounds; Sunga reliefs, Rajput paintings, Gupta temples, Burmese frescoes, textiles, jewelry, sculpture, etc. 400 photos. viii + 423pp. 6⅜ x 9¾. 21436-2 Paperbound $5.00

PRIMITIVE ART, Franz Boas. America's foremost anthropologist surveys textiles, ceramics, woodcarving, basketry, metalwork, etc.; patterns, technology, creation of symbols, style origins. All areas of world, but very full on Northwest Coast Indians. More than 350 illustrations of baskets, boxes, totem poles, weapons, etc. 378 pp. 20025-6 Paperbound $3.00

THE GENTLEMAN AND CABINET MAKER'S DIRECTOR, Thomas Chippendale. Full reprint (third edition, 1762) of most influential furniture book of all time, by master cabinetmaker. 200 plates, illustrating chairs, sofas, mirrors, tables, cabinets, plus 24 photographs of surviving pieces. Biographical introduction by N. Bienenstock. vi + 249pp. 9⅞ x 12¾. 21601-2 Paperbound $4.00

AMERICAN ANTIQUE FURNITURE, Edgar G. Miller, Jr. The basic coverage of all American furniture before 1840. Individual chapters cover type of furniture—clocks, tables, sideboards, etc.—chronologically, with inexhaustible wealth of data. More than 2100 photographs, all identified, commented on. Essential to all early American collectors. Introduction by H. E. Keyes. vi + 1106pp. 7⅞ x 10¾. 21599-7, 21600-4 Two volumes, Paperbound $11.00

PENNSYLVANIA DUTCH AMERICAN FOLK ART, Henry J. Kauffman. 279 photos, 28 drawings of tulipware, Fraktur script, painted tinware, toys, flowered furniture, quilts, samplers, hex signs, house interiors, etc. Full descriptive text. Excellent for tourist, rewarding for designer, collector. Map. 146pp. 7⅞ x 10¾. 21205-X Paperbound $2.50

EARLY NEW ENGLAND GRAVESTONE RUBBINGS, Edmund V. Gillon, Jr. 43 photographs, 226 carefully reproduced rubbings show heavily symbolic, sometimes macabre early gravestones, up to early 19th century. Remarkable early American primitive art, occasionally strikingly beautiful; always powerful. Text. xxvi + 207pp. 8⅜ x 11¼. 21380-3 Paperbound $3.50

ALPHABETS AND ORNAMENTS, Ernst Lehner. Well-known pictorial source for decorative alphabets, script examples, cartouches, frames, decorative title pages, calligraphic initials, borders, similar material. 14th to 19th century, mostly European. Useful in almost any graphic arts designing, varied styles. 750 illustrations. 256pp. 7 x 10. 21905-4 Paperbound $4.00

PAINTING: A CREATIVE APPROACH, Norman Colquhoun. For the beginner simple guide provides an instructive approach to painting: major stumbling blocks for beginner; overcoming them, technical points; paints and pigments; oil painting; watercolor and other media and color. New section on "plastic" paints. Glossary. Formerly *Paint Your Own Pictures.* 221pp. 22000-1 Paperbound $1.75

THE ENJOYMENT AND USE OF COLOR, Walter Sargent. Explanation of the relations between colors themselves and between colors in nature and art, including hundreds of little-known facts about color values, intensities, effects of high and low illumination, complementary colors. Many practical hints for painters, references to great masters. 7 color plates, 29 illustrations. x + 274pp.
20944-X Paperbound $2.75

THE NOTEBOOKS OF LEONARDO DA VINCI, compiled and edited by Jean Paul Richter. 1566 extracts from original manuscripts reveal the full range of Leonardo's versatile genius: all his writings on painting, sculpture, architecture, anatomy, astronomy, geography, topography, physiology, mining, music, etc., in both Italian and English, with 186 plates of manuscript pages and more than 500 additional drawings. Includes studies for the Last Supper, the lost Sforza monument, and other works. Total of xlvii + 866pp. $7\frac{7}{8}$ x $10\frac{3}{4}$.
22572-0, 22573-9 Two volumes, Paperbound $11.00

MONTGOMERY WARD CATALOGUE OF 1895. Tea gowns, yards of flannel and pillow-case lace, stereoscopes, books of gospel hymns, the New Improved Singer Sewing Machine, side saddles, milk skimmers, straight-edged razors, high-button shoes, spittoons, and on and on . . . listing some 25,000 items, practically all illustrated. Essential to the shoppers of the 1890's, it is our truest record of the spirit of the period. Unaltered reprint of Issue No. 57, Spring and Summer 1895. Introduction by Boris Emmet. Innumerable illustrations. xiii + 624pp. $8\frac{1}{2}$ x $11\frac{5}{8}$.
22377-9 Paperbound $6.95

THE CRYSTAL PALACE EXHIBITION ILLUSTRATED CATALOGUE (LONDON, 1851). One of the wonders of the modern world—the Crystal Palace Exhibition in which all the nations of the civilized world exhibited their achievements in the arts and sciences—presented in an equally important illustrated catalogue. More than 1700 items pictured with accompanying text—ceramics, textiles, cast-iron work, carpets, pianos, sleds, razors, wall-papers, billiard tables, beehives, silverware and hundreds of other artifacts—represent the focal point of Victorian culture in the Western World. Probably the largest collection of Victorian decorative art ever assembled— indispensable for antiquarians and designers. Unabridged republication of the Art-Journal Catalogue of the Great Exhibition of 1851, with all terminal essays. New introduction by John Gloag, F.S.A. xxxiv + 426pp. 9 x 12.
22503-8 Paperbound $5.00

A History of Costume, Carl Köhler. Definitive history, based on surviving pieces of clothing primarily, and paintings, statues, etc. secondarily. Highly readable text, supplemented by 594 illustrations of costumes of the ancient Mediterranean peoples, Greece and Rome, the Teutonic prehistoric period; costumes of the Middle Ages, Renaissance, Baroque, 18th and 19th centuries. Clear, measured patterns are provided for many clothing articles. Approach is practical throughout. Enlarged by Emma von Sichart. 464pp. 21030-8 Paperbound $3.50.

Oriental Rugs, Antique and Modern, Walter A. Hawley. A complete and authoritative treatise on the Oriental rug—where they are made, by whom and how, designs and symbols, characteristics in detail of the six major groups, how to distinguish them and how to buy them. Detailed technical data is provided on periods, weaves, warps, wefts, textures, sides, ends and knots, although no technical background is required for an understanding. 11 color plates, 80 halftones, 4 maps. vi + 320pp. 6⅛ x 9⅛. 22366-3 Paperbound $5.00

Ten Books on Architecture, Vitruvius. By any standards the most important book on architecture ever written. Early Roman discussion of aesthetics of building, construction methods, orders, sites, and every other aspect of architecture has inspired, instructed architecture for about 2,000 years. Stands behind Palladio, Michelangelo, Bramante, Wren, countless others. Definitive Morris H. Morgan translation. 68 illustrations. xii + 331pp. 20645-9 Paperbound $3.00

The Four Books of Architecture, Andrea Palladio. Translated into every major Western European language in the two centuries following its publication in 1570, this has been one of the most influential books in the history of architecture. Complete reprint of the 1738 Isaac Ware edition. New introduction by Adolf Placzek, Columbia Univ. 216 plates. xxii + 110pp. of text. 9½ x 12¾. 21308-0 Clothbound $12.50

Sticks and Stones: A Study of American Architecture and Civilization, Lewis Mumford.One of the great classics of American cultural history. American architecture from the medieval-inspired earliest forms to the early 20th century; evolution of structure and style, and reciprocal influences on environment. 21 photographic illustrations. 238pp. 20202-X Paperbound $2.00

The American Builder's Companion, Asher Benjamin. The most widely used early 19th century architectural style and source book, for colonial up into Greek Revival periods. Extensive development of geometry of carpentering, construction of sashes, frames, doors, stairs; plans and elevations of domestic and other buildings. Hundreds of thousands of houses were built according to this book, now invaluable to historians, architects, restorers, etc. 1827 edition. 59 plates. 114pp. 7⅞ x 10¾. 22236-5 Paperbound $3.50

Dutch Houses in the Hudson Valley Before 1776, Helen Wilkinson Reynolds. The standard survey of the Dutch colonial house and outbuildings, with constructional features, decoration, and local history associated with individual homesteads. Introduction by Franklin D. Roosevelt. Map. 150 illustrations. 469pp. 6⅝ x 9¼. 21469-9 Paperbound $5.00

THE ARCHITECTURE OF COUNTRY HOUSES, Andrew J. Downing. Together with Vaux's *Villas and Cottages* this is the basic book for Hudson River Gothic architecture of the middle Victorian period. Full, sound discussions of general aspects of housing, architecture, style, decoration, furnishing, together with scores of detailed house plans, illustrations of specific buildings, accompanied by full text. Perhaps the most influential single American architectural book. 1850 edition. Introduction by J. Stewart Johnson. 321 figures, 34 architectural designs. xvi + 560pp.

22003-6 Paperbound $4.00

LOST EXAMPLES OF COLONIAL ARCHITECTURE, John Mead Howells. Full-page photographs of buildings that have disappeared or been so altered as to be denatured, including many designed by major early American architects. 245 plates. xvii + 248pp. 7⅞ x 10¾.

21143-6 Paperbound $3.50

DOMESTIC ARCHITECTURE OF THE AMERICAN COLONIES AND OF THE EARLY REPUBLIC, Fiske Kimball. Foremost architect and restorer of Williamsburg and Monticello covers nearly 200 homes between 1620-1825. Architectural details, construction, style features, special fixtures, floor plans, etc. Generally considered finest work in its area. 219 illustrations of houses, doorways, windows, capital mantels. xx + 314pp. 7⅞ x 10¾.

21743-4 Paperbound $4.00

EARLY AMERICAN ROOMS: 1650-1858, edited by Russell Hawes Kettell. Tour of 12 rooms, each representative of a different era in American history and each furnished, decorated, designed and occupied in the style of the era. 72 plans and elevations, 8-page color section, etc., show fabrics, wall papers, arrangements, etc. Full descriptive text. xvii + 200pp. of text. 8⅜ x 11¼.

21633-0 Paperbound $5.00

THE FITZWILLIAM VIRGINAL BOOK, edited by J. Fuller Maitland and W. B. Squire. Full modern printing of famous early 17th-century ms. volume of 300 works by Morley, Byrd, Bull, Gibbons, etc. For piano or other modern keyboard instrument; easy to read format. xxxvi + 938pp. 8⅜ x 11.

21068-5, 21069-3 Two volumes, Paperbound $10.00

KEYBOARD MUSIC, Johann Sebastian Bach. Bach Gesellschaft edition. A rich selection of Bach's masterpieces for the harpsichord: the six English Suites, six French Suites, the six Partitas (Clavierübung part I), the Goldberg Variations (Clavierübung part IV), the fifteen Two-Part Inventions and the fifteen Three-Part Sinfonias. Clearly reproduced on large sheets with ample margins; eminently playable. vi + 312pp. 8⅛ x 11.

22360-4 Paperbound $5.00

THE MUSIC OF BACH: AN INTRODUCTION, Charles Sanford Terry. A fine, nontechnical introduction to Bach's music, both instrumental and vocal. Covers organ music, chamber music, passion music, other types. Analyzes themes, developments, innovations. x + 114pp.

21075-8 Paperbound $1.50

BEETHOVEN AND HIS NINE SYMPHONIES, Sir George Grove. Noted British musicologist provides best history, analysis, commentary on symphonies. Very thorough, rigorously accurate; necessary to both advanced student and amateur music lover. 436 musical passages. vii + 407 pp.

20334-4 Paperbound $2.75

JOHANN SEBASTIAN BACH, Philipp Spitta. One of the great classics of musicology, this definitive analysis of Bach's music (and life) has never been surpassed. Lucid, nontechnical analyses of hundreds of pieces (30 pages devoted to St. Matthew Passion, 26 to B Minor Mass). Also includes major analysis of 18th-century music. 450 musical examples. 40-page musical supplement. Total of xx + 1799pp.

(EUK) 22278-0, 22279-9 Two volumes, Clothbound $17.50

MOZART AND HIS PIANO CONCERTOS, Cuthbert Girdlestone. The only full-length study of an important area of Mozart's creativity. Provides detailed analyses of all 23 concertos, traces inspirational sources. 417 musical examples. Second edition. 509pp.　21271-8 Paperbound $3.50

THE PERFECT WAGNERITE: A COMMENTARY ON THE NIBLUNG'S RING, George Bernard Shaw. Brilliant and still relevant criticism in remarkable essays on Wagner's Ring cycle, Shaw's ideas on political and social ideology behind the plots, role of Leitmotifs, vocal requisites, etc. Prefaces. xxi + 136pp.

(USO) 21707-8 Paperbound $1.75

DON GIOVANNI, W. A. Mozart. Complete libretto, modern English translation; biographies of composer and librettist; accounts of early performances and critical reaction. Lavishly illustrated. All the material you need to understand and appreciate this great work. Dover Opera Guide and Libretto Series; translated and introduced by Ellen Bleiler. 92 illustrations. 209pp.

21134-7 Paperbound $2.00

BASIC ELECTRICITY, U. S. Bureau of Naval Personel. Originally a training course, best non-technical coverage of basic theory of electricity and its applications. Fundamental concepts, batteries, circuits, conductors and wiring techniques, AC and DC, inductance and capacitance, generators, motors, transformers, magnetic amplifiers, synchros, servomechanisms, etc. Also covers blue-prints, electrical diagrams, etc. Many questions, with answers. 349 illustrations. x + 448pp. 6½ x 9¼.

20973-3 Paperbound $3.50

REPRODUCTION OF SOUND, Edgar Villchur. Thorough coverage for laymen of high fidelity systems, reproducing systems in general, needles, amplifiers, preamps, loudspeakers, feedback, explaining physical background. "A rare talent for making technicalities vividly comprehensible," R. Darrell, *High Fidelity*. 69 figures. iv + 92pp.　21515-6 Paperbound $1.35

HEAR ME TALKIN' TO YA: THE STORY OF JAZZ AS TOLD BY THE MEN WHO MADE IT, Nat Shapiro and Nat Hentoff. Louis Armstrong, Fats Waller, Jo Jones, Clarence Williams, Billy Holiday, Duke Ellington, Jelly Roll Morton and dozens of other jazz greats tell how it was in Chicago's South Side, New Orleans, depression Harlem and the modern West Coast as jazz was born and grew. xvi + 429pp.

21726-4 Paperbound $3.00

FABLES OF AESOP, translated by Sir Roger L'Estrange. A reproduction of the very rare 1931 Paris edition; a selection of the most interesting fables, together with 50 imaginative drawings by Alexander Calder. v + 128pp. 6½x9¼.

21780-9 Paperbound $1.50

AGAINST THE GRAIN (A REBOURS), Joris K. Huysmans. Filled with weird images, evidences of a bizarre imagination, exotic experiments with hallucinatory drugs, rich tastes and smells and the diversions of its sybarite hero Duc Jean des Esseintes, this classic novel pushed 19th-century literary decadence to its limits. Full unabridged edition. Do not confuse this with abridged editions generally sold. Introduction by Havelock Ellis. xlix + 206pp.   22190-3 Paperbound $2.50

VARIORUM SHAKESPEARE: HAMLET. Edited by Horace H. Furness; a landmark of American scholarship. Exhaustive footnotes and appendices treat all doubtful words and phrases, as well as suggested critical emendations throughout the play's history. First volume contains editor's own text, collated with all Quartos and Folios. Second volume contains full first Quarto, translations of Shakespeare's sources (Belleforest, and Saxo Grammaticus), Der Bestrafte Brudermord, and many essays on critical and historical points of interest by major authorities of past and present. Includes details of staging and costuming over the years. By far the best edition available for serious students of Shakespeare. Total of xx + 905pp.
21004-9, 21005-7, 2 volumes, Paperbound $7.00

A LIFE OF WILLIAM SHAKESPEARE, Sir Sidney Lee. This is the standard life of Shakespeare, summarizing everything known about Shakespeare and his plays. Incredibly rich in material, broad in coverage, clear and judicious, it has served thousands as the best introduction to Shakespeare. 1931 edition. 9 plates. xxix + 792pp.   21967-4 Paperbound $4.50

MASTERS OF THE DRAMA, John Gassner. Most comprehensive history of the drama in print, covering every tradition from Greeks to modern Europe and America, including India, Far East, etc. Covers more than 800 dramatists, 2000 plays, with biographical material, plot summaries, theatre history, criticism, etc. "Best of its kind in English," *New Republic*. 77 illustrations. xxii + 890pp.
20100-7 Clothbound $10.00

THE EVOLUTION OF THE ENGLISH LANGUAGE, George McKnight. The growth of English, from the 14th century to the present. Unusual, non-technical account presents basic information in very interesting form: sound shifts, change in grammar and syntax, vocabulary growth, similar topics. Abundantly illustrated with quotations. Formerly *Modern English in the Making*. xii + 590pp.
21932-1 Paperbound $4.00

AN ETYMOLOGICAL DICTIONARY OF MODERN ENGLISH, Ernest Weekley. Fullest, richest work of its sort, by foremost British lexicographer. Detailed word histories, including many colloquial and archaic words; extensive quotations. Do not confuse this with the Concise Etymological Dictionary, which is much abridged. Total of xxvii + 830pp. 6½ x 9¼.
21873-2, 21874-0 Two volumes, Paperbound $7.90

FLATLAND: A ROMANCE OF MANY DIMENSIONS, E. A. Abbott. Classic of science-fiction explores ramifications of life in a two-dimensional world, and what happens when a three-dimensional being intrudes. Amusing reading, but also useful as introduction to thought about hyperspace. Introduction by Banesh Hoffmann. 16 illustrations. xx + 103pp.   20001-9 Paperbound $1.25

POEMS OF ANNE BRADSTREET, edited with an introduction by Robert Hutchinson. A new selection of poems by America's first poet and perhaps the first significant woman poet in the English language. 48 poems display her development in works of considerable variety—love poems, domestic poems, religious meditations, formal elegies, "quaternions," etc. Notes, bibliography. viii + 222pp.

22160-1 Paperbound $2.50

THREE GOTHIC NOVELS: THE CASTLE OF OTRANTO BY HORACE WALPOLE; VATHEK BY WILLIAM BECKFORD; THE VAMPYRE BY JOHN POLIDORI, WITH FRAGMENT OF A NOVEL BY LORD BYRON, edited by E. F. Bleiler. The first Gothic novel, by Walpole; the finest Oriental tale in English, by Beckford; powerful Romantic supernatural story in versions by Polidori and Byron. All extremely important in history of literature; all still exciting, packed with supernatural thrills, ghosts, haunted castles, magic, etc. xl + 291pp.

21232-7 Paperbound $2.50

THE BEST TALES OF HOFFMANN, E. T. A. Hoffmann. 10 of Hoffmann's most important stories, in modern re-editings of standard translations: Nutcracker and the King of Mice, Signor Formica, Automata, The Sandman, Rath Krespel, The Golden Flowerpot, Master Martin the Cooper, The Mines of Falun, The King's Betrothed, A New Year's Eve Adventure. 7 illustrations by Hoffmann. Edited by E. F. Bleiler. xxxix + 419pp. 21793-0 Paperbound $3.00

GHOST AND HORROR STORIES OF AMBROSE BIERCE, Ambrose Bierce. 23 strikingly modern stories of the horrors latent in the human mind: The Eyes of the Panther, The Damned Thing, An Occurrence at Owl Creek Bridge, An Inhabitant of Carcosa, etc., plus the dream-essay, Visions of the Night. Edited by E. F. Bleiler. xxii + 199pp. 20767-6 Paperbound $1.50

BEST GHOST STORIES OF J. S. LEFANU, J. Sheridan LeFanu. Finest stories by Victorian master often considered greatest supernatural writer of all. Carmilla, Green Tea, The Haunted Baronet, The Familiar, and 12 others. Most never before available in the U. S. A. Edited by E. F. Bleiler. 8 illustrations from Victorian publications. xvii + 467pp. 20415-4 Paperbound $3.00

MATHEMATICAL FOUNDATIONS OF INFORMATION THEORY, A. I. Khinchin. Comprehensive introduction to work of Shannon, McMillan, Feinstein and Khinchin, placing these investigations on a rigorous mathematical basis. Covers entropy concept in probability theory, uniqueness theorem, Shannon's inequality, ergodic sources, the E property, martingale concept, noise, Feinstein's fundamental lemma, Shanon's first and second theorems. Translated by R. A. Silverman and M. D. Friedman. iii + 120pp. 60434-9 Paperbound $2.00

SEVEN SCIENCE FICTION NOVELS, H. G. Wells. The standard collection of the great novels. Complete, unabridged. *First Men in the Moon, Island of Dr. Moreau, War of the Worlds, Food of the Gods, Invisible Man, Time Machine, In the Days of the Comet.* Not only science fiction fans, but every educated person owes it to himself to read these novels. 1015pp. (USO) 20264-X Clothbound $6.00

LAST AND FIRST MEN AND STAR MAKER, TWO SCIENCE FICTION NOVELS, Olaf Stapledon. Greatest future histories in science fiction. In the first, human intelligence is the "hero," through strange paths of evolution, interplanetary invasions, incredible technologies, near extinctions and reemergences. Star Maker describes the quest of a band of star rovers for intelligence itself, through time and space: weird inhuman civilizations, crustacean minds, symbiotic worlds, etc. Complete, unabridged. v + 438pp. (USO) 21962-3 Paperbound $2.50

THREE PROPHETIC NOVELS, H. G. WELLS. Stages of a consistently planned future for mankind. *When the Sleeper Wakes,* and *A Story of the Days to Come,* anticipate *Brave New World* and *1984,* in the 21st Century; *The Time Machine,* only complete version in print, shows farther future and the end of mankind. All show Wells's greatest gifts as storyteller and novelist. Edited by E. F. Bleiler. x + 335pp. (USO) 20605-X Paperbound $2.50

THE DEVIL'S DICTIONARY, Ambrose Bierce. America's own Oscar Wilde— Ambrose Bierce—offers his barbed iconoclastic wisdom in over 1,000 definitions hailed by H. L. Mencken as "some of the most gorgeous witticisms in the English language." 145pp. 20487-1 Paperbound $1.25

MAX AND MORITZ, Wilhelm Busch. Great children's classic, father of comic strip, of two bad boys, Max and Moritz. Also Ker and Plunk (Plisch und Plumm), Cat and Mouse, Deceitful Henry, Ice-Peter, The Boy and the Pipe, and five other pieces. Original German, with English translation. Edited by H. Arthur Klein; translations by various hands and H. Arthur Klein. vi + 216pp. 20181-3 Paperbound $2.00

PIGS IS PIGS AND OTHER FAVORITES, Ellis Parker Butler. The title story is one of the best humor short stories, as Mike Flannery obfuscates biology and English. Also included, That Pup of Murchison's, The Great American Pie Company, and Perkins of Portland. 14 illustrations. v + 109pp. 21532-6 Paperbound $1.25

THE PETERKIN PAPERS, Lucretia P. Hale. It takes genius to be as stupidly mad as the Peterkins, as they decide to become wise, celebrate the "Fourth," keep a cow, and otherwise strain the resources of the Lady from Philadelphia. Basic book of American humor. 153 illustrations. 219pp. 20794-3 Paperbound $2.00

PERRAULT'S FAIRY TALES, translated by A. E. Johnson and S. R. Littlewood, with 34 full-page illustrations by Gustave Doré. All the original Perrault stories— Cinderella, Sleeping Beauty, Bluebeard, Little Red Riding Hood, Puss in Boots, Tom Thumb, etc.—with their witty verse morals and the magnificent illustrations of Doré. One of the five or six great books of European fairy tales. viii + 117pp. 8⅛ x 11. 22311-6 Paperbound $2.00

OLD HUNGARIAN FAIRY TALES, Baroness Orczy. Favorites translated and adapted by author of the *Scarlet Pimpernel.* Eight fairy tales include "The Suitors of Princess Fire-Fly," "The Twin Hunchbacks," "Mr. Cuttlefish's Love Story," and "The Enchanted Cat." This little volume of magic and adventure will captivate children as it has for generations. 90 drawings by Montagu Barstow. 96pp. (USO) 22293-4 Paperbound $1.95

THE RED FAIRY BOOK, Andrew Lang. Lang's color fairy books have long been children's favorites. This volume includes Rapunzel, Jack and the Bean-stalk and 35 other stories, familiar and unfamiliar. 4 plates, 93 illustrations x + 367pp.
21673-X Paperbound $2.50

THE BLUE FAIRY BOOK, Andrew Lang. Lang's tales come from all countries and all times. Here are 37 tales from Grimm, the Arabian Nights, Greek Mythology, and other fascinating sources. 8 plates, 130 illustrations. xi + 390pp.
21437-0 Paperbound $2.75

HOUSEHOLD STORIES BY THE BROTHERS GRIMM. Classic English-language edition of the well-known tales — Rumpelstiltskin, Snow White, Hansel and Gretel, The Twelve Brothers, Faithful John, Rapunzel, Tom Thumb (52 stories in all). Translated into simple, straightforward English by Lucy Crane. Ornamented with head-pieces, vignettes, elaborate decorative initials and a dozen full-page illustrations by Walter Crane. x + 269pp.
21080-4 Paperbound **$2.00**

THE MERRY ADVENTURES OF ROBIN HOOD, Howard Pyle. The finest modern versions of the traditional ballads and tales about the great English outlaw. Howard Pyle's complete prose version, with every word, every illustration of the first edition. Do not confuse this facsimile of the original (1883) with modern editions that change text or illustrations. 23 plates plus many page decorations. xxii + 296pp.
22043-5 Paperbound $2.75

THE STORY OF KING ARTHUR AND HIS KNIGHTS, Howard Pyle. The finest children's version of the life of King Arthur; brilliantly retold by Pyle, with 48 of his most imaginative illustrations. xviii + 313pp. 6⅛ x 9¼.
21445-1 Paperbound $2.50

THE WONDERFUL WIZARD OF OZ, L. Frank Baum. America's finest children's book in facsimile of first edition with all Denslow illustrations in full color. The edition a child should have. Introduction by Martin Gardner. 23 color plates, scores of drawings. iv + 267pp.
20691-2 Paperbound $2.50

THE MARVELOUS LAND OF OZ, L. Frank Baum. The second Oz book, every bit as imaginative as the Wizard. The hero is a boy named Tip, but the Scarecrow and the Tin Woodman are back, as is the Oz magic. 16 color plates, 120 drawings by John R. Neill. 287pp.
20692-0 Paperbound $2.50

THE MAGICAL MONARCH OF MO, L. Frank Baum. Remarkable adventures in a land even stranger than Oz. The best of Baum's books not in the Oz series. 15 color plates and dozens of drawings by Frank Verbeck. xviii + 237pp.
21892-9 Paperbound $2.25

THE BAD CHILD'S BOOK OF BEASTS, MORE BEASTS FOR WORSE CHILDREN, A MORAL ALPHABET, Hilaire Belloc. Three complete humor classics in one volume. Be kind to the frog, and do not call him names . . . and 28 other whimsical animals. Familiar favorites and some not so well known. Illustrated by Basil Blackwell. 156pp.
(USO) 20749-8 Paperbound $1.50

EAST O' THE SUN AND WEST O' THE MOON, George W. Dasent. Considered the best of all translations of these Norwegian folk tales, this collection has been enjoyed by generations of children (and folklorists too). Includes True and Untrue, Why the Sea is Salt, East O' the Sun and West O' the Moon, Why the Bear is Stumpy-Tailed, Boots and the Troll, The Cock and the Hen, Rich Peter the Pedlar, and 52 more. The only edition with all 59 tales. 77 illustrations by Erik Werenskiold and Theodor Kittelsen. xv + 418pp. 22521-6 Paperbound $3.50

GOOPS AND HOW TO BE THEM, Gelett Burgess. Classic of tongue-in-cheek humor, masquerading as etiquette book. 87 verses, twice as many cartoons, show mischievous Goops as they demonstrate to children virtues of table manners, neatness, courtesy, etc. Favorite for generations. viii + 88pp. 6½ x 9¼. 22233-0 Paperbound $1.50

ALICE'S ADVENTURES UNDER GROUND, Lewis Carroll. The first version, quite different from the final *Alice in Wonderland,* printed out by Carroll himself with his own illustrations. Complete facsimile of the "million dollar" manuscript Carroll gave to Alice Liddell in 1864. Introduction by Martin Gardner. viii + 96pp. Title and dedication pages in color. 21482-6 Paperbound $1.25

THE BROWNIES, THEIR BOOK, Palmer Cox. Small as mice, cunning as foxes, exuberant and full of mischief, the Brownies go to the zoo, toy shop, seashore, circus, etc., in 24 verse adventures and 266 illustrations. Long a favorite, since their first appearance in St. Nicholas Magazine. xi + 144pp. 6⅝ x 9¼. 21265-3 Paperbound $1.75

SONGS OF CHILDHOOD, Walter De La Mare. Published (under the pseudonym Walter Ramal) when De La Mare was only 29, this charming collection has long been a favorite children's book. A facsimile of the first edition in paper, the 47 poems capture the simplicity of the nursery rhyme and the ballad, including such lyrics as I Met Eve, Tartary, The Silver Penny. vii + 106pp. (USO) 21972-0 Paperbound $2.00

THE COMPLETE NONSENSE OF EDWARD LEAR, Edward Lear. The finest 19th-century humorist-cartoonist in full: all nonsense limericks, zany alphabets, Owl and Pussycat, songs, nonsense botany, and more than 500 illustrations by Lear himself. Edited by Holbrook Jackson. xxix + 287pp. (USO) 20167-8 Paperbound $2.00

BILLY WHISKERS: THE AUTOBIOGRAPHY OF A GOAT, Frances Trego Montgomery. A favorite of children since the early 20th century, here are the escapades of that rambunctious, irresistible and mischievous goat—Billy Whiskers. Much in the spirit of *Peck's Bad Boy,* this is a book that children never tire of reading or hearing. All the original familiar illustrations by W. H. Fry are included: 6 color plates, 18 black and white drawings. 159pp. 22345-0 Paperbound $2.00

MOTHER GOOSE MELODIES. Faithful republication of the fabulously rare Munroe and Francis "copyright 1833" Boston edition—the most important Mother Goose collection, usually referred to as the "original." Familiar rhymes plus many rare ones, with wonderful old woodcut illustrations. Edited by E. F. Bleiler. 128pp. 4½ x 6⅜. 22577-1 Paperbound $1.00

TWO LITTLE SAVAGES; BEING THE ADVENTURES OF TWO BOYS WHO LIVED AS INDIANS AND WHAT THEY LEARNED, Ernest Thompson Seton. Great classic of nature and boyhood provides a vast range of woodlore in most palatable form, a genuinely entertaining story. Two farm boys build a teepee in woods and live in it for a month, working out Indian solutions to living problems, star lore, birds and animals, plants, etc. 293 illustrations. vii + 286pp.

20985-7 Paperbound $2.50

PETER PIPER'S PRACTICAL PRINCIPLES OF PLAIN & PERFECT PRONUNCIATION. Alliterative jingles and tongue-twisters of surprising charm, that made their first appearance in America about 1830. Republished in full with the spirited woodcut illustrations from this earliest American edition. 32pp. 4½ x 6⅜.

22560-7 Paperbound $1.00

SCIENCE EXPERIMENTS AND AMUSEMENTS FOR CHILDREN, Charles Vivian. 73 easy experiments, requiring only materials found at home or easily available, such as candles, coins, steel wool, etc.; illustrate basic phenomena like vacuum, simple chemical reaction, etc. All safe. Modern, well-planned. Formerly *Science Games for Children*. 102 photos, numerous drawings. 96pp. 6⅛ x 9¼.

21856-2 Paperbound $1.25

AN INTRODUCTION TO CHESS MOVES AND TACTICS SIMPLY EXPLAINED, Leonard Barden. Informal intermediate introduction, quite strong in explaining reasons for moves. Covers basic material, tactics, important openings, traps, positional play in middle game, end game. Attempts to isolate patterns and recurrent configurations. Formerly *Chess*. 58 figures. 102pp. (USO) 21210-6 Paperbound $1.25

LASKER'S MANUAL OF CHESS, Dr. Emanuel Lasker. Lasker was not only one of the five great World Champions, he was also one of the ablest expositors, theorists, and analysts. In many ways, his Manual, permeated with his philosophy of battle, filled with keen insights, is one of the greatest works ever written on chess. Filled with analyzed games by the great players. A single-volume library that will profit almost any chess player, beginner or master. 308 diagrams. xli x 349pp.

20640-8 Paperbound $2.75

THE MASTER BOOK OF MATHEMATICAL RECREATIONS, Fred Schuh. In opinion of many the finest work ever prepared on mathematical puzzles, stunts, recreations; exhaustively thorough explanations of mathematics involved, analysis of effects, citation of puzzles and games. Mathematics involved is elementary. Translated by F. Göbel. 194 figures. xxiv + 430pp. 22134-2 Paperbound $3.50

MATHEMATICS, MAGIC AND MYSTERY, Martin Gardner. Puzzle editor for Scientific American explains mathematics behind various mystifying tricks: card tricks, stage "mind reading," coin and match tricks, counting out games, geometric dissections, etc. Probability sets, theory of numbers clearly explained. Also provides more than 400 tricks, guaranteed to work, that you can do. 135 illustrations. xii + 176pp.

20335-2 Paperbound $1.75

MATHEMATICAL PUZZLES FOR BEGINNERS AND ENTHUSIASTS, Geoffrey Mott-Smith. 189 puzzles from easy to difficult—involving arithmetic, logic, algebra, properties of digits, probability, etc.—for enjoyment and mental stimulus. Explanation of mathematical principles behind the puzzles. 135 illustrations. viii + 248pp.

20198-8 Paperbound $1.75

PAPER FOLDING FOR BEGINNERS, William D. Murray and Francis J. Rigney. Easiest book on the market, clearest instructions on making interesting, beautiful origami. Sail boats, cups, roosters, frogs that move legs, bonbon boxes, standing birds, etc. 40 projects; more than 275 diagrams and photographs. 94pp.

20713-7 Paperbound $1.00

TRICKS AND GAMES ON THE POOL TABLE, Fred Herrmann. 79 tricks and games— some solitaires, some for two or more players, some competitive games—to entertain you between formal games. Mystifying shots and throws, unusual caroms, tricks involving such props as cork, coins, a hat, etc. Formerly *Fun on the Pool Table*. 77 figures. 95pp. 21814-7 Paperbound $1.25

HAND SHADOWS TO BE THROWN UPON THE WALL: A SERIES OF NOVEL AND AMUSING FIGURES FORMED BY THE HAND, Henry Bursill. Delightful picturebook from great-grandfather's day shows how to make 18 different hand shadows: a bird that flies, duck that quacks, dog that wags his tail, camel, goose, deer, boy, turtle, etc. Only book of its sort. vi + 33pp. 6½ x 9¼. 21779-5 Paperbound $1.00

WHITTLING AND WOODCARVING, E. J. Tangerman. 18th printing of best book on market. "If you can cut a potato you can carve" toys and puzzles, chains, chessmen, caricatures, masks, frames, woodcut blocks, surface patterns, much more. Information on tools, woods, techniques. Also goes into serious wood sculpture from Middle Ages to present, East and West. 464 photos, figures. x + 293pp.

20965-2 Paperbound $2.00

HISTORY OF PHILOSOPHY, Julián Marias. Possibly the clearest, most easily followed, best planned, most useful one-volume history of philosophy on the market; neither skimpy nor overfull. Full details on system of every major philosopher and dozens of less important thinkers from pre-Socratics up to Existentialism and later. Strong on many European figures usually omitted. Has gone through dozens of editions in Europe. 1966 edition, translated by Stanley Appelbaum and Clarence Strowbridge. xviii + 505pp. 21739-6 Paperbound $3.50

YOGA: A SCIENTIFIC EVALUATION, Kovoor T. Behanan. Scientific but non-technical study of physiological results of yoga exercises; done under auspices of Yale U. Relations to Indian thought, to psychoanalysis, etc. 16 photos. xxiii + 270pp.

20505-3 Paperbound $2.50

Prices subject to change without notice.
Available at your book dealer or write for free catalogue to Dept. GI, Dover Publications, Inc., 180 Varick St., N. Y., N. Y. 10014. Dover publishes more than 150 books each year on science, elementary and advanced mathematics, biology, music, art, literary history, social sciences and other areas.